Whatever Tomorrow Brings

Embrace Tomorrow
Duet – Book 2

Turning Tree
Press

AMY ARGENT

ISBN (paperback): 978-1-7369405-2-5
ISBN (e-book): 978-1-7369405-3-2

Cover design by Jada D'Lee Designs
Illustrations and Turning Tree Press logo by Jared Pace
Edited by Susan Atlas

Turning Tree Press
First Edition

For Mom and Dad,
who taught me to never give up

ALSO BY AMY ARGENT

THE EMBRACE TOMORROW DUET

Come Back Tomorrow

Whatever Tomorrow Brings

Life always offers you a second chance. It's called tomorrow.

— *Dylan Thomas*

"Will you stay? At least for a few minutes? You're the first visitor I've had."

Intense green eyes, so warm and yet distant. So alone and vulnerable, yet so resilient and strong.

"Can I come back tomorrow?"

So many days spent with him, gaining his trust by giving him my own. Telling him my stories. Holding his hand through pain and fear. Falling in love with him a day at a time. A smile at a time.

"I'm scared, Tori. Jesus, I'm fucking terrified. This is really going to happen, and I don't have any control. I don't know how to deal with this. I feel like I'm falling apart, and there's nothing left to hold on to."

"Hold on to me, sweetheart."

Depression and then resolve. To make peace with the demons from a past full of heartache.

"It's okay, Mom. I'm all right. I'm so glad you could come."

Hope and then disaster.

"Do you have pneumonia?"

"Bacterial . . . I forget . . . the exact name. Evans asked me . . . if I want them . . . . to give me drugs . . . to make me comfortable.

"I told him yes. Too much pain. I couldn't . . . no more."

And then . . . oh God, and then . . .

"Tori . . . I love you. There was nothing for me . . . but now . . . there's so much I want to do . . . so much I want to give to you."

"Tori, I want you to go . . . and I don't want you . . . to come back tomorrow."

And I left.

"Code blue, code blue, room four-twelve. Code blue, code blue, room four-twelve."

And he nearly left this world before I could get back to him. Before he could see the truth of what was between us.

"They're helping him, Tori! Will lifted his DNR. He's letting them help him to breathe."

And now he's fighting for his life against pneumonia. But that's just a consequence of the bigger monster—the cancer that has destroyed his immune system and continues to ruthlessly try to take his life.

"Jenny, is there any hope for him? If he recovers from the pneumonia, does he have any options at all for treatment?"

"Yes, he has options, Tori. He's had options all along, and one in particular that could even be a cure.

He can have another round of chemotherapy followed by a stem cell transplant. The regular chemo alone obviously isn't working for him since the cancer came back twice, but the combination of high-dose chemo with a stem cell transplant has a half-decent rate of success."

He didn't tell me he had options. I was too afraid of his reaction to tell him I loved him. We're quite the pair, aren't we? But now he knows I love him, and now I know the decision he'd been struggling with since he came down with pneumonia. Hell, probably since long before that.

"*I think that's why he lifted his DNR. He loves you, and he's decided to fight —maybe even to go into treatment again. Because he wants to be with you.*"

"*Tori, you need to be there for him and help him fight this. When he recovers from the pneumonia, I'm sure you can talk it out. But he needs you right now. If you're feeling angry—or betrayed—remember that he loves you, and in the end, he chose you.*"

He chose me.

Will chose me, and he's fighting for me. He's fighting for *us*. And I'm going to help him fight with everything I have.

CHAPTER 1

Jenny and I are sitting in the waiting room just down the hall from Will.

The room where she brought me after Will coded, and she told me he'd lifted his DNR and they were helping him.

The room where she confessed that she told him I loved him and that he has treatment options.

The room where I went through his sketchbook and felt his love for me radiating from every stroke of his pencil.

She's been holding me for minutes or hours while I try to put myself together and make some sense of it all. I truly do have the very best friend in the world, and I'm so lucky she was Will's nurse and that she brought us together.

"I owe you—a lot," I whisper, and she just squeezes me tighter.

"You don't owe me anything, and there's still a long way to go. First, he has to survive the pneumonia before we can get to trying to cure him."

I scrub at my face with my hand, my eyes burning from crying and lack of sleep.

"But he'll be okay, right? I mean, the pneumonia won't kill him . . ."

Jenny just smiles at me sadly. "I don't know, Tori. He's very sick right now, and it all depends on how bad this gets. If his lungs can't clear the bacteria . . ."

I squeeze my eyes shut and lower my head, unconsciously wrapping my arms further around myself to fend off her words. "He's going to be okay," I say with stubborn determination.

"I hope so, for both of you. It's going to be a little while before you can see him, and they gave him anesthesia before the intubation, so he's going to be out for the better part of the day. And they'll be moving him up to the ICU."

My breath catches as panic washes over me again. "Oh, Jenny . . ."

"Now that he'll be on the vent for at least a few days, he needs more than we can do for him down here. This doesn't mean it's the end, Tori. It's a good thing, actually, because now that he lifted his DNR, his course of treatment for everything will be more aggressive. They'll take good care of him, and he'll be back down here before you know it.

"While you're waiting to see him, I think you should call Jason . . . and his mother. They'll both want to know he's taken a turn for the worse. They deserve to know, and I suspect he'd want you to be the one to tell them."

"Oh, of . . . of course." I'm still having a hard time wrapping my mind around everything that's happened in the last twenty-four hours, and suddenly, I feel guilty for not reaching out to either of them after Will told me he'd decided to give in. I was just so lost that it didn't even occur to me. *Shit.*

Jenny rubs my back affectionately. "Make your calls, and I'll go check on Will for you."

I nod as she stands.

"I'll come right back and let you know," she says, smiling at me.

I manage a small smile in return, but as she leaves, I let my head fall into my hand. Now I have to explain all this to the only two people Will's allowed to care for him other than me: his mother and his best friend.

I call Jason but I get his voicemail. I don't want to explain everything in a message, so I just say Will has gotten worse, and he should come to see him as soon as he can.

I dial Elizabeth's number, and she picks up on the second ring.

"Tori? Is everything okay?" There's panic in her voice—she knows I wouldn't call unless something bad had happened.

"Hi, Elizabeth. Things aren't as okay as they were. Will came down with pneumonia this week."

"Oh my God, is he all right?"

"He's . . . all right for now." I take a shaky breath. "His lung collapsed this morning, and they had to put him on a ventilator to help him breathe. They're moving him up to the ICU now."

"Oh!" She gasps. "I-I'll come. I'll be on a flight tomorrow morning. Can you recommend a hotel nearby?"

"You're welcome to stay with me, or you can stay at Will's place. I know he was planning to ask you to stay there when you came up to visit, so I'm sure he wouldn't mind."

There's a pause. "I . . . feel strange about intruding into his life that much without his knowing. If you're sure it's no trouble, I'd be happy to stay with you."

"I understand, and it's no trouble at all," I say, a bit relieved. I'm sure Will wouldn't really mind, but I know he's very particular about his things. "Text me your flight information, and I'll pick you up from the airport tomorrow."

"Thank you, Tori," she says tearfully. "If you get the chance to talk to him, tell him I love him."

"Of course. I'll see you tomorrow."

I hang up the phone and collapse back into my chair. It's nearly nine in the morning now, so I call the psychology clinic receptionist and ask her to reschedule all my appointments for the rest of the week. I have no intention of leaving Will's side, much less going back to work, until he's over this.

By the time I'm finished, Jenny is back.

"Hey, sweetie. How are you holding up?"

I sigh heavily. "I'm okay. Elizabeth is coming tomorrow, and I left a message for Jason. How's Will?"

"He's . . . holding on," Jenny says, and my heart flies into my throat.

"They've drained the fluid from his abdomen and put in a chest tube to drain the air and infected fluid from around his lungs. It'll take a few days to clear it all, so when you see him, you'll notice the tube is still in place. And they have him hooked up to the vent. His respirations are good right now, but his fever is very high."

I nod numbly as the reality of how very sick Will is crashes down around me. I need to see him. Now.

"Can I see him, Jenny?"

"Transport took him up about fifteen minutes ago, so they should have him just about settled by now. Come on, I'll walk you up there."

Jenny puts her arm around me, and we go up to the sixth floor together. As we get off the elevator, I'm struck by how very quiet it is, and I'm instantly reminded of a few of the patients I befriended who died in the ICU. I shake my head firmly. I am *not* going to think about death today.

When we arrive at Will's door, Jenny pauses and looks back at me. "Remember, be strong, Tori. In the ICU, patients often look worse than they actually are."

I swallow thickly, then follow her in.

I look at the floor and keep my eyes there until we get to the side of his bed. I'm afraid of what I'll see, but I have to be strong for him. Taking a deep breath, I raise my eyes slowly, but all my air is stolen the minute my gaze falls on him.

He looks absolutely awful. His eyes are closed, but the shadows underneath are dark, making them appear sunken and hollow. His cheeks are ruddy, but the color is too red to be healthy. Sweat is beaded on his forehead, and I realize what's missing is his restless motion. When Will is feverish, he's constantly moving, but he's eerily motionless right now because he's still under the effects of general anesthesia.

They've removed the NG tube from his nose, and white tape goes across his face just below there, holding the tube coming out of his mouth in place. I can hear the positive force of the machine as it forces air into his lungs, and the mere thought that he can't breathe on his own right now almost brings me to my knees.

I take the last few steps to the bed unsteadily. "Oh, sweetheart," I whisper, my voice breaking.

Jenny takes my elbow and guides me into the chair she's placed behind me, and I sit, unable to take my eyes off him. "The shock of it will wear off. You know it's not as bad as it looks, and he's in there, fighting. I'll give you two some time alone. You know where to find me."

She backs out of the room, but I still can't take my eyes off Will's face. He looks so . . . different now that he's not able to smile at me, and I can't see the pout of his lips that always defines his sleep. Now, he truly looks like a cancer patient, and a terminal one at that.

In the blink of an eye, I'm sitting on the side of his bed, but as I reach forward to run my fingers into his hair, I notice he's shirtless. His blanket is pulled up to his chest, but his bare arms are resting on top of it, making the bright red rash that covers them and the scabs where he's scratched his skin raw clearly visible as well as the swollen lymph nodes under his arms. I gasp softly as I take in the damage this disease has done to him. I'm sure they took his nightshirt off because of all the procedures they did this morning, but he wouldn't be happy about being so exposed. I'll have to talk to his nurse to see what we can do to cover him up so he doesn't wake up like this.

I also notice his left arm is pulled away from his body. My curiosity gets the better of me, and I lift his arm gently, pulling the blanket down and away from his torso. A large tube protrudes from his side, gauze and tape surrounding it and holding it in place. The tube goes to a drainage unit attached to the bottom of the bed, and I turn my head away, trying to block out the rest of what I see. This is what's going to save his life, but I can barely stand the sight of it. I carefully put his blanket back in place. My hand finally makes it to his hair, brushing it away from his face.

"Will, I'm so sorry! I came as fast as I could, but I didn't make it! I should have come earlier. I should have known this would happen, and I should have given in and come. I hope you know I'm here, and I'm fighting for you too. I'm going to stay right here until you're better. I promise.

"What you did today . . . I had no idea what you'd been fighting, the decision you were trying to make. And last night, I thought the fight was lost, but you changed your mind, and you chose me—chose *us*. I can't wait to tell you I love you, too.

"I love you, Will, with my whole heart and soul, and I would do anything for you. And I'll do anything I can to help you fight this so you can get better, and we can be together.

"So, you just hang on," I tell him, my voice breaking. "You hang on and outlast this infection, and we'll find a way to get you better."

I must have fallen asleep because I'm startled awake when the door squeaks, announcing the arrival of Dr. Evans.

He smiles at me, then addresses Will. "Hello, Will. How are we doing?" he asks, pulling a mini iPad out of his pocket as he checks Will's IV and the readout on the ventilator. Then he puts a hand on Will's forehead and reaches across the bed and gently takes Will's hand, putting two fingers over Will's pulse point and watching the clock for a few minutes. He puts Will's hand down and makes a few more notes on his device. Then he turns to face me.

"Hello, Tori."

"Hi, Dr. Evans."

The silence is ominous for a moment, but Dr. Evans doesn't let it grow. "I'm here to talk to you about Will's condition," he says, his eyes focused intently on me.

"But . . . I'm not Will's family. Don't the privacy laws prevent you from telling me anything?" I ask, thinking back to everything Jenny had to do to try to help us without losing her job.

"Actually, in this case, they don't. This morning, Will gave you medical power of attorney for his healthcare decisions."

I gasp, all the air leaving my lungs in a sudden *whoosh*. "H-he . . . he did what?"

"He granted you the right to make decisions for him in the event that he couldn't, which is a very good thing because at the moment, he's not capable of deciding anything," Dr. Evans says matter-of-factly.

Will put me in charge of his medical decisions. He put his life in my hands, and he's trusting me to do what he would want with it. He trusts me. I mean, I always knew he did on some level, but this? This is the ultimate. The tears well up and spill over—I'm so touched by what this says I am to him, but at the same time, I'm horrified that it's necessary.

"Are you willing to take on this responsibility?"

"Of . . . of course. I didn't know he'd done that. He was pretty busy this morning before his lung collapsed, wasn't he?"

Dr. Evans nods. "Yes, he was, and it's a good thing, too. I didn't want to see him die that way. Not when he has other options."

Right away, I think of what Jenny told me about Will's treatment options, but I don't ask about it. Until he recovers from the pneumonia, it doesn't matter anyway.

"I'm glad too."

"But let's focus on the present. Will's lung has re-inflated with the help of the chest tube, and his breathing is stable right now, and that's good. We drained the abdominal fluid and the air and fluid from his chest, and we left the chest tube in place to continue to drain the infection as the pneumonia runs its course. My concern right now is his fever. His temperature has been hovering around one-oh-four for almost forty-eight hours now, and that's dangerously high, especially given his weakened condition. We're doing what we can to lower it, but if we can't get it down, it may be only a matter of time until his organs begin to fail. We'll be keeping a close eye on him, but I think the next twenty-four to forty-eight hours will be critical."

I draw in a rapid breath as panic and fear spike through me, and I cover my mouth with my hand.

"Now, calm down," Dr. Evans says soothingly. "This is just what I'm concerned about. It doesn't mean it's going to happen. I just wanted you to be aware of what *could* happen.

"I have faith in him, though. Will has been fighting this disease for more than two years now, and he's tough. You should have faith in him too."

My eyes meet Dr. Evans' reassuring smile, but then they turn to Will. In my eyes, he's as handsome as he ever was, and my mind goes back through all the weeks I've known him, cataloguing his strength, his sweetness, and his incredible talent. And then I think back over all the things he's been through and come out okay on the other side.

I reach over and take Will's hand as I look back at Dr. Evans. "Yes, I have faith in him. He's going to be fine."

"That's the spirit!" Dr. Evans says, giving me another warm smile. "I'll come by to see him every day about this time unless something happens, and I need to come sooner. Hopefully, within a day or two, he'll turn the corner and be on his way to recovery. Please don't hesitate to contact me through the nurses if you have any questions."

Dr. Evans turns to Will and puts a hand on his arm. "I'll see you tomorrow, Will. Be strong."

"Thank you, Dr. Evans." He smiles over his shoulder as he leaves the room.

I lean over Will to kiss him on the cheek, but the minute I close my eyes, a wave of dizziness hits me. It's been more than twenty-four hours since I got any real sleep, and on Monday night I only got a few hours because I was so worried about him.

I grab on to the mattress beside Will's head to steady myself, and when I open my eyes, the spinning stops. I need to take care of myself so I can be there for him when he needs me, but there's no way I'm leaving his side. So I sit back down and rest my head on the mattress beside him.

I bolt up into a sitting position. We're not alone in the room. Will's ICU nurse is standing on the other side of his bed, fiddling with his IV. I glance at the clock on the wall—it's nearly six in the evening. From there my eyes flick to Will. His eyes are still closed, but he's moving his head from side to side restlessly. The tube from the ventilator prevents him from moving much, but he's closer to consciousness than he's been all day.

The nurse glances over at me and smiles kindly. "His fever is still very high, but his breathing is stable. Are you planning to stay with him?"

"Yes, please," I tell her, hoping like hell she's not about to tell me I can't because I'm not family.

"That's fine. I spoke with Jenny, so I know he doesn't have any family here, and it's obvious how much you care about him."

"Thank you, Miss . . . ?"

"Laura. I'm here to make things as easy for Will, and for you, as possible. So please, tell me when you need anything."

"Thank you so much, Laura."

The minute the door closes, I'm perched on the edge of Will's bed, one hand in his hair and the other holding his. He's radiating heat, just like he has been for two days now, and it's scaring the hell out of me. Oh God, I hope the fever gives out before his body does.

"Hi, sweetheart. Today has been a long and tiring day, but I know mine hasn't been as bad as yours has. Your fever is still so high. You have to beat this, okay? You have to come back to me because we have so much to talk about. There are so many things I want to share with you."

As I'm talking, his eyes open, and my heart stutters as I see my favorite green. Even fever-bright and vacant, it's one of the most beautiful things I've ever seen. He's watching me, but it's taking him a lot of effort, so I waste no time.

"I love you. I love you so much, and I miss talking to you. I miss your voice and your touch on my skin. I miss you teasing me, and I miss your smile, and I miss your kisses. Oh God, you kiss better than anyone I've ever known, and I can't get enough of you. I need you to get better so we can do all those things again. I need you more than I've ever needed anyone. We need each other. I love you, Will."

His brow wrinkles a little, and suddenly, I feel his fingers squeezing mine. I smile and laugh as tears flow down my face.

"There you are! I feel you squeezing my hand. I love you, and I'm going to be right here until you're better. Jason and your mom and I, we're all going to be right here. Everything's going to be fine. I promise."

The pressure on my hand slowly eases, and his eyes fall closed as he surrenders to sleep. But he responded. I know he did. He's in there, and he's fighting because he wants to be with me.

CHAPTER 2

Thursday, Friday, and Saturday were as long as Wednesday was, and Will's fever raged on, showing no signs of breaking. Elizabeth, Jason, and I sat with him all day those days, taking breaks as we needed them and talking to Will when his eyes were open. He didn't respond by squeezing anyone's hand like he did for me on Wednesday night, which has me wondering if I didn't just imagine it. I miss him terribly. He's right in front of me, but he's not really here. As I wipe him down for what feels like the thousandth time, I have to remind myself how vibrant and expressive he is when he's awake because it feels like ages since we were together. It's been a long five days.

It's Sunday afternoon, and I'm alone with Will. He's very still right now. He hasn't seemed conscious since early this morning, and his restlessness due to the fever seems to be decreasing. I don't think that's a good sign.

Sighing, I lay my head on my arm wearily. I'm exhausted. The constant worry for Will and lack of restful sleep is taking its toll on me, and I nod off next to him.

I startle awake, nearly falling out of my chair as I try to figure out where I am and what's going on. An urgent beeping sound fills the room, and my eyes widen. Something is wrong with Will. I hit the call button lying on the bed next to him, but before I can even stand up to go find someone, Laura and another nurse are bustling into the room.

Laura goes straight for Will, and I stand quickly, moving my chair back and out of the way. She unhooks the ventilator tube and attaches a hand-ventilation bag in its place. She begins "bagging" Will, while the other nurse checks the display on the vent.

"Low pressure alarm, no other indicators."

"I'm hitting mild resistance," Laura says, as she bags Will with one hand while checking the ventilator tubing with the other. Suddenly, she disconnects the bag and watches Will's breathing.

"No auto-PEEP; I'm going to reconnect," Laura tells the other nurse. She hooks Will back up to the ventilator, and on his first breath, the alarm goes off again. This time his eyes flutter open, and my heart stops.

"Something's not right here," Laura says. "Let's—"

"L-Laura," I say, my voice shaking with panic.

She stops and turns in my direction, her eyes widening. "L-Laura, his eyes . . ." I stutter, and she quickly turns to look at Will.

His eyes are barely open, but it's enough to see that the whites of his eyes aren't white but a sickly yellow color.

"Dammit! Lisa, I need you to get Evans up here right away, and set up for a portable chest x-ray and labs for liver function."

Lisa switches off the ventilator alarm and hurries to comply with Laura's instructions.

I'm still standing behind Laura, trying to get ahold of myself enough to ask what's going on. Before I can manage it, she turns to me, smiling sadly.

"Tori, I'm going to need to ask you to step out for a little bit while we try to sort this out."

"O-okay. What's going on?"

"Well, we don't really know, but he's having trouble breathing right now even with the vent, and as you pointed out, he's jaundiced."

"That happens when your liver isn't working right, doesn't it?"

"Yes," Laura says, nodding. "So we need to run some tests to figure out what's going on. I have your cell number so I can call you when we're finished, or if you want to wait in the waiting room at the end of the hall, I can come get you there."

"I'll go to the waiting room. I don't want to go too far."

Laura puts her hand on my arm and squeezes. "This isn't the end. I'm sure of it. We'll get him sorted out."

I nod and slowly back out of the room. The last thing I see is Will's face —his eyes are closed again, and it looks like he's sleeping. *Please, God, don't let this be the last time I see him!*

I'm halfway down the hall when I hear my name.

"Tori?"

It's Elizabeth. She freezes when she sees the look on my face and nearly drops the coffees she's carrying.

"Oh my God, did something happen? Is . . . is . . ."

"No, no he's not," I tell her quickly. "But we can't be in his room right now."

I take her elbow and lead her down to the waiting room, and while we sit, I tell her what happened. "So Laura is going to come down here when they're finished and tell us what's going on."

"Do you think his body is giving up? That his lungs and liver are failing?"

"I don't know," I tell her shakily.

I call Jason, but it goes to voicemail, so I leave him a message telling him to come as soon as possible. Elizabeth and I sit and hold on to each other, and I do my very best not to consciously think about anything. I just imagine sending all my strength and love to Will and plead with him to stay with me.

After what seems like an eternity, Dr. Evans walks into the waiting room. My heart leaps into my throat, and although my knees feel weak, Elizabeth and I are on our feet instantly. Dr. Evans holds his hands up to calm us.

"It's all right, ladies. Will's fine at the moment. Please sit and I'll fill you in."

I draw in a deep, shaky breath and sit back down. I lean forward, my elbows on my knees and my hands balled together as I stare at him, trying to read his mind because he can't tell me what's going on fast enough.

Just then, the door to the waiting room flies open, revealing a panic-stricken Jason. Before he can get a word out, I fly across the room and throw my arms around him.

"It's okay; he's still alive. But he got a bit worse, and Dr. Evans is here to tell us what's going on. Come sit with us; I'll fill you in on what happened later."

Dr. Evans looks at Jason and nods. "It's good to see you again, Jason. I had wondered if you were still supporting Will."

Jason inclines his head. "Yes, sir, as much as he'll let me."

Dr. Evans smirks, and it breaks the tension in the room because we all know how stubborn Will can be. Each of us knows, loves, and understands Will and would do anything to get him well. At this moment, the bond between us is powerful. I hope it's enough to see Will through this.

Dr. Evans gestures for Jason to take a seat. "Will is stable right now, but I have some not so good news. Will is jaundiced, which tells us his liver isn't functioning properly. We did an ultrasound; his liver is still swollen and inflamed due to the cancer, and I suspect his high fever has put additional strain on it. We don't have his blood work back yet, but I think it will confirm that he's in the early stages of liver failure."

There's a collective gasp in the room.

"Now this doesn't mean his liver *will* fail; it just means that right now, his liver is having trouble doing its job. I'm hopeful if his fever goes down, his liver function will return to normal, but we'll just have to wait and see.

"I wish I had better news for you, but I still have faith he can make it through this. You can go and see him now. I'll be back in a few hours with his lab results, and I'll be keeping a closer eye on him until he improves."

Dr. Evans' statement of "until he improves" and not "if he improves" is not lost on me, and it gives me some comfort. He really believes Will can recover from this.

"Thank you, Dr. Evans," I tell him, the first one of us to find their voice.

Dr. Evans nods and leaves the room.

Silence falls, and the three of us just stare at each other.

"He's going to make it," I say confidently, and I stand on wobbly legs, holding on to the chair for support.

Jason smiles and puts his arm around me, offering his other hand to Elizabeth to help her out of her chair. "Come on, let's go see him."

We make our way down the hall and back into Will's room. Right away, the yellow tinge of his skin strikes me, and I wonder how I didn't see it before. The change must have been so gradual that I didn't notice.

Jason and Elizabeth rush right over to Will, but I'm . . . disjointed. I need to talk to him—to be alone with him, and I won't have that opportunity until this evening when Jason and Elizabeth leave, so I give them the time to be with him now. I sit on the couch, and my exhaustion must have overtaken me because the next thing I know, Jason is shaking me.

"Tori, wake up. It's seven, and Elizabeth and I thought you should get some dinner before we go."

"Thanks. How's Will?"

"No change. Dr. Evans came by and confirmed the results of the liver tests, but he said they aren't as bad as they could be. He said we just have to wait and see."

I drag a hand over my face and glance at Will. Elizabeth is sitting in my usual chair, holding his hand between hers. I don't look too closely because I know if I do, I'll have to go to him, and all the words will spill out of my mouth, but I don't want to do that in front of Jason and Elizabeth. I need to tell him so many things, in case . . .

Jason offers to run out and pick up dinner for me before he leaves, but I decline, instead opting to get a sandwich in the cafeteria.

Jason and Elizabeth say their goodbyes to me, telling me they'll be back in the morning and giving me concerned looks. But they don't say anything. The strain of watching Will slowly get worse is wearing on all of us, and I see fear in their eyes as they tell him goodbye for the night. Elizabeth kisses him tenderly on the forehead, and I have to turn away so she doesn't see my tears. I know they're both wondering how many more days we have. Hell, the thought has crossed my mind more than once even though I promised myself I wouldn't think that way. But things look different after long days, and right now, I'm feeling like this is bigger than Will—bigger than all of us.

Finally, I'm alone with him. The door closes on Jason and Elizabeth, and I wearily turn to face the man I love. His forehead is sweaty, so my detour to his bathroom is automatic—wet the cloth, wring it out, fold it in half, and then again. I hope my efforts to cool him down comfort him. Sometimes, I think their only purpose might be to comfort me.

I wipe across his forehead, refold the cloth, press gently on his neck, one side at a time, then up to his cheeks. It's become a pattern. I didn't want to get used to doing this for him, but somehow I have, and it's become routine. I want to kiss him so much that it becomes routine. I want the feel of his arms around me to become part of me, but not this. *Never* this.

His eyes open as I care for him, and I startle—the neon yellow color is shocking and reinforces how terribly sick he is. His eyelids flutter as he struggles to keep his eyes open, but with his fever so high, there's no way he can focus. But I try anyway. I run my hand through his hair, and he tries to meet my eyes, but he just can't do it. He loses the battle, and his eyes fall closed, but he turns his head a little, leaning into my touch.

I look at him. I mean, I *really* look at him. His skin still looks yellow, and the circles under his eyes are so dark they look like bruises. His body is radiating heat, and the rash that covers his skin is even more inflamed because of it. He looks thin and frail, exhausted. He looks like he's dying right before my very eyes, as if he's lost to me already. I can't lose him. Not like this.

I can't handle the silence—it feels oppressive, like death itself is weighing down on us—so I combat it with words, with connection.

"Today wasn't a good day, sweetheart. You had some trouble breathing, and your liver is starting to fail. Your fever is so high—I don't know how it can stay this high for so long without hurting you. Maybe it can't, and that's why your liver is failing."

I caress his cheek with the back of my hand. His eyes roll under their lids, but I don't think he has the strength to open them again. Suddenly, I feel lost and alone and desperate, and I would give anything, absolutely anything, for him to be able to respond to me, to let me know he's listening and he understands.

"Will, I love you, and I'm not ready to let you go. You can't let go! Not when you just told me you love me, and you've decided to try to beat this. I know you have options—you can go back into treatment and maybe even be cured if you can just fight off the pneumonia. Please, please, Will, don't give up.

"I want to spend my life with you, and I don't think I can live without you. There are so many things I want to do, so much I want to share with you. You are the most amazing man I've ever met, and I don't deserve someone as sweet and wonderful as you, but it seems God gave you to me anyway. But He can't take you away, not after all you've been through—all *we've* been through to get to the point where we could admit we love each other.

"I want . . ." I have to stop because I'm crying so hard my voice fails. "More than anything in the world, I want to tell you I love you and to know you understand. I have to make you understand. I know why you did what you did when you sent me away, but I shouldn't have let you. I should have forced the words out. I should have told you long before that because maybe if I had, things would be different. Maybe you would have decided to lift your DNR sooner, and you wouldn't be so sick right now.

"I need you so much. I feel like I'm dying without you here. Without your smile and your laugh and your touch. I'm . . . lost. And you're lost, so you have to fight off this infection and find me again. We have to find each other. Please, Will, please! I love you."

A sob escapes my chest, and I break down, hard. I put my arms around him, and I get close, as close as I can, and I hold on, my sobs shaking both of us. I beg God and whoever might be listening not to take him from me, to give us the chance to be what we were meant to be, to give him the chance to have the life he deserves. He deserves a long life. And he deserves happiness, more than anyone I've ever known, after all he's been through. He's had enough pain and suffering to last a lifetime, and now he deserves comfort and peace. *Please, God, please.*

I wake up slowly, as I have for the past four mornings, to the soft whooshing sound of Will's ventilator. But . . . something's not right. The sound is too close. As I slowly become aware, I lift my head a little, and Will's hand slides off my head and onto his blanket. I must have fallen asleep here last night after my little freak-out, but how? I look at Will blearily, my brain still foggy. *Did I imagine his hand there?* I don't think I did.

Hope flares in my chest, and a warm smile spreads across my face as I reach up and cup his cheek. "Good morning, sweetheart. Was it your turn to comfort me last night?"

Of course, he doesn't respond, but I just know he did that consciously last night. He had to have. There's no other way it could have happened. As I'm still thinking about it, Laura slips into the room.

"Good morning, Tori. I hope you're not too stiff from sleeping like that. I thought about waking you, but you looked so at peace with Will's hand resting on your head."

"So I didn't imagine it!" I say triumphantly.

"No, you didn't. He must have been aware enough sometime in the night to notice you there and to touch you. I asked the night nurses, and no one's disturbed either of you through the night."

I grin at her as she checks Will over.

"Well, I finally have some good news," Laura says, smiling at me as she finishes taking Will's vitals. "His temperature has dropped—only half a degree, but this is the first time since he came into the ICU that it's been below one-oh-four. So I definitely think it's a good sign."

"That's fantastic!" I lean in to kiss Will's cheek. Maybe I'm crazy, but I think he does feel a little less hot. But he's still yellow. His liver isn't functioning as it should, and it's going to be a waiting game to see if it's going to get better or worse as Will's fever goes down. But I somehow feel as if I turned a corner last night—maybe we both did. This isn't over, but I begged and pleaded with the powers that be to spare him last night, and this morning, we've been given a ray of hope.

"I know you can beat this, sweetheart. You've fought so hard, and it's making a difference now. Keep fighting!"

Monday is a better day, and the days keep getting better after that. Will's fever slowly inches downward, and his liver function starts returning to normal. Jason, Elizabeth, and I are ecstatic, and the atmosphere in Will's room becomes hopeful.

The yellow color slowly leaves his skin and eyes, and as his fever goes down, his restless motion stops. He becomes still—too still, in my opinion, because Will is always moving. By Wednesday, I'm so concerned about it that I ask Dr. Evans. Will's temperature is down to one-oh-one, but he's shown no signs of consciousness since he touched me in the early hours of Monday.

"I think it's exhaustion, Tori. He fought so hard against the infection; now that the threat is diminished, his body is trying to recover. He'll become aware again when his body decides he's recovered enough. You'll see."

It's Thursday afternoon, and I'm reading from my Kindle. I glance perfunctorily over at Will, then back down. *Wait, did he just move?* No, I must have imagined it because I want it so much. I sigh heavily but glance up again anyway. To my utter shock, Will shifts his legs under the blanket, and it looks like a deliberate motion, not just moving in his sleep.

I stand and run my fingers through his hair. "Will? Will, can you hear me?"

His eyes flutter open, and for the first time in eight days, they seem to be focused on me. He blinks slowly but forces them open again.

"Hello, sweetheart," I say, giving him my warmest smile. Inside, I'm turning cartwheels and screaming, but I don't want to scare the hell out of him, so I keep my voice soft and smooth. I continue stroking his hair, but I slide my free hand under his. "Are you with me? If you can understand me, squeeze my hand twice, okay?"

His eyes never leave mine, but I feel his fingers squeeze mine gently once, then a second time. My smile grows even wider.

"Oh, thank God. Sweetheart, you're gonna be okay. You've been really sick for a while, but you're getting better. You have pneumonia. Do you remember? Your fever is going down, and the doctors drained the infection from your chest. If you keep improving, they should be able to take you off the ventilator in a few days. Do you understand?"

He blinks slowly again, and I feel him squeeze my hand twice.

"I love you. I hope it's okay I came back. I couldn't stay away, and after you lifted your DNR and decided to fight, I thought you would want me here."

He squeezes my hand twice more, and I swear it's a little stronger this time. His eyes pierce me, saying one thing and a thousand things all at the same time—that he loves me.

My heart swells, and there's so much I want to say to him, but what he needs most right now is rest. "Sleep, Will. I'll be here when you wake up again—I'm not going anywhere. Now or ever."

He gives my hand one long squeeze as his eyes fall closed, and his hand relaxes.

The minute he's asleep, I slide my hand out from under his and bolt from the room. I jump up and down in the hallway as quietly as I can because I'm in the middle of the ICU. As I'm in mid-jump, the elevator opens to reveal Jason and Jenny. Jason's eyebrows disappear under his bangs, but Jenny knows.

She runs to me and throws her arms around my neck, nearly bowling me over. "He's awake, isn't he?"

"Yes!" My grin is threatening to split my face. "Well, he's not awake now, but he just was! I talked to him, and he responded! Oh God, he's going to be okay!"

Jason scoops us both up, and we're one big pile of hugs and smiles.

"Happy birthday, Tori!" Jenny exclaims.

It's my birthday? I do the math in my mind. I'm thirty-three today. "Oh my, it *is* my birthday, isn't it? I completely forgot!"

Jenny gives me another hug and whispers in my ear. "And Will gave you the very best present!"

CHAPTER 3

The days seem to pass more quickly now that Will is improving. He's been more alert because they're decreasing the sedatives, but he's still desperately tired even when he is awake. For the past three days, he's woken up for five or ten minutes at a time, and then he's out for another hour or two. Yesterday, Dr. Evans came and explained everything that happened to him, and he squeezed my hand to say he understood. Evans also told him they were planning to have him off the ventilator within a day or two, and he squeezed my hand pretty hard after hearing that.

They began weaning him off the ventilator yesterday, and today, they're planning to disconnect it and remove the tube. They've been slowly decreasing the pressure support for his breathing, and right now it's at zero, meaning he's breathing on his own through the machine. He doesn't know the tube's coming out today, but he's going to be so happy about it!

It's ten in the morning, and Jason and Elizabeth haven't arrived yet. I've been awake for about two hours, and I've showered and dressed because this is a big day for Will. Dr. Evans should be coming by soon, so I decide it's time to wake him.

I sit on the edge of his bed and take his hand, rubbing his fingers gently between mine. It's so wonderful that his skin is now just barely warm!

My chest expands with happiness as I smile. He's really going to beat this, and there's so much we need to talk about!

"Will. Sweetheart, it's time to wake up."

His eyelids flutter, then open slowly, and he squeezes my hand.

"Good morning, love." His eyes sparkle at me, and the skin around them crinkles in response. He can't really smile because of the way the tube is taped, but his eyes tell me all I need to know.

"Today's a big day for you. They've had your vent turned down to no support since last night, and you've been breathing just fine, so Evans is going to come and remove the tube this morning."

Will smiles again and moves his other hand on top of mine, squeezing both of my hands tightly in his.

We both startle as the door opens, and Dr. Evans enters, followed by Laura.

"Good morning, Will. Today's the big day. You've been basically breathing on your own since last night, so let's get that tube out of your throat. Does that sound good?"

Will nods, but his eyes speak much louder.

Dr. Evans chuckles. "I know that sounds good. And if all goes well, I'm going to remove the tube from your chest today too. Your drainage is down to almost nothing, so it's time to plug up the hole."

I chuckle, and Will smiles. It's absolutely fantastic to see him awake and happy even if he still has a long way to go until he's fully recovered.

"Well, let's do this," Dr. Evans says, clapping his hands together.

I start to untangle my hands from Will's, but he clutches them, suddenly looking nervous.

"I'll stay, okay? I'm just going to back up to give them room to do the procedure, but I'll be right here."

Will relaxes, releasing my hands so I can step back.

Dr. Evans and Laura move to either side of Will, and Laura disconnects the ventilator. She gently removes the tape from his mouth, and he winces as it pulls at his skin. He's completely breathing on his own now, but they wait for a moment or two, just to make sure.

"Okay, Will, in a moment, I'm going to ask you to breathe in deeply, then try to cough, and while you're doing that, I'm going to pull the tube out. It's going to hurt where the chest tube is, but hopefully, it won't be too bad because you're still on a high dose of morphine. As soon as I get the tube out, we're going to give you oxygen, and you'll need to keep the mask on for a few hours so we can monitor you. If all goes well, I'll come back this afternoon, and we'll remove the chest tube, okay?"

Will nods, but he looks frightened. I think Dr. Evans sees it too because he doesn't give Will any time to think about it.

"Okay, Will. Breathe in as deep as you can and cough. Okay, now!"

Will does as he's told, and within seconds, the tube is out. Laura gently cleans around his mouth and puts the oxygen mask over his face. The mask immediately fogs with Will's breath, and I exhale in a *whoosh*. He did it. He's really breathing on his own.

He brings his hand up to clutch at his throat, and his other arm is curled over his chest. Dammit, he's in pain.

"Will, was that really painful?" Dr. Evans asks.

Will nods.

"Do you need more morphine?"

Will nods again, quickly and decisively, and his breathing has picked up. Fuck, he's in a *lot* of pain.

"Laura, give him an IV push of ten milligrams, and we'll see where we go from there. Will, that went really well, and you're doing great. I'm sorry it's so painful. Have Laura call me if you need anything. Otherwise, I'll be back in a few hours. "

Dr. Evans gives me a reassuring smile as he leaves, and I'm across the room with my fingers in Will's hair before the door closes behind him.

Will's still breathing harshly, but I'm so thankful he's breathing.

"Oh, sweetheart, I'm so sorry that hurt you so much! Laura's giving you more morphine; just hang on," I tell him. He looks exhausted, and I have to remind myself he's still not staying awake for very long, and what just happened probably wore him out. I stroke his hair gently until his hands relax and sleep claims him.

Will sleeps hard until around four in the afternoon when Laura comes in and removes his oxygen mask. He flinches away from her, but he doesn't seem to be in pain, and his eyes open lazily. He's still pretty doped up. Well, it's better than the alternative.

Dr. Evans returns and removes Will's chest tube in a manner similar to this morning's procedure. Laura dresses the wound as soon as the tube is removed, and Will lies back wearily. I move back in and take his hand, and he opens his eyes, his gaze locking on mine. He tries to clear his throat, but the sound is pained, and his hand flies to his throat.

"Sweetheart, don't. Don't try to talk yet. I know we have a lot to say to each other, but you need to give your throat some time to heal. I'll be here. I'm not going anywhere," I say, trying to soothe him.

Frustration flashes in his eyes, followed by what looks like desperation, and he reaches for me, pulling me to him like he hasn't been able to do all this time. I go willingly, but I'm extra careful not to put any weight on his chest.

He holds me tightly for a long moment, and I feel alive again after ten days of being in limbo. I can feel his heartbeat against my chest, and it's strong. I feel as if it's giving us both life right now. He turns his head and breathes against my ear, "I love you," and I swear it's the most beautiful sound I've ever heard even though it's barely a whisper.

"I love you too," I tell him, turning my head to kiss his neck tenderly.

He leans into my kisses, so I keep going, reacquainting myself with his skin since I can't yet reconnect with his soul. When we both can't take any more, he pushes on my arms, silently telling me to back away so he can see my face.

Actually, he wanted me to be able to see *his* face because brilliant green eyes pierce me as he mouths, "I'm sorry."

"Don't be sorry. You did what you thought was best. You were trying to protect both of us. I'm not angry with you. I'm thrilled you lifted your DNR and decided to fight.

"We have a lot to talk about, but it can wait at least a day to give your throat a chance to rest. Can we wait until tomorrow? I just can't bear to see you in any more pain, especially if it's pain that could be prevented. Please?"

Will clears his throat again, and his whole face scrunches in silent misery. He nods at me grudgingly.

He wanders in and out of consciousness for the rest of the afternoon and early evening, but he's becoming more and more aware as the last of the sedative leaves his system. When he's awake, I let Jason and Elizabeth talk to him because I know if *I* do, he's going to try to talk too, and I really don't want him to do that yet.

By seven, Jason and Elizabeth are ready to leave for the night so Will can settle in and get some real sleep now that he's not hooked up to so much equipment. After they say their goodbyes to him, he looks at me and wrinkles his eyebrows.

I chuckle because he looks so cute when he's confused. "I haven't left your side since you were moved up to the ICU. I've been sleeping on the fold-out couch."

The wrinkle in his brow deepens, and he mouths the words, "All this time?"

I nod and smile.

He shakes his head a little. "Go home," he whispers, waving his hand at me. "You look tired."

I'm hesitant to leave him, but just the thought of not having my sleep interrupted by nurses going in and out all night is almost enough to make me whimper. "Are you sure?"

Will nods. "Come back tomorrow," he whispers, his green eyes sparkling as he smiles at me.

Electricity rolls down my spine, and I actually shiver in response. I've missed him so damn much these last ten days; it's like a miracle to watch him come back to me.

"All right, I'll go, but you have the nurses call me if you need anything," I tell him sternly.

He lifts his hand to his forehead and gives me a sloppy salute, and I laugh out loud. Already he's teasing me, and it gives me warm fuzzies in my chest.

I lean in to kiss his forehead, but just as he did on the night he pushed me away, he puts his hands on either side of my face and pulls me down so our lips meet. His are dry and chapped, and the kiss is brief and chaste, but it's hands down the best kiss he's ever given me. Even though we haven't talked yet, it feels like a new beginning.

I pull back and look at him, and I can see the symbolism of what he's just done isn't lost on him. He stares at me intently, a declaration of love and a plea for forgiveness both wrapped up in his gaze.

"I'll be back in the morning," I tell him, and as I stroke the back of my hand over his cheek, he leans into my touch.

It's hard to leave him after all this time, and as I reach the door with my bag slung over my shoulder, I look back again. He cocks an eyebrow at me as if to say "seriously?" and he makes a shooing motion with his hand, but it's weaker, and his eyelids look heavy. He's going to be asleep the minute I shut the door. Maybe it's for the best, then. We'll both get a good night's rest and be ready to talk tomorrow, if he's able.

"Tori. Tori, wake up."

I roll onto my back and stretch lazily, but I tense when I realize there's no sound. No *whoosh* of the ventilator, no *beep* telling me Will's heart is still beating. I sit up abruptly and nearly jump out of my skin when I see Elizabeth standing over me. "Oh!"

"I'm sorry! I didn't mean to startle you. It's nine o'clock, and I know you wanted to go to the hospital this morning, so I thought I should wake you."

Nine o'clock? In the morning? That's right! I came home from the hospital last night because Will shooed me out of his room. And holy shit, I just slept for twelve hours!

I scrub at my face, trying to clear the fog of sleep from my brain. "Thanks, Elizabeth. I wanted to get there before Will woke up this morning, but I'm thinking that might be out the window now."

Elizabeth pats me on the shoulder. "You needed your rest. Even Will commented how tired you looked last night. Do you want to shower, then join me for some breakfast? I was going to make French toast."

My stomach rumbles in response. "Sure. I'll need about fifteen minutes."

We finish our breakfast, and I hurry over to the hospital. It's after ten when I finally get to the ICU, and I'm so eager to see Will, I'm practically vibrating.

I push his door open slowly and revel in the silence in his room. There are no more *whooshes* and *beeps*. The only sound I can hear is the slight wheeze of Will's breathing.

He looks . . . better. His forehead is dry, and all the ruddiness is gone from his cheeks. His mass of auburn hair is still sticking out every which way, but it looks freshly washed. The circles under his eyes look a little lighter, and I grin when I see that his lips are slightly pursed into that little pout that does funny things to my insides. But as I look farther down, I can still see the signs of his cancer—the lymph nodes in his neck are still visibly swollen, and the rash on his arms is bright red and draws my eyes since he's wearing a short-sleeved hospital gown. His belly is almost flat, but there's a pillow lying across his chest. *I wonder why that's there.*

I take measured steps across the room and pull in a deep breath before I pick up his hand between mine.

He opens his eyes, startled, but then I'm swallowed up by the most vibrant green I've ever seen. My heart starts to pound in my chest as his face is transformed by his gorgeous smile, and it lights me up—my own smile struggling to match the brilliance of his. *Oh God, I am so in love with him!*

But suddenly, I'm feeling a little shy. Even though I've been with him all this time, both of us professing our love for each other is a whole new game, and I'm unsure of the rules. It's as if we're starting all over again. I can feel the heat in my cheeks as I whisper, "Hi."

Will tries to return my greeting, but it comes out as more of a squeak, and I can't help but chuckle.

He grins at me, then clears his throat. "Let's try that again. Hi."

His voice is gravelly and rough—it even sounds painful. "How are you today?" I ask, reaching up to caress his cheek.

He breathes out hard and leans into my hand for a second before answering. "Lousy, but better than when I was on the ventilator or before my lung collapsed. It's wonderful not to be struggling for breath or having something breathing for me."

"I bet it is. How's your throat feeling?"

His hand strays unconsciously up to his neck. "It's . . . a bit painful. I have a feeling it would be really bad without the morphine."

"Do they still have you on a high dose?" I had noticed the glassiness to Will's eyes, but he's really alert and doesn't seem high at all.

"Yes, as high as they can give me and still keep me conscious. My liver and spleen are still dangerously swollen, and I think I'd rather die than cough again. With a hole in my chest, the pain is incredible, even with the morphine."

"Can't they give you something to suppress the cough?"

Will shakes his head. "Evans said no. Coughing keeps the mucus in my chest from settling. He said it's how my body's keeping me from getting pneumonia again."

"I'm sure he's right, but I hate that it's hurting you so much."

"Me too."

We lapse into silence for a moment. I desperately want to talk to him, but if his throat is still bothering him, and he's in that much pain, it can wait. "We can talk another day—"

"No, I'm fine. I have some things I need to tell you—"

"Really, it can wait," I say, trying to let him know I'm not upset.

"Please, Tori?" he says, his eyes pleading. "I need—"

He stops abruptly and draws in a rapid, wheezing breath, hugging the pillow across his chest, tight to his body, and scrunching his eyes as he coughs hard. It doesn't sound as involuntary as it did before he was in the ICU, and it's definitely looser, but he cries out in pain as soon as the spasm ends, holding his breath and curling in on himself as much as he can.

I raise my hands over him, but there's nothing I can do to help, and I cringe at the sound of his agony.

He opens his eyes as he tries to get his breathing back to normal and looks toward the table beside him. "Tori, can you hand me that cup with the ice chips?"

He still can't really swallow, and they've been feeding him by IV since he got pneumonia, but I grab the cup to hand to him so he can at least soothe his throat. As he raises his arm, I can see how badly it's shaking. "Here, why don't you let me give you some? You don't look like you're very steady yet."

Will sighs. "No, I'm not. I'm definitely a lot weaker than I was before."

"Hey, that's to be expected," I tell him as I raise an ice chip to his lips. "You just need to give yourself some time."

Will sucks on the ice for a moment then swallows painfully before sighing again. "I know. I just hate that I'm worse off than I was before."

"Well, yesterday you were on a ventilator and had a chest tube, but now, you're not hooked up to any of that anymore."

He smiles, but suddenly, he becomes very serious, and his eyes pierce me with their intensity. "I'm so sorry I told you not to come back. I should never have done that."

"It's all right—"

"No, it's not. And I need to explain. There are . . . a lot of things I need to explain."

I offer him another ice chip, and he takes it before he continues.

"Shit. Where do I start?"

"Just . . . tell me everything," I say, squeezing his hand between mine. "I'm not going anywhere."

He smiles at me, then takes a breath and continues. "The week before my lung collapsed was, hands down, the worst week of my life. Worse than when I attempted suicide or even when I was diagnosed. I was trying to decide if I should just let the pneumonia kill me, but . . . that wasn't all of it. I'll get to what the rest of it was in a minute.

"That day was . . . the worst of the worst. I was in so much pain, and it was so hard for me to breathe—I decided just to give in and let go. By the time you came, the pain was better, but my breathing was worse, and the huge dose of morphine they'd given me made it really hard to think clearly.

"When I saw you . . . God, at that moment, I wished we'd never met. The pain in your eyes when you looked at me—you knew I was going to let myself die—I could see it on your face. And it was killing you. It just tore me apart. The emotional pain on top of the physical was just too much. I couldn't handle it, so I . . . kind of freaked out and pushed you away. I convinced myself this was for the best, that maybe it'd be easier for you to forget if you didn't see the end, and"—he closes his eyes—"I was selfish. I couldn't bear to see you hurting for me even though I knew deep down you still would, even if I sent you away. I tried to make it easier on myself."

He clears his throat, and I give him another ice chip and take advantage of his silence.

"No, it wasn't selfish. You were realizing that you needed to do what you needed for yourself, to get you through to the end. That's what I've been trying to get you to see all this time. It means you're finally ready," I say, tears rolling down my cheeks.

"No, Tori, I'm not," he whispers, and my heart stutters in my chest.

"I just need to get through this," he says, swiping at his eyes and squeezing my hand tighter, his gaze fixed on the blanket in front of him.

"After you left, I felt awful. I was alone and afraid, and I wanted to call you to come back so badly, but I thought I was doing what was best for both of us, and I'd already made my choice to die. So I just tried to hold on.

"And that's how Jenny found me."

Right then, something in Will's demeanor changes. The hand between mine begins to tremble.

"She wanted to know where you were, so I told her what I'd done. She looked so sad that it almost broke me, but I'm a stubborn ass, and I'd already made up my mind.

"But she wouldn't accept it. She kept talking to me—reminding me of everything you and I had done together and pointing out things you did to take care of me that I hadn't even noticed. And she told me you loved me."

I breathe in sharply and our eyes lock, but what I feel from him is pain. In my mind's eye, I can see him sitting there, panting for breath and trying to hold his resolve while Jenny tries to wear him down.

Will closes his eyes and runs his tongue over his lips, and I give him another ice chip. He's getting tired, but I know better than to suggest we talk again later—I can feel his need to get through this so we can move on.

"I got . . . angry. Angry that you loved me, and I'd let it go that far because it tore down my reason for telling you to go. You weren't going to get over this, and I'd sentenced you to God knows what kind of hell when I was gone.

"I told Jenny to leave, and the next hour was the worst of my entire life. I didn't know what to do. I cried, and I prayed, and I beat myself up over the whole thing so badly, it's a wonder I survived it. I wanted so desperately just to let it end, but . . . I wanted you just as much. In the end, I wanted you *more*. I wanted—I *want* a future with you."

He closes his eyes and is silent for a moment, his lip and chin quivering. He squeezes my hand very tightly, and suddenly, his eyes pierce me, full of pain and remorse and begging for understanding. "I love you, Tori. God help me, I've never loved anyone like this before."

My own tears begin to fall, and I sit on the edge of his bed, leaning over so I can place my hands on either side of his face. "I love you too, Will, with all my heart," I tell him, trying to channel everything I'm feeling to him. I want him to have it all, to know that I would do anything and everything for him.

"I . . . know," he whispers. "That's the only thing I remember from the last eleven days, really. Every time I woke up, you were right there, telling me you loved me. I didn't know if it was real or not, but I hoped it was. Sometimes, I couldn't even understand what you were saying, but I knew it was you, and you were waiting for me. I just kept trying to get back to you."

My breath catches in my throat. *What I was doing actually made a difference! Holy shit!*

"Oh, Will! Your fever was so high, I didn't even know if you could hear me or understand me, but I just had to tell you I loved you. I felt horrible that you didn't know how much I cared about you—I should have told you long before that night—"

"Tori, stop. Neither of us can change the past. I think we were both afraid, but . . . I'm not afraid anymore."

"I'm not afraid anymore either," I tell him, reaching up so I can kiss his forehead, and then I press my lips to his.

He pulls away slightly as the tears he was holding back roll down his face. "I haven't been honest with you, and I'm so sorry! I was just trying to protect myself, and I didn't realize—"

"Will, please. Calm down." My words are a plea as I stroke his cheek with my fingers.

He lets out a sob, and it turns into a cough, his hands flying to brace the pillow against his chest as he cringes and whimpers in pain.

I run my fingers into his hair as he tries to pull himself back together, and I give him an ice chip to soothe his throat as soon as he's able to take it. I can't let him suffer through this. Not when I know what he's going to tell me, and I can make it easier.

"Will, I—"

"No. Please, Tori, just let me finish." He coughs a little, but it doesn't turn into a full-blown spasm, and he swallows thickly. "The other battle I've been fighting, the thing I haven't told you . . . is . . . I still have treatment options. I chose to refuse further treatment after my last relapse because I didn't see the point."

He sighs heavily. "I didn't think I had anything to live for. I was estranged from my family, a burden to my friends, and I went through chemo twice, and the damn cancer just kept coming back. It didn't seem like there was any way out, so I decided I wanted it to be over as soon as possible."

My heart breaks for him as I listen because this is the Will I met almost three months ago, lost and alone and looking for an escape.

"But that was before you came into my life. Tori, you turned my world upside down, and you made . . . you *make* me happy. Happier than I've ever been. I love you, and I want a future with you, and I'm willing to do anything to try to make that happen. I want to go back into treatment. I don't know what it will entail, and I don't know if it's even still an option, but I want to try."

He raises his eyes to me, and I'm swept into a stormy green sea of fear and regret. He's terrified I'm going to be angry or push him away as he did to me because he doesn't know he's just answered all of my prayers. I take his beautiful face between my hands. "Sweetheart, I want to be with you too. I'll do anything I can to help you, and I'll stay with you every step of the way."

I lean in and brush my lips over his, and he breathes out shakily before returning the kiss. I want to pull him as close to me as I can and kiss him until we're both breathless, but he's in no shape for that, so I try to pour my passion into every slow, deliberate caress of my tongue and lips.

We kiss until he starts to cough a little, and I run my fingers into his auburn hair. "I love you so much, Will. I know why you did what you did. I understand, and I don't blame you at all! You had made your decision, and you were protecting yourself."

"I'm so sorry. I wanted to tell you I didn't mean what I said about not coming back and that I wanted to fight, but I got so sick so fast, and they put that damn tube down my throat so I couldn't talk . . ."

"It's all right. I knew from the way you looked at me and held my hand that you wanted me here. That was how you told me, and I understood."

He smiles warmly at me.

"And . . . you left me this," I say, pulling his black sketchbook out of my bag. "Will, I don't even know what to say about what's in here. It's unbelievable!"

He turns an adorable shade of crimson as he grins shyly at me. "I always imagined showing it to you myself, but I wanted you to know it wasn't desperation or the morphine talking when I told you I loved you. I'd felt that way for quite a while, but I was too stubborn to admit it. I hoped you'd understand when you saw them."

"Oh, I did! I do! I can't imagine a more special way to tell me you love me. Your sketches are beyond beautiful, and I'll treasure them forever. I've carried this book with me everywhere since Jenny gave it to me, and I've looked at your work so often, I've been worried about leaving marks on the pages!"

"I'll draw you some more as soon as I'm able," he says sweetly. "I love drawing you as much as I love looking at you."

He sighs as his eyes fall closed. He's clearly fighting exhaustion, but he looks more at peace than I've ever seen him.

"Now you know all my secrets," he murmurs, and my stomach clenches. Will doesn't know all of my secrets, and I don't think I'm ready to tell him. Christ, I don't think he even knows I *have* secrets because in all the time I've known him, my energy has been focused on supporting *him*. The time will come someday, but right now, we have to get him better.

Suddenly, he wrinkles his eyebrows as he looks at me. "You were a little less shocked than I was expecting when I told you I have treatment options."

I can feel my cheeks reddening as I stare back at him. "I knew you did."

His eyebrows fly upward, so I continue hastily. "But not for very long. After Jenny gave me your message, I had to know if there was any hope for you, so I begged her to tell me. Please don't be upset with her! She gave me hope, and it helped me get through the last eleven days."

The scowl on Will's face dissolves as quickly as it came. "How could I be mad at her if it helped you? Besides, I have her to thank for convincing me to go back into treatment."

"Really?"

"Yes. She's a persistent little thing. But after I . . . threw her out, I realized what she was saying made sense."

"What did she tell you, sweetheart?"

"She pointed out I had nothing to lose. I've already lost it all, and I have so much to gain if I go through treatment again and achieve remission. I'm sure it won't be easy, but if I can come out on the other side and have a life with you, it'll be worth it."

I smile as happiness bubbles in my chest. "So what do we do now?"

"Well, I think tomorrow we should talk with Dr. Evans about my options and when I could begin. I just hope it's not too late . . ."

"Jenny didn't think it was," I say, trying to assuage his fears. "She said high-dose chemotherapy followed by a stem cell transplant was an option for you and that it could wipe out the cancer completely."

"I hope so."

His eyes close again, and it's only a few seconds before his head lolls to the side, and his breathing takes on the even cadence of sleep. He was obviously anxious to say his piece, and now that he has, he can rest.

Tomorrow will be a very important day—for both of us.

CHAPTER 4

I wake on Monday morning in my own bed after a restful night's sleep. Once again, Will insisted I go home last night, saying it's bad enough that he has to spend the night in the hospital; he doesn't want to be the cause of anyone else doing it.

He was much better yesterday afternoon after he woke up from his nap. He was completely aware, and although coughing still put him in agony, he was in good spirits and eager for today.

Today.

Today, we find out about his treatment options, and he'll have to choose a path that will shape the rest of his life . . . and the rest of mine. And it's likely to determine the length of his life and the quality. I'm nervous, but I'm also filled with hope. A few weeks ago, Will was trying to decide when to die, and now, he's trying to decide how to live. Just the fact that we have this day before us, to face together, is a victory.

Will's room is a beehive of activity when I arrive—Laura and two orderlies are there with him, moving busily about the room.

He's sitting almost upright this morning, and he smiles brilliantly when he sees me. "You're just in time. They're about to move me back down to the oncology floor."

"That's right," Laura says, grinning. "You don't belong up here with the really sick people anymore."

"Why don't I head down and meet you there? It looks like you're about ready to go, and there are enough people in this room right now."

"Okay. Dr. Evans popped by this morning and said he'd see us there after they moved me."

"See you soon," I say, waving.

He waves back, grinning from ear to ear. Today *is* a victory, and my steps are lighter and more carefree than they've been in weeks as I head down the hallway.

When the elevator doors open on four, I'm hit with a wave of déjà vu. I didn't think I'd ever be happy to be coming here to see Will, but after twelve days of tiptoeing through the ICU, the noise and hustle of the oncology floor is homey and welcome.

Jenny is at the nurses' station, but she drops everything when she sees me and comes running over. "He's on his way down, isn't he?"

"Yup, they were just about to move him when I arrived."

"Fantastic! I have his room all ready," she says, bouncing and clapping her hands. "I've missed him."

"He's missed you too," I tell her, marveling at her enthusiasm. I've known Jenny forever and worked with her like this for a number of patients, but I've never seen her as attached to anyone as she is to Will.

The elevator doors at the other end of the hall open, and the orderlies push Will's bed out into the hallway.

"Will! Welcome back!"

Will snorts. "Hi, Jenny. I should have figured you'd be the one-woman welcoming committee when I got back down here."

"You betcha," Jenny says. "You ain't seen nothin' yet!"

Will looks to me and I shrug.

We meet at Will's old room, 412, and Jenny and I follow the orderlies who are pushing Will's bed in. I can hear Will laughing, and as I walk through the door, I soon see why. Jenny has hung a banner that reads "Welcome Back, Will!" in colorful, cartoon-style lettering over where the orderlies are situating Will's bed, and on his bedside table, there's a bouquet of brightly colored balloons, including two mylar ones that say "Welcome Back" and "I Missed You!"

I glance over at Jenny, and she's beaming.

Will shakes his head, still chuckling. "Damn, Jenny, are you really that hard up for interesting patients? I leave for two weeks, and when I come back, you stop one step short of a parade?"

"All my patients are interesting, but some are more special than others," Jenny replies, and I think there's a hint of a blush on her cheeks.

Will's blush is more obvious, and his eyes soften as he looks at her. "Thank you, Jenny. Really. I never thought I'd be happy to be here, but I am. If I have to be in the hospital, there's no place I'd rather be than on your floor."

"Dammit, Will." Jenny swipes at her eyes. "Do you make all the pretty girls cry?"

"Only the ones I care about," he answers, and holds his arms open for her.

Jenny walks to him and they hug, and I have to wipe my own tears away. I don't think I've ever loved Jenny more than I do at this moment.

Jenny pulls back, but Will fixes his brilliant green eyes on her. "Thank you," he says softly.

Jenny nods. "Well, I have patients to check on. Evans should be here shortly for you, and I'll stop back after your meeting, okay?"

"Okay," Will replies, turning his eyes to me.

Jenny winks at me as she leaves, and I nod, hoping she can see everything I'm feeling in my eyes. I'll have to thank her properly later.

"Are you ready?" I ask Will as I cross the room and take his hand.

"I'm as ready as I'll ever be, I guess. It's all I can think about, but since I don't know my options, there's not much *to* think about. I'm mostly just nervous, I guess."

I stroke my hand over his. "I know what you mean. I can't think about anything else either. How are you feeling today?"

Will sighs and closes his eyes. "Better than yesterday but still really tired and sore. I tore my stitches out coughing last night, so they decided it would be better to bind my chest for a few days. It still hurts when I cough, but not nearly as much as before."

"Oh damn. You coughed so hard, the stitches actually split?"

"Yeah. I didn't think you could do that either," Will answers. "But all of a sudden, I was in a ton of pain, and my side was bleeding. Laura restitched it last night, but she said I can't afford to have it happen again —the risk of infection is too high."

As if on cue, Will starts to cough, but I can tell immediately it's better than yesterday. He still winces in pain, but the binding stabilizes him and doesn't allow the stitches to pull.

"Fuck! That still hurts a lot, even with the binding and the morphine. And it's certainly not helping my throat any." He rasps out the words, clearing his throat roughly. "Can you get me some ice?"

"Of course. I'll be right back," I tell him, squeezing his hand before I go.

By the time I return, Dr. Evans is in the room, and they're waiting for me. Will's eyes seek me out, and I move to his side and take his hand, sitting in the chair next to him. He's afraid. He's been excited and hopeful, but now that we're down to it, I think he knows that whatever his choices are, none of them will be easy. The hand that grips mine is clammy, and I can feel him trembling.

"Hi, Tori. Will and I were just discussing his progress, but I think you both had something else you wanted to talk about?"

"Yes," Will says, squeezing my hand tightly. "I've decided I want to go back into treatment for my cancer. I want to make it to remission, for good this time, and have a life with Tori."

I squeeze his hand back and smile encouragingly, and Dr. Evans breathes a sigh of relief.

"I think you've made a good decision, Will. You're too young, with too much life potentially ahead of you, to just give up. I'm glad you've found your reason to try. Now, options. Radiation doesn't have a high success rate for AITL, which is why we didn't do that in the first place, and while standard chemotherapy *does* have a decent rate of success, it's obviously not working for you since you've relapsed twice after treatment. So we're really left with only one option: high dose chemotherapy, followed by a stem cell transplant.

"Basically, you would receive a six-day course of high dose chemotherapy drugs, which would wipe out all of your immune cells, both the cancerous ones and the healthy ones. Then, once we verify all of your immune cells are gone, we would give you new stem cells from a matched donor to repopulate your immune system.

"I'll be honest with you—this is a very intense treatment, and the recovery time is long. It'll take one to two years until your immune system is fully functional again, and you'll be at risk for infection and experience side effects during that time. But, if all goes well, this treatment is a cure for some patients."

As we listen to Dr. Evans explain the treatment steps in detail and all the side effects, Will pales and closes his eyes, and I suddenly feel like I'm going to throw up. *He doesn't think he can do this. Oh God, this was a huge mistake. I can't ask him to do this. He's already been through so much, and we don't even know what the odds are that this treatment would be successful for him.* I'm reeling inside, and I miss most of what Dr. Evans says as my thoughts spiral out of control. *He's still going to die. There's no way out of the pain and suffering for him . . . except one.* I jerk back into the present when I hear Will's voice.

"So what are the odds of this working?"

"Well," Evans replies, "if you're recovered enough to begin treatment in the next few weeks, I'd put your odds of going into remission afterward at about forty percent. They would have been higher if you'd done this four months ago, but the cancer cells have had time to multiply and spread. There's also a chance, maybe twenty percent, that the treatment will kill you. But without it, the cancer will surely kill you, so I wouldn't worry about that. But now, the bad news. Even if you achieve remission, there are no guarantees it will last any longer than the previous two times, and I can't give you any odds on that—it's just too unpredictable. I'm sorry, Will. I wish I had better news for you. Why don't you take some time to think about it, and if you have any questions, let the nurses know, and we can talk again."

"Okay, thank you, Dr. Evans," Will responds distractedly, his eyes still closed.

Dr. Evans gives me an encouraging smile as he leaves the room.

I look at Will as he lies there with his eyes still closed, and I notice how much thinner he's become and how frail he looks. As I watch him, a tear rolls down his cheek. *He can't do this. He won't survive it, and he'll die in pain instead of in comfort.*

Suddenly, his eyes meet mine, full of hopelessness. "Oh God, Tori . . . I don't know if I can do this. I've been through chemo twice before, and both times it nearly broke me, and I was much stronger then than I am right now. Chemo is . . . hell. And this would be six straight days of it at ten times the doses I had before. I don't know how I can—"

"I can't ask you to do this." I blurt the words out, my heart shattering in my chest. "You've been through so much already, and it might not even work. I can't . . . see you suffering because of me."

His eyes well up, and suddenly, there's hurt there. I can see how worked up he's getting, his emotions starting to spiral out of control, but I can't help him because I have no control over my own. He swallows thickly, trying to keep hold of himself. "Does that mean you don't think I should?"

Oh, shit! "No, I . . . I don't know what it means. It means I don't want to see you suffer anymore, but I don't think there's any way out of that, no matter what you choose," I say, my heart pounding painfully.

"What if I did decide I want to do it?" he asks, looking away from me.

"If you decide you want to do it, then I'm going to be here with you. I'll take a sabbatical from work and do whatever I can to make this easier for you."

"Fuck!" Will swears, running his hand through his hair. "I should never have . . . what if I die anyway? I'll have put you through so much more pain—"

"That doesn't matter!" I nearly shout, tears streaming down my face as my emotions overwhelm me. There's so much anger and pain and despair that I don't know what to do with it. So it comes out as cold, hard truth, a truth I've known for weeks now, and it's time he knew it too.

"There's no 'cut my losses' here! It's too late for that! If you die now or you die later, it's going to destroy me either way, because I'm in love with you. That's never going to change. I'll love you if we have a long life together or long after you're gone; it doesn't matter. It's forever."

"Tori, I don't have forever," he whispers, his pain so raw and deep that I clutch at my chest as it assaults me.

My voice breaks as a sob tears from my throat, and I reach for him, but he stops me, eyes closed and brow furrowed, his breath coming in shallow pants.

"D-d-don't . . . I c-c-c—" He starts coughing, and it's long and hard, and I realize after a moment, it's turned into sobbing. I want so desperately to hold him, but he stopped me before, and I just can't take the pain of another rejection. So I stand frozen—trapped in this hell that's descended upon us—and alone.

We are both alone right now even though there are mere inches between us.

I can't bear to watch him, so I dissociate myself, pushing it all away so that it's nothing—I'm nothing— until Will touches my hand.

His eyes are red-rimmed, but he's regained some control, and he looks at me with love, not panic. "Tori, I swear I'm not pushing you away . . . but . . . I need some time to myself. I'm not ready to talk about this yet— I don't think either of us is. I'm overwhelmed, and my thoughts are all over the place. I need to think it through and figure out how *I* feel about it before we can figure out how *we* feel about it. Do you know what I mean?"

I nod mutely. His words sting even though they shouldn't. I want him to let me all the way in, but it's unfair to expect him to be able to change the way he deals with things just because he's told me he loves me. It'll take time for him to learn how to trust and depend on me. After all, even though his choice will affect me profoundly, he's the one who will have to suffer through the treatment.

As I'm telling myself these things, a tear escapes down my cheek, and Will bows his head. When he looks up again, a storm is raging in his eyes.

"I'm sorry. I'm so fucking sorry, but I can't do this any other way! I can't —I don't want to hurt you! I can't even explain it. I just—"

"Will, I understand you need time; I do," I tell him, running my hand up and down his arm. The last thing I want to do is to leave him alone, but I have to. He needs this. I have to let him try to cope in the only way he knows how even if it makes me ache inside. But I know what I have to do before I give him the time he needs—the time we both need.

"It's all right. This isn't like two weeks ago because we both know now that we love each other. I'll go and let you think this through, but there's something I want you to know as you're thinking about it. I said I'd be with you if you go into treatment, but . . . if you decide you're done . . ." My voice breaks badly on the word "done."

"*If* you decide you're done, I want to take you home. You can come to my apartment, or I'll move in with you. I don't care what we do, but I want to be with you for every moment you have left. I can't . . . come here one morning and find out you're gone the way I almost did the day you lifted your DNR. I just can't do it."

I glance up to find him staring at me, and the tidal wave of emotion in his eyes sweeps me away. There's so much pain and heartache and regret—I don't know how he can contain it all. In this moment, I truly understand how awful life has been to him and how cruel it is that happiness is being dangled in front of him at such a price. It's much too high.

"Tori," he whispers brokenly, but the wave takes him under, and he drops his head into his hand.

"Call me when you're ready, and I'll come," I whisper, and I turn and hurry from his room.

I stumble down the hallway, blinded by my tears, until suddenly, I'm wrapped in Jenny's arms. She holds me while I sob, rubbing circles on my back and whispering words of comfort until I regain some control. We somehow make it down to the waiting room at the end of the hallway, and I'm lying in Jenny's lap on the couch.

"What happened, honey? He didn't push you away again, did he?"

"No, h-he didn't push me away. He just . . . he needs some time to himself." I glance up at her, and my heart shatters for the second time today. "Oh, Jenny, it's just too much! He's been through so much already

—he can't do it! I saw it in his eyes—he loves me, but it's not enough. I can't ask him to go through that for me, not when there's a good chance it'll kill him!"

"Tori, the cancer is going to kill him—"

"Yes, but he'll die suffering if the chemo kills him! I can't let him do that! I can't watch him die that way! I want to take him home. This isn't going to work, and I'm sorry he even knows about the possibility. I want to take him home and spend every moment I can with him even if there aren't that many. It'll be better than having false hope and watching the treatment kill him."

"Tori, you're upset. He really *does* have a better chance of going into remission than he does of dying from the treatment. Yes, the whole thing will be brutal, but if he's cured, it'll all have been worth it. You're the one who said if there was even the smallest chance you could win, you would fight. Where did that attitude go? You're tired. You're both worn out, and you weren't expecting the possibility that Will might not be able to handle this. But it's his decision. Maybe he reacted badly too. He's recovering from a severe bout of pneumonia—he's not feeling his strongest. In a few weeks, he'll feel much better, and I know he'll be able to handle the treatment. He just needs some time to think it through."

"It's too much," I say again, resting my head on her shoulder.

"Shh . . . you let Will decide if it's too much. It's his life that hangs in the balance, and he needs your support no matter what he chooses. You'll support whatever he decides?"

"Of course," I tell her, raising my head from her shoulder.

"Good."

"Tori! What happened?" Jason says as he crosses the waiting room, and a new wave of emotion crashes over me when I see him. He holds me just as Jenny did, and I tearfully recount the story of Will's and my discussion with Dr. Evans and the aftermath.

Jason leans against the couch and drops his head back wearily. "How can life be so fucking unfair? Why him? I've asked that so many goddamn times, there ought to be an answer. He deserves an answer!" He pounds his fist on the armrest. "I can't even imagine what's going through his mind right now—as if he hasn't had enough hard decisions in the last few weeks."

I can't hold back the sob that bubbles up in my chest. "I wish I could help him. He's all alone—he's facing this all alone right now, and he's *not* alone! We're here! You, me, Elizabeth, Jenny! He doesn't have to be alone anymore, but somehow, he still is."

Jason rubs my back soothingly. "He's always worked through things on his own, for all the time I've known him. I think he's been doing that since his father . . . since things changed when he was thirteen. He did the same thing after his diagnosis and after both relapses—it's just how he copes with the shit life throws at him."

"I know, and I don't expect him to change right away, or maybe ever. I just have . . . issues with people being alone."

Jason frowns as he looks at me, but I look away—there's no way I'm talking about that today. He sighs heavily. "Well, we'll just have to be there for Will, whatever he decides. I hope he chooses to fight, but if he decides it's too much, then—"

"—then we'll stay with him until the end." I give him a watery smile, and he returns it although it's strained.

Just then, Jenny slips back into the room. Our eyes meet—*oh fuck, did she just go and*—"Jenny, were you with Will?" I ask, sitting forward to peer at her around Jason.

"Yes," she replies, staring at the floor. "He's sleeping now."

"Did you talk to him?"

"Yes, I did."

"He *let* you talk to him? What did you say? You didn't try to convince him to go into treatment, did you? Oh God, Jenny! He needs to decide this for himself! If he does this because he thinks we think he should—"

"Tori, calm down." Jenny tries to soothe me, coming across the room and squatting down in front of me as she takes my hands in hers. "You know I would never do anything to hurt either of you. I care about Will very deeply, and I know he needs to make up his own mind, especially about this. But yes, he did let me talk to him. Will and I have this . . . bond that's grown between us. It's almost as if I'm his conscience or his older sister or something. I just point out things that are important for him to consider while he's trying to make a decision.

"And that's all I did this time. He was very upset when I went in there, so I did what I could to help calm him down, to get him to think rationally. He was exhausted, so he decided to sleep on it for a while and see how he felt when he wasn't so tired. And I think that was a good decision. It's been an emotional day for him, and I think his perspective will be better when he's not fighting exhaustion.

"Please don't be upset with me. I just had to try to help him."

I blow out a heavy breath. "I'm sorry. I'm glad he let you talk to him. I'm just . . . worn out and upset, and I'm not thinking clearly either."

"I know, honey," Jenny says, rubbing her thumbs over my hands. "Why don't you go home? I don't think Will's going to make his decision today —the way he looked, I'm guessing he's going to sleep for the better part of the day now."

"I . . . I can't leave him."

"Tori, you're just as tired and stressed as he is. Give Will the space he needs. He's not alone and suffering right now. He's sleeping because he realized he needed to rest to regain his perspective. I think you should try to do the same. I'll keep a close eye on him and make sure he's not alone and upset. Please, this is such an important decision for both of you. Help yourself by being rested and ready to talk about it when he is."

I stare at her for a long moment, my exhaustion from the emotional stress of the day making me process her words more slowly. She's right —of course she is—but it's so hard to let go. I didn't think we'd both be alone again like this—not after we admitted our love for each other. But I realize I'm not actually alone, and neither is he. I have Jason and Elizabeth to support me, and Will has Jenny, but Will has all of us the minute he decides he's ready to let us be there for him. It truly *isn't* what it was before, and that realization goes a long way toward calming me.

"You're right, Jenny. I'm sorry. Neither of us expected today to go this way. I'll go home and wait for him to work through this. But please, tell him he can call or text me at any time. I'll come as soon as he's ready."

"Of course I will," Jenny says, pulling me in for a hug. She tucks her head into my shoulder and lowers her voice. "This was meant to be, remember? He's going to decide to try, and it's all going to work out. I'm sure of it."

When Jason and I arrive at my apartment, Elizabeth is sitting at the kitchen table waiting, and she rises as I open the door. She pales and covers her mouth with her hand as she looks at us and takes a step backward.

"Oh God, what happened?" she asks, looking frantically back and forth between us.

I turn to Jason. "Would you please tell her? I can't go through it again today, and I really need to lie down."

"Of course," Jason replies, draping his arm over my shoulders. "Go rest, and I'll come get you if anything happens."

I let go of Jason, and Elizabeth pulls me into her arms, squeezing me tightly. She doesn't say anything; she just holds me for a moment, then lets me go. It's so tender and motherly that it almost brings me to tears, but I have none left to cry. I stumble down the hall to my room, grab my phone from my bag, and fall on top of my bed, fully clothed. The weight of my grief takes me under, and I slide into oblivion.

Opening my eyes, I look blearily around the room. It's dark out—*what am I doing here?* I gasp as the events of the day flash behind my eyes, and a wave of hopelessness makes my chest ache and my heart pound. *Oh, Will.* Something vibrates under my hand, and I turn my phone over and sit up abruptly, clutching at it.

Tori, are you there?

I scramble to unlock my phone and type back with shaking fingers.

Yes, I'm here, sweetheart. Are you all right?

Yes. Can you come so we can talk? I know it's late . . .

I glance at the clock. It's nine-thirty.

It's not too late. I'll be there as soon as I can.

I hesitate for half a second, but there's no turning back now.

I love you.

I love you too. I'll see you soon.

As I get shakily to my feet, my nerves go into overdrive. Did he make up his mind? Is he going to ask me what I think he should do? Oh God, I hope not because I have no idea what to tell him! Of course I want him to try, but I can't ask this of him. But I don't know that I can tell him to give up either.

I change into track pants and a t-shirt and grab my phone as I hurry out of the room. Elizabeth is sitting on the couch, watching TV, and she turns and smiles when she sees me. "There you are! Were you able to rest?"

"Will just texted me. He asked me to come and talk."

Elizabeth huffs out a breath, and I think it's in relief. "Well, you need to be on your way, then. Here, at least take a granola bar with you—you haven't eaten since breakfast."

She jumps up and goes into the kitchen, pulling out said granola bar and a bottle of water and handing them to me. She holds on to the water as I grip it and looks into my eyes. "He's going to go into treatment; I know he is. He's strong enough to do this; he just needed some time to wrap his head around it. I know my son. He's going to make the right choice."

I just stare at her as the tears well in my eyes. I want so desperately for him to try, but I don't know what the right choice is. I'm too afraid to hope.

Elizabeth's expression softens. "Go. He's going to make you feel better."

I drive off to the hospital in a daze. I'm feeling . . . nothing. I'm too scared to hope, too worn out to cry. I'm just . . . here.

Until I get to the familiar doorway of room 412. I push it open without pausing, but I stop dead the moment my eyes fall on him. He's awake and watching the door, waiting for me. His brilliant green eyes pierce me, brimming with so much love and . . . *need* that it almost brings me to my knees. I glance up at his tousled auburn hair and down at his chiseled jawline. I see none of the signs of his illness and all the signs he's everything I need. And suddenly, I'm feeling *everything*.

I fly across the room and into his arms. He pulls me close, and I feel the warmth of his skin, the beat of his heart—he's alive, and we still have time! No matter what he decides, we still have time.

"I'm sorry," he whispers over and over, and he holds me as tightly as he can, our tears and heartache mingling together and washing away like so much rain. I curl into his shoulder. He nuzzles his cheek against my forehead and electricity zaps through me, but it's not sexual. It's love, pure and simple.

I'm alive again. I'm back with him, the world is turning again, and we can face this together.

He rubs his cheek against me again, and I look up into his eyes. The need is still blazing there. I lift my chin, and he drops his so his lips brush against mine. The contact ignites a fire in both of us, and suddenly, we're kissing passionately, our hands roving and touching, *feeling* everything we can, as much as we can, all at once. Will moans, and the sound goes straight between my legs, but we're way past what he should be doing right now as sick as he's been. As if on cue, he breaks off the kiss, panting and gasping in pain as he curls an arm midway between his chest and belly.

"Are you all right?" I ask tenderly, cupping his cheek as he bows his head, eyes closed.

He stays that way for a moment; then he meets my eyes. "Yeah. I just got a little carried away."

Now it's his turn to cup my cheek, and he raises my chin so we're looking intently into each other's eyes. "I'm *so* sorry I left you alone like that. I know I shouldn't have—"

"Will, stop," I tell him, stroking my fingers over his cheek. "You're under so much stress—you're trying to make the biggest decision of your life! And I know this is how you handle things. I don't expect it to change overnight, or maybe ever, just because we love each other. If this is what you need, then take it."

"Are—are you sure? I thought you were upset—"

"I didn't say I liked it. I said I understand it." I glance down nervously. "Did it help?"

"Yes, it did."

I look up, and the sea of green is calm.

"I've decided what I'd like to do. I want to go back into treatment. I want to have the high-dose chemo and the stem cell transplant."

He looks to me for affirmation, but now, I'm the stormy sea of emotion: hope, fear, sorrow, pride, love. I don't know what to say to him although, in the back of my mind, a spark of hope is kindled.

"Tori, I have to do this. I have to do it for you—"

I open my mouth to interrupt him, but he raises his hand and shakes his head.

"—and I have to do it for me. As tempting as it is to give in and spend whatever time I have left in as much comfort as I can with you, I just can't give up that way. Not now. Not when I know . . ." He swallows hard. "If this treatment kills me, at least I'll know I did everything I could to have what I want—to have what we want—a life together."

"But it's going to be so hard . . ." I stammer, unable to truly believe he's willing to do this, the spark of hope wavering.

"Yes, it *is* going to be hard, but I realized if there's even the smallest chance I could recover from this, that I could have a life with you, then I have to take that chance."

"Sweetheart, are you sure?" I ask, fanning the spark into a small flame.

"I'm sure. I love you with all my heart and I want a life with you. I want *you* more than I've ever wanted anything. And if it doesn't . . . work out . . . then at least you'll know I loved you enough to try. After all you've given me, it's all I have to give to you, really."

"Will—" I begin, but I'm struck dumb. He's giving me . . . his life. He's going to put everything he has left into trying to beat this just so he can be with me. He loves me enough to try, and win or lose, this is his gift to me. *Is that really what he just said?*

He blushes and looks down. "I can't date you like a normal guy would and bring you flowers and take you places to show you I love you, but . . . I *can* give you this."

Holy. Fucking. Shit! The flame explodes into a bonfire, and I throw my arms around him. "Will, I love you so much! I can't even—that you would do this for us—that you'd give this to me, I . . . I don't know what to say."

"Don't say anything, other than you'll help me," he answers, his eyes downcast. "I've told you what I *want* to do, but now, we have to decide what I'm *going* to do. It's true I'm the one who has to go through the treatment, but I'm going to need lots of help and support for a long time afterward. If it's too much—"

"Will," I say, taking his face between my hands, "losing you is too much. I love you, and I'll do anything and everything that's needed—more than what's needed—to get you better. I want a life with you, too, and *I'm* willing to do anything to make that happen. And I'm not the only one. Jason, Jenny, and your mom are ready and willing to commit to taking care of you too. You're not the only one who's been thinking these last few days. We're all ready to help you in any way we can."

"Really?"

"Yes, sweetheart, really. You can ask them yourself tomorrow, and they'll tell you the same. They love you, and we all want you to have a long and happy life. You deserve it after all you've been through. No one deserves it more than you."

I had thought my words would comfort him, but his brow creases even further.

"But . . . what if it doesn't work, and I put everyone through hell with me? I'm scared, Tori. I'm afraid to hope this could actually be a cure."

"You have to believe in it, Will. There's no proof that attitude has a psychological effect on cancer, but I believe it does—I've seen it help people with my own eyes. If you're going to do this, you have to believe it can help you."

Will looks down, but I raise his chin gently.

"*I* believe it will cure you," I tell him. "I believe in *you*. I believe you can do this, and when it's over, we're going to be together . . . forever. We *will* have forever. I won't accept any less."

A smile slowly spreads across Will's face, and it's the first one I've seen since we talked to Dr. Evans this morning.

"I love you," he murmurs, pulling me close and kissing me sweetly. Those amazing green eyes capture me, and there's no one in the world but him. "Do you know how much you've changed things for me? For the first time in years, I want to do more than exist. I want to *be* more . . . for you. And I'm happy. Even with all this shit going on, despite the sickness and the pain, I'm *happy*. That's something I haven't been in a very long time."

If a heart could burst from sheer bliss, I swear mine would be doing it right now. It's one of those moments where time seems to stand still, and I know I have to soak it up and savor it because it's the kind of moment that only comes along a handful of times in an entire lifetime. And I'm sharing it with Will.

We stare into each other's eyes, and I know I should say something, but I can't. For this instant, it's enough just to *be*. The tears well up and over-flow, but for the first time today, they're happy tears.

Will's brow furrows, and he reaches up to gather the moisture with his thumb.

"I'm happy too," I whisper, unable to say anything more. The moment is too perfect to complicate it with words.

Will chuckles and shakes his head, but it turns into a cough, and I'm reminded that he's only been breathing on his own for two days. He grips his chest and winces as the fit subsides, and reality settles firmly around us again. We need to get him better so he can begin treatment.

He looks at me wearily.

I reach out and stroke his arm. "Sweetheart, I think it's time you got some more rest—you need to get over this so we can get to the business of curing your cancer. Tomorrow, you can tell Jason, Jenny, and your mom what you'd like to do, and then we can let Dr. Evans know."

"Jenny, too, huh?" he asks as a grin tugs at the corner of his mouth.

"Are you really surprised? She only annoys the people she cares about."

"Annoy would be one word. Badger would be another good one. It's like I've stepped into my own personal fairy tale, and I've been given a Jiminy Cricket who's going to help me become a real boy."

I laugh as an image of Jenny in a blue top hat and opera gloves flashes through my head, but the analogy is spot-on.

"I've been given an angel *and* a conscience—the powers that be must want this to work out all right," Will muses, shaking his head.

"That's the spirit!" I encourage him, marveling at his change in demeanor. "But now, you really need to get some rest."

Will looks down, then glances up through his eyelashes with the best puppy dog eyes I've ever seen. But they're not over the top—they're tentative and shy—and my heart melts into a puddle before he even opens his mouth.

"Would you stay tonight?"

He had me at "would." "Of course, if you want me to," I reply, glancing over at the couch.

"No, I meant . . . here," he says, patting his mattress with his hand.

"Are you really well enough for that? I don't want to hurt you."

Will snorts. "I'm on so much morphine, I'm pretty much only in pain when I cough . . . although I might keep you awake if I'm coughing," he says, looking crestfallen.

"Well, why don't we give it a try, and if it doesn't work, I can move to the couch."

Will brightens immediately. "Deal. Will you help me though? I can't move over by myself right now." He's trying to hide his emotions, but I know how upset he is that he's weaker than he was before the pneumonia.

"You'll get your strength back. And until then, I get to touch you more."

He smirks at my joking, and the moment is lighter as I help him shift to the side of his bed. When he's comfortable and settled again, I climb up beside him and tuck my head into his shoulder. He snuggles up to me and sighs in contentment.

"Someday, we'll do this right," he murmurs as his eyes close, and I bite my lip as I smile. If there's a someday in his mind, then Will has hope.

CHAPTER 5

I wake curled around Will, and even though we're cuddled together on a hospital bed, it feels fantastic. It's been almost three weeks since the first and only time I slept with him like this. I feel . . . rested. He woke up coughing a few times during the night, but he tried his best to be quiet and not disturb me. I woke up every time, but after the first one, I pretended not to so he wouldn't be upset about it. After each spasm ended, and his pain subsided, he'd cuddle into me again and kiss my forehead tenderly. It was all I could do to stay still and not smother him with kisses, but I knew he needed rest more than he needed me to jump him in the middle of the night.

As I stare at him now, sleeping peacefully, I think through everything that happened yesterday. He's really going to do this, and there's a chance he'll be cured. *Oh my God, he could be cured!* We could have a normal life together—share an apartment, go out on dates, have friends over for dinner—everything a normal couple would do; it could be ours a year from now. I want it more than I've ever wanted anything.

He can do this; I know he can. Yesterday, I thought it was bigger than he is because I was worn out and afraid. I'm still afraid for him, but his determination to try, his willingness to do this for us—for me— convinced me he's going to be okay. Jenny says this is meant to be, and I'm just going to go with that. I have to be strong for him because he's the one who's likely to waver, given what he's about to endure. I have to be the rock he clings to when the storms of doubt and despair rage.

And I will be. I promise.

Will begins to cough, and I duck out from under his arm as one hand goes to cover his mouth and the other arm curls around his chest. When the spasm finally stops, he rests his head back and slowly opens his eyes.

"Are you all right?" I whisper, and he startles, seemingly unaware I was there. A lazy, blissful smile spreads across his face.

"I'm fine now. Best morning I've had in weeks," he says huskily, his deep, sleepy voice causing my stomach to twinge and flip.

I reach up and run my fingers into his hair, and he sighs in contentment.

"Thanks for staying with me."

Those gorgeous green eyes twinkle at me, and for a moment, I'm unable to breathe, let alone reply. He chuckles, and it frees me from my stupor.

"No need to thank me for something I wanted to do." He grins even wider, and the warm fuzzies spread outward from the center of my chest until I feel like a puddle of goo.

"You have another big day today. You need to talk to Jason, Jenny, and your mom, then let Dr. Evans know what you've decided."

"Yeah," he answers, eyes and fingers going immediately to his afghan.

"This'll be nothing compared to making the decision itself, honestly. I told you, everyone knows what they're getting into, and they want to do this with you. It'll be no big deal," I say, shrugging.

"I know. I'm sorry, I'm just . . . tired. It's been a hell of a few weeks."

"I know, sweetheart. But you'll get some time to rest and recover before the treatment begins. I'm pretty sure you're going to have to be completely over the pneumonia before they'll give you chemo."

"You're probably right," he replies, relaxing and closing his eyes again.

"Listen, why don't you rest for a while longer, and I'll go grab some breakfast and call Jason and Elizabeth. Your mom knew I came here last night, so I'm sure she's anxious to know what's going on, and I wouldn't be surprised if she called Jason and filled him in too."

Will smiles with his eyes still closed. "There's quite the little conspiracy around here, isn't there? It's nice, though. It's been a while since so many people cared about me like this."

I swallow thickly at his words. They're genuine and honest, but I feel bad all the same. I wish I could erase the last few years for him and put a life with me in their place. But I choke back my emotion. "Well, you better get used to it because everyone plans on sticking around."

"Good," he answers, already drifting toward sleep.

I slide off his bed as gently as I can, and I actually manage not to jostle him. *Thank God for morphine.* I slip out of his room, opting to freshen up in the nurses' lounge so I don't disturb him, and run smack into Jenny.

She stops abruptly, but a cheesy grin spreads across her face. "Did you spend the night?"

"Yes, I did." Even though there's no reason for me to be blushing, I can feel the heat creeping up my cheeks anyway. "He texted me around nine-thirty last night and wanted to talk, and then he asked me to stay, so I did."

"Did he make his decision yet?"

"Yes, and he wants to talk to everyone this morning, you included. He just fell back to sleep though. He woke up coughing a little earlier, and I don't think he was ready to be awake yet."

"I'll only peek my head in for now, then. I don't want to disturb him."

She cocks her head to the side and appraises me. "You don't seem upset. Does that mean he's decided to go back into treatment?"

"Yes." I'm unable to hide my smile.

Jenny bounces and claps her hands. "I *knew* he'd make the right choice! Now we're one step closer to your happily ever after."

I snort. As if this is some fairy tale with a scripted ending. So many things could go wrong, but I love Jenny's enthusiasm all the same.

"I need to clean up and call everyone. I'll see you in a bit?"

"Of course," Jenny says as she tiptoes into Will's room.

<hr />

I sit on Will's bed and hold his hand as Jason, Jenny, and Elizabeth file into his room. He squeezes my hand, and I look over to find a perplexed expression on his face as he stares at Jason and Jenny. I grin as I realize they're holding hands.

"Jay?" Will asks, raising his eyebrows.

"Jenny and I started dating a few weeks ago," Jason explains, blushing to the roots of his hair as Jenny beams at Will.

Will's eyebrows disappear completely into his hairline, and he shakes his head in disbelief. It takes him a moment to recover, but then he smiles at them. "That's fantastic! I'm so happy for both of you."

"Thanks, man," Jason replies, grinning.

Will tenses as he squeezes my hand again—now it's time to get serious. He's still nervous despite what I've told him. Maybe because he's been through this before, and his friends didn't stick by him? Whatever the reason, he's barely got a handle on his anxiety.

Jason, Jenny, and Elizabeth each take a seat in the chairs Jenny brought in, and Will begins.

"Thank you all for coming this morning. I have a big decision to make. I've decided what I *want to do*, but in order to figure out what I'm actually *going to do*, I need input from all of you because . . . I'm going to need your help."

He takes a deep breath and huffs it out, and I squeeze his hand reassuringly. I can feel sweat on his palm. His eyes shift from their faces to his afghan, and he clutches it with his free hand as he continues.

"I've decided I want to go back into treatment, but I can't do it alone. The only option really left for me is high-dose chemotherapy followed by a stem cell transplant. I have to recover from the pneumonia first, but then I would have six days of high-dose chemo which would wipe out my immune system, and then they'd give me stem cells from a donor to replace my cancerous ones.

"The chemo is going to make me extremely sick, and I'll be in the hospital for at least a month after the stem cell transplant. When they say I can finally go home, I'm going to need lots of help because I'll be too weak to take care of myself for a long time—the total recovery time from the stem cell transplant is a year or more. Tori has committed to going through this with me, but . . . I'm going to need more help than one person, even someone as fantastic as Tori, can provide."

I squeeze his hand and smile at him, but he doesn't look up. His hand trembles in mine.

"So . . . I guess I'm asking if you're willing to help me. You all know how I hate to be dependent on anyone, but with this course of treatment, I really don't have a choice. I'm asking if you'll help me try to take my life back from this disease so I can spend it the way I choose to."

The only sound in the room is Will's harsh breathing until Elizabeth rises from her chair. She walks around to Will's other side, gently releases his fingers from the afghan, and holds them between hers.

He squeezes my hand tighter as he begins to tremble a little harder.

"Will, I wish you didn't have to ask that question. I wish you already knew I would help you, but my past choices have landed us here, and I'm sorrier for that than you'll ever know. I'm going to be here for you, whatever you need. I haven't been here for you these last four years, and there's nothing I can do to change that, but from now on, I want you to know you can depend on me, no matter what. I love you, honey, and I'll never abandon you again."

Will bows his head and bites into his lip hard, and a tear rolls down his cheek. He frees his hand from mine to swipe at his eyes before raising them to look at her.

"Oh, Mom," he whispers brokenly, and he pulls her into his arms.

"Will, I'm so sorry." She sobs into his shoulder, and they hold each other as their tears mingle.

I have to wipe away a few tears of my own as Elizabeth raises her head to look at her son. "Thank you for giving me the chance to make it up to you—to prove to you that I want things to be different. I have to go back to San Francisco for a little while to take care of some things, but I'm going to come back when you begin treatment."

"But what about Dad? Won't he—"

"Never mind about your father," Elizabeth says, cutting him off. "You have enough to worry about. I'll do what I need to do, and then I'll be back here to support you, all right?"

Will glances at me, but I smile back reassuringly. I know Elizabeth is planning to leave Will Senior and move up here permanently, but she doesn't want one more thing on Will's already over-anxious mind as he gets ready to fight his cancer again. She'll tell him after his transplant when it's all over and done.

"Okay." Will agrees, giving her a watery smile.

"Will," Jason says, getting to his feet so Will can see him without having to raise his head from his pillow.

Will looks at him, and I can see his conflicting emotions bubbling under the surface. They talked everything out after Jason found out where Will was, but the wound of Will's decision to be alone is still fresh for both of them.

"Will, I'm in. I was in the last time you relapsed, even when I couldn't find you. I was here when you were diagnosed; I took care of you through your first relapse—I was even here when things were at their very worst for you . . ."

Jason pauses and Will bows his head. Jason takes a deep breath, and when he continues, his voice is rough with emotion.

"I've always *been* here, and I'll always *be* here. You're my best friend, and you don't . . . deserve . . . any of the bad things that have happened to you. If I could change any of them or go through any of this in your place, I would.

"I want to help you beat this and have a long, happy life with Tori. You deserve happiness more than anyone I know. So . . . I'm in."

Will raises his eyes, and they lock with Jason's, and so much healing seems to transpire in the silence between them.

Jason steps around the bed and clasps Will's hand, but Will tugs him into an embrace.

"Thank you," Will says quietly. "You *have* always been here—more than anyone else in my life. I forgot it once, but I won't ever again."

When Jason steps back, all the eyes in the room are wet, but no one pays it any mind.

Jenny stands up and saunters over to Will's bed, perching herself on the corner opposite me. She winks at Will and wiggles her eyebrows, and he chuckles and blushes. "I've always liked you—right from the moment you yelled, 'Get that goddamn needle away from me, bitch!'"

Will gasps. "I really said that?"

"Well, all but the 'bitch' part. I added that for a bit of dramatic flair," Jenny replies, smirking.

Will laughs, but it ends in a cough that leaves him clutching his chest.

"Anyway," Jenny continues, ignoring his illness as years of nursing have taught her, "I liked you from the very beginning which is why I went to Tori about you. And look how that turned out. Now she's your girlfriend, and you ended up returning the favor without even knowing it by bringing this sweet man into my life." She gestures to Jason, who smiles and bows.

"See? Karma isn't always a bitch, and the way I see it, she owes you even more. This is meant to be, Will. You and Tori are meant to be together, and you're meant to be happy; I just know it. I started this adventure, and by damn, I'm going to see that it finishes the way it's supposed to. I don't let my best friend fall in love with just anyone, and I don't pester the living hell out of my patients when I think they're doing boneheaded things. You're just special, I guess." She finishes with a grin.

Will chuckles again and shifts his leg against her playfully. "I never had a sister, but I feel like I do now—complete with badgering and telling me what to do."

Now he turns on the charm. "Thank you, Jenny. If it weren't for you, I would have died in this hospital weeks ago, alone and afraid. I owe you more than I can ever repay, and I'm honored that you're willing to continue to help me."

Jenny just stares at him for a moment, then shakes her head. "Damn, Will! Those eyes of yours need to be registered as a lethal weapon! If I weren't dating *him* and terrified of the wrath of *her*," Jenny says, pointing at Jason and me in turn, "I'd be in your lap right now."

Will snorts.

"See, sweetheart? You have a whole team of people who love you and are ready to support you."

"Yes, it appears I do." His smile is radiant as he glances around the room.

Just then, the door opens and Dr. Evans pokes his head in. "Wow, there's a party going on in here. Should I come back later?"

"Actually, you're the next person I need to talk to, so please, join us," Will says, motioning Dr. Evans in. Will closes his eyes wearily, and I squeeze his hand to get his attention.

"Are you sure you want to do this now?"

"Might as well get it over with, and this way, everyone can listen in. I'm tired, but I'll rest better once this is over and done with."

He turns his attention back to Dr. Evans, who is standing at the foot of his bed. "I've decided I want to have the high-dose chemo and the stem cell transplant. The people in this room are going to be my support team for my recovery."

Dr. Evans's eyes fall on Jenny. "You too?"

"Yes, sir," Jenny replies, grinning. "Will is more than just my patient."

Will smiles at Jenny, and Dr. Evans glances between the two of them, bemused.

"Well, I think you've made a good decision, Will. You're strong, and having seen all you've been through, I know you can handle this. We'll have to wait a few weeks before we can get started though. You need to be completely recovered from the pneumonia, and I'd like to see your white cell count drop to a certain level before we begin. The treatment will kill your white cells, but it's best to take advantage of your body's natural method of destroying them while we can as you recover from the pneumonia.

"Also, I'm concerned about your liver. Your enzyme levels haven't yet returned to where they were before you got sick. Between that and the dangerous amount of swelling, I suspect there may be some permanent damage there, but we won't know for sure until you're fully recovered. The chemo will put additional stress on your liver, so we need to give you as much time to heal as we can before we begin. It's a delicate balance, but I think you'll be ready in two to three weeks.

"In the meantime, I'd like to keep you here in Oncology to recover so we can monitor your condition closely and begin as soon as possible. Is that all right with you?"

"That's fine, Dr. Evans," Will replies. "About the liver damage—is it serious?"

"Right now, I think it's just at the level where you're going to need to say goodbye to your barhopping days, but it could become more severe under the stress of the chemo. We'll monitor you very closely and do whatever we can to minimize it. But for now, you need to focus on resting and recovering."

As if on cue, Will yawns, and we all glance at each other knowingly.

"Sweetheart, why don't you take a little nap, and we'll all go have an early lunch. You've had a stressful day already, and it's not even noon yet."

Will nods grudgingly. "I wish I could argue with you, but I'm having trouble keeping my eyes open."

Everyone rises and we all shuffle out of Will's room, with me being the last one to go.

"Tori?" he calls sleepily.

"Yes, sweetheart?"

"Can you come back later?"

"Of course. I'll come back in a few hours."

Will's sleepy smile is the last thing I see as I close his door.

Lunch with Jason and Elizabeth is a relaxed and happy affair—everyone is relieved that Will's made his decision and eager for his treatment to begin. I'm happy too. I feel like our feet are finally set on a path even though it's going to be a difficult one to walk.

Jason takes Elizabeth home afterward so she can make arrangements to return to San Francisco, and I go back to Will's room, sitting beside him and reading until he begins to stir.

He shifts on the bed, wincing as he does so, and he suddenly begins coughing. The spasms rattle him awake, and he's left panting and cringing from the effort.

"Fuck, that hurts!" he mutters, and I rub my hand over his arm soothingly.

He jumps a little as his eyes fly open, but he relaxes when he realizes it's me. "I didn't know you were there," he says in his sexy-as-hell, sleepy voice, and I have to mentally shake myself before the fantasies take over.

"I've been sitting here reading," I tell him, gesturing at my Kindle.

"I'm glad you came back. There was something I wanted to talk to you about."

I tense immediately. No discussion that starts with those words is likely to be pleasant, and right away, I'm thinking of a million different things that could be wrong. *Did he change his mind? Did I do something to upset him? Did—*

"Tori, relax," Will says, gripping the hand that's stopped massaging his arm. "It's nothing bad. Just . . . something Jenny said that stuck with me today, and I wanted to talk to you about it."

"Okay," I reply, absolutely clueless as to what it could be. I move from my chair to sit on the side of his bed and take his hand in mine.

A delicious blush floods his chest and paints his cheeks, and I can't help but smirk. I'll never get tired of seeing this man blush.

Will looks down at first, but then he takes a breath and forces himself to meet my eyes. "Well . . . Jenny said you're my girlfriend . . ."

Oh.

Well, that statement's a minefield I wasn't expecting.

"Um, I hadn't thought about it—"

"We kind of skipped that part and went right to saying we loved each other." Will blurts out the words nervously. "To be honest, I think of you as more than my girlfriend at this point, but as far as anyone else is concerned, I think girlfriend will do."

He runs a hand through his hair and grips the back of his neck. "That didn't come out right."

I've never seen Will this flustered before, and I can't help but laugh and shake my head.

"Laughing? You're . . . laughing while I'm sitting here feeling like I've just stuffed both feet in my mouth." He's complaining, but his green eyes sparkle as he smirks at me sidelong.

"You're just adorable when you're flustered, and it's a side of you I've not seen much of since I've known you," I tell him, grinning. "But I know what you mean. I think of you as more than just my boyfriend, too, but to everyone who sees us, that's what we are."

"*That's* what I meant!" he exclaims, looking relieved . . . but it doesn't last. "We did this completely backward, and I'm so sorry about that. I'm supposed to dazzle you and sweep you off your feet—take you to exciting places and show you what an interesting guy I am—but instead, you've seen the worst of me, and I can't take you anywhere."

"Sweetheart, I don't care that we didn't meet in the 'usual' way. I fell in love with you for who you are. That's what matters. The rest of it's just . . . fancy ways to get me to see the real you. But I saw the real you even though you were protecting yourself. And I loved you even when you were pushing me away and falling apart. I think our relationship is much stronger because of what we've been through together. I don't think either of us will ever underestimate the importance of each moment we get to spend with each other, and that's something most couples don't figure out in a lifetime."

Will huffs out a breath. "I knew you'd understand. But I still feel bad. I want to . . . bring you flowers just because it's Tuesday. I want to take you on moonlit walks and hold your hand. I want to whisk you away for the weekend and not let you out of bed except to feed you incredible food. I want . . . God, there are so many things I want, I can't even tell you . . ." He trails off, staring down at his afghan.

I'm stunned. *Did he just say he wants to bring me flowers? And walk in the moonlight? And have a sex-in at a B and B somewhere? Do I know this man?* "Will, are you a romantic?"

He blushes again and looks down. "Maybe. Just because I can't cook doesn't mean I don't know how to spoil a beautiful woman. There are lots of things you don't know about me. All you've seen of me is my apartment and me trying to push everyone and everything away. I don't have a lot of choices here, stuck in this bed."

He's right. Because of our situation, I really don't know much about his likes and dislikes or how he interacts with people. He's obviously charming, and he loves chocolate, high-end Italian food, and cats, but I've never seen him out in the real world. *Oh my.* Now that's something I'm really looking forward to!

"Well, you haven't seen me outside of this hospital either, and I *can* cook," I tell him, grinning.

"It sounds like things will be pretty interesting when this is all over and done with," Will says with a smile, but it reminds me of something else we should talk about.

"While we're on the subject of outside the hospital, we should talk about what's going to happen when you do get to leave here."

78

Will's eyes immediately shoot downward, and the afghan pattern-tracing begins, but I have no intention of allowing him to feel uncomfortable. I already have a plan.

"I've been reading about aftercare for stem cell transplant patients, and wherever you stay for your recovery is going to need to be super clean and prepared in advance. So I—"

"Wait, you were reading about this?" he asks, giving me a peculiar look.

"Well . . . yeah. I want to know everything I can about what's going to happen to you and how best to take care of you afterward. Is that okay?"

"Of course, it's okay. I was just . . . Wow, you really do love me, don't you?"

"Yes, you silly man! How many times do I have to tell you?" I exclaim, leaning over and kissing him. "When I said I was going to do anything and everything, I really meant it. That wasn't a romance novel I've been reading all afternoon. I've been reading everything I can find about AITL and this treatment."

His smile is brilliant, warm, and sappy, and I can feel the love and happiness radiating off him. "Thanks, Tori. It really means a lot to me, the things you're doing."

Sweetheart, you ain't seen nothin' yet! I think to myself as I remember all the things I've read. I lean over and kiss him again. "We're in this together, as much as possible, right? So don't think of it as you and me; think of it as us. Then you don't have to thank me."

He grins at me. "Okay, we're an 'us.' I like the sound of that."

"Me too. Anyway, we're going to need to prepare someplace in advance for you, so I was thinking I could get your apartment ready over the next few weeks and while you're recovering from the transplant and . . . relocate my things?"

"You mean like . . . move in? You would do that?"

"Well, yeah. I kind of figured you'll need me around the clock, and it makes no sense for us to have two apartments if I'm always going to be at your place—unless that's not what you want."

"Other than remission, I don't think I've ever wanted anything more," he tells me, bringing my hand up to his lips and kissing the back of it tenderly. "I love you, Tori. Will you move in with me?"

It sounds so much like a marriage proposal that I can't breathe for a moment, and euphoria rocks through me as I think of all the possibilities for Will and me together.

"Yes, I'll move in with you," I tell him, leaning in and touching my lips to his. He responds immediately, kissing me softly and sweetly as my head swims, drunk on the love I feel for him. He breaks the kiss way too quickly for my liking, resting his head back and closing his eyes.

"You know I really want to keep kissing you, but I think I'm reaching my limit." He wraps an arm around himself and grimaces, and I'm forcefully reminded of the hole in his chest and the fact that he was on a ventilator a mere three days ago.

"You're right. I'm sorry."

"No, don't be sorry. *Never* be sorry," he says, reaching up and cupping my cheek.

"Why don't you sleep now, and I'll read some more about how much I have to clean your apartment."

Will chuckles. "Don't you mean *our* apartment?"

"Yes, I suppose I do." I agree, grinning.

"Are you sure you wanna give up yours though? We could—"

"Will, your apartment is to die for, and it's the perfect space for your painting. I have a generic apartment in Wedgewood."

"You really like my place?" he asks, stifling a yawn.

"I *love* your place, but we're going to have to talk about it another time because you have a date with your pillow right now."

He rolls his eyes dramatically, but they drift shut despite his best efforts to keep them open.

"You can stay for a bit," he instructs me sleepily, "but go home and have dinner with my mom tonight since she's leaving."

"Okay, sweetheart, I will," I answer, but I think he's already asleep.

I spend the remainder of the afternoon reading beside him, but he barely stirs.

I leave for home around four-thirty, telling Jenny I'll be back in the morning. She gives me a hug and a warm smile, and I can't help but return it. I *am* happy even though I feel like I could sleep for days.

CHAPTER 6

Over the next few days, it becomes apparent exactly how hard Will pushed himself to make his decision—he sleeps almost around the clock for the next two days. In the little time he's awake, he convinces me to go back to work.

"You're going to take time off when I start treatment, and it's not like I'm going to be doing anything exciting over the next few weeks. I'll sleep while you're working so we can spend some quality time together when you get off," he tells me. And he has a point. My boss is understanding, but I know she'll be more sympathetic if she sees I'm actually trying to keep up with my patients. So, I started back yesterday.

It's three in the afternoon, and I'm already headed up to see Will. My last patient cancelled, and while I have a mountain of paperwork I could catch up on, I missed seeing him this morning because I was running late. He was sleeping yesterday morning when I stopped by though, so I probably only missed watching him sleep.

A smile spreads across my face as I think about it. I love watching him sleep. I guess that's a good thing because after his treatment, he'll be spending much more time asleep than awake for the first few months.

I open his door slowly and as my eyes fall on him, I draw in a shocked breath. His eyes are closed, and I can see beads of sweat at his temples and on his forehead. He's huddled under his afghan, shivering violently. My stomach drops to my shoes, and I feel as if the world has tilted on its axis. He can't get sick again; he just *can't*. He has to get better and go into treatment so we can have our life together. We knew it was a very real danger, but it *can't* be happening so soon! He's not even over the pneumonia yet!

I grab onto the door for support and try to force myself to calm down, but it's just not working. I stumble across the room but manage to pull it together a little before I open my mouth—I don't want to upset him any more than he already is.

"Sweetheart, you're feverish!" I exclaim as I put my hand to his forehead.

He opens his eyes, but they're dazed and glassy. "T-Tori," he whispers as I reach under his afghan to take his hand.

"Have you been like this all day? I was running late this morning, so I didn't stop by. I figured you'd be asleep anyway."

Will nods his head a fraction. "Y-yes, it's b-been since early this m-morning. And I've either b-been freezing or r-roasting the entire time, so I haven't been able to s-sleep."

God *damn* it! I should have come by! It seems like every time I'm not right here, something bad happens!

"Have they . . . could it be an infection?" I ask, trying to keep the fear out of my voice and failing miserably.

"No, they did b-bloodwork this morning, and my wh-white count is still going down. This is just the c-c-cancer doing its thing," he says, his teeth chattering.

I release the breath I was holding, but I'm only relieved for a moment. "Goddammit, this cancer never gives up, does it? We're right back to the same old shit and before you've even had a chance to recover from having pneumonia!"

When I look up at him, his eyes are closed. "Wh-what did you expect? That the s-symptoms would d-disappear because I d-decided I want to live? C-cancer is a good k-killer, Tori. It knows to k-kick you when you're d-down."

His words stop me cold. He's upset already, and my anger and negativity are only making things worse.

"I'm sorry, sweetheart. I'm just frustrated for you. It is what it is, and all we can do is hope everything works out for your treatment. I'm relieved it's 'just' the cancer symptoms and not a new infection that would delay your chemo."

"Yeah, I g-guess that's something to be g-grateful for," Will says, but he sounds pretty far from grateful. "D-dammit, it hurts to sh-shiver." He wraps his arms more tightly around his chest.

My heart aches for him as I glance around his room, trying to think of some way I can help. Suddenly, I have an idea—several, in fact. Will switched back to his green afghan after I cleaned the blood off it, but he never gave the cornflower-colored one back to me, so it should still be with his things.

I open his closet and find it neatly folded at the bottom. As I unfold the afghan and lay it over him, he opens his eyes. He gives me a small smile as I cover him, tucking in the edges around his legs and drawing it up to his chin. When I'm finished, I run my hands down his arms from shoulder to elbow, and then back up again.

"Does that hurt?"

"N-no. The only pain I can feel is my chest and b-belly, and these damn ch-chills are rattling them b-both pretty good," he says miserably.

I continue rubbing my hands up and down his arms, and he realizes what I'm trying to do.

"It m-might help."

Suddenly, he raises his eyes to me, and I see desperation there. "T-Tori, what if this d-doesn't work? What if I don't even m-make it to the chemo and s-some other infection gets me f-first? I d-don't know how much more of th-this I can take . . ."

My blood runs cold. He's voicing the fears that have been chasing each other around in my head for the last five minutes . . . hell, ever since he made his decision, if I'm honest. But he has to believe in order for this to work. We both do.

"Sweetheart, everything's going to be fine. I just know it." I try to soothe him, running my fingers into his hair. "You're going to rest and get well over the next few weeks, and then the treatment is going to be success-ful. You only have to put up with this for a little while longer, and then the cancer is going to be gone."

An idea strikes me—a way to help him focus on what he needs to do and to believe in it. Will is strong, but he's recovering from a serious illness, and he still has the awful symptoms of his cancer to deal with. He's worn out and afraid, but this treatment and recovery are going to be the fight of his life, so he has to be ready to meet it head on. He needs to keep his eyes on the prize, so to speak, and know what it is he's suffering for. And I know just how to help him.

I'm no artist like Will, but I need to paint a picture for him—a picture of our life together after the cancer is gone. It needs to be so vibrant that he can see it and feel it—know how wonderful it's going to be. And I need to make him want it so much he can taste it, enough to get him through even the worst days of his treatment. He's giving me the gift of life with him, so I'm going to give him the gift of making that life as easy for him to get to as possible and as wonderful as it can be once we get there. It's the least I can do after everything *he's* doing.

"Let's talk about that—when the cancer's gone, that is. I don't know about you, but I have a whole *list* of things I want to do when the cancer is gone."

Will opens his eyes to watch me, but there's still doubt and misery churning in their green depths.

"Let's start with an easy one—one we already know we're going to do.

"When the cancer's gone, I want to move into your apartment because I love old buildings, and I want to be surrounded by your artwork."

"S-so it's the b-building and the artwork, is it? N-not the c-company?"

"I'm not done yet, smartass. When the cancer's gone, I want to wake up with you wrapped around me every morning because you're my home now, and it doesn't matter where we are."

The ghost of a smile touches his lips.

"When the cancer's gone, I want to make love to you on the floor of your art studio, and I want you to do very naughty things to me with paint brushes."

His eyes widen, and he drops his chin as he stares at me. "Whoa. Y-you put some thought into th-that one."

"Yes, I did. Would you like to know exactly how much?"

"Y-yes, actually, I would," he replies, smirking.

"Another day. I don't want to get you all worked up when you aren't feeling well. And you *will* get worked up when I tell you about my fantasy."

He adds a blush to the smirk, and I know this is working.

"I won't f-forget about that."

"I'm counting on it," I tell him, slowing down my rubbing on his arms as his shivers subside. "What about you? What do you want to do once the cancer's gone?"

He closes his eyes for a few moments, and that's when I remember how hard it is for him to focus when he's running a fever. But this is important, and I won't question him for very long. Today is only the beginning of this.

He opens his eyes lazily, but the shivers have completely stopped.

"When the cancer's gone, I want to take you to Il Terrazzo Carmine and eat fancy Italian food with you. I want to bring you flowers *every* Tuesday and maybe some days in between. I want to hold your hand wherever we go whether the moon is out or not."

My smile is so wide, my cheeks hurt. He's going to do this with me. He's going to play along, even though I don't think he truly realizes how much he's going to help himself—how much he's going to help us both.

"When the cancer's gone, I want that 'sex-in' thing you were talking about, where you don't let me out of bed for the weekend except to feed me."

"Oh, yes, how could I forget that one?" he says, yawning.

"Sweetheart, you look like you could sleep. Why don't you do that, and we'll add more to the list later?"

"Okay," he answers, closing his eyes and yawning again. But they flash open one last time. "Thank you, Tori. I needed something to look forward to."

"I know you did, and we're going to keep adding to that list. We've got nothing better to do while we wait this out, so let's plan our future."

"That's an excellent idea," Will says as he drifts off, and I smile to myself in satisfaction.

The days go by, and Will continues to improve, despite his cancer's best efforts to the contrary. The hole in his chest from the tube heals without infection, and his cough turns from thick and wet to raspy and dry. It still stays with him, but Dr. Evans explains that it's from irritation in the small spaces of his lungs caused by the pneumonia and not from lingering infection.

He gets stronger, too—he's able to stay awake pretty much as long as he did before the pneumonia, and he's able to move himself in bed again and grip things without his arms shaking.

Despite his recovery from the pneumonia, Will's cancer is relentless. The swelling in his liver and spleen remains at dangerous levels, and his belly slowly starts to fill with fluid again. It reduces his pain, but every time I look at his distended belly, I know time is working against us, and we need to break the cycle of his disease as soon as we can before something else bad happens. He's feverish every three or four days, usually lasting for about forty-eight hours. It exhausts him, and I can see the misery in his eyes on those days, but he doesn't break down again like he did the first time . . . maybe because we're spending most of our time planning for our future.

I've stayed true to my promise to myself, and every day for the last two weeks, we've added to our "When the cancer's gone" list:

"When the cancer's gone, I want to watch you paint in your studio."

"When the cancer's gone, I want to take you to Lake Washington and lie on the boat dock with you so we can watch the sun glint off the water."

"When the cancer's gone, I want to go to Europe with you and see all the skylines you've painted in person."

"When the cancer's gone, I want you to meet my dad."

"When the cancer's gone, I want to paint a portrait of you—my drawings don't do you justice."

"When the cancer's gone, I want to take you to my favorite place in the Olympic Forest. We can take a picnic lunch, and I'll draw you under some pretty trees."

"When the cancer's gone, I want to make love to you, slow and sweet, until we're both begging for release."

"When the cancer's gone, I want to marry you."

That last one nearly gave me heart failure, but Will proclaimed it so sincerely and so sweetly that it curbed my panic instantly. But it proved to me he really *is* planning ahead and believing in what we've been doing. The picture we've been painting is now vibrant and has a life of its own, and we can both see it clear as day. And we want it. More than anything in the world, I can see we want it, both for and with each other.

For the most part, Will is happier than I've ever seen him. He's pleased that he's recovering, and he's put a lot of enthusiasm into planning our future. That's what he talks about most, rather than the past or the present, and the light in his eyes as he tells me all the things he wants to do with me makes me tremble with joy on the inside. On the outside, I just smile and go along with whatever picture of what's to come he's painting. His ability to paint mental pictures is almost as good as his ability to paint physical ones, but every once in a while, I catch him staring off into the distance, and there's fear in his eyes.

My afternoon drags because I'm spending all my spare brain cells thinking about the meeting Will and I have with Dr. Evans at four o'clock. He ordered major blood work for Will yesterday, and I have a feeling the time has come, and Evans is going to set the date for the start of Will's chemo. I'm terrified, but I know we're walking a fine line between allowing time for Will to recover and risking his developing another infection.

I head up to Will's room a little past three-thirty and find him awake and anxious. His eyes are on me as I walk into the room, and although he smiles, he's not really there. The fingers of his left hand are tracing squares on his afghan purposefully.

"Hi, sweetheart. How are you this afternoon?" I ask as I cross the room to sit on his bed.

"I'm fine, I guess," he answers distractedly, his gaze sliding away from me.

"Hey," I say, cupping his cheek in my hand, drawing his eyes to mine.

He gives me a lopsided grin. "I'm sorry. I'm just nervous about this meeting."

"Why? I have a feeling Dr. Evans is going to tell us we've waited long enough, and it's time to move forward with your treatment. That's what we've been hoping for, right?"

"Right," Will responds uneasily, and he looks away again.

"You're scared, aren't you?"

"I've been through this twice already, Tori, and both times were horrible. This course of chemo will be shorter, but the doses will be so much higher, and the side effects will be extremely intense. I guess I hope Evans *does* give me the go-ahead today because the anticipation is really starting to get to me. It's just hanging out there over my head, and I want it to be over with."

"Sweetheart, I'm sorry this is worrying you. I don't know how bad it's going to be, but I'm going to stay with you every step of the way. We'll get through this together, okay?"

"Yeah," Will answers, giving me a small smile. "You always know just what to say to make me feel better, do you know that?"

"At least I'm good at something." As I tease him, his smile widens.

We both jump as the door squeaks, and Dr. Evans peeks his head around it. "Knock, knock."

"Come on in," Will says with a smile.

Dr. Evans inclines his head and goes straight for Will's chart, pulling out his iPad as he does so. "How are you feeling today, Will?"

"I can't complain. Nothing is worse today than before, and I'm not feverish, so it's a good day as far as I'm concerned."

"That's good to hear," Dr. Evans says, taking a seat in the chair on Will's other side.

"I reviewed your blood work from yesterday, and based on that, I think it's time for you to begin treatment. You've completely recovered from the pneumonia, other than a bit of residual cough, and your white cell count has dropped to the level I wanted to see. Your liver enzymes are still a little elevated, but I doubt that's going to improve further anytime soon, and I think we've pushed our luck far enough, given your odds for new infection. The risks of waiting are now outweighing the benefits, so it's time to make our move. Are you ready to do this?"

I look over at Will, and for a few seconds, I see fear in his eyes, but suddenly they harden, and there's determination instead.

"Yes, I'm ready. Let's get this over with," he says confidently, and inside my head, there's a resounding "Yes!" I would jump up and punch the air, but somehow I don't think anyone else would find it appropriate.

"Excellent. I'd like to set the start date for your chemo as Tuesday, then. There are a few things we need to do first. I'm going to schedule you for insertion of a central line tomorrow because I want to give you a few days to recover and ensure the line is placed correctly before we start your chemo. It's a simple procedure—it can be done right here in your room. You'll have the central line from now until at least Day 100 of your recovery after transplant."

"Wow," Will says. "I'll be going home with it?"

"Yes, but it will only be two small tubes coming from an incision in your chest, which we'll cap when you're not here in the hospital. We'll deliver your chemo and the stem cell transplant through the central line, and you'll also need it for blood transfusions during those first hundred days after your transplant. The catheter is threaded into a larger vein than we can use with a PICC line, which is needed for the types of drugs you'll be receiving. And it'll save you from having to get stuck every time you come in for a blood transfusion, which will be a few times a week right after your transplant."

Will nods, taking it all in, and I squeeze his hand reassuringly.

"On Monday, we'll drain the fluid from your abdomen and do one more round of blood work in prep for the chemo; then, we'll start on Tuesday morning."

Will nods again, looking a bit overwhelmed.

"Okay then, I'll come check on you tomorrow afternoon after your line insertion. It'll all be over soon, Will; then you can move on with your life," Dr. Evans says with a wink and a smile.

I smile back at him, but Will is staring straight ahead distractedly.

Dr. Evans's eyes tighten in concern, but he nods and departs.

"Are you okay?" I ask as soon as Evans closes the door.

Wills shakes his head as if to clear it. "Yeah, I . . . Our discussions have been so focused on what drugs I would be getting and for how long, I guess I didn't think to ask how they would be delivered. I didn't know the central line procedure was coming."

"I'd read that a central line is usually used for high-dose chemo and stem cell transplant. It doesn't seem too bad, though. You'll just have two little tubes sticking out of your chest instead of your arm, and from what I've read, it's not hard to take care of."

Will snorts. "You're all over this, aren't you?"

"Yes, of course I am," I respond seriously. "This is a big deal, and if we mess it up, it could mean your life. I want to know everything I can so I can take care of you properly when I get to take you home."

"I'm glad," Will says, smiling. "And I like the sound of that."

"What? Me getting to take you home?"

"Yes," he says huskily. "I've been dreaming about sleeping with you in a normal bed and being woken up by someone other than a nurse."

"Me too. I'm going to wake you up like this every morning," I say, threading my hand into the hair on the back of his neck as I kiss him tenderly.

Will moans into my mouth as he returns the kiss, and the sound is so needy that my belly twinges in want. We've been making out regularly over the last two weeks, when he's felt up to it, but he hasn't made a move to touch me anywhere else.

His tongue swipes against my teeth, and I open wider, tangling my tongue with his and moving in closer as the familiar warmth heats my chest. God, I love kissing him. Some days I think I'd be happy with just doing this forever, but then there are others where I yearn for much, much more. I know *he* wants more—it's there in every lingering touch, in every sweet nip of his teeth, and in the urgency with which he kisses me, like he's doing right now.

Will's hands are cupping my cheeks, his lips devouring me. He lets out an intense groan, and I wonder if I could burst into flame. His lips move to my neck, nipping and sucking as he pants for breath and hums in satisfaction. Goosebumps shoot down my leg as he finds that spot just under my ear that drives me wild. "Oh, Will . . ." I moan, and he laughs against my neck.

"That's a sound I want to hear every day for the rest of my life." He purrs, feathering my collarbone with kisses.

"You do this every day, and I promise you, you'll hear it."

His kisses are passionate and playful—full of the love and hope for the future we've been sharing for the last few weeks. We break apart, gasping and smiling. We seem to have this unspoken agreement that we're not going to go any further until we're able to do it properly. The fantasies we've shared with each other are detailed and steamy and don't involve hospital beds, pain, or catheters. I think we've spoiled ourselves and don't want the imitation.

We cuddle up on his bed and watch *Jeopardy*, and by seven-thirty, he's yawning and droopy-eyed.

"I'll come in the morning and be here for your procedure," I tell him, and he mumbles "Love you" as I quietly close his door.

───── • ◦ ─────

By the time I arrive at Will's room on Saturday morning, they've already placed his central line. I frown at him, and he's quick to try to comfort me. "I'm sorry, Tori, they came in here bright and early, and I couldn't convince them to wait."

I chuckle and shake my head at his backward logic. "I didn't need to be here for *me*, I wanted to be here for *you*!"

"It was fine—it didn't really hurt when they removed the PICC line, and they gave me a local anesthetic when they inserted the central. The whole thing took about twenty minutes."

I breathe a sigh of relief that it wasn't an ordeal for him; then I inspect his new hardware—a small tube sticking out of his chest that's divided into two, with clamps attached to each piece. The clamps are open, and there's tubing attached to both ports since, at the moment, the central line is serving as Will's IV. A dressing covers the exit site to protect it, and there's a small incision just above his collarbone that's bandaged and must have been part of the procedure. His arm is also bandaged where the PICC line was, and a nasty-looking bruise is visible.

"It doesn't look so bad. I think it'll be better than the PICC line because now, at least, I can move my arm more easily," he tells me.

I'm amazed that despite everything that's going on, he's able to find something positive in all this. I think he's finally managed to get into the frame of mind he needs to get through this treatment.

We spend the rest of Saturday and Sunday watching movies and cuddling, and Will is relaxed and happy.

Monday, however, is another matter. It's my last day at work for at least two weeks, so I go in, finish up last-minute paperwork, and make sure all my patients will be covered by other psychologists while I'm gone. Not that I'm going anywhere—I'll actually be right upstairs, but I know I won't have another thought about my patients once Will's chemo starts.

When I arrive at his room, he's sleeping, so I wake him by gently caressing his cheek with my hand. His eyes snap open, and I know in an instant that the peace and contentment of the last few weeks is gone. The fear is out in full force and with it, a heavy dose of anxiety.

I decide to take the casual approach. "Hey, sweetheart, did you have a good nap?"

Will smiles, but it's forced and doesn't reach his eyes. "I—no, not really. I'm a bit worked up about tomorrow."

I close my eyes, happy and sad at the same time. Will has been opening up to me so much more over the last few weeks, and the fact he's able to admit his fears to me without my probing for information is a huge step in the right direction.

His eyes meet mine, a storm of confusion and doubt.

"Tori, this is gonna be really rough. I'm going to be so sick and miserable. Are you sure you want to be here for this?"

I bark out a laugh, and he furrows his eyebrows. "You've got to be kidding me right now. Seriously? You're the one who has to go through all this pain and suffering, and you're trying to give me an out from having to *watch* you? Christ, Will, if I could do this *for* you, I'd jump at the chance! You don't know how much I wish I could do something other than *sit* here!"

After he gets over his shock from my outburst, he looks at me sheepishly, but he still seems unsure.

"Sweetheart, I'm not leaving. I'm going to be here every minute. I'm going to hold your hand and run my fingers through your hair and cuddle you if you're feeling up to it. I'm going to do everything I can to make this easier for you, no matter what it is."

Will closes his eyes and puts a hand to his forehead. "I'm sorry. I didn't mean to sound like I was pushing you away. I'm just so jumpy about this. I wish the wait was over."

"It'll be over soon, sweetheart," I tell him, taking his hand in mine and rubbing his fingers gently. "Tomorrow is going to change everything for you and get us one step closer to our life together. I know how anxious you are, but try to remember all the things we have planned for when the cancer's gone.

"'Keep your eyes on the prize,' as the saying goes. I moved the last of my things into your apartment yesterday."

Will grins at me. "Really? Everything is all moved in?"

"Not . . . everything. I'm not planning to sleep there until you're ready to go home and be there with me, so some of my things are still back at my apartment."

"But . . . aren't you planning to give up your apartment? What are you going to do until then?"

Shit.

"Don't worry about the details, Will. You have enough on your plate. I'll be staying right here with you for at least two weeks for your chemo and transplant."

He looks at me quizzically. I should have worded that better so it wouldn't have caught his attention. Elizabeth is actually taking over my apartment, but Will still doesn't know anything about Elizabeth divorcing his father and moving up here, and I have no intention of being the one to tell him. So I try to divert him as best I can.

"I'm sure you're going to hate me living in your apartment. You're so neat, and my shit's going to be everywhere—"

"Tori, as long as it's yours, I'll be happy it's there."

"Sure, you say that *now*. Wait until you're tripping over my stuff and swearing; then you'll be singing a different tune."

"If I make it that far, I'll be singing a happy tune, no matter what." He looks down and away, doubt and despair written all over his face.

"Will," I say softly, running my fingers into his hair. He leans into my touch and sighs.

"I need to ask you to do something for me. If it comes to it, it might be the hardest thing you ever have to do, but I'm afraid of how this is going to go, so I have to ask."

"What is it? You know I'll do anything," I tell him, my mind racing through a thousand possibilities at once.

He stares down at his afghan, pressing it into the mattress with his index finger as he traces the box weave. "Tori, you know I want to spend the rest of my life with you. Nothing is going to change that. In my heart, you'll always be the one, and I'll always want to be with you."

"Will, you're scaring me."

He huffs out a breath and covers his eyes with his hand for a moment. "I'm worried this is going to get really bad, and I'm going to try to . . . back out of it. My worst fear is that I'll get in the middle of this chemo, and the pain or the sickness will convince me it's not worth it, or it'll be so bad that I'll just want to die instead. I don't want to hurt you, so I want you to understand what I want and how I feel *now*, when my judgment isn't clouded by whatever else is happening to me. And . . . I want you to promise to help me if I do tell you I want to stop because it's not what I really want."

I stare at him for a moment, absorbing his words and the gravity of the situation he's describing.

He thinks this treatment is going to break him.

He thinks this treatment is going to break him, and he's asking me to help hold him together.

Of course, I'm going to say yes, but oh God, could it really come to his begging me to let him stop? As I stare at the man before me, I can't even imagine what would lead us to that point. But said man is staring back at me, his doubt coalescing into fear because I'm just looking at him and not responding to his request.

"I'm sorry, sweetheart," I say, raising my hand to his cheek. "I wasn't debating my answer. I got lost in trying to imagine a situation where you'd say that to me. Of course I'll convince you not to stop if you need convincing. I promise."

Will closes his eyes, and when he opens them again, the fear there is raw and wild. "Tori, I love you so much. But I'm so scared of this. What if the chemo kills me? What if the transplant doesn't work? What if we go through all of this and I die of some damn infection anyway?"

I lie on my side next to him and pull his head onto my shoulder, holding him as he sobs softly against me.

"Sweetheart, there are so many what-ifs right now, you'll go crazy if you imagine them all. Let's talk about what *is*. I love you with all my heart, and you love me the same. I'm going to stay with you and love you, no matter what happens. Even if you . . . die, we'll have been together every moment, and you'll have done all you could do. I can't ask for any more than that, and you can't ask any more than that of yourself. You, me, the doctors—we're doing everything we can, but when it comes down to it, we don't have control. We just have to hope and pray you're strong enough to make it through this and that nothing bad happens.

"I believe you're going to make it through this, Will. I believe you and I are meant to be together, and you deserve a long and happy life, and you're going to get it. That's why I've been planning the future with you. Because I believe it's going to happen. I know how much harder it is for you to believe because of what's happened to you in the past and because of the path you're staring down right now. But you need to try as hard as you can to believe because that's what's going to see you through. Believe that we're going to live together and do all the things couples do and have amazing sex involving paintbrushes. Believe it, and you can make it happen through the strength of your belief and of our love.

"Just . . . let it go and believe. You have no control, so just believe and let God."

Will lifts his eyes to look at me, and I see the storm is quieting. The fear is being replaced by acceptance, the doubt by faith.

"I love you so much, Tori. You're the best thing that's ever happened to me," he whispers, tears rolling down his cheeks, but this time, they're happy tears. I cuddle him in close, and as I kiss his forehead, he relaxes against me.

"You're the best thing that's ever happened to me too," I tell him, holding him tightly.

CHAPTER 7

I wake to the feel of gentle fingers running through my hair, and my lips part in a smile before I'm even fully aware. Will's deep chuckle vibrates against me, and I open my eyes to a sea of brilliant green. He's smiling, and I take in the beauty of his face for a moment, bringing my hand up to caress his cheek. Today's the day. I stare at him and do everything I can to commit his amazing smile to memory because I don't know when I'll see it again.

"Good morning, sweetheart. You're up early," I say, glancing at the clock to see that it's barely past seven.

"I've been awake for a while. I couldn't sleep," he answers, running the tips of his fingers over my eyebrows and down to the tip of my nose.

"You should have woken me! I would have kept you company." I scold him gently, but he shakes his head.

"It's all right. I needed some time to center myself, and I like watching you sleep."

A blush heats my cheeks. "I like watching you sleep, too, and that's a good thing because I think I'll be seeing more of you asleep than awake over the next few weeks."

"That's very true." He continues to trace the contours of my face with his finger, leaving my skin tingling in its wake.

"What are you doing?" I ask, capturing his hand in mine and bringing it to my lips, kissing each of his fingers.

He exhales heavily. "I'm reminding myself why I'm doing this because, soon, I'm going to be too sick to touch you like this."

I squeeze my eyes shut as I continue to kiss him, now on the back of his hand and down to the scar on his wrist.

"Why do you do that?" he asks. "That's not the first time you've kissed those scars. You've done it before when I've talked about my suicide attempt."

"Well, they mean something to me. They remind me how strong you are."

"Strong?" Will scoffs, shaking his head. "I always thought they were a sign of weakness—that I couldn't handle what life gave me."

"Oh, no. You may have done this in a moment of weakness, but when I look at these scars, I see what came after. You're still here. You got the help you needed, and you fought your way out of your depression. You turned your life around and became a better person because of it. And then, you were brave enough to endure two rounds of chemo to keep on living, and you never once went back to this," I say, lifting his wrist.

"You're a survivor, Will. That, to me, is strength. That's what I see when I look at these scars. I'm so glad you didn't succeed in that moment of weakness because what came after brought you to me. I know you can do this, too." I kiss my way up his palm.

"I hope so because I want the day to come when we can wake up like this every morning."

He moans softly as I pull his index finger into my mouth, and suddenly, he's breathing heavily. "Kiss me, Tori. I don't know when I'll be able to kiss you again—"

I cut off his words with my lips, and his arms surround me, fingers buried in my hair and tongue begging for entrance. I kiss him with all the passion and love and anger and fear I'm feeling. I give it all to him, hoping he'll understand—and he gives it right back, ravishing my mouth with desperate purpose, clinging to me and pouring all his love into each movement of his lips against mine. I feel the love foremost but also his own fear and desperation. *What if this is the last time I get to kiss you like this? What if I die during treatment? What if we go through all of this and it doesn't work?* It's all there in the pressure of his lips, in his need to consume me. I get lost as his emotion threatens to overwhelm us both, and our teeth clack together with the ferociousness of the kiss.

But, suddenly, he slows down, and there's a shift in his demeanor. The need turns to worship; his lips become soft and gentle on mine, and all I feel is his love, simple and true. Heat begins to build in my chest and spread outward, making my arms tingle. One of his hands remains buried in my hair, but the other comes around to stroke over my breast, circling my nipple through my bra and causing it to peak. He moans against my mouth, the sound so erotic and sexy that my own hand wanders to his chest, pinching his nipple gently between my fingers. He gasps against my mouth, and I know he's aroused, and though I want so desperately to reach down and touch him, today's not the day. So I back off a bit, focusing on what I can tell him with my lips and the stroke of my fingers over his collarbone.

We kiss softly and sweetly for long moments, soaking up the feel and taste of each other, until he finally pulls away.

The look in his eyes stops my heart.

"I love you so much, Tori." But I hear so much more, so many things we've said over the weeks, but he doesn't have to say them now because I already know.

"I love you so much, too," I answer, unable to contain my tears.

"It's gonna be okay," he tells me, pulling me against him.

I feel the strong beat of his heart and the strength in his arms, and oh God, I hope it's enough. "I know."

Jenny pokes her head in the door, her smile faltering for a second as she sees how we're wrapped around each other. Her professional bedside manner snaps into place as she pushes the door open.

"Good morning, Will! Today's the big day! We need to get you cleaned up and ready because your infusion starts at nine."

Will stares at me lovingly for another moment, then, with a sigh, forces himself to look away.

"Hi, Jenny. I'm ready. Let's get this show on the road."

Another woman enters the room behind Jenny. Her long brown hair is tied back into a ponytail, and her deep brown eyes hide behind a pair of studious-looking glasses. She wears a short, white coat, and her smile is warm and caring.

"Hello, Will," she says brightly. "I know it's a big day for you, and you have a lot on your mind, but I wanted to stop by and meet you before your treatment began. My name is Jill Walker, and I'm going to be your transplant coordinator."

She approaches and holds out her hand, and Will takes it, giving her a tentative smile.

Then she turns to me. "And you must be Tori. Nice to meet you as well. Jenny has had nothing but good things to say about you."

I take her hand, and her handshake is strong and confident.

She turns back to Will. "As I'm sure Dr. Evans already explained, I'll be watching over you after the transplant and determining when you need blood transfusions and any other support you may require.

"You won't be feeling very well at the point when I become involved in your treatment, so I wanted to come and introduce myself today and wish you good luck. I'll do my very best to see that you have everything you need after your transplant and that you recover as quickly as possible."

Will smiles at her gratefully, and her eyes widen as he pins her with those amazing green eyes of his. I don't know how he's made it this far in life without some woman snapping him up, cancer or no.

"Thank you, Jill," Will says. "It sounds like I'll be in very good hands."

Jenny pipes up. "The best. I chose her for you myself. Only the best for my favorite patient."

Will smiles warmly at her. "Always looking out for me, aren't you?"

"*Someone* has to; otherwise, who knows where you'd end up?" As Jenny teases him, Jill looks a little confused, but the affection between Jenny and Will is easy to see.

"Well, now that I know you're Jenny's *favorite* patient, I'll be giving you my very best, for sure," Jill says, grinning.

And with that, we get busy with our tasks. I go shower and get some breakfast, and Jenny helps Will clean up in preparation for the long week ahead. When I return, it's almost nine and Will is alone, staring downward with his afghan clenched in his fists.

He looks up when I enter, trying to calm the storm, but I see it in his eyes for a few seconds before he gets it under control.

"Hey, it's gonna be okay, remember?"

"Yeah. I just want to get it over with. I don't do well with anticipation."

"I'm getting that," I tell him as I take his hand. "Your wait is over though. I saw Jenny getting things ready as I passed the nurses' station."

As if on cue, Jenny comes through the door holding two IV bags. She smiles at him kindly. "Okay, Will, it's time to get started. Are you ready?"

Will nods because I think he's too anxious to speak right now, and Jenny catches on right away.

"Nothing's going to happen right away with this drug. It'll probably cause nausea and vomiting but not until a few hours after the two-hour infusion is over. And we're going to give you medication to counter the side effects. So relax and try to sleep, if you can. This is going to get rough later on, so you should both get all the rest you can now."

Will relaxes visibly, and I squeeze his hand. The wait is over, but at least we have a little more time before the really bad stuff starts happening.

As Jenny hooks up the IV bags, Will looks at me nervously. "Would you lie on the bed with me for a while?"

"Of course, sweetheart! From now on, anything you want or need, just ask and I'll do it. I'll cuddle with you, I'll rub anything that hurts—absolutely anything, okay? No request is too big or small."

"Thanks, Tori," he says, kissing my hand.

I crawl onto the bed beside him, and he rests his head on my shoulder and snuggles against me. The first infusion actually seems to make him sleepy—he's out within a few moments, and I follow not long after.

I wake sometime later to Will moving next to me. I glance up at the clock. It's nearly one in the afternoon, and his infusion ended almost two hours ago. We both must have been more tired than we thought! He's still asleep, but he can't lie still—his arm is gripping his stomach, and he moans a little in his sleep as he turns to face me. I don't want to disturb him, so I lie quietly beside him, hoping he'll be able to rest for a while longer.

My hope is short-lived as he wakes with a groan ten minutes later. "Oh God, I'm really nauseated," he says, swallowing thickly.

I turn to face him, causing the bed to move slightly, and he moans and clutches his stomach.

"Sweetheart, I think you need your space now. Why don't I get off your bed so you have more room to find a comfortable position."

"Yeah," he says weakly.

I slide off the bed as gently as I can, but it still causes him to moan again. "I'm sorry!"

"S'all right. Not your fault," he answers, head in his hand. "Tori. This is already . . . getting rough. I might not talk much . . . over the next few days. I have to deal with this in any way I can . . . and in the past that's been by . . . focusing inward. I just wanted . . . you to understand."

"I do understand. You do whatever you need to do, and I'll be here in whatever way you need me, okay?"

I go and tell Jenny he's nauseated, and she gives me a sympathetic look.

"Okay, I'll be down shortly. In the meantime, I left a stack of basins in his bathroom in case he gets sick."

I hurry back down to his room to find him in the same shape as when I left. He endures the nausea for almost two hours, moaning and shifting position, but he can't stay still for very long. Finally, at around three o'clock, he asks me to call for Jenny.

When she comes, he speaks to her in a monotone voice laced with misery. "Stop whatever you're giving me for nausea and vomiting. It's controlling the vomiting, but the nausea is unbearable. I feel like I'm drunk, and I really need to throw up, but I can't. I'd rather vomit and feel better for a while than put up with this for six days."

"Of course, Will. Whatever you need. If you change your mind, let me know."

About twenty minutes later, Will starts vomiting.

And so begins our descent into hell.

Chemotherapy is poison. Cancer is a rebellion of the body's own cells, and very little distinguishes the ones that have become cancerous from the healthy ones. Chemotherapy focuses on those differences, but it still kills the healthy cells too. The theory is that chemo should kill more cancer cells than normal cells, and the chemotherapy should kill the cancer before it kills you. In theory. But when it comes right down to it, receiving chemotherapy is allowing yourself to be poisoned.

Watching Will be slowly poisoned is, hands down, the worst experience of my life.

He's awake for the rest of the first day, and I lose count of how many times he vomits. I hold the basin for him and run my fingers through his hair, aching for him, but it's all I can do.

Jason arrives around seven in the evening, and I slip out for a little while and get myself some dinner since I skipped lunch. My sandwich tastes like sawdust in my mouth because I know Will couldn't keep anything down right now if he tried.

I go back to the room to find Jason rubbing Will's back as he retches, and I can't stop the tears that flow down my cheeks. I wonder if I'll be able to stop the tears at all over the next six days.

Jason is on night shift with Will so I can get some sleep on the couch on the other side of his room. The first night is horrible—Will is either vomiting or dry heaving about every twenty minutes, and I wake up every time. At three o'clock I finally give up on sleep and go help Jason with Will.

The next day is even worse because Will receives two half-hour infusions of a different drug and a two-hour infusion of yet another. This is the regimen he has to endure for the next four days. He develops flu-like symptoms—fever, chills, and severe body aches—in addition to the intense nausea and vomiting. I've never seen a human being as sick as Will is . . . and it just goes on and on; the days and nights start to run together.

Will doesn't talk. At all. His focus is turned completely inward, fighting with all he has to make it through this, to resist the urge to tell them to stop and let him die. I tell him I love him a million times, and he answers by squeezing my hand because he can't say the words right now. I run my fingers into his hair—sometimes he leans into my touch, and sometimes he flinches away, and I let him be. He speaks occasionally, saying "I'm thirsty" or "I'm gonna be sick," but it's monotone and with no recognition of who's around him. He keeps his eyes shut most of the time, and when they're open, he never raises them to look at me. I think right now it's just too hard and would bring him that much closer to breaking.

On the third day, he becomes jaundiced again, his liver struggling to clear all the toxins he's allowing into his body.

By the fourth day, Will can't help but flinch away and curl into a ball when Jenny brings in the IV bag containing each infusion. It's a psychological reaction he just can't get past. But he says nothing, stalwart in his decision to see this through. I cry every time I see those damn IV bags and count the minutes until it'll finally be over.

That day is also when the pain really begins for him. His liver is failing, and between the increase in toxins and byproducts and the dangerous swelling that was already there, the pain becomes excruciating. I beg Dr. Evans to increase his morphine, and his response freezes my heart.

"As much as I want to, Tori, I can't give him anything more, and in fact, we've had to reduce his morphine. Morphine is processed through the liver, and if I increase it, I'll be giving him a death sentence. If his liver truly fails, there's no way he'll survive a transplant since we just destroyed his immune system, and he'll die. We have to hope he can endure the pain and that his liver will keep functioning until we get through the chemo course. I'm sorry, but there's nothing more I can do."

I stumble back into Will's room to find him vomiting into a basin Jenny is holding for him, clutching at his upper right side and panting, a moan escaping with every labored breath. Two more days. He has two more days to endure this, and after that, the side effects won't even stop right away. Oh, dear God, how can he do it? As I look at him, in utter misery, my heart cries out for me to tell him to quit. This is too much—I don't know how he's going to survive it—but I can't betray him like that. He's the one who's suffering, and he has to make the call, and if and when he does, it's my duty to try to talk him out of it because I promised him I would do everything I could to help him see this through. The tears fall as I go to him—I feel like I've been crying nonstop for days.

On the fifth day, the real crises hit. Will starts having muscle spasms, and around one in the afternoon, he has a seizure. I'm alone with him at the time, and somehow, my training takes over and I roll him onto his side and position him correctly, then call Jenny for help. It only lasts a minute, but by the time she gets there, I'm hyperventilating and completely freaking out. I collapse on the couch while she sees to Will, but she's by my side in a few minutes as the room fills with people.

Dr. Evans and two other doctors hurry in and consult in hushed voices on the other side of the room. I stare at them vacantly as Jenny tries to pull me back together.

"Tori. Tori! Snap out of it! Will needs you!"

I look up at her blearily, but her words finally register, and my brain kicks into gear again. "What the hell happened, Jenny? What would cause him to have a seizure?"

"Tori, this just got really serious. Dr. Evans wants to talk to you, but you have to remember how badly Will wants this—how badly you both want this. This isn't the end. I know he can do this. He only has to survive one more day of chemo, and then everything will get better, I promise you. This is a crisis, but it *will* pass, and you'll have your life together. Do you believe me?"

Jenny stares at me intensely, willing me to buy into her words, and somehow, I manage to draw strength from them. "Yes, I believe you."

"Good," she says, sounding relieved. "Now you can go and talk with Dr. Evans."

I begin to get up, but thankfully, Dr. Evans comes to me because I don't know how steady I'd be on my feet. He sits on the couch next to me, and he takes my hand. I freeze in fear. Dr. Evans has *never* taken my hand before, and the implication of his action scares the shit out of me —as if I'm about to need comfort. He must see the terror in my eyes because he starts in immediately.

"Tori, we need to talk about Will. His symptoms today mean we have a new problem, and it's a serious one. He's developed tumor lysis syndrome, which is a fairly common occurrence with high-dose chemotherapy. Basically, his cells are dying so fast that his body can't keep up with the byproducts, and it's thrown his electrolytes out of balance. The muscle spasms are being caused by a decrease in calcium, and we've also detected increases in phosphate and uric acid. This means he's in renal failure, and we're going to need to start dialysis in order to help his body clear all the cellular byproducts. After today, he's done with the two drugs that are causing this to happen, so I think he'll still be okay as long as we go ahead with dialysis. If this had happened two days ago, I'd say his chances for survival would have been slim if he tried to complete the treatment. But as it is, I think if we treat this aggressively, everything will still work out for him. Do I have your permission to go ahead with the treatment?"

I realize belatedly that I still have power of attorney for Will, and Dr. Evans is asking me to make the decision for him.

"What will happen if he doesn't have dialysis?"

"If we don't go ahead with dialysis, he won't live out the week," Dr. Evans says. "This is serious, but it's treatable, and he only has one more dose of chemo tomorrow, and it's a different drug that the dialysis will actually help his body process. If this had to happen, right now is really the best time."

My gaze falls on Will. He looks . . . awful. His skin is a sickly yellow color, his eyes sunken from lack of real sleep and constant pain. He's lost weight over the last week—I can see it in the thinning of his arms, and for once, his belly is almost completely flat. But as I watch, his lips come together into that pout I fell in love with, and I sob brokenly. My heart is screaming that he's suffered enough, that I should let him go even though it will kill me.

I shake myself from my moment of weakness and don't let myself think about it because Will and I have already made our decisions. It's my job to act for him and to see this through.

"Yes, I give permission for the treatment. He's worked so hard and suffered so much to get here. He needs to have the chance to see it through."

"Thank you, Tori. I think you're making the right decision. This is what Will would want, and I really feel we can get him through this." He squeezes my hand, then hurries off to make the arrangements.

Within minutes, there's a flurry of activity in Will's room as the nurses bring in the equipment for dialysis. They're going to use Will's central line and filter his blood continuously until his kidneys can do the job for themselves again.

I take a deep breath. This is okay. Dr. Evans said this is okay, and Will can get through this. This isn't the end. His body just needs a little help, that's all.

But I stare fearfully at the equipment, knowing we're one step closer to Will's body failing.

He's been unconscious since the seizure, but now he moans and clutches his side, turning feebly in his bed.

I go to him and stroke the side of his face, but he flinches back, crying out from the pain of the sudden movement. He pants out a few hard breaths, then moves his arms to grip his stomach.

"I'm gonna be sick," he mumbles, and I have just enough time to grab a basin before he heaves. I rub his back until the episode is over, and he lies back wearily against the bed, panting and moaning.

For the first time in five days, he raises his eyes to me, and my heart stops. Will's face looks haunted—as if he's fleeing from an invisible demon he can't escape. His eyes look dead—frozen—with no trace of the warmth and brilliance and love I've gotten so used to seeing. But somewhere in their depths, his pain is an unquenchable fire. I see it, and it burns me. I almost recoil from his gaze, but somehow I find the strength to look back at him and not cower away.

"Tori," he rasps out, and I know what's coming. Oh God, I know what's coming. My worst nightmare is about to come true.

"Tori, tell them to stop. I can't do this anymore," he says woodenly, and I can't contain the cry of anguish that bursts from me.

"I'm in so much . . . pain. So sick I can't . . . take it. Let me die. Right now . . . I . . . want to die. It has to be . . . better than this." He gasps, clutching his side and squeezing his eyes shut.

No, this can't be happening. Not after I just had to convince myself not to tell him to do this. Not after he made me promise. *No!*

I touch him again, and this time he doesn't flinch away. I caress his cheek, and he leans into me, but I know it's no comfort. "Will, you can't give up. You only have one more infusion left, and the sickness won't stop now, even if they stop treating you. You have to hang on. It's only one more day; then it'll be over."

"Tori . . . please . . . make it stop."

My heart shatters. It's shattered so many times before, but this time, it's so painful I clutch at my chest, gasping for air.

He's falling apart. The pain and sickness are driving him beyond reason, just as he feared. Deep inside me, panic begins to bloom.

"Will, I love you so much, but I can't do that. There's no way for me to stop it. You have to hang on.

"I love you, Will, and we're going to have a life together. 'When the cancer's gone,' remember? We have a whole list of things we're going to do, and I wrote them all down. They're right here so you can see how many there are," I say, reaching over and pulling the list out of my bag. I show it to him with shaking fingers, but he closes his eyes and bows his head.

He raises his eyes to me again, wells of misery and hell on earth, and he starts to sob. "Tori, I'm sorry . . . it's not enough . . . I love you, but it's not enough . . . I don't have . . . anything left . . . I'd do anything . . . to make it stop. Please . . . let me go . . ."

Oh God, what do I do? I can't—I'm not—

And that's when I break down.

Completely.

I sob uncontrollably, anguish pouring out of my soul. "I promised! Oh God, Will, I promised you I wouldn't let you give up! Don't make me go back on my promise! Don't make me! Please! Don't ask me to do this!" I'm begging now, clutching his hand desperately.

My hysteria gets his attention, and he puts his hand on my head. "I love you so much, Will! You can't leave me! I promised! You made me promise!"

He tries to pull me up and into his arms, and I go willingly, clinging to him as we cry together. Finally, he pulls back, resting wearily against the mattress.

"I won't . . . make you. But I don't . . . know how . . . to keep going," he whispers brokenly.

"What can I do? There's got to be something. What can I do to make this easier for you? I'll do anything. If I could suffer this *for* you, I would."

"Hold me," he whispers. "I keep waking up and thinking . . . I'm alone, and I can't remember what's wrong with me . . . and why I'm doing this."

Oh Jesus Christ. My chest tightens so much I can't breathe, and I close my eyes and clench my teeth to keep the wail of anguish from escaping. Somehow, I manage to hold it together.

"Of course I'll hold you. I'll hold you every minute until this is over."

There's no way he can move by himself, and even though I shift him as gently as I can, he still screams from the pain. I don't even bother to wipe away my tears as I settle him against me—I know they're not going to stop until this is over.

Jenny comes running in, probably because everyone on the floor could hear Will screaming. She stops dead at the sight of us.

Will is still panting and whimpering, eyes closed as he clings to me, and I have to swallow thickly before I can speak.

"Jenny, I need Jason. Can you please call him and ask him to come?"

Jenny just nods and backs out of the room. I see the fear in her eyes—she doesn't even have to ask what's going on. She's seen people break under the strain of chemo before.

Will may be broken, but he's not defeated. He's going to make it through this.

I run my fingers into his hair and whisper words of love to soothe him, but he doesn't respond. His focus is turned inward again, trying to cope with his suffering in any way he can, and I can only hope my words and my touch provide some small comfort.

Suddenly, Jason is beside me, rubbing my arm gently. "Tori, what—"

"He asked me to tell them to stop, and he told me he wanted to die . . . but I talked him out of it. He's barely hanging on, and he can't remember what's going on, so he asked me to hold him to remind him."

Jason's face is a mask of horror, his eyes brimming with tears. "Oh God . . ."

"I made him a promise, Jason. I promised I'd see him through this, and I wouldn't let him give in. I have to hold him together until the end of the last infusion tomorrow. Will you help me?"

"Of-of course I will! Whatever you need."

I nod gratefully, trying to pull myself together enough to keep going. I'm beyond exhausted, and everything seems to be moving in slow motion, but I'm also trying to gear myself up for the fight ahead.

"I'm not going to move from this spot until sometime tomorrow, so I need you to take care of whatever else he needs."

"Absolutely," Jason replies, his eyes never leaving Will.

At that moment, Will starts breathing more heavily, and Jason is already scrambling for a basin when Will mumbles, "Gonna be sick" and leans forward, heaving into the basin Jason holds in front of him.

The next eighteen hours are the hardest of my entire life. I have never seen a human being go through so much misery. I bite my tongue until it bleeds to keep myself from telling him I'll make it stop right now.

He whimpers and moans in the grip of his pain, and sometimes, it's sharp enough that he cries out. Tears of frustration and agony roll down his cheeks, and he bites the inside of his mouth so hard it begins to bleed.

I hold him as tightly but as gently as I can and whisper a hundred thousand million times, "It's gonna be okay. I love you. Just a little longer, and it'll be over. It's gonna be okay."

The tears keep sliding down my cheeks, and I can't stop them, can't stop the outpouring of raw, unimaginable pain from my heart.

I go on autopilot as the hours drag by.

I stroke his hair.

I kiss his forehead.

And I pray.

I pray to God, and I ask Him to give me just this one thing in my whole life.

I reason with Him that Will deserves the happiness that waits at the end of all of this for all the bad things that have already happened to him in his short life.

And I beg.

For strength.

For help.

For mercy.

For relief.

The words flow from my lips in a constant mantra—any time I'm not saying words of comfort to Will, I'm begging, "Please, please, please."

I will him through the night.

I hold him together, and I give him everything I have and things I didn't even know I had or was capable of giving.

This night defines who I am as a person and what I'm willing to give and endure for another. And the answer is that, for Will, I'm willing to give everything.

I watch the sunrise, but it's no new beginning—it's another day in hell for us. I pray that when the pink of the sunset colors the sky, there will be hope in it.

When Jenny finally comes in with the last infusion, Will loses it.

"N-n-no, n-no!" he whimpers, struggling feebly in my arms, but I hold fast.

"Last time, last time. One more and it's over," I whisper. "Just close your eyes and hold on to me, and it'll be all over."

He's completely broken as he sobs against my shoulder, but he does what I ask. He fights through the pain and the sickness until, finally, it *is* completely over.

He's still in terrible pain, clutching at his side and whimpering, so I hold him tightly and run my fingers through his hair. About two hours after the infusion ends, Will starts vomiting again, but by this point, he's delirious with exhaustion and can't even tell us when he's about to be sick. He's so out of it that Jenny suggests we try an anti-emetic again —Will didn't like the way it made him feel at the beginning of the chemo, but at this point, he's not really going to know the difference. The drug appears to help because his vomiting becomes less frequent, but he can't really rest because of the intensity of his pain.

Finally, at around three in the afternoon, Jenny comes in and tells us Dr. Evans left an order to increase Will's morphine because enough time has passed that most of the last drug will have been processed through Will's liver. And oh, thank God, it's enough. About twenty minutes after the increase in dosage, Will's grip on his side slackens, and he falls into an exhausted sleep.

Tears course down my face as I watch him, and I thank God and every other deity I've ever heard of that Will's suffering has ended. It's not over, but somehow, he's made it through this part. I smile at Jason, and then sleep claims me too.

CHAPTER 8

Something jolts me awake. *Where the hell am I?* I look around blearily, and I'm lying on a couch in . . . the nurses' lounge? I'm at the hospital . . . *Will!*

I jump to my feet, but I have to grip the back of the couch as a wave of dizziness washes over me. I raise my hand to my forehead, and suddenly, Jenny is holding me up.

"Jenny! What's going on? Where's Will?"

Jenny sits me back down on the couch. "He's fine, Tori. He's doing okay. I had Jason carry you in here last night, so you could get some real rest."

"But . . . has he been alone? I promised I wouldn't leave . . ."

"I stayed and sat up with him last night. Jason was almost as bad off as you were, so I sent him home. Will's still waking up to vomit every few hours, but he's sleeping in between, and he doesn't seem to be in any pain. He's still on dialysis, but his kidney function is slowly improving, and his electrolytes are starting to normalize."

I breathe a sigh of relief. It's over. It's really over, and he's going to get better now. But then I run through the list of everything that's gone wrong since Tuesday. "And his liver?"

"No change yet, but that will probably take longer." She looks up at me, suddenly very serious. "You got him through it. You held him together that last day by sheer strength of will. He's strong, but in the end, it was too much for him and he needed you, and you gave him everything you had. You were amazing."

I smile at her tiredly. "He's the one who survived. I just held his hand."

"You did a lot more than that. He would have given up without you."

I nod, unable to argue. "I love him, Jenny. More than I ever thought I could love anyone."

"I know," she says, smiling at me. "And you're both going to get the happiness you deserve."

Jenny yawns widely. "Come and get some breakfast with me. I'm exhausted, but I'm also starving. Jason's with Will now—you can go join him after you feed me."

I grin at her, knowing this is her way of getting me to eat, too. I'm desperate to see Will, but I have to take care of myself if I'm going to be any good to him. "All right. Let me brush my teeth and change, and we'll go."

After breakfast, I'm feeling much steadier, and I hurry down the hallway to Will's room. But Jenny stops me before I reach the doorway. "The chemo has already killed off most of his immune system. He's under isolation protocol now, and we're all going to need to wear masks and gloves when we go in to see him to protect him from infection."

I nod, fear suddenly coursing through my veins. Will may not be physically ill at the moment, but he's weaker than he's ever been because his body can't protect him. Something as small as a cold could be fatal because he has no way to fight back.

Jenny puts her hand on my arm. "It's okay, Tori. As long as we're careful, he'll be safe. And as soon as we know the transplant took, we won't need to wear them anymore. It'll only be two or three weeks."

"I know. I'm fine. It's just a lot to take."

"I know, honey. The worst is over though. The rest isn't easy, but the chemo is the scary part, and he's already through that."

Nodding again, I put on my gloves and mask so I can enter the room I left just hours ago. As I push the door open, my eyes are immediately drawn to Will. I bite my lip painfully—he still looks awful, but . . . he looks at peace. His skin is still yellow, and his eyes are shadowed and sunken, but he's sleeping soundly, and there are no signs of pain. His muscles are relaxed, and the skin around his eyes is smooth. He made it. *He made it!*

"There's my hero," Jason says as he stands up and gives me a hug.

"I didn't do anything," I mutter, embarrassed. Will's the one who survived this. I watched and felt no pain at all.

"Do you even know what you did? You held him for nearly twenty-four hours and whispered it was almost over and that he'd be okay. I watched you, and I still don't know how you did it. I don't know how you held it together for him like that because even I had to walk out a few times. But you stayed, and you didn't let go of him—not for one second—until he finally got relief from his pain."

I stare at him as his words wash over me. That was twenty-four hours? A whole day? "Wow, I . . . I didn't realize . . ."

Jason and Jenny are both looking at me, and I can tell that they're smiling by the crinkling of the skin around their eyes.

"How has he been?"

"I've only been here about an hour, and he's been asleep the whole time."

"He vomited around five this morning, but he's been sleeping ever since," Jenny chimes in. "The side effects are waning."

I walk over and run my gloved fingers into his hair, and a handful of auburn strands come away with my hand. I gasp in surprise as tears well up in my eyes. Jenny puts her hand on my shoulder.

"He's going to lose it all. The drugs he's had are strong, and three out of the four cause hair loss. It'll grow back, though, in a few months."

I close my eyes and nod, unable to say anything. I did know this was coming, but knowing and watching it happen are two entirely different things. Sighing, I shake my head—he's got bigger problems than this. This one isn't life threatening.

Dr. Evans strides into the room, and he pauses when he sees us all gathered there. "How's my support team this morning? A little better rested?"

Jason and I nod as Dr. Evans moves to check Will's chart.

"I'm glad you're all here because I was going to try to meet with you today to update you on Will's progress."

"How is he?" I blurt out, my eyes straying back to Will.

"He's doing better than I expected, considering everything that happened this week," Dr. Evans says. "But we're going to have to change our plans slightly. He was actually scheduled to receive the stem cell infusion today, but I'm going to delay it because of the tumor lysis syndrome and the issues with his kidney and liver function. He needs to stabilize, and the transplant will cause some additional stress on both organs, so I want to give him a few days to recover. We'll proceed with the transplant as planned as soon as his body is ready.

"I'm optimistic we'll be able to take him off dialysis in two or three days, and hopefully, he'll be stable enough for transplant by then. In the meantime, he'll start receiving blood transfusions to replace the immune cells that are dying.

"We're getting there," Dr. Evans says, smiling at me. "He's made it through the hardest part. It should be easier from here."

Suddenly, I'm overwhelmed with gratitude for this man who's doing everything he can to see that Will survives. "Thank you, Dr. Evans," I say, hugging him.

He freezes, then holds me firmly. "You're welcome, Tori. Thank *you* for coming into his life. I've known Will for almost three years now, and I've never seen him as happy as he is with you. You're his reason for living."

Warmth floods my heart for the first time in days, and I chuckle. "He's my reason for living, too, although I'm not quite so dramatic about it," I say, and it's everyone else's turn to chuckle.

We settle into a routine of watching over Will as we wait for him to improve enough for transplant, and we all recover from our own exhaustion from the previous week. Will continues to be sick every few hours, but the amount of time between each episode is lengthening, and his body is slowly stabilizing. He sleeps almost constantly, only waking when he's sick, and with the same reduced awareness he had during the chemo. I start to wonder if he understands that he's already finished the chemo, but he never stays awake long enough for me to really talk to him, and I don't have the heart to try to wake him up to explain.

On the third day after the chemo ended, I'm sitting beside Will, reading, and suddenly, I'm greeted by my favorite shade of green. I'm on my feet in an instant, grabbing the basin on the table next to me in one swift motion. "Are you gonna be sick?" I ask him, holding the basin near his chest.

He furrows his brow and shakes his head. I'm guessing he doesn't remember that pretty much every time he's been awake for the last ten days, it's been to throw up.

His eyes are barely open, and he looks as if just lying there watching me is taking most of the strength he has. "Am I still . . . alive?" he whispers.

I inhale sharply as hope flares in my chest. This is the first time he's asked a question since before all this began. For the last nine days, he's had no idea what's been going on around him, or even inside of him— he's been too sick to care. I smile and take his hand between mine. "Oh, yes, you're very much alive. How are you feeling?"

"Awful. Why can't . . . I breathe?" His voice is quiet and weak, and he takes in air in small pants despite the nasal cannula that's giving him oxygen.

"You're anemic, sweetheart. It's going to make you tired and short of breath. You finished the chemo three days ago, but you're still experiencing the side effects. They've been giving you blood transfusions to replace what the chemo destroyed, and as soon as you stabilize, they're going to give you the stem cell infusion."

"Three . . . days?" he asks, looking bewildered.

I have no idea what he remembers, and I'm not about to remind him of the hell he went through. "Yes, three days. You've been asleep most of the time since the chemo ended, other than when you've been sick. The worst is over, sweetheart. It's only gonna get better from here," I tell him, squeezing his hand.

His eyes flutter closed as the corners of his mouth turn up in the faintest of smiles, but to me, it's as if the sun just came out. It's the first time I've seen him smile since he started the chemo. Although a sob borne of relief threatens to break free, I hold it back because I don't want to scare him.

He opens his eyes again, and they zero in on me, his eyebrows wrinkling in confusion. "Mask?" he asks.

I smile sadly behind the surgical mask I'm wearing. Fuck, it hurts to see him like this. It's worse now than it ever was, even right after he had pneumonia. I reach up and cup his cheek with my gloved hand. "I have to wear it now, but only for a couple of weeks. The chemo wiped out your whole immune system, and until the stem cell transplant takes, and you start producing new cells, we have to be really careful."

"Can't see . . . you smile," he whispers, and I grin behind the mask as a few tears slide down my cheeks.

"You're gonna have a long time to see me smile, sweetheart. Right now, we need to keep you safe," I tell him, stroking his cheek.

He angles his face into the touch, and I can't hold back the sob this time. He's still here, and he's still fighting.

His eyes open wider at the sound, and his brow furrows. "Hey . . . s'okay. Mm'okay," he murmurs, squeezing my hand.

I shake my head, trying to get a grip. "I know, sweetheart; you're going to be fine. It's just been a long time since we could talk like this, and I've missed you, that's all."

"Missed you . . . too," he replies, then squints at me. "You look . . . tired."

I chuckle and run a hand over my forehead. That's a fucking understatement. It's been the longest nine days of my life.

But I don't even consider mentioning any of that. "Keeping up with you is hard work," I tell him with a wink and a smile.

He exhales heavily, and I think that was his best attempt at laughing. Again, his lips curve into a faint smile, and I'm beside myself with excitement.

"Love . . . you," he whispers as his eyes fall closed, and his head lolls to the side. He's out again, but I'm going to be wearing this smile until the next time those beautiful green eyes open.

The next day, Dr. Evans's afternoon visit brings good news. I look up from my book as he enters the room, and I grin as I see the crinkling around his eyes—a sure sign he's smiling underneath his mask.

"Good afternoon, Tori. And it *is* a good afternoon because I have good news. Will's blood work shows that his electrolyte levels are stable, and his kidneys are functioning normally, so we're going to stop the dialysis and give him the stem cell infusion tomorrow."

My grin grows even wider, but as I glance over at Will and see the yellowish tinge to his skin, I'm reminded of the other big issue. "That's fantastic! But what about his liver?"

Dr. Evans frowns a bit. "His liver function is improving, but it's not back to normal yet which is why he's still jaundiced. I don't think his liver is going to fail, but it's been significantly damaged, and only time will tell how well and how much it will heal. The process will be slow since we've killed off many of the cells involved in helping to restore its function. It's going to take time, but we can't wait any longer to do the stem cell infusion because Will won't survive long, unable to regenerate his own blood supply. His liver will continue to heal as he recovers from the transplant."

Dr. Evans puts a hand on my shoulder. "It'll be all right, Tori. I'm not worried about it right now. I'm more concerned about keeping him going until the transplant takes."

I just nod. While the chemo looks like the scary part, the scariest part is actually the wait for the stem cell transplant to take, when Will is completely defenseless against infection.

***

Day 0

I wake up early, and for the first time since Will's chemo, I'm actually excited for the day. Today is the day he gets his stem cell infusion, and we get to move one more step forward. The road has been long, and it's going to be longer still, but this is the last piece we're dependent on the hospital for. The rest is up to Will.

When I arrive, Jason is already there in his mask and gloves, sitting beside Will and holding his hand.

Will looks much the same as he has for the last few days. He's very still as he sleeps, and his skin is a sickly yellow color. I haven't seen my favorite green eyes since the day before yesterday, but Jenny assured me this is all normal.

"He's probably going to be pretty out of it until his body starts to produce new blood cells. His own cells are still dying off from the chemo, so at this point, even though he's so still, he's actually getting worse and not better. As the anemia gets worse, he's going to be too exhausted to talk and too confused to hold a conversation anyway. It'll get better when his body starts producing new cells. You're going to witness a miraculous transformation."

God, I hope so because right now I'm more than a little afraid. The days after the chemo have been as terrifying in their stillness as the chemo was in its violence.

I sit beside Jason, and we wait together for the appointed time. The hour seems to drag by, but finally at around ten o'clock, Jenny and Jill enter the room.

My eyes are immediately drawn to the IV bag in Jenny's hands. It looks ordinary—the same as any of the other blood transfusions they've given Will since the chemo ended. But I know better. This one is different.

Jenny follows my stare and grins. "Yes, this is the one. This is no ordinary bag of blood. This is the moment you've been waiting for—the moment when Will's life begins anew."

I smile, and I can't help the tears that roll down my cheeks. But Will needs to know. If at all possible, he needs to know this is happening today.

As Jenny sets up the infusion, I perch on the side of Will's bed and run my hand into what's left of his hair. It's been falling out steadily, and I swallow thickly as I see the clumps on his pillowcase around his head. I know it'll grow back, but dammit if it doesn't make me cry every time I see it!

I shake my head to clear the thought and speak softly to him. "Will? Sweetheart, can you hear me? The big day is finally here, and I want you to open your eyes and see it with me."

He shifts a little but doesn't open his eyes, so I keep stroking his head and the side of his face and talking to him. After a minute or two, my persistence is rewarded, and my heart pounds in my chest as he slowly opens his eyes.

He looks at me blearily, and I can't tell if he recognizes me or not, but it doesn't matter. He's *here.*

"There you are! I've missed those gorgeous eyes of yours! Today's the day, sweetheart. You're about to get your new stem cells."

I reach up and turn his head gently to the side, and he raises his eyes to stare at the bag of blood.

"There it is, Will. Your new life is in that bag. All we have to do is wait for it to start helping you."

He blinks slowly, and I turn his chin back to face me and take his hand between mine.

"I love you. Today is the first day of your new, cancer-free life, and I'm so glad I get to share it with you."

As I watch, I see the corners of his lips move, but I don't think he has the strength to raise them into a smile. His hand also moves in mine, and I feel soft pressure as his fingers grip the side of my hand.

It's enough.

It's *more* than enough.

I turn to Jason, and unshed tears glisten in his eyes. He's watching, and he saw the very same things I did—Will's here, and on some level, he understands.

Tears flow down my cheeks, and I hold Will's hand a little tighter as the infusion begins.

Of course, it doesn't go smoothly. Nothing ever seems to for Will.

About an hour into the infusion, he grows very restless—a huge sign that something is wrong, considering he's been almost completely still since the chemo ended. As I look closely at him, I see a sheen of sweat on his forehead.

"Jenny, I think he might be running a fever," I say, looking over my shoulder at her.

Jenny and Jill are both sitting on the other side of Will's bed, but since everything has been going smoothly, they were talking quietly. They both stand and move in to check on Will.

Jenny pulls her sleeve up a bit and lays the back of her arm above her glove against his forehead. "Yup, he's feverish. Dammit! Jill, let's cut the infusion rate in half and see if we can keep it from getting too high."

"This is normal, right?" I ask nervously.

"Yes, it's a fairly common side effect. It's not a sign of infection; it's his body reacting to the stem cells. Slowing down the infusion sometimes helps." Jill explains to me.

Thankfully, in Will's case, it does help, and he's able to complete the infusion without his fever going too high or any other side effects developing. A few hours after the infusion, the fever breaks, and he returns to stillness.

But my relief doesn't last long.

The days after the transplant are terrible. Will is severely anemic. His body doesn't have enough red blood cells to carry oxygen to his tissues, so his hands and feet are freezing, and he's completely exhausted. He sleeps almost constantly, and when he's awake, he's so weak he can't move. Even saying a few words is a tremendous effort, so he's silent most of the time. His breath comes in small pants—his body's way of demanding more oxygen, but lack of oxygen isn't the problem; it's the lack of cells to carry it. They're giving him oxygen through a nasal cannula, but I don't think it's helping. They continue to give him blood transfusions multiple times a day, trying to replace, if only temporarily, the cells he's missing.

He's still jaundiced—if anything, I think it's a little worse—and on the second day after the transplant, they begin monitoring his heart because Will's anemia is so severe. Dr. Evans explains that anemia causes the heart to beat faster to try to compensate for the lack of red blood cells, and over time, that can lead to permanent heart damage.

I feel so helpless. There's absolutely nothing I can do, except watch and wait. It's as if Will's had his trial by fire, and now we're waiting to see if he'll rise from the ashes.

On the fifth day after Will's transplant, Elizabeth arrives. Jason and I have been holding each other together, with help from Jenny when she can manage it, but another person to bear the burden with us will make things easier, I'm sure.

Jason's and my routine changes with the addition of Elizabeth: Jason comes and spends the morning with Will while I go to work; then I spend the afternoons with him. Elizabeth comes to the hospital in the late afternoon, and we both stay until early evening then leave together.

Will's condition remains the same, day after day. He's confused and mostly silent, his breath still coming in pants, and his hands are freezing to the touch. But as the days go by, I start to notice a few subtle changes—the kind you would only pick up on if you were here every single day. The rash on his arms and torso is fading—it's gone from an angry red to a fainter pink. And I swear the lymph nodes in his neck are becoming less swollen, but I can't be sure. I hope it's not just wishful thinking on my part.

Day 12

I arrive at Will's room and start putting on my mask and gloves to begin my afternoon watch over him. I'm about to push the door open when Jill comes striding down the hall.

"Hi, Tori. I have some news. Can I join you in Will's room?"

She's smiling, and my stomach does a nervous flip. Could this be what we've been waiting for?

"Sure," I say, waiting for her to gear up.

I hold the door open for her, and Jason turns around as we enter.

"Afternoon, ladies. Will and I could use some company of the female persuasion." He grins at me and winks.

"You and Will are both taken, I'd like to remind you, so you'd better watch what kind of company of the female persuasion you're propositioning!" I scold him, cuffing him playfully.

"Yes, ma'am," he responds, rubbing his head.

"You have some news for us, Jill?" I ask as I glance at Will, noting that he looks the same as he did yesterday. I go around Jason and stand next to Will, stroking my gloved fingers on the side of his head. He rolls his head on his pillow but doesn't open his eyes.

"Yes," she answers, and I can hear the excitement in her voice. "Will's blood work from yesterday revealed the presence of immature differentiated cells in his bloodstream which is usually the first sign when a transplant begins to take."

I grin widely and turn to Jason, but he's already on his feet and pulling me into his arms. "Oh, thank God," I say as he squeezes me, laughing as he lifts me off the ground in his exuberance.

"That's fantastic, Jill! What will happen next?" Jason asks.

"Well, if the transplant is truly taking, we'll see an increase in Will's cell counts, and his anemia will start to improve. Once the process starts, it's pretty rapid, and you're going to be amazed by how quickly he starts to get better."

"I can't wait," I say eagerly, looking back at Will. We've waited so long for this—it's time for things to finally start to progress.

"Thanks, Jill," I say, putting my hand over hers.

"You're welcome. Let me know if anything changes for him," she says as she nods at us, backing out of the room.

"I hate to leave now, in case he wakes up," Jason says as he stands.

"I doubt anything will happen today," I say, giving him another hug. "But now we have something exciting to look forward to."

"Indeed." Jason covers Will's hand with his own. "You stay out of trouble while I'm gone, and don't do anything I wouldn't do," he tells Will, and I chuckle and shake my head.

After Jason leaves, I sit down next to Will and take his hand.

"Hello, sweetheart. Today's a great day! You're finally showing some improvement, and it's only a matter of time until you start feeling better."

To my utter astonishment, Will opens his eyes. But it's not like the other times over the last twelve days when he's opened them and not seemed to see anything. This time, his eyes focus straight ahead, and then he rolls his head slightly so he can see me.

The minute his eyes fall on me, his lips turn up in a small smile. *Holy shit, I think he actually knows it's me.*

"Will?" I ask, holding my breath.

His lips turn up a little more. "Tori..."

I laugh in sheer relief, my happiness at his recognition of me bubbling over. "Hi, sweetheart! How are you feeling?" I ask, grasping his hand more tightly between mine. I want to move to the side of his bed and at least hug him, but he hasn't moved at all other than opening his eyes, and I don't want to cause him any pain.

"I don't . . . know," he responds dazedly. "Tired. Really tired. What . . . day is it? When did I finish the chemo?"

His amazing green eyes are focused on me—clear and bright and begging me for answers. I have no idea what he might remember, so I try to keep the details to a minimum.

"It's October thirty-first. Halloween. You finished the chemo two and a half weeks ago."

"Two and a half *weeks*?" he exclaims softly. "Holy hell, that's a long time. When was the stem cell transplant?"

"Thirteen days ago."

He closes his eyes wearily. "Did it work?"

I smile behind my mask as warmth fills my chest. "Yes, so far so good. Your blood work yesterday showed the presence of immature blood cells which could only get there if you're making them yourself. And you're awake and talking to me, and not confused, which means your anemia is a little better."

He lies there quietly for a few moments, but suddenly, he furrows his eyebrows as if he's in pain. When he looks at me, there's confusion in his eyes. "What happened? Something went wrong, didn't it?"

My heart starts beating faster, and my breathing picks up. I don't want to tell him if he doesn't remember. It's bad enough *I'll* have those memories for the rest of my life.

"On the fifth day, your cells were dying so fast, your body couldn't keep up. Your electrolytes got all out of balance and . . . you had a seizure."

Will's eyebrows go up, but if I'm going to get through this, I have to keep going. I gaze down at his afghan and force myself to push through it.

"Your kidneys started to fail because they couldn't keep up with all the cell death, so you had to be put on dialysis. And . . . you . . . asked me to tell them to stop your chemo."

Will squeezes my hand tightly, and when I look up, his eyes are closed, his face scrunched up in pain. "I remember. Oh God, I remember! Jesus, I'm so sorry!" A tear rolls down his cheek.

"No! Don't be sorry," I tell him, unable to stay away. I perch on the side of his bed and lean over, resting my head against his chest and holding on to his shoulders.

He leans his cheek against my head. "You held me after that. I remember the feel of you, even through all the pain. You told me so many times that you loved me and that it was gonna be okay. Oh, Tori, I remember!"

"Don't think about it, sweetheart," I say softly, my head snuggled into his chest, right over the strong beat of his heart. "It's over now. You made it through, and we're past that. It was awful, but it's over."

"I love you, Tori. I love you so much!" He rubs his cheek against me. "I'm here because of you. I would have given up that day if it weren't for you."

I break down, crying tears of sorrow and heartbreak and relief against his chest, and I feel a few of his own land on my forehead. I wish I could kiss him right now. So much.

"It's all right." He tries to soothe me. "You're right; it's over now. I made it through, and it's over."

He holds me as my tears turn into sniffles.

"What happened after the chemo?" he asks quietly.

I sit up to wipe my eyes, and he smiles at me—the first real smile I've seen since right after the chemo ended. I can't help but smile back; I'm so happy he's able to talk to me. And now that we've gotten through the chemo part, I can tell him the rest more easily.

"Well, you were supposed to get the stem cell infusion the day after the chemo ended, but because of everything that went wrong, Dr. Evans delayed it by five days. In that time, we waited for your electrolytes to normalize and for you to be well enough to go off dialysis. After that happened, you had the stem cell infusion, and since then, we've been watching and waiting for the transplant to take."

"I remember asking you why you were wearing a mask, and I think I remember the day of the infusion, but why don't I remember anything after that. Have I been awake?" he asks, a little fear in his voice.

"You were conscious some of the time, but I wouldn't call it 'awake.' You've been so severely anemic that it made you confused and out of it. You talked to us sometimes, but I'm not surprised you don't remember. We've been waiting for today, the day when we would get some sort of indication the transplant had worked and you showed some improvement. God, Will, I'm just so happy you're here!"

He smiles again, but his eyes drift closed. "I'm happy to be here, believe me."

"Are you in any pain? Is there anything I can do for you?" I ask, suddenly remembering I need to let Jill know that he's awake and lucid.

Will shifts his hips and winces. "My belly is still tender, but I can tell I'm still on morphine. It's fine as long as I don't move, and that's not really a problem because I don't have the energy to move right now anyway. I'm a little cold, though. And this may sound weird, but my head in particular is cold."

I smile as I touch his cheek. "No, it doesn't sound weird at all." I gently lift his arm and support it so he can feel the top of his head, and his eyes widen when he touches bare skin.

"Shit, I forgot that was going to happen," he murmurs. "It all fell out already?"

"Yes, it happened pretty quickly after you finished the chemo. And it's the anemia that's making you feel cold. Your hands have been freezing for days now."

I go over to his closet and pull out the cornflower-colored afghan, and he smiles tiredly at me. "Do you want me to bring you a hat to keep your head warm?"

"Actually, I have a few that I like from the last time I lost my hair. They're in the coat closet at my apartment. Will you bring them for me?"

"Of course I will, sweetheart," I say, stroking his cheek.

He leans against my hand and closes his eyes.

"You've been awake for a long time now. Why don't you rest for a while? I have a surprise for you later this afternoon, and I want you to be awake for it."

"Okay," he mumbles, already headed toward sleep.

The minute I'm sure he's out, I tiptoe out of his room and dash to the nurses' station.

"Jenny! He's awake! We talked for about fifteen minutes, and he wasn't confused at all!"

Jenny jumps a mile in the air because I scared the shit out of her, but she's too excited by my news to scold me. She flies out of her chair and hugs me as we twirl around.

"I *told* you he'd be okay! Everything's going to get better so fast now— wait 'til you see! I am *so* happy for you guys!"

I hold her as my tears start again, but for once, they're happy tears. Will's going to get better now. It's really going to happen!

135

"He woke up, didn't he?" It's Jill's voice, and as I look up, she's walking down the hallway, smiling.

I pull back from Jenny and nod enthusiastically. "Yes, and he was completely lucid. He asked me about what happened to him, and he told me what he remembered—I think the anemia must have improved a bit."

"Yes, that's highly likely, and it's only going to keep getting better from here. Was he in any pain?"

"He said no, but he was too weak to really move around much. And he said he was cold, so I put his other afghan over him, and now I'm going to run to his place to get him some hats because his head is cold."

"Good idea, Tori," Jill tells me. "I'll keep an eye on him while you're gone."

I grin and wave as I head down the hall, and I call Jason as I drive to Will's place. I'm not going to tell Elizabeth, though. She'll be here in a few hours, and she and Will can be each other's surprise today!

Will's hats are right where he said they'd be—two black knit beanies that I can easily imagine him wearing after his previous rounds of chemo to keep his bald head warm and to ward off the obvious questions. But this time is going to be different. This is going to be the last time he ever has to do this.

I glance around his apartment—I haven't been back here since I finished moving all my stuff in more than three weeks ago. Now that Will is starting to improve, I'm going to have to begin the real work of getting this place cleaned within an inch of its life and ready to house someone with almost no immune system. The task seems daunting, but between Elizabeth and me, I'm sure we'll get it done.

I hurry back to the hospital, wanting to beat Elizabeth there so I can see her face when Will wakes up. Will is still sleeping when I go in, but the moment I touch his cheek, those amazing green eyes open, and I'm filled with joy.

"Tori," he murmurs sleepily. "I love when I wake up and the first thing I see is you."

"I have plans for me to be the first thing you see every time you wake up," I tell him, cupping his cheek and rubbing it.

"Mmm . . . I like the sound of that." He purrs, flashing a brilliant smile.

"Did the afghan make you any warmer?"

"Yeah, but my head still feels cold and strange with no hair up there."

"Well, you're in luck because I ran to your place while you were napping and got your hats for you," I tell him, pulling one out of my bag.

Will grins even wider. "You're too good to me, do you know that?"

"Hardly," I reply, waving him off. "Can I put this on for you?"

"Please," he says, and I gently lift his head and situate his hat down over his ears.

"Much better. My head feels warmer already, and I can't really tell I don't have hair when I'm wearing a hat. I remember that now from before."

Wow, he does look better with the hat on—less like a cancer patient anyway.

"So what was the—"

But he's interrupted by Elizabeth walking through the door, eyes down as she adjusts the gloves on her hands.

"Hey, Tori, I—"

She raises her eyes and stops in her tracks, gaping at her son.

"Mom!" he exclaims, and Elizabeth is across the room in a heartbeat.

"Will? Oh, Will, you're awake! And you look so much better today!" she exclaims, squeezing his hand. "Nice hat!"

Will chuckles. "My head was cold. When did you get here? I didn't think you'd be coming until I was ready to leave the hospital."

Elizabeth smiles at him warmly. "I got here about a week ago, and . . . I'm here for good."

"What do you mean?" Will asks, furrowing his eyebrows.

"I mean I moved up to Seattle. I'm taking over Tori's apartment since she's moving into yours. I left your father, and I filed for divorce."

"Oh, Mom," Will says, looking shocked.

"I'm okay, honey. I should have done this a long time ago. It was long overdue. I'm just sorry I missed out on this much of your life because I was doing what *he* wanted. I'm tired of being controlled."

Will smiles at her. "Good for you, Mom. I'm so glad you're here."

"I'm glad I'm here, too, honey. There's nowhere I'd rather be."

We visit with Will for the rest of the afternoon, and although he nods off a few times, he's awake for longer than I thought he would be. Jill and Dr. Evans come to see him, and both are thrilled with his progress.

As six o'clock approaches, Elizabeth and I decide it's about time to leave so Will can get some more rest.

"Sweetheart, it's time for us to go and get some dinner and for you to get some more sleep. I'll stop by in the morning; then I'll be back around noon to spend the afternoon with you."

"You're not staying?" Will asks softly. I can see he's trying not to be needy, but for him, it's as if he's been gone for a few weeks.

"No, love. I wish I could, but I can't. You're in isolation now, and until they lift it, I'm not allowed to stay with you. I think they're actually bending the rules by letting us visit as long as we do every day. You're not supposed to be close to anyone so you don't pick up any germs. I think we'll be able to stop wearing the masks and gloves within a few days, though, as soon as they confirm that your transplant worked."

"I miss you," he says tiredly.

I feel the familiar pang in my heart, but there's nothing I can do. We have to keep him safe. "I miss you, too. I wish I could kiss and cuddle you, but we're going to have to wait just a little longer. But I promise you, as soon as I can, kissing you is the very first thing I'm gonna do."

Will chuckles, but his body betrays him, and his eyes seem to close of their own accord.

"I love you, and I'm so glad you came back to me today," I whisper as I stroke his cheek. He nuzzles into my hand, but he's already mostly asleep.

Elizabeth and I go out to dinner, and although I'm sad and missing Will, we're another step closer to having a life together. Definitely something worth celebrating.

CHAPTER 9

Day 31

From the day Will woke up, everything began to change. His blood work the next day confirmed he's now producing his own blood cells, and I was so happy, I could barely contain myself! We celebrated by going over our "when the cancer's gone" list, and there was a sparkle in Will's eyes as he read off everything we're going to do together.

Dr. Evans declared we can stop wearing masks and gloves when we visit Will, but we still need to wash our hands when we go into his room and avoid close contact as much as possible. Will was fine with this for everyone but me, and Dr. Evans conceded that if we shared a kiss every now and then, it would be unlikely to do any harm. Well, you can just imagine Will's response to *that*. Needless to say, he's pretty much been kissing me any time he damn well pleases because I have absolutely no ability to tell him no.

Will's still fighting constant exhaustion, but he stays awake as much as he can to spend time with everyone and to do whatever Jill asks him to do. His anemia is improving, and he's no longer panting for breath. He's gone from receiving multiple blood transfusions a day to one a day, and soon, he should be dropping down to one every other day. When it's time for a transfusion, the anemia is bad, and he gets dizzy and short of breath, but the symptoms disappear as soon as he has the transfusion.

His liver function is also slowly improving, and although it's gradual, the jaundice is clearing.

But the best part? The best part is his cancer appears to be in remission, and his symptoms are disappearing. His rash continues to fade, and the itchiness that had always plagued him has finally stopped. He still has a little bit from the morphine, but he tells me it's nothing compared to what it was before.

And the swelling he had is going down, pretty much everywhere. I can see the difference in the lymph nodes in his neck, and he tells me the ones under his arms and in his groin are doing the same. It's a slow process, but he can tell it's happening because the lumps are softer and less painful. But the bigger deal is the swelling in his liver and spleen is decreasing. His belly is growing progressively smaller and less tender. He's had two ultrasounds since the transplant, and each time, the size of both organs has been smaller than the last measurement.

Two days after he woke up, Will did a swallowing test, and we discovered he could swallow liquids again. Jill started giving him clear fluids, and although it was a rocky start, after a few days, he was able to keep something down. Apparently, the digestive system doesn't take kindly to chemotherapy or to being bypassed for two months by intravenous nutrition. A few days later, he had a test for swallowing solid food, and he passed that with flying colors too. His transition back to eating for himself has been slow, and he's still eating more liquid than solid food, but Jill is doing her best to work him up to a normal diet again.

As the days go by, Will continues to get stronger, and Jill continues to prepare him to leave the hospital. She has him up and walking every day—to the bathroom at a minimum and even in the hallway on a good day. He can't do it without assistance yet, so it's either one of us helping him, or he's using a cane. He's not happy about the cane, but I remind him it's better than a wheelchair or still lying in bed.

Jill is also switching him to all oral medications and preparing me to manage everything for him. The number of pills he needs to take is unreal—antibiotics, antivirals, antifungals—his body can't fight off anything yet, so we have to rely on the medications to protect him until he can protect himself again.

Will is excited by the idea of going home, but as November wears on, I'm increasingly anxious. Dr. Evans and Jill are doing all these things to get him ready, but they've made no mention of when he might actually get to leave, and Thanksgiving is fast approaching. I so want to have him home and cook him a nice turkey dinner instead of having to come here and spend the holiday with him at the hospital.

On Monday of Thanksgiving week, I'm sitting with Will when Dr. Evans comes breezing in.

"Good afternoon, Will! Oh, hi, Tori! I'm so glad you're here too because I have fantastic news."

Like everyone else who enters this room, his first stop is the sink by the doorway to wash his hands. As he turns around, Will's eyes meet his, and I can see the hopefulness on Will's face. Evans smiles back at him and nods.

"It's time, Will. Your cell counts are high enough that we can let you out of here. I'm putting discharge orders in for tomorrow, so you'll get to spend Thanksgiving at home."

I can't stop myself from jumping up and down and squealing, and the smile on Will's face is absolutely stunning.

"Really? I get to go home, just like that?"

"Just like that. You're eating on your own; you're on your feet regularly; you're off morphine and onto all oral meds—there's no reason for you to have to be here.

"Of course, you'll be back every few days for blood transfusions . . . but it's time to go sleep in your own bed so we can give this one to somebody who actually *has* cancer," Evans says, grinning at him.

Will laughs—one of those joyous laughs that bubbles up from inside of you when you just can't contain what you're feeling, and I swear it's a sight I'll remember for the rest of my days. I've never seen him so completely happy—hell, I don't know if I've ever seen *anyone* so completely happy!

"Thank you, Dr. Evans," Will says, swallowing thickly, "for everything you've done for me. I know I wouldn't be here if it weren't for you. You never gave up on me even when I wanted to give up on myself."

"You're welcome, Will," Dr. Evans says, coming over to squeeze Will's hand. "Somehow, I think this young woman has more to do with your still being here than I do, but I'm thrilled this story has a happy ending rather than an unfortunate one. I'm so glad you made the choices you did and that I've gotten to be part of your journey from despair to happiness. You've done well, son, and I think you have an exciting future ahead."

Will grins even wider, tears brimming in his eyes.

"Get some rest tonight; tomorrow will be a big day for you," Dr. Evans says as he nods at Will, then winks at me.

As soon as Evans is out of the room, I throw my arms around Will and kiss him soundly. "Oh my God, oh my God, you get to go home! It's really happening! Tomorrow night, you'll get to sleep in your own bed again!"

Will can't wipe the grin off his face. "I can't believe it. There have been so many days when I never thought I'd get to leave this hospital. And now . . . *poof*! I'll be leaving tomorrow."

"Oh *shit*!" I exclaim, slapping a hand to my forehead. "I only have two days to get Thanksgiving dinner together! Your mom and I were going to skip it because we were planning to spend the whole day here with you."

"You don't have to do that—"

"Will, if you think I'm going to miss the opportunity to make you a fantastic Thanksgiving dinner for our first holiday together, you are *sorely* mistaken," I say, leveling my gaze at him.

His eyes widen. "Oh. Um . . . okay then," he says, looking a little frightened.

I laugh, realizing I've gotten ahead of myself. "I'm sorry; I'm just excited. Do you like turkey? Can I make us a nice dinner?"

Will chuckles. "Yes, I like turkey. I can't promise I'll eat three helpings because I still don't have much of an appetite, but if it's not too much trouble, that would be great."

He's humoring me. I don't think he gives a rat's ass if we have Thanksgiving, but since he now knows I want to, he's going to go along with it. "Did you have Thanksgiving dinner last year?"

"No," he says, looking away. "I was just finishing up chemo, and I was in no shape for anything like that."

Shit, I hadn't even thought about the fact that he would have been in chemo last fall, too—barely a year ago.

"Besides, Thanksgiving is kind of a family holiday, so . . ."

". . . so you haven't had a real Thanksgiving since you stopped talking to your parents, have you?"

"No. The holidays were really hard for me after we left San Francisco, especially when I was sick. Jason dragged me home with him once, but after that, I stayed around here and hung out with friends who had stayed in town."

"Well, then, I'd like to start a new tradition, if you don't mind. Thanksgiving at our place with your mom?"

"Our place . . ." Will says, smiling. "Tomorrow it'll be 'our place.'"

"Yeah, you get to see how I trashed your immaculate apartment with all my stuff."

Will shakes his head. "I told you, I'm going to be so happy to see your stuff that I'm not going to care where you've put it."

I grin at him. "How did I get so lucky?"

He snorts and shakes his head. "*I'm* the lucky one. After all you're doing for me, do you really think I'm going to care about where you put things? As long as you're living with me, I'm going to be the happiest guy around."

I laugh as I lean in and kiss him. "I'm happy, too, but I'd be happier if I had a turkey in the fridge—I need to go call your mom and get organized!"

"Okay, okay," he says, waving me off. "You go talk to her, and I'll rest for a while. You'll come back?"

"Of course I will," I tell him, caressing his cheek. "I'm so excited!" I squeal again as I bounce out of the room, and the last thing I see is Will smiling and shaking his head.

I skip down the hall, heading straight for Jenny. The grin on her face when she sees me matches my own—she already knows.

"Oh, Tori, I'm so excited for him! I didn't think it would be so soon. I thought he'd have to spend the holiday here," she says as she hugs me.

"I know; me too! What are you and Jason doing for Thanksgiving? Elizabeth and I are going to cook dinner now. Can the two of you come?"

"We both decided to stay here to spend the holiday together, but Will's getting to be home for this is huge. I'm sure Jason will want to be there," Jenny says. "And I want to be there too."

"Are you sure? If you were planning on spending Thanksgiving just the two of you—"

"Pfft," Jenny says, waving me off. "We decided to stay here because our families have too much drama, but you guys are family we actually *like* to hang out with! Besides, we have the whole weekend for alone time, and if we're lucky, many more to come," Jenny says with a twinkle in her eye.

"So . . . this is serious between you and Jason?" I ask, elbowing her in the ribs.

"Yeah, I think it is. We get along amazingly well; we have more in common than I thought, and he's so sweet and attentive. I really like him, Tori. Will has good taste—first Jason, and now you. The guy's batting a thousand, in my opinion, even with all the other bad luck he's had."

I chuckle and shake my head. "Yes, he seems to be a good judge of character. And you know how I feel about Jason already. He's such a loyal and devoted friend to Will; how could I not adore him?"

Jenny grins at me. "Yeah, I was hoping when Will's better, we might be able to double date."

"I was thinking the same thing, but maybe a bit sooner than that. After a few weeks, I think he's going to be going nuts cooped up in the apartment—maybe we can do a double date for dinner and movie at our place."

"That would be fantastic!" Jenny says, beaming. "I'm sure Will would love that, and you're right, although he's ecstatic now, he's going to get sick of being in the apartment before long."

"Right, so if he can't go out into the world, I'm planning to do what I can to bring the world to him," I tell her, nodding decisively.

"That's a fantastic idea, Tori. I hope he realizes how lucky he is to have you."

"Oh, I think we both realize we're lucky."

Elizabeth is over the moon that we get to have Will home for Thanksgiving, and between the two of us, we work out a menu including some of Will's favorites that Elizabeth used to make and some of my own recipes that I want him to try.

I return to Will's room to find him asleep, but I'm used to that after the past few weeks. He's still spending more time asleep than awake, but it's slowly getting better. He's only a month out from his transplant, and the severe fatigue may last up to a year.

I take his hand in mine and rub my fingers over the back to wake him, not wanting to startle him from his nap.

He squeezes my hand and smiles, eyes still closed, and puckers his lips.

I grin and giggle, leaning over to put my lips over his. The kiss is slow and warm, as if he's still waking up, and he stops when a smile over-takes his face.

I chuckle and back away, but only slightly because I'm immediately held in thrall by brilliant green.

"I hoped it was you. I figured Jason never holds my hand to wake me, and my mom wouldn't kiss me if I did that."

"I said I'd be back," I tell him, leaning in to kiss him again.

I jump when I hear a throat clearing behind me, and Will and I break away from each other, both blushing fiercely.

"Yup, you're ready to leave," Jill says, grinning at us.

Will laughs and squeezes my hand. "So all I had to do was let you catch me kissing Tori to get you to believe I was ready to go?"

"Hardly, but it's a sure sign you're feeling better," she says with a wink and a smile. "So, since we're going to spring you tomorrow, I wanted to go over some things with you. Tori already knows most of it because we've been getting her ready to take over your care, but you should be aware of it all, too—particularly the things you need to watch out for. Is now a good time?"

"Sure," Will says, looking at me and smiling. His excitement about getting to leave is like an energy force in the room.

Jill begins by explaining what goes into the decision to discharge a transplant patient, and she reviews the symptoms and side effects that Will will still have once he's at home.

Then, she goes over the list of things we have to do. We've already been cleaning the apartment according to Jill's instructions because that's where Will's going to be for most of his time for the next few months. Until at least Day 100, he's not supposed to go anywhere other than home and the hospital, and any time he leaves the apartment, he has to wear a surgical mask. There's a list of foods he can't have because of the risk of bacteria, and he needs to shower every day to stay as clean as possible. Everyone else needs to continue to wash their hands before they come anywhere near him, and Sebastian, Will's cat, isn't allowed in the apartment until at least Day 100. That one damn near breaks Will's heart—I can see it on his face—but I knew about that, and Jason has already agreed to keep him until he can come home with us.

We also have to watch Will extremely carefully for signs of infection. We'll have to take his temperature twice a day, and at the first sign of a fever or any other new symptom, we have to go straight to the ER. Even a little sniffle could get out of control quickly and kill him, so we can't take any chances.

By the end of Jill's long explanation, Will looks a little like a deer in the headlights, and he doesn't ask any questions. I, however, ask several, and that seems to help him relax a bit. If he's worried I can't handle this, he's in for a pleasant surprise. Ever since he woke up, I've done nothing but read about everything I need to do to take care of him. It's all new to me, of course, but at least knowing what needs to be done has helped me to relax—maybe Will needs the same reassurance.

When Jill leaves, I put my hand over his. "Hey, don't worry. I've got this," I tell him, smiling confidently.

"So you knew about all that?" he asks, his brow furrowed.

"Yes, I've been reading about everything you need for weeks now. The apartment is ready, and I have all the lists I need for everything else—

it's going to be fine, sweetheart. All you need to worry about is not wearing yourself out too much. I've got the rest."

He smiles at me, but some of the happiness is gone, and I'm not sure what it's been replaced with.

I squeeze his hand. "I'm sorry. I should have told you about all of this sooner. You've been working so hard to get to this point, I didn't even think about talking to you about all this other stuff yet."

"That's okay. I should have read about it myself, but I'm still so tired all the time that it's hard to get motivated to do anything. Thanks for keeping everything organized for me."

"That's my job," I tell him, smiling and rubbing my hand up his arm. "Like I said, don't you worry about it. You just get the rest you need and stay healthy. The rest is easy compared to your job."

Will smirks at me. "I have the hard job, eh?"

"Absolutely. I just have to grocery shop and go to pharmacy school." I deliver my sarcasm deadpan, smirking right back.

He laughs, but it ends in a yawn.

"Speaking of doing your job, Jenny should be here with your dinner any minute, and then you should get a good night's sleep. Tomorrow is going to be so exciting! And I need to drop off a few last-minute things at the apartment and get you some clothes to wear out of here."

Will grins and shakes his head. "I still can't believe I'm going home."

I lean in and kiss him, and the thought that tomorrow we'll be sleeping in the same bed is almost enough to make me moan aloud, but I don't want to get him going now because he needs to rest. "Believe it, sweetheart. Starting tomorrow, you're all mine."

He smiles as I make my way out of the room, and I hear him whisper, "I was already all yours."

CHAPTER 10

Day 32

Today's the day! Today's the day! When I wake at my old apartment, Will is my first thought, and I hurry to get ready so I can get to the hospital early.

Elizabeth is excited as well, and we share a cheerful breakfast before heading out. She managed to get everything we needed at the store yesterday, so we're gearing up to do some serious cooking once we get Will settled in.

When we arrive, he's already awake and all smiles, eager to be on his way.

"I'm so excited for you!" Elizabeth exclaims as she hurries over and hugs him first.

He grins even wider as he squeezes her. "Hi, Mom."

"Good morning, sweetheart," I say, leaning in and kissing him next. "Has Jill been by? Do you know what needs to happen before we can leave today?"

"I don't think very much. I need to get dressed and get everything together, mostly. Jill said I'll need to come back tomorrow for a transfusion, so there shouldn't be any blood work or anything today."

I frown at his statement about the transfusion. For the last eight days, Will has been having a transfusion every other day, and today he's due for one. Jill must be thinking he's now ready to go two days between transfusions.

"Okay then. Let's get you dressed and ready."

Will is already in sweatpants and a white t-shirt, but I've brought him a very warm-looking U Dub sweatshirt that was in one of his drawers and a pair of sneakers I found in his closet.

I help him slip on the sweatshirt, then put on his shoes and tie them for him. He frowns and cocks his head as I finish.

"What?"

"Nothing, I . . . it's been five months since I've worn shoes. They feel . . . strange."

"I bet they do," I say, grinning. "You won't need to wear them for long, though. Most of the time, you'll probably be walking around our apartment in socks—those hardwood floors are cold!"

Will smiles brilliantly. "I can't wait to be walking around our apartment. There are so many things I like in that sentence: 'walking,' 'our,' 'apartment'—no trace of 'hospital' or 'nurse' there at all!"

I chuckle. He's so happy and so ready to be out of here. We chat easily as I gather up all his things, and then we wait for Jill to come.

She shows up about twenty minutes later, a huge smile on her face. "Well, this is it. Are you ready?"

"I've never been more ready for anything in all my life," Will says fervently before he breaks into a smile.

"Well, let's get this show on the road, then. You're all good to go. Dr. Evans has signed the discharge order, and you're scheduled for blood work and a transfusion at ten tomorrow. I'll call transport, and after that, there's just one more thing you need to do before you're on your way."

Will furrows his brow as he looks at her, but her words were enough to tip me off. I know what he has to do before they'll allow him to leave.

I grin at Jill, and she winks back, sharing the secret with me. Will will find out soon enough.

Jill leaves, and we wait.

And wait.

And wait.

Finally, around eleven, transport shows up with the wheelchair we'll be taking with us for Will. He's able to walk short distances now, but the walk from the car to our apartment is long, as is the walk through the hospital when we come back for transfusions. He'll be using the chair until he's strong enough to walk that far himself.

The orderly's smile is infectious as he grins at Will. "You ready, man?"

"Absolutely," Will replies.

The orderly puts on Will's surgical mask for him and helps him to stand, watching as he takes the few steps over to the waiting wheel-chair. Will needs a little help, but once he's situated, he looks up at me. "Aren't we going to put on my coat?"

"We will, but there's something you have to do first," I tell him, rubbing his shoulder.

He's just about to ask me what when Jill comes through the door. "Okay, Will, everything's ready. It's time for your last procedure here."

The orderly pushes Will's chair out the door into a hallway lined with people. All of the oncology staff is there as well as some of the patients who are mobile, and they're all smiling at Will.

Suddenly, his eyes light up in understanding. He knows what he has to do.

Will is wheeled over to the wall next to the nurses' station where a golden bell hangs from a wooden plaque. Next to it, there's another plaque with the inscription:

Survivor's Bell

Ring this bell
Three times well
Its toll to clearly say,

My treatment's done
This course is run
And I am on my way!

As the sailing ships of another generation relied on their ship's bell to signal their position in the fog, may this bell enable you who ring it to navigate your way through life free of cancer.

Dr. Evans steps forward from the crowd and puts his hand on Will's shoulder. Then he says in a loud voice, "This is Will Everson, a stem cell transplant patient whose angioimmunoblastic T-cell lymphoma is now in remission. He is a survivor, ready to begin his life anew, free of cancer. Today he rings the Survivor's Bell three times, once for love, once for hope, and once for courage to celebrate his own victory and to inspire those who hope to follow the same path. Congratulations, Will!"

The crowd is silent as Will raises a shaking hand to the bell pull, his eyes red-rimmed. He looks to me and I nod encouragingly, my happiness and pride in him bubbling over.

His first ring is tentative, but the next two are loud and strong, and the hallway erupts in thunderous applause. Jenny and I both let out a whoop, and Dr. Evans squeezes Will's shoulder. No one comes any closer to him because they know he's a transplant patient, but every one of the staff makes eye contact with him and either salutes or flashes a victory sign as they go back to their work.

Jenny, Elizabeth, and I all wipe the tears from our eyes, and I see Will swipe at his too.

Jenny bounds over to him and puts a hand on his arm. "I am *so* excited for you! I'm gonna miss you like crazy, but it'll be much nicer seeing you at your apartment instead of here. I'm stuck at work today, but I'll stop over as soon as I can, all right?"

Will smiles at her warmly. "Thanks, Jenny. I'm going to miss you too. But something tells me I'll still be seeing you—that is, if Jason has anything to say about it."

"Mmm, I certainly hope he does, then," Jenny says in a playful voice. "Now, get out of here! You're no longer part of the sick people club!" She squeezes Will's arm before she walks away.

Now it's just Elizabeth and me standing with Will and the orderly, and the floor has resumed its normal activities.

"Are you ready?" I ask Will.

"Yeah, let's go," he says, grinning again.

We make our way through the hospital, and I walk beside Will, watching him the whole time. He still looks happy but thoughtful as he watches all the people going about their day. It occurs to me that he hasn't seen this many people in months; his exposure has been limited to the hospital staff and the few visitors he's gotten. I wonder if it seems strange to him.

We get to the main lobby, and Elizabeth helps Will put on his coat while I go get my car. I leave it running at the curb, and I expect to see the orderly wheeling Will out already, but I don't.

I walk back through the glass doors and find Will still sitting in his chair with a determined look on his face. His coat is on, but Elizabeth is still holding the scarf and gloves I brought for him, and she looks frustrated.

"Will, what's wrong?" I ask as I walk up to stand in front of him.

"I want to walk out of here. I didn't come here of my own free will, so I didn't get to walk in, but I want . . . I *need* to walk out. I can't explain it; it's just something I need to do."

"Okay, sweetheart," I say, taking the scarf from Elizabeth's hands and wrapping it around his neck.

He narrows his eyes at me, but I pay him no mind.

"It's cold outside. It's going to take you longer to walk out of here than it would to leave in the wheelchair, so I want you to be warm, all right? You get your way, but I also get mine."

He snorts and shakes his head. "Fine."

Elizabeth loads Will's things into the car while I flip up the footplates on his chair and retrieve his cane.

"He's not supposed to—" The orderly begins to object, but I silence him with a look.

"He survived cancer. If he wants to walk out of here, then that's what he's going to do."

Will looks at me appreciatively, and I put an arm under his shoulder and help him to his feet. It takes him a moment to steady himself, but then he begins taking slow, shuffling steps toward the door, leaning heavily on his cane.

I know this is a bad idea, and he's going to be exhausted after this, but I can't argue with the determination in his eyes. Will rarely takes a stand on anything, so for him to insist on this, it must be really important to him.

I walk beside him, but as he reaches the open glass doors, a gust of cold wind assaults him, and he takes a gasping breath. He stops and sways, and I put my shoulder under his and my arm around his back.

"Are you all right?"

He closes his eyes wearily. "Yeah. But . . . can you help me the rest of the way? I'm really tired, and I'm afraid I'm going to fall."

"Of course I can," I tell him, my heart aching that he couldn't do this completely on his own. "And I'd never let you fall."

We make it to the car, and as soon as I help him sit, he lies back against the seat, completely exhausted. I help him get settled, reclining the back so he can rest more comfortably, and by the time I'm done, his eyes are already closed.

The orderly loads the wheelchair into the trunk, and I hurry around to my side of the car. Will is already asleep, and not even the slamming of the car door makes him stir.

I reach for the gearshift, but my hand never gets there because I glance over at Will, and suddenly, it hits me—I hold his life in my hands now. It's not the same as being responsible for making his medical decisions when he couldn't, where whatever I decided was carried out by trained professionals. No, I'm directly responsible now —responsible for making sure he takes all his medications, responsible for making sure the apartment stays as germ-free as possible, responsible for doing everything he can't do for himself, and responsible for watching him for even the smallest sign of illness. The enormity of it floors me.

I look over at him, passed out from exhaustion after being awake for two hours and walking fifty feet. He's still so weak, and he looks so . . . frail. I notice the thinness of his fingers resting on his lap and the pallor of his skin. He's still wearing his black beanie to keep his bald head warm and his surgical mask to protect him from the germs of others. He looks as if a stiff wind could blow him over, and it nearly did as he tried to make his way to the car. *Oh God, can I really do this? What if he gets sick and it's my fault? After all he's endured to get here, what if I fail him?*

A twinge of panic shoots down my spine, and I grip the steering wheel tightly. *How the hell am I going to do this?* Just as my thoughts begin to spiral out of control, I nearly jump out of my skin as there's a sharp rap on the window. The security guard is standing there, looking at me with concern. I nod at him, putting my hand on the gearshift to pull out, when I suddenly feel Will's touch.

"Everything okay?" he asks groggily, his beautiful green eyes meeting mine, his gaze full of love and trust.

And just as quickly as it came, the fear is gone. "Everything's fine, sweetheart. We're going home."

He smiles at me as his eyes drift closed again, and he's out almost immediately.

I *can* do this. He's suffered through so much to get here—he's done his part, and now I have to do mine. He believes in me now, just as I believed in him when he went through the chemo, and I believe in us— I always have. Sure, this is scary as hell, but it's not the hardest part. He made it through the hardest part because he believed what I was telling him, and if I have to, I'll tell us both again until we get through this. *It's going to be all right. Everything is going to be fine.*

This time when I look over at him, I don't see the weakness or the frailty. I see the man who survived chemotherapy and a stem cell transplant against the odds because he wanted to be with me. I see the man I love and would do anything for because he's already done the impossible for me.

I pull away from the curb as the warmth of my love for Will floods my chest. It's time to take him home.

The drive is uneventful, and Will sleeps the whole way until I pull up in front of the apartment building. Jason is standing just inside the doors, and he comes out as soon as he sees us.

"Will, we're home," I say softly, rubbing my fingers over his.

He opens his eyes, and I see the crinkles in the corners as he smiles.

"It's so strange—I left here at the height of summer, and now it's basically winter. It really brings home how much of life I've missed."

"You didn't miss it; you just spent it somewhere else," I say, but the smile has faded, "somewhere I could meet you and fall in love with you." The smile comes back again.

"Good point," he says, jumping a little as Jason taps on the window.

Jason grins at him excitedly, and he already has Will's wheelchair set up and ready.

Will turns back toward me, and again I see that determined look in his eye. "I can walk up to the apartment."

Argh, I want to let him do this, but again, it's a colossally bad idea, and this time, common sense needs to win out.

"Yes, you can, but I'd really rather you didn't because I'd still like to spend some time with you today."

"Tori—"

"Wait a moment; I'm not finished," I tell him gently, raising my hands to calm him. "I have no doubt you could walk all that way, but when you got there, you'd be totally exhausted and probably sleep for the rest of the day, and I wouldn't get to spend any time alone with you on our first day living together."

His eyebrows go up a fraction, but he's still scowling at me.

"And, on the off chance you can't make it all that way, what if you get so tired you trip and fall, like you were worried about at the hospital? Then we'll have to take you right back there, and this won't be your first day home after all."

He opens his mouth to argue, but I don't give him the chance.

"Please, sweetheart? Just for getting back and forth from the hospital until you're stronger? You probably won't need to use it in the apartment—"

The look in his eyes tells me I need to back away from that one quickly.

"Okay, you *won't* need to use it in the apartment, but the hallways are long to get to and from the elevator, and since you're still not steady, you'll be touching the wall the whole way, and Lord knows if and when it ever gets cleaned. Is it really worth it?"

He sighs, and I know I have him with that one. I hate to use his fear of getting sick against him, but if it'll help me to ensure he doesn't overexert himself, then I'll stoop that low.

"All right, but soon, I want to be walking to and from the car," he says, the fire still in his eyes.

"Sweetheart, as soon as you're able, I'll be the loudest one in the cheering section." I put my hand over his. "I'm only doing this because I love you, and I don't want to see you have a bad day today."

"I know." Will concedes to my logic, his green eyes now warm instead of blazing. "I'm sorry. I'm just frustrated and a bit on edge. You're right about the wheelchair, at least for now."

That's more concession than I thought I was going to get, so I accept it with a smile. "No worries, sweetheart. But let's get out now. Jason looks cold."

Will looks back over at Jason, who looks a bit windswept and is hunching his shoulders. "Oh, oops," he says, the tension finally leaving his voice.

I get out of the car, and Jason takes that as his hint to open Will's door. "It's about time. I thought you'd changed your mind and decided to go back to the hospital."

"Shut up, smartass, and help me get out of the car." Will snaps at him, but I can hear the smile in his voice.

"Yes *sir!*" Jason answers smartly, and I breathe a sigh of relief. Will's finally relaxing a little bit.

Jason gets Will situated in his chair, then puts his hand on my shoulder. "Why don't you take him up, and I'll park the car. This is a big day for you two."

I smile at him appreciatively. "Thanks, Jason."

"Although I hate to miss seeing Will lose his shit when he sees what you've done to his apartment," Jason says a little louder so Will can hear him, and the look Will gives him when he turns assures me that Will would be beating the crap out of Jason right now if he were able.

"Don't mind him, Tori," Will tells me. "I'm not going to flip out, no matter what you did to my apartment. I'm just happy to be home."

"I know, sweetheart." At least Jason managed to lighten the mood.

Will's all smiles again as I push him through the lobby, looking around eagerly at everything.

"Has it changed much?" I ask as we stop in front of the elevator.

"No, but I've been staring at the same four walls for so long, it's nice to see something different and familiar. I love this building."

"I do too," I say, putting my hand against the worn bricks that form the walls of the lobby. "This is my home now—our home now."

Will's eyes dance as he smiles at me, but something is . . . off. It's as if he's trying too hard. But I bite back the question that's burning on the tip of my tongue; if there's one thing I've learned, it's that Will will tell me what's bothering him when he's good and ready and not a moment before. Pestering will only make him defensive and stressed, and that's the last thing I want right now. So I grin back at him and wheel him up to the apartment.

Jason catches up to us just outside the door, and Elizabeth has already gone in with Will's things.

"Here we are, sweetheart," I say as I open the door, and Jason steps behind Will to wheel him in.

Will takes a deep breath and nods, and I wonder what he's thinking because he looks like he's preparing himself for something unpleasant rather than a happy homecoming.

Jason wheels him in and stops a few feet inside the door, giving Will the chance to look around at the home he hasn't seen for five months. Although I've officially moved in, I tried to change very little of the look of Will's apartment, its meticulous order having tipped me off that he's particular about his things despite his claims to the contrary.

I put most of my furniture in storage, figuring Will and I can go through it when he's well enough and decide what we want to keep. The one thing I did keep out, though, is my black leather recliner. That thing is the comfiest chair I've ever sat in, and I have a feeling Will might appreciate it too, given the long convalescence ahead of him. It doesn't exactly fit the décor of the room, but some things are just necessary.

Will looks around the living room, his eyes taking in all the new and rearranged items, and lingering on the recliner a little too long. Pfft . . . wait 'til he sits in it!

"Welcome home!" Elizabeth says excitedly as she comes down the hallway, her earlier irritation with Will forgotten.

"Do you want to take your mask off?" I ask, coming up beside him.

"Please," he says, and I reach up and take it off his ears.

He takes a few deep breaths, then rests his forehead against his hand.

Jason and I share a look over Will's head.

"Why don't we get you out of that chair and settled?"

Will looks up at me and nods, and there's that overly cheerful smile again. *Dammit.*

Jason starts to wheel Will over to the couch, but I put my hand on Will's shoulder. "Oh no," I say, shaking my head. "Bedroom. You've had enough adventures for today. You can brave the couch tomorrow."

He smiles, and this one looks genuine—maybe all he needs is some time alone to rest.

Jason wheels Will into the half bath to wash his hands, and when they've finished, he wheels Will down the hallway and into his—our—bedroom. Jason helps him stand and shuffle over to the side of the bed closest to the bathroom, lowering him down to sit on the side. Will is breathing heavily, and as I watch, he swipes at his eyes with his hand. Something's wrong.

I motion to Jason with my chin to leave the room, and he wrinkles his eyebrows at me but complies. Sitting down next to Will, I put my head on his shoulder. "Hey. Are you all right?"

He takes a shuddering breath, then nods. "Yeah. This is just . . . a little overwhelming. I never thought I'd see this place again. I had myself convinced I'd die in that hospital, even after the transplant—hell, *especially* right after the transplant. It's a lot to take in all at once."

There it is. It took him half the day to tell me, but he's slowly getting better at opening up, and this is an emotional and stressful day for him.

I reach up to wipe away a tear that's making its way down his cheek. "You're afraid something's going to go wrong, aren't you?"

His teeth catch his bottom lip, and he nods tightly. "Aren't you?"

For a moment, I think back to my little breakdown in the car, but it's my turn to do for him now, and I *will* get us through this.

I rub his back, trying to soothe him. "Yes, of course I am, but not as much as I thought I would be. You're doing absolutely fantastic, sweetheart. I know your recovery isn't going as quickly as you'd like, but three months ago, you were dying of lymphoma, and now, you're cancer-free and sitting in your own apartment. You've worked so hard and been through so much; you deserve for everything to be okay now. God, the universe, karma—someone owes you this, and I believe it's gonna happen. We'll just take it slow and be really careful. But I know everything's gonna be okay. I'm sure of it."

"I love you," he says, reaching up to cup my cheek in his hand.

I put my hand over his and squeeze. "And I love you. And I'm so proud of you for all you've accomplished. Today really *is* a day to celebrate."

Will rests his chin on top of my head. "Can we celebrate . . . later? I'm really fucking tired right now."

"Of course. Why don't we get you settled in here, and you can nap for a while. It's a few hours until dinner yet."

He smiles at me gratefully from under droopy eyelids, and I help him stand again so I can pull down the covers for him. Slipping off his shoes, I tuck him under his thick down comforter. He breathes in deeply and lets it out with a contented sigh. "It smells like home."

He inhales again. "Home and Tori."

I chuckle, then lean in and kiss him on the forehead. "Sleep well, sweetheart, and call me if you need anything," I say, putting his cell phone on the nightstand.

As I straighten up to step away, he grasps my hand, reminding me of another day, what seems like an eternity ago. My skin tingles at the contact, just as it did that day, except now I understand why.

"Will you stay? At least until I fall asleep?"

You're the first visitor I've had echoes in my mind. "Of course, I will. I'll stay right here until you fall asleep."

He smiles as his eyes drift closed, and I climb up onto the bed beside him.

His eyes flutter open again, but as I begin stroking his forehead down to his temple, they close and he snuggles into my hand. I don't disturb his beanie because I know his head is cold even when he's indoors, but I run my fingers gently along it until I'm sure he's sleeping soundly.

I slide off the bed and make my way into the living room where Jason and Elizabeth are sitting and talking. They both look up as I enter.

"How is he?" Elizabeth asks.

"He's all right. He's sleeping now," I say, not volunteering any more details.

But Jason is having none of it. "What was the matter?"

I sigh in resignation. "He was just a bit overwhelmed by coming back here. He never expected to, you know? And he's afraid something's going to go wrong—that he'll get an infection or the cancer will come back."

Elizabeth frowns, but Jason cocks his head to the side. "That doesn't really surprise me. He always was a bit of a worrier, and it has to make him feel vulnerable not to have the support of the hospital around him."

Jason has a good point. I hadn't thought about it that way. For the last five months, any time something went wrong for Will, trained staff were always there to deal with it, and he's been in isolation to protect him. *Shit.*

"Well, then, we have to work to convince him we can handle this and that he's just as safe and supported here with us as he was there. I think if everything goes well for the next few days, he'll gain some confidence in the new arrangement."

"I hope so," says Elizabeth. "He looked happy today coming home, but I could see the fear in his eyes when he thought we weren't watching. I think you're right, though, Tori. Once he sees we've got this, he'll relax a bit."

She grins at me, and I feel better about the whole thing.

"Well, I think I'm going to head out," Jason says. "I'll be back in the morning to help you get him to his appointment."

"Thanks, Jason. I'm sure I'll be able to get him there myself before too long."

"Hey, no worries," he responds. "I need to be here to give him shit about his first night alone with you anyway."

I chuckle and shake my head at him. "What are we, in junior high?"

"Guy stuff. You wouldn't understand," Jason says loftily with a twinkle in his eye.

"All right, all right, just don't make him want to kick your ass so badly that he wears himself out trying," I tell him, punching him in the shoulder.

"Yes, ma'am," he says, dipping his chin smartly.

When Jason heads out, Elizabeth goes into the kitchen to begin getting things ready for Thursday, and I decide it's time to organize the pharmacy we brought home from the hospital for Will. I pick up the tote bag and take it to the kitchen table. Taking a deep breath, I remove all the pill bottles and begin the slow and difficult task of sorting through everything and arranging it into pill organizers. Will is taking twelve different medications—some once a day, some twice, some that need to be taken with food or water or on an empty stomach, some that need to be taken before others. I sort through all the instructions and make the notes I'll need and then arrange a week's worth of medications for him. By the time I'm done, I have a headache, but I forget all about it as I hear my phone beep from across the room. Will's awake.

I hop up from the table and quickly put the bottles away in a cabinet in the kitchen. Will already knows how many different medications he's taking, but the sight of all those bottles makes me feel discouraged; I can only imagine how it would make *him* feel.

I hurry down the hallway to the bedroom, and dazzling green eyes meet mine the minute I open the door. Oh God, am I in love with the fact that I get to see him all the time now!

He's still lying on his back—he pretty much has to because of the central line. If he lies on either side, it squishes up the skin around the line and hurts him. He smiles brightly as he sees me and turns his head to the side for a better view.

"Well, hello there, sweetheart. Did you have a nice nap?" I ask, lying down next to him and curling up so we're nose to nose.

"I did. It's a shame I had to wake up alone though," he answers, stroking my eyebrow lazily with a fingertip.

"Don't worry. I don't intend to let that happen often." I raise my own hand to cup his cheek affectionately.

"Good."

We lie there and just touch each other, reveling in the ability to do so uninterrupted, until Elizabeth speaks from behind me.

"I hate to disturb you two, but it's time for supper. Tori, I made us some sandwiches, and Will, I have yogurt and a milkshake for you."

We both glance over at her, and she smiles. "Should we all eat in here?"

"What an excellent idea," I say, sitting up.

I help Will sit up, then prop a few pillows behind him so he's well supported, and we eat picnic-style on the bed.

Will is relaxed and happy, and Elizabeth and I take our cue from him, and we have a pleasant meal together.

After dinner, Elizabeth makes her excuses and heads back to my apartment, and Will and I are finally alone. I walk her to the door, then clean up the dishes in the kitchen before returning to the bedroom.

Will is still awake when I get there, and he smiles at me as I sit down on the bed.

"Hey, sweetheart, how are you doing?" I ask, taking his hand. It feels a little cold, so I rub it between my own.

"I'm all right," he answers, looking down at the comforter.

Suddenly, he looks back up at me. "I'm sorry about today. I wanted everything to be so happy and good, but I've just been all over the place emotionally. I'm so excited to be home, but . . . I'm scared and nervous and just . . . upset at the same time."

"Will, everything you're feeling is normal and understandable," I say, moving a little closer to him. "This isn't a fairy tale. There's good and bad, ups and downs, and no day is going to be perfect, not even when you're completely recovered. As far as I'm concerned, today was a good day. Your bell-ringing ceremony made me cry tears of joy, you got to leave the hospital, and now here we are, alone in *our* apartment for the very first time. I can't imagine how today could be any better, even if there were a few not-so-happy moments."

"You're right," he says, pulling me down to lie on his shoulder. "It's been an amazing day. I just wish I could shake the fear I'm feeling. I feel . . . exposed—like there are so many things that can hurt me or go wrong. I hate feeling this way."

Dammit if Jason didn't hit the nail right on the head. He keeps this up, I'll have to start calling him "the Will whisperer."

I snuggle in closer and put my arm around his waist. "It's just going to take time. The hospital protected you, and people were always there to fix whatever went wrong. But your mom and I have put a lot of time into getting everything ready for you, and I think we're about as prepared as we can be.

"This apartment is as clean as we could make it," I say, gesturing around, "and I'm confident you're safe here—as safe as you can possibly be. And I think after a few days of nothing going wrong, you'll start to feel that way too.

"But please, tell me when you're scared or nervous or upset. We're in this together, and earlier today, you kept a lot of that to yourself. Burdens are lighter when they're shared, and I want to share everything with you, the good and the bad."

"For better or worse, eh?" he says, grinning.

"In sickness and in health," I add, continuing the vow. "And death isn't going to part us anytime soon if I have anything to say about it."

Will chuckles and reaches over, grasping my chin and pulling it up so I'm looking at him. Those amazing green eyes melt me into a puddle every time, and now is no exception.

"I'm so in love with you," he says huskily, his eyes burning with the strength and depth of his emotion.

My stomach clenches, and suddenly, I can't breathe. He may not be healthy, but his heart and soul are completely undamaged and undaunted, and I feel the force of his love as he looks at me. He's so passionate, and when he directs those feelings at me, I'm just obliterated.

"I don't know how I got lucky enough to have you walk into my life, but I'm never going to let you go, and I'm going to do everything I can to make you happy."

I swallow thickly, trying to keep the tears back, but my voice shakes with emotion. "I already *am* happy, so just keep doing what you're doing."

Will laughs, and I feel as if my heart's about to burst, the sound is so joyful and happy and *right*.

"I'm so in love with you, too," I say, leaning up to capture his lips. We haven't kissed like this since yesterday, and being able to do it cuddled up on the same bed is more than arousing.

Will's lips move hungrily against mine, and I moan as the familiar heat spreads from my chest and down into my belly. I deepen the kiss, thrusting my tongue into his mouth eagerly, and the moan of pleasure I'm rewarded with makes me rub my thighs together.

His hands are all over me, touching, teasing, and caressing every inch of skin he can reach. I pull him closer, sliding my hand up the back of his neck and under his beanie, gently running my fingernails over his scalp. He moans deeply, and his hat slips off, his self-consciousness forgotten in the heat of the moment.

We kiss until he's out of breath, but the smile on his face is the most beautiful thing I've ever seen.

He's *happy*.

And his happiness is like a drug to me, so I look into his eyes and enjoy the high until he finally regains his breath.

I curl into his shoulder again, and we just lie there cuddling and snuggling until Will shifts position and winces. I had been dozing off, but when he moves, I'm suddenly awake, and I glance over at the clock. Seven-thirty. We should get him ready for bed—I'm sure he's tired.

"Tori, I um . . . need to—"

"You haven't been to the bathroom since you got home, have you? I'm sorry. I should have asked you," I say, getting up and going around to his side of the bed.

"I didn't need to until now," he says, sounding nervous.

What's going on? Is he not feeling well? "What is it?"

Will looks down at the comforter, a blush creeping up his neck and cheeks. He sighs. "I know I need your help, but . . . this isn't exactly the way I wanted you to see me naked for the first time."

Jesus, he's embarrassed. I look at him critically for a moment, in the way I've taught myself not to, and I can easily see why. He's severely underweight and doesn't have a single hair on his head, including no eyebrows. He *looks* like a cancer patient, or a prisoner from a concentration camp; he can't be feeling very attractive. But he shouldn't be worried about that now; I'm certainly not.

I stroke my hand up and down his arm. "I know this isn't the way you want things to be, but it's okay that they're different. When we're able to be together that way, we'll already be comfortable with each other. It'll be even better."

He glances up at me, clearly unconvinced. And I can see he's still uncomfortable. *Fuck.*

"Come on, sweetheart, let me help you so we can get you settled for the night," I tell him, pulling back the covers a little.

He frowns, steeling himself, and lets me help him stand and take slow steps into his bathroom. He bites his lip before slowly dropping his pants, and I'm treated to the sight of his cock for the very first time. It looks . . . normal. The swelling in his lymph nodes is completely gone, and his rash has faded. Other than being thin, there's no difference from any other guy I've ever seen. Well, actually, there is *one* difference. He looks as if he's rather . . . well endowed. My stomach gives a giddy twinge as I imagine what his cock looks like when he's hard. *This is not what I should be doing right now.*

Will sits down unsteadily, but he does manage to do it himself, and then he raises his eyes to me, embarrassment written all over his face.

"Call me when you're finished," I tell him, cupping his cheek before I turn to leave. As I cross the room, an idea hits me, and I start stripping off my clothes as I walk back into the bedroom. I'm nervous for Will to see me naked too, but right now, I would do anything to wipe that look off his face—absolutely anything.

He calls me after a few minutes, and I can't hide my smirk as I walk back in completely naked. I'll remember the look on Will's face for the rest of my days. He looks over, and his eyes go wide as his jaw unhinges.

The shock is followed immediately by lust as he swallows nervously, and his eyes become hooded.

"Tori, what—"

"Well, you *have to* show me, so I figured it was time I showed you. Now, we're even," I say, standing with my hands behind my back just out of his reach.

"Oh, we are *far* from even," he mutters, swallowing again. "God, you're beautiful."

He reaches for me, and I take two steps forward, my skin sizzling where his hand makes contact with my hipbone. His body may be damaged, but his eyes haven't changed, and right now, they're devouring me and making me feel like the most beautiful woman in the world. And it doesn't matter where we are; I love him, and when he looks at me like that, my stomach does backflips. I hope it always will.

He strokes his thumb over the prominence of my hip, beginning where my leg and center meet, and I shudder as electricity courses through me. His eyes are glued to my pussy, and I can't help but blush and giggle under the intensity of his stare.

I grin at him mischievously. "Do you feel better now?"

"Better?" He laughs. "Well, my dick is trying to convince me I'm up for this, but the rest of me knows I'm clearly not. I think you may have started a war."

"Well, I know whose side *I'm* on."

I take his hands and help him to his feet, and—sweet Jesus—he's hard as a rock. His cock juts out prominently, and . . . damn! Now that he's erect, I can clearly see there's not a hair to be found anywhere on him. All of his skin is smooth and soft and—oh my—I had no idea that no hair there was such a big turn on for me! My mouth goes dry as I stare at him, trying to stop the wild fantasies that are playing out in my mind. He's not ready for that—he's not even cleared for light exercise, let alone the type of workout I'd like to give him. But I know one thing I *can* do for him that will feel normal and take his mind off his anxiety.

As he drapes his arm over my shoulder, I reach down and take him in my hand, stroking firmly over his smooth, velvet skin from base to tip. The groan I'm rewarded with makes me weak in the knees, and Will leans into me.

"Ohhh, please don't start anything we can't finish. This day is already hard enough—"

I stroke him again, and his words are swallowed by his own moan of pleasure.

"Yes, it is, but so are you. And who says I'm not going to finish it?"

Will's eyes light up, but they dim quickly as he frowns. "You know we can't—"

"Yes, I know we can't, and I know you can't touch me, but that doesn't mean *I* can't touch *you*," I explain, pointing to my chest and his for emphasis.

He draws in a rapid breath, and his eyes widen as understanding dawns, but there's a little bit of fear there too. "Oh, Tori, I don't know . . ."

"It's still going to be weeks yet until we can make love, or I can do this with my mouth. And no one told us I couldn't touch you if you're feeling up to it. Let me make you feel good, please?"

On the fence for probably a dozen reasons, not the least of which is exhaustion, he purses his lips. But his mental health is just as important as his physical health, and he's been so upset today that I think he needs this.

"You did say *he* was ready." I motion toward his cock, which twitches right on cue, nodding, if you will, as if he were listening to the conversation. I cover my mouth with my hand to stifle my laughter, but Will notices anyway and blushes deeply.

"Tell you what—you can make it up to me later. When you get to one hundred days, I want you to taste me and make me come with your tongue."

That does it. "Ohhh," he groans. "I want to do that *so* much!"

I grin as I help him out of the bathroom, his pants and his insecurities forgotten behind us on the floor. He sways a bit as we get to the bed, closing his eyes and gripping me a little tighter.

"Are you all right?"

"Yeah; just a little dizzy," he replies as he sits on the side of the bed. "It'll pass."

He sits with his head in his hand until the dizziness passes, and then I help him lie down flat with a single pillow under his head. He rests for a minute, but then he opens his eyes and stares at me expectantly. He looks exhausted, not moving any part of himself that he doesn't have to, but his eyes sparkle and dance, and his cock is still standing at attention.

"Are you sure you're up for this?" I ask, hoping I haven't pushed him too far.

"Are you kidding? Do you want to see my dick start weeping? And I don't mean in the 'I'm gonna come' way; I mean in the 'crying bitter tears and threatening to never cooperate again' way. Unless . . . *you* don't want to . . ."

I sit down next to him and run my hand over his tip and down, and he can't help the soft moan that escapes him. "Oh, I want to. I just wanted to make sure I wasn't the only one."

Will chuckles. "You and he are on the same side, remember?" he says, smirking at me and nodding toward his erection.

"Well, let's get acquainted, then," I tell him, crawling over his legs and stretching out next to him on the bed.

He grins at me and closes his eyes, waiting for my touch. And I don't intend to disappoint him. I start by gently cupping his balls and massaging them, and Will lets out a shaky breath that ends in a moan. My clit is instantly alive and pulsing, and I have to remind her rather sternly that she'll be getting no attention tonight, at least not from Will.

I slide my fingers up his length, gripping more firmly as I get to the tip, and Will inhales sharply and tenses, holding his breath before letting it go in a whoosh.

"Oh God, Tori, do you know how much I've wanted this? It's not—ahh! —everything I want, but it's"— he hisses in time with my stroke—"a good start."

I chuckle softly. He's babbling because he's either still nervous or he's excited, but either way, it's adorable.

"Sweetheart, hush up and enjoy this," I tell him, stroking a little harder. He gasps in response, and my whole body reacts, a shiver running down my spine as heat floods my senses. Fuck, I want him so badly. My head knows we can't do this now, but other parts of me aren't as easily persuaded. So I close my eyes, just as his are, and imagine it's a few months from now, and he's healthy and strong, and we're able to do this the right way.

The smooth skin of his shaft slides under my fingers, bunching up a little as I get to the top and twist a bit, slipping onto the silky surface of the tip. Will groans at the twist, and his breath starts coming in pants as I repeat the motion, a little faster this time.

"Fuck, this isn't going to last—ohhh—very long." There's already a touch of urgency in his voice. He's moaning with every downstroke of my hand now—needy little sounds of pleasure that are slowly setting me on fire.

I reach down again and massage his balls, and his guttural moan sends electricity shooting straight to my center—almost enough to make me touch myself. I'm going to resist, though. This is for him, not me, and I'm not going to make him feel bad that he can't reciprocate.

I open my eyes as I feel the bed shift, and the sight of Will writhing and bucking into my hand is almost enough to make me come. He's rolling his head from side to side, and he just can't stay still as he lifts his hips to meet me, thrusting into the hollow of my fingers. I tighten my grip even further.

"Oh, f-f-fuck, I'm close." He's panting now, thrusting in time with my firm strokes.

Suddenly, I feel him harden even more in my grip.

"ToriI'mgonnacome." He blurts the words out in a rush before he cries out, streams of come pulsing onto his chest and belly with every cry. When he finally stops, his body goes limp, but he's still breathing hard, trying to get himself back together.

I reach up and stroke his head as if he had hair because in my mind, he does, and he relaxes. "Was it good for you?" I ask playfully.

He doesn't open his eyes, but a slow smile spreads across his face. "It was fantastic. Can we do it again?"

I laugh because I know there's no way he could handle that again today. I think he barely made it through the first time. "Honey, your dick is convincing your mouth to write checks your body can't cash. You know that, don't you?"

"Sure. Just practicing . . . for when I can say that and mean it," he answers, slurring his words a bit. He's truly exhausted now, but he's happy. Mission accomplished, but now I need to get him to bed.

"I'll go get something to clean you up, okay? Then it's time for you to get some rest."

"Yeah . . . thanks," he says softly, barely awake.

My clit is still sensitive and throbbing as I walk into the bathroom, and it only takes a little finger action and one run through what I just witnessed before I'm shuddering and shoving my fist into my mouth to keep from waking Will.

When I go back into the bedroom, he's asleep just as I knew he would be, but his amazing smile remains. He barely stirs as I clean him up, so I decide not to torture him any further. I'm sure he's not feverish, and if I cover him up well, he should be fine sleeping with no clothes from the waist down. And if I'm honest with myself, I'm exhausted too. Today was a difficult day for everyone, and all I want to do is crawl into bed beside him. So after slipping on my pajamas, that's exactly what I do.

As I curl into his shoulder, he slides his arm around me, and I think I see his smile widen a little. "Welcome home, Will," I whisper, kissing his chest as he mumbles softly in his sleep.

CHAPTER 11

Day 33

I wake to soft kisses against my temple, and it takes me a moment to figure out what's going on. Will came home yesterday, and he's in bed with me. I chuckle and smile in pure happiness before I even open my eyes. My fingers trace gently up the side of his chest, and he laughs, tensing and pulling away from me. I had no idea he was ticklish there. I have no idea about so many things about him.

I raise my chin and open my eyes to find him staring at me; this morning, the brilliant green I adore is warm and golden like honey.

"I didn't know where I was this morning," he says, his voice still gravelly from sleep. "It was too quiet, a nurse didn't wake me up, and something warm and soft was snuggled up against me."

"Was it a good way to wake up?" I ask, continuing to stroke his chest but not in the newly discovered ticklish spot.

"Best morning I've had in years," he replies, pulling me a little closer. "How about you?"

"Mmm . . . this definitely beats the couch in your room, and I think it even edges out sleeping in my apartment alone."

"Edges out? Hmph." Will grumbles, and I burst out laughing as I snuggle further into him.

"This is wonderful. I was smiling before my eyes were even open when I realized where I was and that you were here with me."

Will kisses my forehead. "Good. I may not be able to do much right now, but cuddling is on the short list of things I *can* handle."

"Well, I guess we'll need to do a lot of cuddling, then," I tell him, tucking my head into the crook of his arm. It truly is fabulous to be able to get this close to him, finally. No tubes and wires, on this side anyway, and no swollen and tender parts to contend with. I sigh in contentment.

We lay quietly for a while, savoring the moment. I rest my head against his chest, feeling his heart thrumming strongly under me. He's here—he's finally home, and it's even better than I ever thought it could be. My fingers continue to wander over his chest, and his snake around my waist to stroke the side of my hip. Suddenly, they stop, and he stares down at me, looking puzzled but very serious. "I know I was really tired last night, but . . . did you get me off before we went to bed?"

I laugh, gently shaking us both. "Did you think you imagined it?"

"Yes. I'm still wondering if I imagined it. In fact, maybe I'm not even awake right now."

"You're awake, and I can prove it happened. If you look under the covers, and you're naked from the waist down, then it was real."

Grinning, Will lifts the covers so he can peer down at himself, and I lift them on my side so I can see too. I smirk as I see that he's pitching a tent for me again this morning.

"See? *He* remembers," I tell him, nodding my head toward his erection.

"I do, too," Will says, brushing his lips against mine. "I'm sorry I can't . . . that we can't—"

"You have nothing to be sorry for. There'll be plenty of time for that when you're stronger, and by God, I've watched you suffer so much that if I can do something—anything—to give you pleasure, I'm gonna do it. I want you to be happy because seeing *you* happy makes *me* happy."

"I don't deserve you," he says, his voice rough. He kisses me sweetly.

Electricity rushes through me, but I don't deepen the kiss. As much as I'd like to lie here with him all morning, he's due at the hospital in a little while, and we have a lot to do to get him ready.

"Yes, you do deserve me. You deserve better than me, in fact, but I guess I'll have to do." He looks like he's about to protest, so I continue quickly. "How are you feeling this morning?"

"Tired," he answers, stretching. "But I get to lie here with you, so I can deal with it."

"Actually, you don't get to lie here with me. It's time for your medication; we need to take your temperature this morning, especially since we didn't do it last night; and you're due at the hospital at ten."

"Argh." Will groans. "I guess the pretending I'm normal is over for today."

My heart clenches at his words, but I can't argue them. He's far from recovered and still has a long road ahead of him. But his happy moments are becoming more frequent. I hope it's going to be enough to see him through.

"Normal is overrated. You're sweet and cuddly—that's better than normal," I say, rubbing his head. "So, I don't think you're ready for the table yet, but do you want to try for breakfast on the couch?"

"Sure, that sounds doable," he answers as I slide out from under his arm and out of bed.

He watches me as I walk around the bed, but I fake him out and keep going into the bathroom. I peek my head back around the corner. "I'll be right back."

I return to find his eyes shut—*damn, did he fall back to sleep?* "Will," I say softly, and he opens his eyes to stare up at the ceiling.

He sighs heavily. "Fuck, I can't believe I'm this tired still, this long after the transplant and after a full night's sleep."

"Hey, we're only on Day 33, and you're doing great. Are you ready to get up?"

Will nods, and I help him sit up and swing his legs over the side of the bed. Something's wrong, though, because he nearly topples over sideways.

"Whoa," he says, raising a hand to his forehead. "I'm really dizzy."

"Do you want to lie back down?"

"Yes, but I have other needs at the moment," he says, gripping the side of the mattress. "Can you help me into the bathroom?"

"Of course," I tell him, grasping his forearm and hoisting him to his feet. He leans on me heavily, keeping his eyes shut as he shuffles across the tile. I get him settled and give him some privacy, scurrying to the kitchen to put some coffee on.

When I return, he's on his knees, elbow braced on the toilet bowl and his forehead resting in his palm. "Oh, sweetheart!"

"The dizziness was too much for my stomach. I really need to lie back down."

Anger surges through me. Will was due for a transfusion yesterday, but Jill wanted to see if he was producing enough red cells to go another day before his next transfusion. "Dammit! I knew you needed a transfusion yesterday! I should have insisted before they sent you home!"

"It's all right," he mutters. "It'll get better after today's transfusion."

"But if they'd done it yesterday, you wouldn't be going through this now. Fuck!" I swear, trying to keep my anger and frustration under control. I take a deep breath and let it out slowly. "Okay, let's make a new plan: no breakfast; we'll hold your meds until we get to the hospital; I can help you get dressed lying down on the bed, and then you can rest there until I'm ready to go. Does that sound okay?"

"Yeah," he replies as I pull him to his feet. He nearly takes us back down, both of us scrambling to grasp the countertop to keep from falling as he sways, completely off-balance.

"Let's get you off your feet," I say, throwing his arm over my shoulders. "Close your eyes like you did before, and I'll lead you."

Will doesn't respond, but he closes his eyes, and I slowly guide him over to the bed. By the time we get there, he's completely out of breath.

"Fuck . . . I'm gonna . . . pass out." He pants out the words as he stumbles, pitching forward so I have to catch him under his armpit with my other hand.

"No, you're not! Sit . . . sit!" I ease his weight onto the bed as he clutches at it, and my heart breaks for him. *Holy fucking shit—I'm gonna rip Jill a new one for this as soon as we get to the hospital!* This was completely unnecessary today. As if he isn't anxious enough about being home for the first time, she had to go and try to push his limits physically? Go*dam*mit!

"Sweetie, I'm gonna lay you down so we can try to get you stabilized, okay?"

"Yeah," Will mumbles, holding onto my arm tightly.

I shimmy him backward a little, then swing his legs up onto the bed. I move with him as I lay him back, holding the back of his head and lowering him very slowly.

When I finally get him flat on his back, he still has his eyes closed, but at least he's panting less frantically. He's still gripping my arm, though, and he's pale and clammy. "Are you still with me, sweetheart?"

"Yeah. I didn't faint . . . so that's good . . . right?"

"Yes, that's good."

"I nearly did though. My ears were ringing . . . and when I opened my eyes . . . everything was . . . still black."

Now that's just scary. "Can you see if you open your eyes now?"

Will rolls his head to the side and opens his eyes, but he squeezes them shut again quickly.

"I can see you, but this is . . . really bad. I'm so dizzy, I can't keep . . . them open."

"Keep them closed, then. It should get better once your blood pressure has a chance to go up—at least, until we have to get you up to go to the hospital."

"Fuck," Will mutters, finally starting to breathe normally.

"I'm going to call transplant and tell them we're coming as soon as we can since you're in such bad shape, and I'm going to ask them to have blood ready for you when we get there."

"Thanks, Tori," he says, smiling a little.

I start to wiggle my arm out of his grip, but he squeezes a little tighter.

"Can you stay here? When I'm this dizzy, I get panicky if I don't have someone to hold on to."

I think back to his dizzy spells in the hospital when he needed a transfusion—yep, he gripped my hand every time I was there, but I had no reason to leave his side.

"Yes, I can stay here, but I need to get my phone so I can call the hospital, and then I'll call Jason to come sit with you while I get ready. He was coming over later anyway to help us; I'm sure he won't mind coming sooner. Will you be all right for a minute?"

"Yeah," he answers shakily, but the minute I let go of his hand, he's clutching the bedspread for dear life.

I run and grab my phone, then make my calls while Will clings to me, and Jason shows up about twenty minutes later. By now, Will is resting peacefully, and he even dozes for a bit while I get ready.

Getting Will to the car is an ordeal because the minute he sits up, his world is spinning again, and the two steps he takes to his wheelchair leave him out of breath. I try to put the surgical mask on him, but he waves it away, telling me it's too hard to breathe with it on when he's like this. *So much for following the rules.* We repeat the process at the car, and Will vomits again as soon as Jason pulls away from the curb, the motion of the car running counter to the spinning in his head.

He rests his head back, and I let him hold my hand, doing whatever I can to stabilize him against the motion of the car. His hands are cold as ice, reminding me of the days before his transplant took, when his anemia was so severe he could barely move.

Jason drives as smoothly as he can and stops and starts slowly. I call transplant again and tell them we're going to come to the ER because I think Will needs oxygen as soon as possible, and they say they'll be ready.

Finally, we make it to the hospital, and by then, all my anger and frustration has coalesced into a tight ball in my stomach with one name on it—Jill.

The ER staff is waiting in the ambulance bay when Jason pulls up, and they swiftly get Will out of the car and onto a gurney. A nurse is there at the ready, and she holds an oxygen mask over Will's mouth and nose.

"Tori?" he calls, reaching out blindly, and I step up to him and take his hand.

"I'm here, sweetheart. Everything's going to be fine."

"I know," he says, meeting my eyes. "I'm okay."

Does he know I'm about to lose my shit? Is he trying to calm *me* down? *He's* very calm right now. Normally, this kind of crisis would be enough to give him a panic attack, or at least an Ativan-worthy dose of anxiety, but not today. He's certainly not happy about the state of affairs, but he's not freaking out over it either.

Rather than stay in the ER, we take Will up to transplant anyway because it's really the safest place in the hospital for him. I hold his hand the whole way, but his grip has slackened from what it was in the car.

When we arrive in the isolation hallway, Jill is waiting for us, talking to Jenny.

Jenny takes one look at me and flinches—she's seen me furious before.

Jill immediately walks over to Will and puts a hand on his shoulder. "Hey, tiger. I thought we turned you loose yesterday. You were supposed to walk back in here like you own the place."

"Next time," Will says weakly, but he's smiling under the oxygen mask.

"We'll have you good as new in no time. Mark will get you settled," Jill says, gesturing toward the guy standing next to Jenny, "and I'll be down in a moment."

Will nods, and Mark starts to wheel him away to the transfusion room. Jenny tries to catch my eye, but I'm too focused on what I'm about to do to pay her any mind.

"A word, Jill?" I say, my tone dangerously clipped.

She narrows her eyes at me. "Sure."

I turn on my heel and walk toward the empty waiting room, and as soon as I get there, I round on her.

"What the hell, Jill? Did we really have to try to stretch him to three days right now? He's anxious about going home, and he's terrified something's going to go wrong, and then this morning, his first morning away from the hospital, he gets up and he can't even stand?

This was *not* necessary right now, and it's caused him added worry and stress."

"We need to see that he progresses—"

"Yes, we do, but not at the expense of his mental well-being. This could have waited until the weekend or next week—any time other than his very first day away from the hospital in five months!"

I'm glaring at her, but she doesn't flinch—I'm sure I'm not the first family member to advocate aggressively for a patient.

"You're right," she says, still meeting my eyes, "but I really did think he would be fine. Otherwise, I wouldn't have done it. I'm just as surprised as you that he came in this way this morning."

"Well, don't do it again," I say, unable to keep the snippiness out of my voice. "It's too late for Will, but don't do this to other transplant patients and risk ruining their first day home. It's too important a day for them."

"Thanks for the advice," she replies. She doesn't lose her cool, but it's obvious we're both annoyed with each other.

"I'm going to go sit with Will."

"I'll be down in a few minutes so we can discuss our next steps," she says, and we both leave the room and go our separate ways.

When I get to the door of the room where Will is, I can hear him talking, so I stop for a minute to listen.

"You know your girlfriend is out there giving Jill a tongue-lashing for not transfusing you yesterday, right?"

Will chuckles. "What can I say? I'm a lucky man."

"I've seen wives and husbands of patients not get that worked up over things like this. You said you met her *after* you were diagnosed?"

"Yes, we met in July when I came in with an infection. I guess you could say we became a couple in September."

"Damn, dude, you *are* a lucky man. You're gonna make it through this if that one has anything to say about it. If I were you, I'd hang on to her."

"I plan to," Will answers, and suddenly I'm grinning from ear to ear. This is the first time I've really heard him talk about me to anyone else.

Just like that, my anger evaporates because despite everything that happened, Will's unfazed. He's feeling well enough to have a casual conversation, so the transfusion must be helping.

He's actually sitting up when I walk into the room, and he's no longer wearing the oxygen mask. Seeing those things does more to relax me than even overhearing his conversation did. The minute he sees me, his green eyes dance, and he flashes me a brilliant smile.

I head straight over to the sink to wash so I can touch him. When I take his hand, it's much warmer than it was in the car, and his cheeks are starting to pink up again. It's amazing what a few hundred million red blood cells can do.

"Are you feeling better?" I ask, bringing our hands up so I can kiss the back of his.

"I'm starting to," he answers. "I'm not out of breath anymore, and the dizziness has stopped. I'm not sure what would happen if I stood up, but before, I couldn't even raise my head without everything spinning, so I'm making progress."

I grin and shake my head. I'm thrilled he's not upset about all this, but I can't fathom why not.

"Don't take this the wrong way, sweetheart, but you've been awfully calm about this whole thing."

"And you're wondering why I didn't freak out and have a panic attack?"

"Well, kinda . . . yeah," I admit as my cheeks heat.

"So that's my MO now when things go wrong, eh?" he asks, smirking.

"No, of course not. But yesterday was such an up and down day for you, and you *were* worried about something going wrong—"

"Yeah, but this wasn't an unexpected thing. I knew what this was right away and how to fix it. If I'd started running a fever or something, I would have been much more upset. This has been happening for weeks now. I'm used to it."

"Why did *you* get so upset? Mark said you were out there trying to take Jill's head off."

I blush again because now that I've calmed down, I realize some of my reaction was probably residual stress from yesterday. "I didn't take her head off, but I was pretty pissed this happened to you today. You had enough to worry about; there was no reason to try to push you to go another day without a transfusion on your first day home. You didn't need any more worry and stress, and I was afraid it was going to make you panic about being away from here."

His eyes soften as he looks at me, and he squeezes my hand. "So you were looking out for me, as usual."

"Of course," I reply, a bit sheepishly.

"Well, you can relax. Now that I'm getting my power up, all I wanna do is get the hell out of here again and go back to our apartment."

I caress his cheek and he leans into my hand, and we settle in to wait for his transfusion to finish.

When he's done, he has more blood work, and we schedule his appointment for Friday. Based on how anemic he was this morning, Jill thinks we should wait a bit before trying to go to every third day for his transfusions. *Damn straight.*

He's able to stand and walk the few steps to his wheelchair without getting dizzy, so we leave the hospital that way. Even though I can't see his mouth because of his mask, the crinkles around his eyes tell me he's grinning from ear to ear about leaving again.

By the time we get home, Elizabeth is already there and preparing things in the kitchen. Tomorrow is Thanksgiving, and we're having turkey dinner for five, so it's time to get the bird prepared, the stuffing made, and the pies baked.

Will slept the whole way home in the car, and at the moment, it looks like it's taking all he has to remain sitting up, but he stops Jason when he begins to push him toward the bedroom.

"I wanna be in the living room today if you guys are going to be out here cooking," Will says, his pleading eyes on me. "It's lonely back there, and I have a feeling I'm going to be spending quite a bit of time cooped up in the bedroom over the next few weeks."

"But, sweetheart, you look as if you're about to fall asleep sitting up. It'll be quiet back there, so you can rest—"

"I'm so exhausted that nothing is going to disturb me when I fall asleep, but at least this way, I'll already be out here when I wake up. Please?"

I've never been able to say no to him. Those eyes just melt me into a puddle, and at warp speed when he's doing the damn puppy dog thing.

"Okay, but why don't you try the recliner today? I saw the looks you were giving it yesterday, but I really think it'll be more comfortable for you than the couch."

He eyes both it and me dubiously, glancing back and forth.

"I'm giving a little. Now you give a little, too. It's called a compromise. When have I ever steered you wrong?"

He laughs and agrees, and as soon as we have him settled in it, I can tell he's comfortable. He lays his head back and sighs, then shoots a stealthy look in my direction to see if I noticed. He admits nothing, but the fact he's asleep in under three minutes tells me all I need to know.

The day passes in a blur of cooking, and Will wakes up after a few hours and watches us work. We chat and laugh and have a lovely afternoon, and Will has dinner sitting in the recliner before I take him back to get him settled for bed.

This is the first "normal" evening we're having, so I try to set out a routine for us of getting him cleaned up and ready, followed by medication, and last, taking his temperature.

"We have to do this twice a day from now on?" he asks around the thermometer.

"Yes. Now be quiet until the reading is done, or I'm going to have to do it again." As I scold him, I watch the numbers blink on the device.

Will rolls his eyes at me, but he shuts up and waits until the thing beeps.

"Ninety-eight point four," I proclaim, grinning as I write it down in our logbook. He relaxes a little after I read out the verdict. I have a feeling this is going to be a stressful time of day for him until he gets a few more days at home under his belt.

"Shit, you didn't get a shower today," I say, fretting. He's supposed to shower every day, but things were so crazy this morning, and I didn't remember until now . . .

"Tori, I'm way too tired to tackle that tonight. Let's plan to do it in the morning from now on, when I have some energy. I'll be okay until tomorrow, I'm sure," he says, leaning toward me to kiss my neck.

I put my hand on his chest before he can make contact with my skin. "Oh, no. I've been out today, and I haven't showered since yesterday. No kissing any parts of me until I'm clean."

"You're really going to be a stickler about this, aren't you?" he asks, leaning back against his pillows and closing his eyes.

"Remember yesterday and this morning when you were telling me how scared you were that something bad was going to happen? Well, I'm scared too, which is why we're going to do everything we can to prevent it. I can't break the rules because if I do and you get sick, I'll never forgive myself."

His opens his eyes again and gives me a small smile. "I'm sorry; you're right. I guess I'm tired of jumping through hoops, but now isn't exactly the best time to stage a revolt. There are just a lot of new things to get used to."

"I know there are, but you've been doing wonderfully. We'll get the medical and hygiene stuff down to a routine, and then you'll hardly notice it. It'll just be slow going until we figure out how best to work everything. But I have faith in us."

"Me too," he says, his smile and his soft green eyes warming me from the inside out. "Now hurry up and shower because I want to cuddle up with you."

"Sweetheart, you're gonna be snoring inside of two minutes."

He purses his lips, but he can't bring himself to deny it.

"How fast can you shower?"

I chuckle as I get up from the bed. "How about this? I'll go as fast as I can, and even if you're asleep when I come out, I'll still cuddle up to you. I'll be here when you wake up in the morning, and you can touch me all you want . . . well, all that you're allowed." He pokes out his pouty lip as I amend my words.

"Dammit, Will—"

"Okay, okay," he says, throwing his hands in the air. "I know. I'm just teasing you. I'll be a good boy and go to sleep, but tomorrow morning, you better be ready for me because I plan on being a bad boy then."

Warmth floods my cheeks and my center, and I laugh as he waggles his eyebrows at me. "When did you get so cute, anyway?"

"I've always been this way," Will says with his nose in the air. "I've just been too busy with other things lately to show it. But I've got all the time in the world now, and I plan on using it to show you exactly who I really am because I'm not that anxious, broken man you met in the hospital."

I stop and stare at him for a moment because only once since I've known him has he ever mentioned the differences between his former self and the man I met in July. "Well, I look forward to getting to know this 'new to me' Will, then, because if the other one made me fall in love with him, I can only imagine what kind of havoc this one will wreak."

Will chuckles, but his eyes fall closed. He's done for tonight.

"Go to sleep, love," I say, leaning down and kissing him on the forehead. His lips rise in a semblance of a smile, but even as I watch, his head lolls to the side.

CHAPTER 12

Day 34

Something's tickling me. I'm lying on the dock by the lake, but there must be a mosquito after me—or something—so I bring my hand up to brush it off my neck . . . and I run into something much bigger. As I startle awake, the first things I see are brilliant green eyes twinkling at me.

Will laughs and shakes his head, and I narrow my eyes at him.

"What were you doing?" I demand of him, still scowling and half-asleep.

"Well, I had been sleeping, but you were lying next to me so warm and soft, and part of you started calling to me. This part, right here," he says, tracing his finger down my collarbone. "How could I not answer its plea? So I started kissing you right there, and then the other side got jealous, and soon half your body was demanding my lips! So when you woke up, I was doing the best I could to keep all of your parts satisfied, like a good boyfriend should."

He gives me his very best puppy dog eyes, the charm turned on at full blast, and I ask you, how in the name of God can I be angry when he's putting this much effort into getting out of trouble? And that line of bull he just fed me? Oh my God, if this is the way he's going to be from now on, I am in some *serious* trouble.

I wrinkle my nose, still trying to look angry, but my lips betray me and keep pulling up at the corners.

His own smile spreads wide because he knows he has me. He keeps tracing my collarbone, then slowly slips his index finger down between my breasts.

"What am I going to do with you? I was dreaming and I thought you were a mosquito; I was about to swat you!"

"Mmm . . . that could be fun," he says, bringing his lips down to take over for his finger.

"What has gotten *in*to you?" I ask, sighing softly as he takes a nipple into his mouth.

"I told you I was going to be a bad boy this morning." He complements his reminder with the most innocent look I've ever seen, then returns his attention to my breast.

"You certainly weren't kidding," I say, arching my back and moaning as pleasure shoots down my spine.

His soft hands start exploring me as he continues to work on my nipple, and a warm flush rushes through me until every single part of me is awake and tingling.

I start to explore, too, running my hands down his arms. His skin is so smooth and soft—it dawns on me that it's because he no longer has any arm hair. Of course, I knew that, but exploring his body is showing it to me in ways I hadn't thought about . . . and I like it.

My fingers slide under his shirt to caress his chest, and he pulls back even though I'm on the opposite side from his central line.

He squeezes his eyes shut with a grimace.

"What's wrong? Did I hurt you?"

"No, I'm fine," he answers, eyes still shut.

"Will."

His teeth dig into his lower lip, and he sighs in frustration. "I'm just ... a little lightheaded. Fuck," he says, bringing his hand up to his forehead.

"Okay, lie back," I say, gently pushing on his chest.

He makes an irritated noise, but he lies back, frowning.

"Goddammit." He sighs heavily.

"Better?" I ask, caressing his cheek with the back of my hand.

"Yes, but I wasn't finished." He's pouting now and puffing out that adorable lower lip.

I lean forward and suck said lip into my mouth, nibbling until I feel him relax. "Who said we were done? I just think that until you're a little stronger, it would be better if you were the one on your back, hmm? I want you feeling high from orgasms, not lack of oxygen."

Will chuckles, and he can't help but grin at me. "All right. But I think you just like to be in control."

"You might like me in control, too, if you pipe down and let me have my wicked way with you." I purr at him, sliding my finger down his front until I reach his navel.

His eyes widen, his pupils dilating a little. "Oh," he groans hungrily, and I can't help but laugh. He's so stubborn sometimes, but certain things just grab his attention immediately—particularly things involving me and sex in any form.

I lean over and capture his lips, moving carefully to make sure he's all right.

He's having none of that though. As soon as our lips touch, his hand slides up my back to clutch at the base of my skull, and he angles to the side so his erection is pressing into my thigh. He wriggles against me for a little friction, and I swallow his moan before it escapes, thrusting my tongue into his mouth.

His kisses are needy and eager as he swivels his hips to rub against me, and my clit pulses at the closeness of his erection.

Just once. What can it hurt? A little voice inside my head pleads.

It can land him in the hospital again, my better judgment replies. *Discussion over.*

But his proximity is setting me on fire, so I slide my palm over him firmly.

"Ohhh." He moans deep in his throat, and if my panties weren't already wet, they certainly are now.

"Can I touch you?" I ask, low and breathy, as my hand presses against his cock and rubs up and down.

"God, please," he begs, his breath coming faster as I slip my hand down into his sweats.

My fingers encounter the silky tip first, and then my fist slides over the smooth, velvety skin of his shaft. He's rock hard as he writhes against me, gasping a little, but I continue my journey downward. My fingers brush the unbelievably soft and completely bare skin of his balls, and we moan simultaneously.

His eyes snap open. "I know why I'm moaning..."

I blush. "Um...you have no hair."

"Oh," he says, his own face flushing as he looks down.

Shit. "No, I...it kind of...turns me on?" I look up at him shyly.

His eyebrows knit together. "What?"

"It turns me on," I say with more confidence. "I like you bare down there. Your skin is so soft and smooth..." *I wonder what it tastes like.*

Now he raises an eyebrow. "You're serious."

"Yes." I cup his balls and massage them between my fingers. "Can you feel that I'm serious?"

"Yesss," he hisses, closing his eyes again and going back to enjoying what I'm doing.

I stroke and fondle him, and he hums his pleasure, but the waistband of his pants against my forearm is irritating me. He looks at me questioningly as I sit up, but a smile tugs at his lips when I grab both sides of his sweats and raise my eyebrows for permission. He nods and lifts up for me, and I can't help but snake a hand underneath him to give his ass a little attention too, squeezing a bit as he chuckles.

But my focus shifts immediately to his cock, standing at attention and slick at the tip. Will follows my line of sight and lowers a hand to cover himself, but I stop him before the self-consciousness can take hold.

"No," I whisper. "I want to see this time. You're beautiful."

He closes his eyes and swallows, but all that's forgotten the minute my hand returns to his cock.

"I want to watch you come, Will," I tell him, low and sultry, as I start a slow rhythm up and down his shaft. He sighs, but soon, he's wanting more, his hips bucking up against my hand. So I grip him more tightly, making a slick hollow for him to thrust into, and he tenses, gasping.

Will throws his head back against the pillow, his neck deliciously exposed for me, but I'm more interested in sucking on other things right now. He's moaning on the exhale every time I stroke his swollen tip with my thumb and thrusting urgently into the wet home I've created for him.

"Fuck, I'm close." He words are a desperate pant as he squirms and writhes against my hand.

I know I can't put my mouth on his cock for fear of infection, but nobody said anything about other parts. I kneel up and lean over his body, bringing my head down to pull one of his balls into my mouth.

I swirl my tongue, and he lets out a shout as his sac tightens between my lips, and I feel his release pulsing under my fingers. Will moans in time with every pulse, and the feel and the sound are so erotic that my clit tightens, and I get a head rush. *Holy fuck, I can't wait until I'm able to just tackle him and have my way with him! He's so damn responsive and sexy!*

Will collapses bonelessly on the bed, a quivering heap of post-orgasm bliss, and I deftly clean him off with a tissue, then curl into his shoulder. He pulls me in close and holds me until his breathing finally slows.

"Happy Thanksgiving, sweetheart. Are you thankful?"

He cracks one eye open and glances at me. "I am the most thankful motherfucker on the face of the planet right now," he answers, bringing his lips down to meet mine.

I giggle as he tries to kiss me, and we both dissolve into laughter.

"That was . . . wow. I'm not even sure what you did at the end there; I was so close to coming when you did it."

"You couldn't tell?" I ask, smirking.

"Um . . . no. I know you did something with my balls, and it felt incredible, and then I had an out-of-body experience."

I laugh again. "Well, I'll just have to keep that trick in my back pocket for next time."

"Aw, come on, Tori! What did you do? That was an amazing orgasm, and it sucks to have a new favorite thing and not even know what it is. Please?"

Here come the puppy dog eyes, and he sweetens the offering by peppering my lips and cheeks with kisses.

My center starts to warm again as he lavishes me with his attentions, and as always, I give him exactly what he wants.

"Well, let's put it this way: the next time someone says 'suck my balls' to you instead of telling you to fuck off, you should seriously consider that offer."

Will's jaw drops and his eyes widen, and he makes a cute little spluttering noise. A blush floods his chest and enflames his cheeks, and he grins like a little boy on Christmas.

"I *am* the luckiest man alive," he murmurs under his breath, but I hear every word.

"What?"

"Nothing! You *were* really serious about the no hair thing, weren't you?"

I grin and nod.

"Well, maybe I'll keep them that way then. I think the hardest part is probably shaving them in the first place, but I'm already over that hurdle."

"Mmm . . . I think I'd like that."

Will shakes his head. "There's so much I don't know about you. But if today is any indication, I'm going to enjoy the hell out of learning!"

I bring his hand up and kiss the back of it. "Well, I didn't know about that one, either. Maybe we'll learn some things together."

His eyes light up eagerly. "That sounds even better!" he exclaims, running his fingers up and down my arm.

"But we're not going to work on that now," I say, swatting his hand away. "We have things to do, and I have a turkey to get in the oven."

Will frowns, but as soon as he sees me looking at him, he smiles to hide it.

"What is it?"

"Nothing."

"Hey," I say, raising his chin so he meets my eyes.

He huffs out a frustrated breath. "It's nothing really. I just . . . This is quickly becoming my favorite time of day. I wake up and you're right here with me; I'm not exhausted, and I can pretend things are different for a while. I'm sad to see it end."

I lean down and kiss his perfect lips, and he can't help but respond, pulling me closer and warming me from the inside out with his affection. We break apart, breathless, and I lean my forehead against his. "Soon, every day will be like this. I promise. Every day proves you're getting better and stronger, and every morning brings us one day closer to your being completely well. I know it seems a long way off, but look how far you've come already. I'm so proud of you, Will."

A small, satisfied grin creeps across his lips, and he kisses me chastely. "You're right. While I hate being sore, tired, and over-medicated, it beats the hell out of dying of cancer. Glass half full, right?"

"Exactly! Maybe things could be better, but they could also be so much worse, so now's really not so bad."

"I love you," Will says, his fingertips soft on my cheek.

"I love you, too. Now, let's get you up and get our day started!"

I sit up and offer him my hand. He takes it gratefully, sitting up and swinging his legs over the side of the bed. He groans softly as I help him stand, closing his eyes and holding on to my shoulder.

"You okay?"

"Yeah . . . just sore—and stiff. My joints have been in one position for too long. It's always like this when I first get up. It gets better the more I move around."

Shaking my head, I put my shoulder under his arm and help him into the bathroom. He leans on me heavily, his movements slow and pained. He's told me before that the joint pain from the cancer was worse, but I don't know, the pain from the treatment looks almost as bad right now.

"Listen, why don't you have your breakfast in bed this morning so you can take your medication, and while you're doing that, I can get the turkey situation under control. When you're finished, you can take your shower, and then we'll get you set up in the recliner. Sound good?"

"That sounds fantastic. I can't tell you how good it feels to be doing something other than lying in a bed!" His eyes dance, and I feel his excitement. He really is ecstatic about being home!

Unlike yesterday, today things go according to plan, and Will has fruit and cereal for breakfast and takes his medication on time while I get the turkey in the oven.

When I go back into the bedroom, he's just finishing up, and I'm thrilled to see he's cleaned his plate. He still doesn't have much appetite, and sometimes his stomach is really out of sorts, but today seems to be starting off well. I hope he'll be able to have some turkey and stuffing.

"Are you ready to get cleaned up?" I ask, and his brow furrows a little.

"Sure," he answers, but his tone is as hollow as the smile he's giving me.

"Hey, remember two days ago? For better or worse? I can see the 'worse' on your face right now, and I don't want you to bear it alone. Tell me?"

Will frowns and huffs out a breath.

"Please don't tell me this has anything to do with being self-conscious about taking your clothes off . . ."

His eyes are suddenly on the comforter. *Fuck.*

I caress his cheek until he raises his eyes to mine. "I thought we got past this the other night—"

"Yeah, but now you're going to see all of me, all at once," he says, his gaze hard.

"Sweetheart, I'm in love with you. *All* of you. I've touched every part of you, whether I've seen it or not, and I think you're beautiful. How many times do I have to tell you until you believe me?"

"Until I gain thirty pounds," he replies stubbornly.

Sighing, I shake my head.

"I'm sorry. This is harder than last time. I'm much thinner than I was, and I've lost my hair absolutely *everywhere*—I think I look awful, so I can imagine what everyone else thinks."

"Everyone who loves you thinks you're in recovery, and everyone else can go to hell! Will, when I look at you, I don't see someone who's thin or hairless or weak—I see someone who's very brave. I see someone who went through hell because he wanted to be with me and is still recovering from that ordeal. When I look at you, I see the man I fell in love with. And if you remember, I fell in love with you when you were a terminal lymphoma patient. And although I personally think you're gorgeous, what I really fell in love with is here." I touch his temple. "And in here." I touch to his chest.

"Your hair will grow back, and you'll put on weight, but the parts I'm most concerned with are already perfect and whole—neither the cancer nor the treatment has tainted them. So you see, it doesn't bother me at all. As I said, I think you're beautiful. Will you . . . let me show you?"

Will furrows his brow, looking equal parts nervous and confused.

"Let me take care of you," I whisper, coaxing him to sit up.

His teeth catch his lower lip, but he says nothing, and although he's agreeing, I know this is hard for him. He wants to be independent and whole so badly, and he and I have never had this level of intimacy before. It's a stressful combination on top of everything else he's dealing with. But I plan to go out of my way to make this easy and comfortable, and I'm hoping it'll be an experience he won't soon forget.

I help him stand, and we take slow steps to the bathroom, but his motion is more fluid than it was earlier, and he seems to be in less pain. He sits on the toilet seat while I start the shower and get everything ready for him, the lines around his eyes conveying his stress.

When I'm finished, I stand before him, drinking in the beauty I see there. He's in sweats and a t-shirt, and he's wearing his hat, but all I see are mesmerizing green eyes and smooth, soft skin. Nudging his knees apart, I stand between his legs and begin by kissing his forehead. I leave a line of soft kisses along the edge of his beanie, and very slowly, I push it back with my lips, loving every inch of his bare scalp as I reveal more skin. When I reach the crown of his head, his hat slips off, but I continue my attentions until I've kissed every inch of him.

He's panting a bit by the time I finish, and I step back to look into his eyes. I can't quite decipher what I see there, but it doesn't appear to be shame, so I continue. Taking the hem of his t-shirt, I pull it over his head, doing his left arm first and maneuvering carefully around his central line.

Will hunches self-consciously, but I rub my thumbs over his shoulders until he relaxes. He flinches a little as I lean in, but I hear a soft sigh as I trail feather-light kisses around the dressing that covers his central line. Reaching behind me, I retrieve the clear plastic patch and very gently cover both the dressing and tubes with it.

I take his hand and kiss his palm as I pull him to his feet, running my nose down his wrist to nuzzle the scar there. His brow furrows, but he doesn't break the moment by speaking, and I get down on my knees before him. I carefully slide his sweats down over his hips, and although he's semi-hard, I don't pay any attention right now—that's not the point of what I'm doing. He lifts his feet one by one as I pull off his pants then his socks, and I wince at the coldness of his toes. I hate having cold feet, and Will's have been freezing for weeks. I'll have to try to do something about that.

He's completely naked now, but I don't draw any attention to it by roving my eyes over his body. I'd certainly like to, but I know I won't like his response, and I don't want to make him any more uncomfortable. He sways a little on his feet and grasps my shoulder.

"I don't think I can stand for long enough—"

I place a finger over his lips. "You don't have to stand, sweetheart. We put a seat in the shower for you and had a hand-held showerhead installed. All you need to do is sit, and let me do the rest."

"You really did think of everything, didn't you?" He winds his arms around me, but I know we're pushing the amount of time he can comfortably spend on his feet, so I nudge him over toward the shower.

He sits down heavily on the wooden bench and leans his head back against the wall. Taking advantage of his inattention, I slip out of my clothes, and before he's even aware, I'm in the shower naked with him. He startles when I take his hand, and his eyes widen appreciatively as he takes in the view. His thumb finds the prominence of my hip, and I let him stroke as I lather up my hands and begin massaging his fingers.

He groans in contentment and closes his eyes, his thumb pausing, completely distracted. I return that hand to his knee, then use both of my hands to massage him, slipping from his fingers to his hand then back to his forearm. I massage every inch of his arm, including his shoulder, and when I finish, I give the same treatment to his other side, cleaning him while I try to rejuvenate his tired muscles. Will hums in the back of his throat as I work, completely relaxed and boneless as he leans against the shower wall.

I rinse him off with the showerhead, and his eyes open lazily as I kneel before him. He looks like he's going to speak, but I shake my head, not wanting my worship of his body disturbed. He smiles and his eyes flutter shut, and I return to my task. I spend a long time rubbing his feet, pressing and kneading in all the right places if his groans are any indication. By the time I finish, I think they're a little warmer, so I move my attentions to his calves. He's sporting a good semi from me rubbing his inner thighs by the time I'm done, and a shiver rolls down my spine as he moves restlessly on the bench.

No, we're not doing that now, I firmly remind myself, but it's hard to take my eyes off his cock as I soap his belly, running my fingers over his abs. He shivers under me, and suddenly, his head is buried in my chest.

"Will, are you all right? How are you feeling?"

"I feel . . . beautiful, Tori. Thank you," he says against my skin, and I wrap my arms around his neck and stroke his bald head.

"You *are* beautiful, Will, inside and out, and I love you with all my heart."

"I know. I could *feel* it just now. All of it," he says, pulling my chin down so he can capture my lips. The kiss is passionate but not steamy—it's worshipful—both of us pouring our love for each other into the movements of our lips and tongues. It's perfect.

"Are you ready to get out? We'll get you settled, and then I'll come take my shower—"

"You could just shower now." He casts his eyes downward, but they come back to my breasts as if drawn there. "I could . . . watch."

"Would you like that?"

"I would. Very much."

I straighten up and begin to wash myself, fully expecting to receive some "help" along the way, but Will keeps his hands to himself. He watches though. No movement of mine escapes him, and his stare is so lustful, I swear I can feel it burning my skin. It's my turn to feel beautiful—and desired.

When I finish, I help him out of the shower. We get him ready for the day, but now he's sluggish, and he leans on me more heavily as I help him walk to the living room. He's tired—I can see it in the way he collapses onto the recliner and lies there with his eyes shut for a moment, but he tries his best to hide it, grinning up at me as if he's ready to go.

"Sweetheart, take a nap. I know you're tired, and you're not gonna miss anything this morning. Rest so you're feeling refreshed when company gets here."

"Company? Is someone other than my mom coming?" he asks, suddenly nervous.

"Jenny and Jason are coming—they stayed in the city for Thanksgiving, and once we found out you'd be home, I asked them to join us. Is that okay?"

A wide grin spreads across Will's face. "That's fantastic! Everyone I really care about will be here today. What a great way to spend our first holiday together!"

I chuckle and smile at him, his excitement warming my heart. I'm amazed how his moods can bounce back and forth from self-conscious and brooding to almost giddy. It's as if carefree Will is trying to break free, but careworn Will just can't let go. I wonder if the balance will shift as he gets better.

We get him situated in the recliner—his feet up and a pillow behind his head and shoulders, and I tuck his green afghan closely around his legs and feet. I look up as I'm finishing, and he's already sound asleep, his chest rising and falling softly and his lips already pursed into that adorable pout. He looks . . . comfortable. It's such a world away from how he looked in the hospital. He looks like he belongs here, like he's healing even as I watch. We can do this, he and I. We can make him well again.

Elizabeth shows up a while later, and we work quietly in the kitchen so we don't disturb Will, but we're both giddy with excitement that he's home, and we all get to spend the day together. Jenny and Jason show up around noon, just as we're getting ready to take the turkey out of the oven, and I glance over at Will, worried we're going to wake him.

Elizabeth clinks two dishes together in the kitchen, and Will's brow furrows before he opens his eyes. He blinks owlishly, but as his gaze falls on his table, set for dinner, and on all of us in the doorway, the most amazing smile spreads across his face. I swallow thickly—if there's a fairy who grants wishes on Thanksgiving, then I've just gotten mine. Our eyes meet, and his gaze softens—how the hell does he melt me on the spot with those lady-killing green eyes of his? Every. Single. Time.

"How's Will?" Jenny asks, drawing my attention back to the conversation.

"I'm over here," Will calls from the recliner.

He blushes as four sets of eyes fall on him, but Jenny is across the room and kneeling next to him before the rest of us manage to blink.

"You look *so* much better today. How does it feel to be home?"

"It's fantastic. I love being in my own space again and being up and around. It's slow going, and it's different, but it beats the hell out of the hospital."

"I bet it does," Jenny replies, winking. "And I'd wager the nursing staff here is a little more . . . *attentive* than at the hospital."

Will's gaze meets mine as he blushes adorably, and Jenny giggles at his embarrassment.

"Slightly," Will says with a smirk.

"Jenny, quit making my boyfriend blush. That's my job." My scolding makes Will color even more as his eyes widen in surprise.

I laugh out loud and go over to them, shoving Jenny out of the way playfully so I can lean in and kiss him. Will grasps the back of my head and holds me there, trying to deepen the kiss until Jason wolf-whistles from across the room. We break apart, and he's still red in the face, shooting daggers at Jason as I straighten up.

"See?" I say to Jenny, batting my eyelashes as Will narrows his eyes at both of us.

Jason sits down with Will while Jenny and I go to the kitchen to help Elizabeth get everything set out on the table.

"How is he doing really?" Jenny asks as soon as we hear the boys strike up a conversation.

"He's . . . fine. His fatigue is a lot to deal with, and it's been a bit bumpy working through all the things he needs to do, but we're getting there."

"And he's happy," Jenny says, and it's not a question.

"Yes, he *is* happy, and so am I," I tell her, contentment brimming in my chest. "I never thought one person could make such a difference in your life."

"Of course they can! Look at the difference you've made in his."

Thinking back to the man I met in July, I realize she's right, but even if it's not as obvious, he really has done as much for me as I have for him.

We get down to the business of setting out a large meal, and soon, everything is steaming on the table. I walk over and stand beside Will, and he glances up expectantly.

"We're ready. Do you want to try eating at the table?"

"Sure! I think I'll be okay, but if I get too tired, I can always come back here."

I just grin and shake my head. Who is this positive, easygoing person in my recliner? Being home has wrought such a change in him already, and it hasn't even been three days.

He notices my expression, and his brow creases. "What?"

"Nothing," I reply, smiling down at the most important person in my life. "I'm just happy."

His smile is so beautiful, it dazzles me, but I'm brought back to earth by Jason.

"Come on, Will, that turkey isn't gonna eat itself!" he says, rising from the couch. He extends his hand. "Let's get you to the table."

Will chuckles and takes Jay's hand, and while the two of them negotiate the room, I fetch a few pillows to cushion Will's sore body from the hard wood of the kitchen chairs.

Once we get him settled, we all take our seats, and everyone's gaze turns to Will.

He clears his throat uncomfortably, but as he looks around at each of us, his cheeks widen into a smile. His eyes fall on Elizabeth last. "When I was growing up, we used to have a tradition of going around the table and saying what we were thankful for. If no one has any objections, I'd kinda like to do that now."

We all nod as a serious atmosphere falls over the room, and I reach over and take Will's hand.

He squeezes my fingers. "Well, since it was my idea, I'll go first.

"I'm thankful for . . . this morning." I gape at Will, shocked, but he just smiles and continues solemnly. "And for every morning I wake up because I know now what a precious gift that is. Life has thrown me some curve balls, but I've also been given the support I need to make it through those hard times." He glances around the table meaningfully at each of us. "I'm thankful for everyone at this table because each of you has saved my life, and if it weren't for you, I wouldn't be sitting here today. But most of all, I'm thankful for Tori, who walked into my hospital room one day and changed everything. Tori, you *are* my life now, and I've never been happier. I truly have a lot to be thankful for."

He squeezes my hand again as he finishes, his eyes affirming his words and so much more. I cover my mouth with my hand, and I can't help the tears that spill down my cheeks. He's so perfect—I have no idea what I ever did to deserve the love and happiness I've been granted.

"Tori," Will says softly, and I suddenly realize everyone is staring at me.

"Sure, get me all choked up, and then tell me it's my turn." I tease him, and everyone laughs, which gives me a minute to regain my composure.

"I'm . . . not good at speeches." I hesitate, but Will rubs his thumb over my knuckles, and as I look into his eyes, I find the courage to continue. "I'm thankful for . . . my dad, who's with us in spirit today, and for my job at the hospital. But this year, I'm thankful for some things I haven't been before. I'm thankful for friendship. Jenny, you're the best friend a girl could have, and Jason, your friendship with Will has helped him through so much—it inspires me, and I hope I can be as good a friend as you are. And Elizabeth, you're more like a mother than a friend, but your help and advice have meant so much to me over the past few months. And I'm thankful for fate or chance or whatever force made it possible for Will and me to meet because it's changed my life and shown me that just one person can make all the difference in the world. And I'm thankful he's here with us today and that he's getting better."

Will's eyes are watery, and he squeezes my hand as we all look to Jenny. As she and Jason share what they're thankful for, I glance around the table at the four people who mean so much to me. I'm shocked as I realize that at this time last year, I only knew one of them, and I was living with Peter. It's amazing how life can stay the same for so long, and then in an instant, everything changes. What Will said was exactly right—the day I walked into his hospital room changed everything, for both of us. Thinking further on it, that day changed everything for all of us because otherwise, Jason and Jenny wouldn't have met, and Elizabeth would still be with Will Senior.

Elizabeth's voice draws me from my reflection.

"I also have a lot to be thankful for, and the most important thing is my son. Thank you, Will, for reaching out to me and letting me back into your life. I can't change the past, but it means so very much to me that I get to be part of your future."

A tear slips down her cheek and Will takes her hand.

"And, Tori, thank you for all you've done for Will. I don't know what would have happened if you hadn't intervened, but I don't think he'd be where he is now, and I'm thrilled you're part of his life, and now mine. And thank you all for welcoming me into your lives and helping me make a fresh start."

We all look around the table at each other for a moment, and I can feel the love and hope that radiates around the room. It seems we all have new beginnings this year and so much to give thanks for.

Jason breaks the silence.

"And I'm also thankful for the turkey and that it'll be in my belly and not on that platter five minutes from now. Let's eat!"

We all laugh and start passing dishes around the table. I glance over at Will, and he seems to be doing all right. He's resting his head against the high back of the chair, and he has this perpetual grin on his face. So much of life has passed him by over the last few months. I wonder if today is making him feel like he's alive again, like he's part of something again. God, I hope so.

We eat quietly for a few minutes, but as everyone's initial hunger is satisfied, conversation begins. Elizabeth glances thoughtfully around the room, then covers Will's hand with hers.

"Will, your artwork is simply stunning. It was always beautiful, but I can see you've improved a lot over the last four years."

"Thanks, Mom," Will says, blushing.

"I didn't want to look until you could show me, but we needed to clean the whole apartment, so there was really no way around it. One day when you're feeling better, I want you to take me into your studio and give me the grand tour."

"Of course I will," Will responds, smiling at her. "My career was really starting to take off, but then I got sick, and I couldn't keep the momentum going. I'm hoping when I'm well, I'll be able to start promoting my work again."

"That shouldn't be a problem," Jason chimes in. "There are still a good number of inquiries about you at the openings and showings. All of our friends usually refer any inquiries to me, and I've gotten the word out that you're on sabbatical for medical reasons, but you hope to be back soon."

"Really? Wow, Jason, thanks," Will says.

Jason nods and smiles. "You have enough work back there that you could hold a gallery show. I hope that's something you'll think about when you're back on your feet."

"I'm already thinking about it," Will says, looking down at his plate. "But I think it's gonna be quite a few months yet until I can really consider trying to do it. It's a lot of stress and a lot of palm pressing, and I'm not going to be in a position to handle either until at least the summer."

"The time will go by fast, and maybe you'll be able to produce some new work in the meantime," Jason says.

"Yeah, I don't think I'll be able to work on anything large because standing takes too much energy right now, but I'm hoping I'll be able to sit and paint after Christmas."

I smile at the optimism in Will's tone. This is the first time he's mentioned painting or his artwork since his transplant. He's starting to plan his future again, and this time, no "when the cancer's gone" list is required.

"I think you'll be able to sit and paint for a few hours a day by the time the holidays are over," Jenny says. "Your cell counts should go up rapidly over the next few weeks."

"That'll be fantastic," I say, and Will grins at me.

We chat comfortably through the rest of the meal, and I'm pleased to see that Will samples a little bit of everything.

When it looks like everyone has finished, Elizabeth picks up her plate and stands. "Is everybody ready for dessert?"

"Wow, Mom, I don't think I can eat another bite," Will answers, leaning his head back and closing his eyes.

I glance across the table, and Jason is staring at me, a knowing look in his eyes. It only takes two seconds for me to realize we're on the same page.

"Come on, Will, let's go watch the Lions lose. At least this year, it'll give Seattle an extra win," Jason says, standing.

Will opens his eyes as a grin spreads across his face. "Sure. I really haven't watched any football this season. I didn't even think about it when I was in the hospital."

I smile gratefully at Jason, and he winks at me as he circles behind Will to help him up. Jenny, Elizabeth, and I watch as Jason helps Will to stand, and they make their way slowly across the living room. Will's movements are stiff, and he hisses a few times, reminding me that it's time for him to have more pain medication, among other things.

Elizabeth looks worried, but Jenny shakes her head and puts a hand on Elizabeth's arm. "He's fine," she mouths, smiling to reassure her.

Elizabeth forces a smile, and she and Jenny start on the dishes while I fetch Will's medications.

He's settled in comfortably by the time I make it to the living room, and honestly, if it weren't for how thin he is, I'd think it was just another day watching TV in the recliner. I give him his pills and a glass of water, and although I want nothing more than to stay right here, Thanksgiving dishes don't wash themselves.

"I need to go help with the dishes," I tell Will. "You watch some football, and I'll be in to sit with you in a little while."

"Thanks, Tori," he says, his gaze warm and soft. "Dinner was wonderful, and I'm having a fantastic day."

My heart soars, and I smile so widely I think my cheeks might split. "I'm having a great day too," I say, leaning in to kiss him before returning to the kitchen.

I look over on each pass as I clear dishes from the table, and Will is asleep within five minutes. We all expected as much, so we clean up quietly, then cluster on the opposite side of the living room to talk.

We all have a lovely afternoon together. Will is in and out of the conversation, taking catnaps as he needs to, but he's smiling all the time when he's awake, and he seems to really enjoy just being with everyone. We pull out the leftovers and throw together some cold turkey sandwiches in the early evening, and then everyone heads home.

I let Will sleep in the recliner while I straighten up a bit, and then I wake him for medication and all the other things we need to do to get him ready for sleep. When we finally crawl into bed, he snuggles up to me and buries his nose in my hair.

"Today was wonderful. The best day I've had in . . . God, I don't want to even try and figure out how long because it's depressing."

"Then leave it at, 'today was wonderful,'" I tell him, tipping my chin up to brush my lips against his.

Will hums, pulling me closer. "Okay, consider it left. Thank you though. I know it took a lot of effort to have a big meal and company over while we're still trying to sort out all my . . . details, but I really appreciate it. I just felt so alive today; I haven't felt that way in a very long time."

A thrill of pure joy tingles down my spine—Will really is coming back to life.

I kiss him, telling him with my lips how perfect he is and how head over heels in love I am with him. He resists for a second, but then he throws himself into the kiss, thrusting his tongue into my mouth and whimpering as I ravish him. The heat begins to build, but I break the kiss before it gets out of control, knowing he's too tired for anything more and not wanting to tempt him.

He pants quietly, trying to catch his breath. "Wow, what was that for?"

"Because you're the most wonderful man I've ever met, and I'm so in love with you," I tell him, pressing myself against his side.

Will chuckles softly. "Just wait, Tori. You ain't seen nothin' yet," he murmurs, and I fall asleep wondering what he could possibly mean.

CHAPTER 13

Day 39

I t's Tuesday afternoon, and I'm finally done seeing patients for the day. I hurry out to my car, eager to get home and see how Will's doing. Today is not a good day.

First thing in the morning is, hands down, my new favorite time of day. Will is always awake before me since he sleeps so much more, and for the last week, I've woken to soft hands and warm lips pulling me from sleep and into his eager embrace. He's happy and playful in the morning—we snuggle a bit, explore each other—I've even done a bit more exploring below his waistline with my hands and my tongue! It's like our little bubble outside of time—until reality sets in.

But not this morning. Today, I was the first one up, and when I kissed Will awake, reality was right there with us. He woke with a hiss and a groan, his joints stiff and aching, and I was out of bed and fetching him pain medication before we'd even said a proper good morning. And it didn't get any better from there. He had absolutely no energy, and everything was a struggle. I coaxed him into the shower where I did my best to massage away his soreness, and although he was grateful, his movements were still slow and painful even after a half hour under my ministrations and the steaming water.

The transfusion didn't help either. Jason and I got him to the hospital on time despite the shape he was in, and as the nurse hooked him up, I could see the eager light of hope in his eyes, but that's not the way it works. The transfusion staved off his dizziness and put the pink back in his cheeks, but the terrible soreness and fatigue remained.

I'm supposed to go to work and let Jason take Will home, but today, I wanted to stay with him. He was having none of that though.

"You just went back to work yesterday; you can't be taking off already! And besides, there's nothing you can do for me. I need to go back to bed, try to sleep this off, and hope tomorrow is a better day," he told me as we helped him into Jason's car.

"Go to work. Maybe I'll feel better by the time you get home," he said, doing his very best to convince me.

And so I went, but my thoughts kept straying from the patients I was seeing back to my own sweet patient, and I had to stop myself from calling to check on him a good half dozen times. Things had been going so well, I guess we were both surprised by today.

I arrive home to find Jason on the couch, but Will's nowhere to be seen.

Jason gives me a soft smile as I put down my bag and keys. "He's all right. He's still really sore, but he managed to fall asleep. He's been out since about two."

"Thank God for that. No new symptoms or anything?"

"No, and although he's frustrated, he's not upset. He knows what this is. He had days like this after both his previous rounds of chemo. 'Fatigue days,' he used to call them. Things should be better by tomorrow."

In my head, I know he's right, but knowing about 'fatigue days' and actually seeing Will have one are two totally different things.

"He'll be fine, Tori, honest," Jason says, coming over and putting an arm around me. "Do you want me to stay for a while?"

"No, I got this. Jenny told me you were going to make dinner for her tonight. A hungry Jenny is a scary thing, and I'm not going to be responsible for that."

Jason chuckles as he gives me a squeeze. "Okay. You call us if you need anything, all right? And I'll be back at eleven-thirty tomorrow."

"Thanks, Jason," I tell him, hugging him tightly.

"Anytime."

As soon as Jason's out the door, I head straight back to the bedroom and Will.

I round the corner and stop to take in the sight of him sleeping, as I almost always do. He's flat on his back, but his head is angled toward me. His arms are tucked under the white comforter because he's always cold, and his chest rises and falls in the steady rhythm of sleep. I raise my eyes to his strong jaw, which looks even more angular without a dusting of stubble, and I shudder, remembering what it felt like under my tongue yesterday morning. But my eyes are drawn to his lips, puckered into that perfect little pout that makes me want to straddle him and have my way with him. Do all men look like innocent little boys when they sleep? And how can he look sexy as fuck at the very same time? I never noticed before Will, so maybe I'm one of the lucky ones.

Taking a step toward him, something red on the pillow beside him catches my eye. It's a rose. Will left me a rose. Warmth bubbles in my chest, and I start to smile, but then, I freeze as panic shoots down my spine. We can't have flowers in the house. They can have bugs and mold and germs and, oh my God, if he gets sick because he wanted to do something romantic for me—

I lurch forward to snap up the offending article, and it nearly flies out of my hand, much lighter than I expected. It's . . . paper? As I pull it up to my nose, I realize it's not alive at all but an intricately folded piece of red paper, its stem made from green tissue paper-wrapped wire with an expertly folded green leaf sticking out of the side. It's exquisite.

The sound I make is somewhere between a chuckle and a sob. Will found a way to give me a flower without endangering himself. He didn't buy it; he *made* it, because what else would an artist do after all? But the part that has tears rolling down my cheeks is that he made it today even though he was hurting. Even though he felt like hell today, he was thinking of me.

Suddenly, my legs feel weak, and I drop down onto the bed, forgetting that I might disturb him.

Will winces, drawing in a sharp breath and scanning the room with those mesmerizing green eyes until he finds me. His features soften into a smile, but the skin around his eyes remains tight.

"Tori . . . are you all right?" he asks, grimacing as he pulls his hand out from under the covers to reach for me.

"I'm . . . You made me a flower." I stammer, holding it up as I sniffle and wipe at my eyes.

"Well, it's Tuesday, and this is the first one where I've been in any position to give you a flower . . ."

When the cancer's gone, I want to bring you flowers every Tuesday and maybe some days in between.

I make that chuckle-sobbing sound again as joy and pain twist my heart.

He drops his gaze. "You don't like it."

Gasping, I quickly grab his hand. "Like it? Will, it's gorgeous—one of the nicest things anyone's ever done for me."

"Then, are those happy tears?"

"Yes—no—yes . . ." I lay the flower down and move closer to him, caressing his cheek with my fingertips. "You amaze me. You're having such an awful day, and I was upset about that all afternoon, and then I come home to find that even though you're miserable, you were thinking of me and made me a flower? Where did you even learn to do that? I'm just—" I stutter to a halt, tears still streaming down my face.

"This is not quite the reaction I was hoping for," he says deadpan, quirking what would be an eyebrow if he had one.

I laugh and wipe my face again. "I'm sorry. I really do love it. I was already upset for you, and your being sweet on top of it threw me over the edge."

Will smiles, and warmth spreads through my chest and slows my tears.

"I think I understand now," he says, squeezing my hand. "First of all, I'm fine. Yes, I'm sore and tired today, but it happens after chemo. I don't like it, but I'm not worried about it, so you shouldn't be either."

I give him a watery smile, and he pulls on my hand, inviting me to crawl under the covers and curl up on his shoulder. Once I'm cuddled up next to him, he continues. "Second, it's only a little flower. I told you I wanted to give you flowers, and for some dumbass reason, I chose Tuesday, and I wanted to hold to that as soon as I could. I've been thinking about it for a few weeks, but I couldn't figure out how to do it since I have so many restrictions. But today it finally hit me. Mom taught me to make paper flowers when I was little to stop me from pulling up half the garden and making an ungodly mess just to give her a posy. So . . . I figured that might work for now. And making it this afternoon took my mind off the pain, so it was a good thing."

"It's not 'only a little flower,' Will. Well . . . not to me, anyway."

"What is it to you, then?" he asks, brushing his lips against my temple.

"It's beautiful and sweet and clever. You put more thought into this than any man ever has when doing something nice for me. And you did it to fulfill something on our 'when the cancer's gone' list, and other than my moving in here, it's the first thing on the list you've been able to do. So to me, it means that you're a romantic and you love me, and you're actually starting to get better, and you have hope."

Will shakes his head. "Damn, that's a lot for one flower to say! What'll happen when I make you a bouquet?"

I start to giggle, but he winces, bringing my thoughts back to his day. "Are you still in a lot of pain?"

He nods tightly, his jaw flexing.

"Do you want to go back to sleep? I can wake you later for dinner—"

"No, I'm actually wide awake, but I don't have the energy to do anything. Could we just—"

"Cuddle?" It's more of an offer than a suggestion, and he smiles at me gratefully.

"Yeah. I just want to hold you and talk to you, hear about your day."

I grin as his words touch me in places that no one really has before. He's so attentive, and he makes me feel important. "Okay, but why don't I get you your meds first? It's time, and I don't want you to be hurting any more than absolutely necessary."

His gaze softens and he strokes his thumb on my hip. "Thanks, Tori. You take such good care of me."

"I love you," I say simply, stretching to capture his lips. He winces again before I can even get there, so I change course and get up carefully instead.

He juts out his lower lip in a glorious pout, but I'm unmoved. "I'll kiss you after we get your pain under control. I promise. It's hard to enjoy it when you're wincing, and I know you're hurting."

Will sighs and nods.

I head to the kitchen to retrieve his suppertime medications. Now that he's been home a week, I know his med schedule like the back of my hand, and I'm no longer nervous about it. I pour him a glass of apple juice, then empty the pill sorter compartment into my hand. Only four. That's not too bad.

As I turn to leave, I spy the Raisinet bag next to the cookie jar. I grasp it between two fingers, smiling as I return to the bedroom.

Will's eyes are closed when I walk in, but they open lazily when he hears the familiar rustle of the bag. He raises an eyebrow at me.

"What? Bad days are what chocolate was made for."

"Who am I to argue with that?" Will asks, cringing as I help him sit up.

"Take your meds, then we'll try some chocolate and Tori snuggles therapy," I tell him, and he grins from ear to ear.

He takes all his pills and finishes his juice. Then I snuggle into his side, my hand in the Raisinet bag I've placed on his stomach. I know he's too tired and sore to move, so I feed him Raisinets as I tell him all about the afternoon's patients. I'm actually surprised I remember as much as I do since all my thoughts were focused right here in this room all day.

And that's how our evening goes. We chat and cuddle until I hear his stomach rumble, then I get up and reheat us some of the beef stew I made yesterday. I don't even ask if he wants to try to feed himself because I saw how shaky his hands were when I helped him into the bathroom earlier. His smile is a little sad as I feed him, but he knows it's not worth fighting it today. He's content to let me take care of him.

Thankfully, Jason was right, and Will *does* feel much better the next morning. He wakes me with gentle kisses to my temple, and he's playful and happy. And as the week goes on, his condition continues to improve. He still sleeps a lot, but he spends more time in the recliner in the living room than he does in our bed. And although he still puts his arm around my shoulder for his first stiff shuffle to the bathroom in the morning, he's started using his cane to get around during the day. God, the smile on his face when he first figured out he now has some independence! Watching him get stronger and make progress every day is like watching a flower bloom.

Speaking of flowers, when I get home from work on Friday, there's a bouquet of five red lilies waiting for me on my pillow. The paper he's used is different because there's a single white pinstripe down each lily petal, and this time, the stems are green pipe cleaners with a piece of yellow curling ribbon holding the bouquet together.

He's asleep in the living room when I find them, and my heart melts as I stand with my bouquet in my hand, watching the love of my life slumber like the angel he is.

I loved him just the way he was when he was sick, but now, there's so much . . . more.

Day 44

"Can I touch it?"

"No."

"Aw, come on!"

"No!"

"Please? Just for a moment?"

Will makes a frustrated noise and tries to keep from smiling, but he's hard-pressed. He's not upset; he's ecstatic his hair is starting to grow back. I'd thought his head felt a little rough over the last few days when I touched it in the shower, but he keeps his hat on almost all the time, so I really couldn't be sure. But today, all of a sudden, there's a fine coat of light-colored, barely-there hair. It feels like touching a duckling—all soft and fuzzy—and I can't keep my hands off it!

Will's ears and cheeks turn a delightful shade of pink, and he smirks as he pulls his hat off. I eagerly run the pads of my fingers over his latest sign of recovery, and he laughs out loud as I hum in contentment. We've had breakfast and our morning shower, and since it's Sunday, we came back to the bed to lounge a bit before doing anything else with our day.

"It's not *that* big a deal."

"Nonsense! It's a *huge* deal!" I exclaim, rubbing the side of his head as he closes his eyes. "You've recovered from the cancer symptoms, but your recovery from the chemo and the transplant are much harder to see. Now, all we have to do is look at your head every day! And personally, I'm planning to touch it every chance I get until your hair's long enough that I can run my fingers through it again."

"You like that, don't you?"

Now it's my turn to blush, but I'm not really embarrassed. I've accepted that I have a hair addiction, and Will's coppery locks are my drug of choice. "Maybe," I respond coyly. "When you were sick, it was one of the few things I could touch without hurting you, so other than your lips, it kind of became where I channeled all my . . . enthusiasm."

"Mmm . . . and I like your *enthusiasm*." He purrs, pulling me close so he can capture my lips.

The kiss builds in intensity until I feel as if I'm ablaze, and Will starts fumbling with the buttons on my shirt. I'm almost swept away, but I grasp his hand to still him.

He looks at me in confusion, but I need a minute to catch my breath before I can speak. "Hey, you already had a taste of my enthusiasm this morning, and I don't think you're ready for seconds. And besides, Jason will be here shortly."

"Jason? But it's Sunday. Why is Jason—"

"You'll see," I answer, unable to contain my grin.

Will narrows his eyes at me. "What are you two up to?"

"Me? I'm not up to anything."

He continues giving me the evil eye—does he really expect me to break? I just smile back at him.

"Well, you're in on it, at the very least," he says, pulling out the pouty lip.

I pluck at it with my thumb until his smile makes it disappear. "Sometimes secrets are a good thing. Come on, we should get up before Jason gets here.

"Oh, and you should put your sweatshirt on," I say, tossing it to him.

He raises an eyebrow at me, but I just shrug and look as innocent as possible. He smirks and shakes his head but pulls it on anyway.

As we reach the living room, there's a knock at the door, and I smile as I move past him to answer it. I glance to the right, but I'm careful not to turn my head so that Will doesn't notice. A large drop cloth-covered canvas sits propped against the wall near the dining room table—Jason's stealth mission while Will and I were in the shower was obviously successful.

I open the door to a grinning Jason and usher him in. "Your timing is perfect. We just came out of the bedroom," I tell him, gesturing toward Will, who's making his way to the recliner.

"Hey, Will. Don't sit down yet. There's something I want you to see," Jason says, hurrying into the kitchen to wash his hands.

Will stops in front of the recliner and furrows his brow, doing a quick scan of the room. His eyes fall on the canvas, and his brow furrows even further. "A painting?"

"No, something even better," Jason says, taking Will by the arm and leading him to one of the large living room windows.

I hold my breath, worried about his response, but the moment he glances down, his face is transformed by a radiant smile.

"Since we can't have visiting hours, this was the best alternative I could come up with," Jason explains, opening the window as far as possible.

Will takes the last few steps over to the sill, and as he leans against the low, narrow ledge, he's greeted with cheers from below.

I approach slowly and stand back with Jason, but I'm close enough to see there are a good twenty people down on the sidewalk, cheering and clapping.

"Hey, guys," Will calls, but he quickly looks back to Jason with the hugest grin on his face.

"Damn, Will, this is worse than the zoo," a male voice calls, and Will laughs loudly.

"Thanks, Jeremy; you always know how to make me feel better."

"You're laughing, aren't you?" Jeremy responds, and Will chuckles and shakes his head again. "We miss you at Trinity."

"I bet you do. I was the best DD you guys ever had. Don't worry; I'll be back at it soon. I think my drinking days are now officially over."

"How are you doing, Will?" a female voice asks, and my heart flutters as Will's smile remains and maybe even grows a little wider.

"I'm all right. I'm in remission again, and I'm hoping this time I'll stay that way. I'm still tired a lot and stuck in the apartment until my immune system recovers. It's not so bad though. I have a girlfriend now, and she's taking good care of me."

Will blushes as wolf whistles sound from below, and he beckons me over to him.

"This is my Tori," Will says, pulling me closer. "I'll bring her out as soon as I can so you can all meet her. Thank you, guys, so much, for coming to see me. You've really made my day."

"Oh, we're not done yet," Jason says, walking toward the canvas on the back wall. "We all made you something to brighten your days since winter in Seattle can be so gloomy."

With a flourish, Jason pulls the drop cloth off the canvas and reveals a gorgeous mural.

There are so many vibrant images to look at, but the Golden Gate Bridge draws my eye, and I realize they've painted San Francisco for him. A bright orange and yellow sunset casts its golden glow on the skyline, and the resulting shadows bring it into sharp relief. There are rolling hills dotted with cheerful-looking houses, and in the foreground, there's a park and a few brightly colored gatherings that look like festivals.

Will's breathing is shallow beside me, and he slowly stands so he can see the whole mural.

"They . . . You all did this?" he asks, casting a glance over his shoulder then back at Jason.

"Yeah. We've been working on it since your transplant took."

Will buries his face in his hand and sways a little, so I put my shoulder under his.

"We love you, Will! Get better soon!" Words of encouragement float up from the sidewalk, and Will gasps, overcome with emotion. He leans into me, and I support him while he tries to pull himself together. After a moment or two of shaky breaths, he lowers his hand and leans toward the sill again, so I help him sit.

"Do you like it?" the same female voice as before asks, and Will grins through his tears.

"Yeah, Kate, I love it. It's beautiful. I can't even tell you how much this means to me. It *will* brighten my days, even the bad ones. Thank you all *so* much."

"You just get better, Will," a male voice calls. "We're all pulling for you, and if there's anything we can do, let us know."

"I think you've already done it, but thanks, Ryan."

Will sways again—he's had enough, and it's time for him to rest. Ever watchful, Jason notices too.

"Thanks for coming, everyone. I think Will has a date with his recliner now."

"We'll see you again soon, Will!" "Hang in there!" "We love you, Will!" "Take care, Will!"

Will waves to them, and his smile is spectacular.

Jason puts his hand on Will's shoulder, and as Will moves to stand, Jason supports him, knowing how tired he is.

But Will didn't just want to stand up—he throws his arms around Jason and squeezes him tightly.

I back up a few steps, feeling as if I'm intruding on something private, but I still hear the words Jason says into Will's shoulder.

"They asked about you every time we all went out, but I never told you because you were in such a bad place, and I knew you felt they'd betrayed you. I didn't want to cause you any more pain. But I thought maybe now you were ready. They really do care, and they haven't forgotten you, even though they flaked a bit when you needed them."

"I . . . I don't know what to say. I thought they didn't care anymore. It was like the sicker I got, the less I existed."

"You were always in their thoughts, but I convinced them to give you some space because you had enough to deal with. I hope you'll let them back in now. They really are still your friends—if they weren't, they certainly wouldn't have taken the time to make this."

"Thank you, Jason," Will says, and the rest of the conversation doesn't take place out loud, but I can see all I need to.

Will's grin returns, but he's nearly stumbling as Jason helps him over to the recliner—that was the longest he's been on his feet since he left the hospital.

"Are you all right?" I ask as I tuck his afghan around him.

"I'm fine. Just tired," he answers, but as he closes his eyes, the smile still lingers on his face.

"Are you happy?"

"Yeah. That was really something. I guess there are more people who care about me than I thought."

How could anyone know you and not *care about you?* I think, shaking my head. Where we are now is such a far cry from where he was when I met him, alone and afraid. He did what he needed to do to survive his ordeal, but I'm so glad he now has the chance to see what his life is worth to so many others—few people get a second chance like that.

Will sleeps for a few hours after that, and when he wakes, he's cheerful and smiling.

The events of the day change something else, too. In the afternoon, he gets up to use the bathroom and is gone for so long that I get worried, so I head down the hallway in search of him. I find him standing in the doorway of his studio, leaning against the frame.

I put my hand on his shoulder, and he looks over, his lips turning up in a small smile.

"I think it's time I reacquainted myself with this part of my life," he says, glancing around the room. "I think my hands are steady enough most days that I could draw, and I'm still hoping by the start of the year, I'll be strong enough to sit and paint for short sessions."

"I think there's a pretty good chance," I tell him, nudging my shoulder into his so he wraps his arm around me. "And I can't *wait* to watch you paint."

"Oh?" he says, raising his sparsely regrown eyebrow.

I giggle as I lean my head on his shoulder. "Hell, yes! The mere idea of you creating things right in front of me—it's incredibly sexy."

Both eyebrows go up now.

"And besides, we have a date with a few of those paintbrushes, and I can't help but think about that every time I come into this room."

Will blushes, his grin all but confirming he's plotting mischief. "Well, I guess I better start training for that now," he says, leaning down to give me a scorching kiss. We spend the rest of the afternoon in the bedroom, doing our very best to build Will's stamina.

CHAPTER 14

Day 48

I open the door of the apartment to silence. I had expected Will would be in the recliner watching TV, but the living room is empty. Maybe he's taking a nap?

He's been home alone for a little while this afternoon. Now that he's up and around, we've been giving him a little time to himself before I get home since he's had people on top of him every minute for months now.

I drop my purse and keys on the kitchen table and head back toward the bedroom, but before I even get there, I can hear that he's vomiting.

Oh God . . .

I stop next to the dresser and put my hand on it to steady myself. I breathe deeply—I can't let him see my panic. There's no reason to panic. It could mean so many different things. Nothing and everything.

Pushing myself forward, I make it to the bathroom doorway where I take in the sight of Will curled over the toilet, his face as white as a sheet.

"Oh, sweetheart!"

He looks up at me, his eyes glassy and a little vacant.

I kneel down beside him and lay a hand on his forehead. "You're feverish."

"I know. I've been shivering for a while now."

"Why didn't you call me?"

He drops his head into his hand. "I wanted to, but it came over me so suddenly—I had to hurry to make it in here. I didn't grab my phone, and I've been too sick to go get it," he answers, clutching at his stomach and groaning.

"I'm sorry, Will. I'm just—"

"I know. Me too." Then he retches again.

"When did this start?"

"Um . . . maybe a half hour ago? Fuck!" He slaps his open palm against the wall next to him.

I caress his cheek, and he closes his eyes. "Hey, we can't panic. This doesn't mean the cancer has come back. It could be an infection, or . . . my money is on graft-versus-host disease from the stem cell transplant. Evans told us it was pretty common and to watch for these kinds of symptoms."

"I know. I'm just . . . frustrated. And so damn tired of being sick!"

"I know, sweetheart. But this is only a little bump in the road; I'm sure of it. Will you be okay here for a minute while I call the hospital, or do you want to go lie down?"

"No, I think I better stay here. I'm still feeling really nauseous."

As I leave the room, I hear him vomit again. *Oh please, God, please! Let this be something other than the cancer coming back!*

I take another deep breath. I have to keep it together because I'm the one in charge here. I have to get him to the hospital and try to keep him from panicking until we figure out what's going on.

As I expected, Jill tells me to get Will to the ER as soon as possible, so I call Jason next. The adrenaline is really kicking in now, and as I think of Will on the floor in the next room, my composure starts to slip. I grip my phone tightly as I hear him vomit again, and Jason picks up.

"Hey, Tori, what's—"

"J-Jason, I need your help. It's Will—"

Jason inhales sharply. "What happened?"

"H-he's feverish and vomiting. We have to get him to the ER."

"Oh *fuck*! I was just there! What the hell happened?"

"I don't know!" I yell, my voice rising in frustration. "He said he was fine, and then all of a sudden, he wasn't! Oh God, what if—"

"No, Tori, don't go there. He's fine. Everything's gonna be fine. Get him ready to go as best you can. I'll be there in ten minutes."

"O-okay," I answer, my voice quavering.

I end the call and wrap my arms around myself tightly, willing my body to get in line. Will needs me, and I can't be weak, not after everything he's been brave enough to get through.

The minute I round the corner to the bathroom, my own fears are forgotten because Will is a mess. He's still curled over the toilet, but I can see sweat on his forehead now, and he's shivering violently. He raises his eyes to me, wide with panic and terror.

"No, no, everything's going to be fine. Don't panic! I promise, sweetheart, it's going to be fine."

"I feel . . . awful." He pants between words, moaning and clutching his belly.

"I know, I know." I rub his back gently. "We're going to get you to the hospital and get this all straightened out. Jason's on his way, but we need to get you ready, okay? I need you to help me."

"I'll ... try," he murmurs, his fist pressed tightly to his forehead.

"Okay, I'm going to get your chair and bring it to the bathroom door, so all you have to do is walk the few steps to get there, okay?"

"Yeah," he says, but before I can stand, he grabs my hand and squeezes it, grunting sharply.

"Are you in pain?" I ask, trying to keep my voice from shaking.

"Yeah. I don't know ... how I'm going to stand."

"We'll do it together. But we need to get out of here, and the first step is for me to get your chair. I'll be right back."

"All right," he says shakily, and I dash from the room. We need to go as soon as Jason gets here, so I take a moment to grab Will's duffel bag and put a change of clothes and his medications into it. I also grab a trashcan and line it with a plastic bag—I think we're going to need it.

I position his chair in the bathroom doorway and kneel beside him.

"Okay, Will, it's time to stand up now. Tell me how to help you."

He swallows thickly. "Go ... slow. I'm so ... nauseous."

"We'll go slowly, I promise. Put your arm around my shoulders."

Will puts his shaking arm around me, and I can feel the heat radiating from it.

I start to lift him and Will gasps, biting into his lip. I get his feet under him, but when I try to straighten him up, he whimpers.

"Can't ..."

"All right, we can walk like this. Hold on to the wall if you need to."

"Can't," he says again, clutching at his belly.

Eyes closed, he takes one shuffling step forward and swallows ominously. He goes as still as he can, and I see his jaw flex.

"Tori!" Will gasps, and I get the trashcan under his chin just as he heaves. When he's finished, he's shaking even harder, and he brings a hand to his sweaty forehead.

My own breath is coming in gasps because other than during his chemo when it was expected, I've never seen him so violently ill. "Will, we have to keep going. We've got to get you help. As soon as I get you situated, I'm going to call an ambulance."

"N-n-no. No . . . ambulance. I left here that way last time, and I almost didn't make it back. I can't do it again."

"But—"

"Please, Tori. I can't," he says, his breath quickening as he raises desperate eyes to me.

Oh God, the last thing he needs right now is a panic attack. "Okay, sweetheart, no ambulance. Try to be calm, all right? Getting upset will only make you feel worse."

Will nods but regrets it instantly, clutching at his midsection and groaning.

"Let's keep going. You're almost there." I encourage him, setting down the trashcan and gripping the wall to steady us.

It takes us a few minutes, but Will manages to shuffle the last few steps to his chair. As soon as he sits down, he retches again, then hunches over, his arm gripping his belly.

Panic is still flaring at the base of my spine, and I want to press him about calling an ambulance, but he's pretty close to panic himself, and I don't want to throw him over the edge. So I bite my lip and give him the now-empty trashcan to hold, just in case, as I wheel him slowly into the living room.

As we reach the coffee table, Jason hurries through the door and stops in his tracks as he takes in the scene before him.

"Jesus, Will."

Jason looks to me, and I purse my lips and shake my head, hoping he'll get the message. He immediately looks down and closes his eyes, but Will doesn't even seem to have heard him.

Jason pulls it together quickly and comes to my side. "Why don't you grab whatever you need, and I'll stay with him?"

I can't answer him for fear of the sound that might escape if I try to speak, and I'm sure my eyes reflect the terror that's surging through my veins. But his gaze is calm and sympathetic as he grips my arm.

"It's okay. Everything's going to be okay," he whispers, and I can feel his calm spreading through me.

I take a deep breath and give him half a smile, then turn to gather up everything we need. Out of the corner of my eye, I see Jason put his hand on Will's shoulder, whispering soothingly to him.

Running through the apartment, I grab Will's bag and my purse and keys, and we begin the slow trip to the car. Will is so nauseated that he asks us to stop every few feet, trying desperately to keep from heaving.

Getting him into the car is an ordeal, but finally, he's lying curled up on the back seat, his head in my lap and the trash can on the floor between my feet. He clings to my thigh, his nails biting into my jeans.

He vomits again as soon as the car starts moving, and I run my fingers through his sweat-soaked hair to try to soothe us both. When he's finished, he groans, clutching at his midsection with both arms.

"Oh God, this can't be happening!" Panic is lacing his words and so clear in his eyes as his breathing accelerates.

"Hey, we don't know *what's* happening," I remind him gently.

"No . . . I *do* know. It's not only . . . fever and vomiting. The pain . . . it's so bad . . . it hurts like it did . . . when my liver and spleen were swollen. The cancer is coming back," he says, his voice breaking on a sob.

Fear trickles down my spine in an icy chill, but I fight against it. He's sick and he's terrified, so I have to be the one who looks at this rationally. "Your liver or spleen could swell from infection, too. Let's get to the hospital and let Jill check you out, okay?"

"Tori, I'm so sorry! It didn't work! I'm gonna die this time!" He sobs, and suddenly, he's hyperventilating.

"Can't . . . breathe . . ." He gasps, his breaths loud and frantic, and it takes everything I have not to go right along with him.

"Shh . . . shh . . ." I try to soothe him. "You're having a panic attack. But everything's going to be okay. Just listen to my voice—"

He's breathing so fast that he can't be getting any oxygen, and he goes rigid for a moment before slumping in my arms.

"Will? Will!" I scream as I place my fingers to his neck. After a second, I feel a thready pulse there. *Oh, thank God!*

"Tori," Jason calls from up front, terror in his voice.

"He's . . . all right," I say, out of breath myself. "He had a panic attack and passed out. You can go faster now—I think he'll be out for a few minutes."

Jason floors it, and I can't control the sobs that burst from my chest as I cradle Will's head in my lap. *What the fuck is going on?*

We make it to the hospital in record time, and Jason flies out of the car to get help.

Jill is the first one out of the building, and she opens the door on my side.

"Tori, what—"

"He needs Ativan and morphine right away," I tell her, trying to keep my voice steady.

"Morphine? He can't be hurting that badly if he's sleeping—"

"He's not sleeping; he's unconscious! He had a panic attack in the car, and he passed out!"

"Fuck! Okay, let's get him out, and we'll get the Ativan and morphine going. Then we'll sort this out."

Like two weeks ago, an orderly lifts Will out of the car and lays him on a waiting gurney. Will moans, and he's vomiting before his eyes are even open, taking the staff by surprise.

"Tori? Tori, what happened?" Jill asks, pulling me from the car and trying to get my attention.

My eyes never leave Will as I rattle off his symptoms, and as I watch him get sick yet again, I can't stop my own panic from taking over.

"He said the pain feels like when his liver and spleen were swollen. He's freaking out because he's sure the cancer's back. Oh God, is that really what this is?"

"Hey, it's gonna be okay," she says, putting an arm around me. "I don't think it's a relapse. This is too . . . violent for that. It's either an infection or graft-versus-host, and we can take care of both. Don't assume the worst, Tori. This looks scary, but I don't think it's as bad as it seems."

Her words comfort me, but I have no time to dwell on them because we've reached the isolation corridor, and Will's calling for me.

I rush to his side, taking his hand and stroking his cheek as one of the nurses starts a morphine drip and gives him a dose of Ativan. "I'm right here, sweetheart. We're at the hospital, and we're going to get you straightened out."

"Wha happn'd?" Will asks groggily, and I wonder if it's the fever or maybe disorientation from fainting.

"You're not feeling well, but the nurse gave you medication that's going to help. Let me hold your hand until it starts working, and then I'll explain everything, okay?"

Will nods, but he swallows thickly and grips his belly a little tighter. "'m nauseous . . . and my stomach hurts."

"I know, sweetheart. Just rest for a few minutes."

He's quiet for a moment, then he grimaces. "Fuck, this really hurts—" His eyes widen as he squeezes my hand. "Oh God, the cancer! Tori—"

"No, Will, Jill doesn't think so. But we'll have to—"

Before I'm even done speaking, Jill comes through the door with a nurse in tow.

"Hi, Will. I'm sorry you're feeling so poorly today. We'll get you sorted out. Can you tell me your symptoms?"

He's breathing faster again, and he winces as he curls an arm over his midsection. "Fever, nausea, and . . . fuck! My stomach hurts *a lot*. The cancer's back, isn't it? It has to be!"

"Now, now, it could be a few different things," Jill says, squeezing his arm gently. "We've given you morphine for pain and Ativan for anxiety, and now I want to take some blood to see what's going on. Can I give you an anti-emetic for the nausea and vomiting?"

"Yeah," Will answers, and that's when I know it's bad because he hates those drugs. "Throwing up feels like my stomach is on fire."

"Okay, we'll get that set up in a few minutes, and Dr. Evans is on his way down. We'll probably need to run a few other tests, but let's see what your blood work shows first. Don't worry, Will. I know this is scary, but you're going to be fine."

Jill gives him an encouraging smile, then she and the nurse leave the room with a few vials of Will's blood.

The nurse comes right back with yet another IV bag and adds it to the two already hanging from the pole and feeding into Will's central line. His eyes are closed, his face scrunched as he whimpers in pain.

"The morphine should start to work soon," I tell him, stroking the side of his face. "Can I do anything for you?"

"Water?" he asks, opening his brilliant green eyes to stare at me wearily. "My throat is raw from all the vomiting."

"Of course, sweetheart. I'll be right back." I almost get him a cup of water, but then I think better of it. He's been so sick he probably shouldn't have anything by mouth for a while, so I opt for ice chips instead. That should be enough to soothe his throat without upsetting his stomach.

When I return, his eyes are closed, and when he does open them, they're even glassier than before, and he smiles lazily.

He accepts the ice chips I put on his tongue, and he tries to stay with me even though the morphine is trying to knock him out.

"I don't . . . remember how I got here," he slurs, his head lolling to the side.

"We came in Jason's car, but you had a panic attack and passed out halfway here. That's why you don't remember."

"Oh, shit! 'm really f-fucked up, aren't I?"

"No, Will, you're gonna be fine. Right now you're high on morphine, but we're going to get the rest of this straightened out."

"Morphine? Oh. Ohhhh—" He moans as he grips his belly, swallowing hard and panting. "Gonna be sick," he mumbles, and I barely have enough time to get a basin under his chin before he's heaving again. *Goddammit.*

When he finishes, he's shivering. I help him lie back against his pillow and I pull his blanket up to his chin. *Shit.* I wish I'd thought to grab his afghan from the apartment.

"I'm s-s-sorry," he murmurs as I cup his cheek.

"Don't be sorry, sweetheart. You have nothing to be sorry about. This isn't your fault."

"D-d-didn't want . . . be here again. Don't wanna be . . . s-s-sick."

Pain slices through my chest, paralyzing and sharp, because things have been good for a while, and I'm no longer used to this. It takes me a moment to find my voice. "I know. I don't want you to be sick either. Why don't you try to sleep? I'll wake you when Dr. Evans gets here."

"'kay," he mumbles, and his breathing soon slows and evens into sleep.

I drop my head into my hand, trying to calm my *own* rapid breathing. *Jesus Christ, what a day!* Will was fine at lunchtime, and according to Jason, he was still fine at four-thirty. Poor Will! To get so violently ill so suddenly, all alone! But I know that's not why I'm still shaking. Jill's words comforted me, but the fear that this is a relapse still lingers in the back of my mind, making me tense and edgy. After all Will's been through and how happy he's been over the last few weeks, to lose it all now would be utterly devastating.

And not just for him.

He's my whole life now—my first thought in the morning as he kisses me awake and my last thought in the evening as I snuggle into his broad shoulder. I can *exist* without him—draw air into my lungs and go through the motions—but I can't *live.* He's breathed life into places I thought were dead forever after . . . my mother, and without him, it'll all turn into a vacuum, cold and dead. Without him, there's . . . nothing. Nothing for me to be and no one for me to care about—not the way I care for him.

I stifle a sob, desperate not to wake him, and Jason chooses that moment to poke his head in the door. He takes one look at me, and then he's kneeling before me, pulling me into his arms.

"Hey, did you hear something?" he asks, lifting my chin so he can look into my eyes.

I shake my head.

"Then we still don't know anything, and there's no reason to cry. I went to Jenny, and she thinks it's graft-versus-host disease. She said the symptoms of a relapse would be more gradual, not acute like this."

"That's what Jill said," I murmur tearfully.

"There, you see? Two intelligent women who know what they're talking about, both with the same opinion. They must be right."

I give him a watery smile.

"That's what I wanted to see. How's he doing?"

Taking a deep breath, I wipe my eyes and try to pull myself together.

"He's all right. They have him on morphine, Ativan, and something for the nausea. He was sick again after the morphine kicked in, but then he was able to fall asleep. Jill took blood to run tests, and we're waiting for Dr. Evans to come by."

"Everything sounds like it's in order, then. Can I sit with you?"

"You don't have to do that—"

"Do you really think I'm gonna sleep tonight until I know he's okay?"

I smile again and shake my head as Jason pulls up a chair.

The wait for Dr. Evans turns into several hours, and although Will sleeps for the first two, he's awake and vomiting again by the time Dr. Evans finally arrives.

Evans strides into the room, his expression softened with concern. "Hi, Will. I'm sorry to have kept you waiting. How are you feeling?"

Will opens his eyes to answer him, but instead, he vomits into the basin I'm holding. When he's finished, he lies back wearily against the pillow and closes his eyes. "Awful," he whispers.

"Well, it took me long enough to get here that your tests are already back, and the good news is, this isn't a relapse. Your blood work was clear as far as the cancer goes."

Oh, thank God.

Will squeezes my hand tightly, and his lips turn up in a small smile, although he doesn't open his eyes.

"But your blood work did show that you're having a graft-versus-host reaction, and that's what's making you sick. I want to keep you for at least a day or two to get you stabilized, and I'm going to start you on another round of immunosuppressive drugs."

Dr. Evans puts his hand on Will's shoulder. "This is fairly common for transplant patients, and one round will usually clear it up. You're still doing fine—this is only a little bump in the road."

I grin as Evans echoes the words I said back at the apartment.

"You should be feeling a bit better by tomorrow, and I'll come see you then, so we can decide if you get to go home, all right?"

"Yeah," Will answers, swallowing ominously, and I suspect we're in for a long night.

Sadly, I'm not mistaken. Will is sick through the night, and neither of us gets much sleep. His fever breaks, but his stomach pain and nausea continue despite the medication, and he can't keep anything down even though clear liquids are all they're giving him. He spends the next day in a morphine-induced haze, slipping in and out of consciousness and asking me again and again why he's here. My answer seems to be making him more upset every time I have to repeat it.

Dr. Evans is perplexed by Will's lack of improvement, so he orders an endoscopy in the afternoon. When he gets the results, he comes to see Will.

"The lining of your stomach is extremely inflamed—that's why the pain and nausea haven't stopped. I'm afraid we're going to have to give your digestive system a rest and a chance to heal, so I'm going to put orders in for nothing by mouth and IV nutrition. That should reduce your symptoms and give the medications a chance to work, but unfortunately, it means you're going to have to stay until things improve. I'd say a week, at a minimum. I'm sorry, Will. This bump is a little bigger than I'd originally thought, but you're still in remission, and your cell counts are rising nicely. And although it's miserable, this is a very good sign for your transplant—it means the stem cells we gave you are producing mature, fully functional immune cells. They'll be able to protect you as soon as we convince them that they and your stomach are on the same side."

Will closes his eyes and sighs, but I give Dr. Evans a warm smile. He doesn't have to try to cheer Will up, but Evans cares about him, so I guess it's second nature.

"Thank you, Dr. Evans."

He nods at me and squeezes Will's shoulder before he's on his way.

"Fuck." Will swears, but he's still too blitzed on morphine to really talk about it, and I don't want to upset him even more.

"Hey, this is no big deal. You'll be feeling better before you know it."

"Yeah," he says woodenly, his eyes still closed. "Tori, I'm tired. Why don't you go home tonight and get some real rest and come back in the morning? I'm still out of it from the morphine, and I keep falling asleep."

I look at him critically, but there's no way for me to tell if he's shutting me out or if he's really telling the truth. Maybe it's both, and he needs a little time to come to terms with this.

"All right, sweetheart, if you're sure you'll be okay."

My words seem to break through a bit because he opens his eyes slowly. "I'll be fine. 'm just tired," he slurs, and I decide to do as he says.

"I'll be here first thing in the morning." My heart breaks as I leave his hospital room. *Dammit*, this wasn't supposed to happen again! He's been doing so much better, and we've become so close, but now I feel like there's a wall between us, and I don't know what he's thinking. Hell, maybe *he* doesn't even know what he's thinking.

I turn the key in the lock of our apartment, and the darkness and silence that greet me are deafening. I've never stayed here alone before —my first night here was two weeks ago when Will came home. It's wrong to be here without him. For a split second, the thought of coming home without him permanently flashes through my mind, but I shove it away before the pain can well in my chest.

This is only temporary. Everyone says so. He's not that sick, and he'll be home before I know it.

I repeat the words as I clean up the dishes from yesterday and pick up his cane from our bathroom floor.

He's not that sick, and he'll be home before I know it.

I curl up on his side of the bed because the sheets still smell like him and add a "Please, God," before my mantra as it lulls me to sleep.

Day 50

I wake with a start, alone. *Where's Will?* And I'm . . . lying on his side of the bed. *Oh, fuck! He's back in the hospital.* The events of the last two days assault me, and I throw my arms over my eyes, trying to keep the tears at bay.

He's not that sick, and he'll be home before I know it.

The words have more power this morning than they did last night, but the tears still slide down my cheeks. Everything had been going so well. Why couldn't it have stayed that way? I allow myself a few moments of despair, but I can't afford to think like this. Of all the things that could have happened, this is actually the least dangerous. He doesn't have some life-threatening infection, and the cancer hasn't come back to claim him. He's miserable, but he's *safe*. His stomach just needs some time to recover, and then he can pick up right where he left off—getting stronger and putting his life back together.

But he *is* miserable. And today, he's probably going to be coherent enough to realize it. I need to be strong for him and help him keep what's happened in perspective. My breath catches as I remember the way we parted last night. I hope he's not going to pull away from me again and try to deal with this by himself. So much has happened since his decision to go through with the transplant. I don't know if I can handle his pulling back after we've become so close and learned to live as a couple.

As I walk up to the door of Will's room, the déjà vu is overwhelming, so I stamp my foot to snap myself out of it. *This is* not *the same. This is only temporary. Everything's going to be fine.*

Taking a deep breath, I put on a smile and push open the door . . . and my face falls immediately as my gaze falls on Will. He's awake, his chin angled to the side and down so he's facing slightly away from me. He looks broken, plain and simple. He's staring down at his blanket with the saddest look I've ever seen, and as I watch, he raises his hand and brushes a tear from his cheek.

"Will." He turns his watery gaze to me, and I dash across the room, throwing my arms around him and pulling him close. He whimper-grunts in pain, and I release him, but he doesn't let go, pulling me in more gently and resting his head on my shoulder.

"Tori," he whispers brokenly, and I run my fingers over his back, up and down.

Suddenly, my composure shatters, and I grip him tightly. "Oh God, you scared the shit out of me!"

"I'm sorry," he whispers, holding on just as tight.

I give us a moment, both of us soaking in the feel of the other before I pull back and cup his cheek in my hand. "How are you feeling today?"

Will snorts as his perfect lips twist into a frown, and he tries to pull away.

"No, Will, please. Don't pull away from me. Tell me what's going through your head right this second."

He looks at me, his green eyes stormy and desperate.

"I'm not pulling away, I just . . . I wanna go home. Thursday morning, I woke up in your arms, and today, I woke up sick and alone. I can't *be* here."

My teeth dig into my lip painfully. "Do you remember everything that happened?"

He heaves a sigh. "No, but I don't want to be here. Can't you take me home?"

I bite my lip even harder as my face scrunches to hold back a sob. "I want to take you home more than anything, but I can't do that right now. You have graft-versus-host disease, and it's inflamed your stomach. You can't even keep water down, so they have you on IV nutrition."

"We could do that from home," he says, his tone pleading.

"No, sweetheart, we can't. Well, maybe we could, but I can't give you your meds by IV all by myself, and they've added quite a few since you got here. That's the big issue, Will. You can't be throwing up your meds —they're too important, and since I can't give them to you by IV, you're stuck here until you can keep down your meds and enough liquid to keep you hydrated. Dr. Evans said your digestive tract needs to rest and heal, and the only way to do that is to bypass it for a few days. It won't be that long, and then you'll get to go home again."

"Fuck! I was fine! I'd even had some energy the last few days. What the hell happened?"

"Sweetheart, tell me what you *do* remember, and then I'll fill in the blanks, okay? I'll tell you everything I know."

Will's teeth grab his lip again. "I remember Jason leaving on Thursday, and suddenly, I felt awful, and I was running for the bathroom. I remember you finding me there and everything until we got to Jason's car, but after that, it's only bits and pieces. I think Evans was here, and he told us this wasn't a relapse, but it's all a haze of vomiting and pain, and I don't remember much of yesterday at all. I only know it's Saturday because you left my phone here beside me and it says so."

I run my hand from his temple to his cheek, and he leans into the touch. "No, it's not a relapse. You're still in remission; they checked your cell counts yesterday and everything looks good. It's only the graft-versus-host disease, and it's actually a good sign because it proves your new immune cells are working—they're just attacking the wrong thing.

"You don't remember the whole trip here because you had a panic attack in the car and passed out. You were terrified this was a relapse, do you remember?"

"Yeah," Will says, rubbing his forehead. "I really freaked out when the pain got so bad. I was sure my liver and spleen had both swelled up again, and I couldn't handle it."

"Of course you couldn't! I would have lost it too," I tell him, stroking his cheek. "You came around when we got to the hospital, but they gave you morphine, and that's why you don't remember yesterday. You slept most of the day, and when you were awake, you were high as a kite and not making much sense."

Will looks down and swallows hard. Then my heart stops as he raises those beautiful green eyes, now consumed by fear. He caresses my cheek with the back of his hand. "I'm . . . scared. I didn't think I'd ever be back here like this again, and I'm afraid I'll never leave."

I close my eyes and take a deep breath as his words echo my fears from last night and this morning. We both need to convince ourselves this is different—everything is different from the way it was before. But the thought that's almost enough to make me smile is that he confessed his fears to me. He didn't pull away and try to deal with it himself; he turned to me instead.

"Sweetheart, you're not 'back here like this.' Everything is different this time. You're not a cancer patient. You're in remission, and you're going to stay that way. You're only on this floor because you're immunocompromised, and this is the safest place for you. And you're not bedridden this time. You can get up and walk around, and as soon as you feel well enough, I think you should so we don't lose all the progress you've made. This time, you're only here so they can monitor your meds; otherwise, you could go home. Let's not treat it as if it's the same, okay? Nothing else is going to go wrong. This is not me coming to see a terminal cancer patient; this is me coming to see the man I love, who took a little detour in his recovery."

Will gives me a half-hearted smile as if he really wants to believe me.

I lean in and kiss him softly on the lips, then back away to see his smile grow a little wider. With my index finger, I tease at the corners of his mouth, grinning goofily, until he chuckles and gives me a true smile.

"*There* you are! I knew I hadn't lost you! How *are* you feeling today? Is your stomach any better?"

Will swallows hard, as if thinking about it has made it worse. "I'm . . . still really nauseated, and it still hurts, even with the morphine. It's not like before, though. Now it's a burning pain, like everything in my stomach is on fire."

He grimaces and wraps an arm around his belly. "I was so distracted, I forgot I had been feeling really sick." He swallows again and pales. "Oh fuck, I'm gonna throw up again. Tori, you don't need to be here for this."

I raise my eyebrows at him and laugh, and he gives me a confused look.

"I stayed with you through six days of high-dose chemotherapy. Do you have any idea how many times I held your head while you threw up?"

"No, I really don't," he says, swallowing noisily.

"Probably best that way," I say, patting his arm as he retches into the basin I'm holding.

He whimpers as he heaves, clutching his belly, and my heart breaks to see him in this much pain again. It's so reminiscent of the way things were before that I have to look away before the memories can overtake me. *This is not the same, this is* not *the same . . .*

When he's done, he collapses back against his pillow, the happiness I managed to coax out of him replaced by despair.

"Fuck! Why did it have to be my stomach? Haven't I had enough pain and vomiting already for one lifetime?"

I fight to hide my smile because it isn't funny, but his sarcasm is so much better than what I saw in his eyes a moment ago. Anything active is better than giving up, losing hope.

"Well, you actually got lucky that it's not your liver because with the damage you already have, it probably would have killed you. And you've definitely had enough rash and itchiness to cover several lifetimes, so I'm glad it isn't your skin either."

"I wouldn't have been able to touch you then, like this," I say, running my fingers along his jaw. "Or this." I pick up his hand and start to massage it gently.

Will closes his eyes, and his head rolls to the side, sighing in contentment.

I continue to massage up his arm, loosening his stress-filled muscles as I go. "Just focus on my touch. Imagine we're at home in the shower together. Can you hear the water running? Let the steam and the heat wash over you, and feel the tightness leaving your muscles under my fingers. Can you feel it?"

"Yeah," Will murmurs, far away from this hospital room, and I grin—he's better off than I thought he was going to be. I was afraid he'd plunge into depression as he did last time when he couldn't eat. But I realize he's stronger than that now—he's in a better place, and he wants what we have together, and deep down, I think he really believes he can be well again.

I massage his arms and legs for him, and by the time I finish, he's a puddle of goo.

"If my stomach didn't hurt so much, I'd be in heaven right now," he tells me.

"It should start getting better soon. This isn't like the cancer where you were always waiting for things to get worse. Dr. Evans is treating the problem, and you're going to get better."

His bright green eyes seek me out. "I'm sorry, Tori. I *am* trying to be positive. I can't seem to be anything but miserable right now."

"I know, sweetheart. I don't expect you to be positive when you're hurting. As long as you remember we're in this together, and I'm here to help you. You did that today, and it made me really happy."

Will smiles, but it turns into a grimace as he curls an arm over his poor stomach. "God, I hope this stops soon. I don't wanna be sick anymore."

Unfortunately, Will doesn't get his wish for a few days—the pain and nausea continue, and he's so uncomfortable that he stays in bed unless he absolutely has to get up. Finally, his discomfort eases late in the day on Monday, and he gets some much-needed sleep.

When I arrive on Tuesday morning, his mood is greatly improved, and he asks Dr. Evans about going home.

"It's going to be a little while yet," Evans tells him as Will tries to hide his disappointment. "Your symptoms have eased because the inflammation is starting to clear, but we still need to give your digestive tract a few more days' rest before we try to get it working again. And I won't lie; that part isn't going to be easy or pleasant. You're going to feel better for now, but when we start to introduce liquids again, the pain and nausea will come back. Once you're keeping water and your meds down, we'll let you go home, but it's going to take you a few weeks to get back to solid foods."

"Do you think he'll get to go home in time for Christmas?" I blurt out, unable to stop myself.

"Yes, I think he will," Evans says with a smile. "He's tough, and this is nothing compared to where he's been."

Will grins, his upbeat attitude returning. And I get the sense he's bored, now that he's not in pain, because when I return after seeing patients, Jason is with him, and there's a bouquet of eight multi-colored paper lilies on his little rolling table.

I grin as I realize it's Tuesday. Even in the hospital, Will has somehow managed to keep his promise.

On Wednesday morning, I bring him his charcoals and an empty sketchbook. "You said you wanted to start drawing again," I tell him. "Why should being in the hospital stop you?"

"You're absolutely right," Will says, giving me a brilliant smile. "I said I didn't want to be here, so I should stop acting like I belong here."

And that's exactly what he does. For the rest of the week, Will spends as little time as possible in his hospital bed. He walks whenever the nurses will let him, his cane in one hand and his IV pole in the other, and when he's tired, he sits in his recliner and draws or reads. I'm surprised to discover that Will is an avid reader since I never saw him with a book while he was a cancer patient.

"I tried to let go of everything when I thought I was going to die," he explains. "It was too hard to see all the things I'd be leaving behind, so I left them behind by choice. Except for drawing. I found I couldn't bear to leave my art behind, and by the time I asked you to bring my sketchbooks, I had some . . . *one* I really wanted to draw." He blushes, but the smirk he gives me is anything but shy—it's playful and adoring.

The days pass with Jason and Elizabeth coming by to cheer him and Jenny popping in during her shifts. Elizabeth and I take advantage of Will's absence and give the apartment another thorough cleaning, and before we know it, Dr. Evans orders another endoscopy and proclaims that Will's stomach has healed.

Will's ecstatic, but it doesn't last long because the first glass of water they give him results in instant pain and vomiting. The next week is trying for him because he's nauseated most of the time, and he brings back up more liquids than he keeps down. He's frustrated, but he fights through it like he did with his chemo, and finally he's able to keep down water and about half the liquid diet they're giving him.

Christmas is fast approaching, and I'm getting nervous, but Dr. Evans gives Will the go-ahead for discharge on December twenty-first. He'll have to come back if he can't keep down meds or if he becomes dehydrated, but after sixteen days as an inpatient, Will's champing at the bit to get out of here.

As soon as Evans leaves, I throw my arms around him. "I can't *wait* to get you home! Our first Christmas together! I'm so excited!"

"As long as it doesn't involve any food, I'm excited too," Will says, head in his hand.

"We'll get this worked out like we worked out your meds and showers and all the other things we had to do the first time. Once you're home, I have some new recipes to try. We'll find something that agrees with your stomach, don't worry."

"With you taking care of me, I never worry," he says, giving me his warmest smile, and at that moment, it hits me. There are no more obstacles between us—no boundaries. He trusts me completely and implicitly, and he's mine, just as I am his. I hug him again and bury my face in his shoulder so he doesn't see my tears because even though they're tears of joy, I don't think I can explain. Christmas just came early, but I think there's even more happiness to come.

CHAPTER 15

Day 66 – Christmas Eve

I clean up the remains of our Christmas Eve dinner—a big bowl of applesauce for Will, which is the only semisolid food he can keep down, and a ham sandwich for me—as he makes his way into the living room.

As I'm putting the ham in the fridge, I hear music coming from the living room, and when I close the door, I'm plunged into semi-darkness. I try not to smirk as I head for the living room—Will is definitely up to something.

The only light in the apartment is the Christmas tree, bathing the room in a soft golden glow. Will is sitting in the recliner, but just as he used to do in his hospital bed, he's shifted over so there's an empty space beside him. He grins wickedly and waggles his eyebrows, patting the spot beside him as a smooth jazz version of "Baby, It's Cold Outside" plays softly in the background.

I chuckle and cover my mouth with my hand as joy and love bubble up inside me. My God, could he *be* any more adorable and romantic? He raises his eyebrows high as if to say, "How can you possibly resist this?" and I'm done for—but I can dish it out as well as take it. I saunter across the room, swaying my hips a bit and giving him my best "smoky" stare, and I fight down my smile as I see his Adam's apple bob from a deep swallow. *Gotcha.*

But he's not done yet, and it's my turn to swallow thickly as his own gaze turns dark and steamy in the half-light. "We don't have a fire, but would you sit and enjoy this lovely Christmas tree with me?"

The lump in my throat is suddenly too big to talk around, so I nod as he raises his arm, and I crawl underneath it, curling into his side. He inhales deeply and lets out a sigh as I snuggle into him, his closeness warming my heart just as the afghan he's thrown over me is warming the rest of me.

He squeezes me a little tighter, and we both lie there holding each other and looking at the tree.

"You know, you really saved my life, Tori. You helped me to see past the narrow world I'd restricted myself to, to see what I could have if I was willing to fight for it. And now look where I am—where we are. I have a life again, with you, and I believe I can be healthy and strong again. You've given me the best gifts anyone can ever receive: love and hope. And I really *am* thankful every day for you."

"Will!" I gasp as I inhale sharply, tears welling in my eyes. I'm about to thank him for helping me to live again, too, until it hits me at the last second that he wouldn't understand. He still doesn't know that I wasn't really living before, or why, and now the lump of emotion in my throat isn't love, it's shame. I've kept this from him up to now because he's had enough of his own problems to deal with, but he's getting stronger and better every day. He needs to know me—*all* of me—even though it will be hard to burden him after all he's been through. But I owe it to him, and more and more, I *want* him to understand.

But not today. It's Christmas and this is a time for happiness, and right now, I don't want to relive my past Christmases that were ruined. I want to revel in the amazing gift I've been given—the wonderful man before me.

"Merry Christmas, Tori. I love you," he whispers, kissing the top of my head.

I don't trust myself to speak, so I look into his eyes, and the love that's reflected there takes my breath away. Will is so passionate, and I'm seeing it more and more every day as he comes out of the stasis he was in—as he again becomes the man he was before the cancer took over. I caress his cheek and move my lips to his, softly answering his words with my own silent declaration of love and saving and hope.

We begin slowly at first, our kisses warm, chaste, and adoring. But suddenly, he runs his tongue against my teeth, and it ignites a fire in my belly; we haven't kissed like this in more than two weeks. I plunge my tongue into his mouth, and his guttural moan makes my stomach twinge and flip, the fire turning molten. My fingers slide up the back of his neck and into the soft, downy hair that now covers his head—he's stopped wearing his hat since he got home from the hospital, and I've been longing to do this, but he's been feeling so sick that I've barely touched him. His own fingers caress my neck, pressing harder at my collarbone, asking permission.

"Yes," I murmur against his lips, and he slides his hand into my bra, cupping my breast before focusing his attention on my nipple. He rolls his finger over it until it forms a tight peak, and I gasp into his mouth. I feel his smile against my lips for a second before he goes back to plundering me with his tongue.

I scratch my fingernails against his scalp, pulling him closer, and he groans deeply when his arousal makes contact with my thigh. The sound is electric—it strikes me like a bolt of lightning and I clench my thighs as my center melts. I want to make love to him so badly I can taste it, but it's too soon, so I focus on his mouth, tangling and devouring.

He starts to rock against my leg, the friction pulling needy sounds from him. I palm over his erection, and he hisses and arches against me, throwing his head back and offering me the underside of his delectable jaw. My lips are drawn to the soft, smooth skin under the bone, and I lay eager kisses there, searching for the spot that drives him crazy. He gasps and writhes against me when I find it, and I lick and suck there, my clit beginning to pulse from the sounds of his pleasure. I continue to nibble as my hand slides over his erection again.

"Tori," he moans, thrusting into my hand. *His* hands are everywhere, scrabbling under my shirt and lifting my bra so he can fill them with tender skin as he seeks out my lips and kisses me with barely contained passion. A shiver tears down my spine—I'm high on this power I have over him, the way I can make him feel. I want *more. Now.*

My hand slips into his sweats as I kiss my way down his neck, my fingers itching for the feel of smooth, velvet skin. I graze the tip—

"Fuck!" He gasps, gripping my side and dropping his head to my shoulder. Oh God, I *need* to watch him come. I need to see him lose control, swept away by the pleasure I'm giving him. And I grin as I realize I have the power, and he's well enough for me to do it.

I sheath his cock with my hand and his hips undulate against me, his eyes squeezed tightly shut, his mouth fallen open in an "o." His cheeks are flushed, his breathing harsh and rapid, and I squeeze a little tighter on my next pass, my center pulsing and tightening as he lets out a glorious, guttural moan.

My clit is *begging* to hear that again, so I move a little faster, sliding my hand down the velvet steel of his cock and then pulling, drawing primal sounds from him as I reach the tip, squeezing and twisting as he bucks against me. My heart pounds in time with his frantic breaths, and as I start to stroke him faster and harder, he grasps my other hand tightly, his eyes locking with mine, desperate and frenzied with lust.

"Tori, touch yourself. Come with me, *please.*"

I nearly come right then as the rawness of his desire bleeds through his words and consumes me, twisting my center as my thighs clench and goosebumps erupt on my legs. I nod because there's no way I can speak, and I plunge my hand into my panties to stroke the throbbing there, so anxious for release.

I gasp as I press on the nub with two fingers, slowly beginning to circle as my breath hitches.

"Yes, that's it," Will croons, his voice rough and husky. I realize my other hand has stilled, so I stroke him again, and his head flies back and thumps against the chair.

"Oh, f-f-fuck," he murmurs, unable to keep his hips still, and I circle my clit harder as I glide over his shaft in an ever-quickening rhythm. I'm panting, but he's moaning more frantically with every sweep of my hand, my center tingling as the sounds of his impending orgasm drive me toward my own. He's completely wild, consumed by pleasure and aching for his release. And, oh sweet Jesus, it's the sexiest thing I've ever seen *or* heard!

As he moves against me, I can feel the tightening in his thighs, the erratic desperation of his thrusts as he hardens even further in my hand. "I'm so—oh, G-G-God, I'm gonna . . . come so h-hard." He stammers as he goes rigid, crying out as he pulses over my hand.

The sight and feel and sound overload me, and I explode, my walls contracting as my legs rock, and I shudder through the waves of pleasure. I'm adrift for a few minutes, but I can feel the smile on my face as I come down, and when I open my eyes, I'm plunged into a sea of brilliant green. Will is leaning back against the chair, but his half-open eyes are staring at me in wonder and adoration.

"Jesus," he whispers. "That was . . . fuck . . ."

I grin as my heart expands so much I swear it's going to burst out of my chest. "That was fantastic."

"Fantastic doesn't even begin to cover it," he says as his breathing finally starts to slow. He reaches up and caresses my cheek, and it's one of those moments—the kind you remember forever. He's amazing and he's beautiful and he's mine; he's all I need—all I want—forever.

"I love you," I tell him, but the words seem inadequate, so I lean forward and gently brush his lips.

"I love you, too. Always and forever," he whispers. No matter what tomorrow brings, I've already had the best Christmas ever.

Day 67 – Christmas Day

I wake slowly, warm and cozy and comfortable. *Will's home.* And yesterday, we finally found something he could eat, and we had a romantic and steamy Christmas Eve. I roll to my side and open my eyes, expecting to see my favorite pout, but the space beside me is empty. I sit up, listening for any sound from the bathroom. It's quiet, but I crawl across the bed anyway and peer in, at once relieved and worried when I don't see him there. *Where the hell is he?*

I'm in the process of crawling back across the bed to get up and search for him when the bedroom door opens, revealing Will carrying the tray I usually serve him breakfast on.

He swears under his breath as I hop out of bed, take the tray from him, and set it down. But the minute my hands are free, he pulls me into his arms. "Merry Christmas, Tori," he murmurs, smiling and leaning in for a tender, chaste kiss.

"Merry Christmas to you! What have you been up to?" I ask as he shuffles over to the bed and slowly sits down.

"Well, I woke up early and I was hungry, and I figured I'd better do something about that before it turned into nausea. So I got up and ate some applesauce, then I sat for a bit until I had the bright idea that I could make *you* breakfast this morning. So . . . ta-da! I'm no chef, but I *can* spread cream cheese on a bagel."

I look down at the tray beside him, and indeed, there's a bagel with cream cheese along with a small bowl of fruit and a bouquet of origami poinsettias. "You made me flowers!"

"Well, it *is* Tuesday," he answers, shrugging. "I made you coffee, too. Only I didn't trust myself to carry it with no hand to use for balance. Let me go get it for you."

He rises stiffly, grimacing as he straightens, and I'm filled with warmth and gratitude for all the effort he's put in. "I've got a better idea. Why don't you crawl back in bed and rest, and I'll go get the coffee, then sit here and have my breakfast."

He frowns, so I put my arms around him. "This is fantastic, sweetheart, truly. I just don't want you to wear yourself out."

He leans down and captures my lips, and instantly, there's nothing but him. He's gentle but insistent, so I open to him, our tongues seeking and tangling. Memories of last night flash through my mind—he was so passionate and *alive*—I can't wait to see what he'll be like when we can actually make love, and better yet, when he's fully recovered. The memories morph into fantasies—God, the things I want to do to him—and I moan into his mouth as I pull him against me.

He groans in response as his erection presses against my thigh, but he pulls back and looks at me quizzically. "Whoa there, tiger. What's gotten into you this morning? I thought you wanted breakfast?"

"I do, but I was thinking about last night."

"Oh," Will says, an adorable blush flooding his cheeks.

I laugh and swat him playfully. "Last night was amazing, and I was thinking ahead about what some other nights might have in store for us."

"Well, I like the way you're thinking, then," he answers, smirking. "But go get your coffee because I wanna open Christmas presents." He's literally bouncing in place, he's so excited. *He's like a kid on—well, it* is *Christmas morning*, I remember, giggling.

"Who says you got presents?" I ask, running my thumb under his chin.

"Okay, then I wanna give *you* presents!"

I stop and stare. "You got me presents?"

He rolls his eyes dramatically. "Of course, I got you presents. It's Christmas!"

"But you've been in the hospital for the last two weeks—"

"Well, I had a little help, but I've had plenty of time to think about what I wanted to give you," he says, his eyes dancing. "Go get your coffee. I'll stay here and rest like a good patient."

He shoos me out of the room, and I shake my head as I walk down the hall. *What did he get me that he's so excited about?*

When I return, he's resting as promised, but he sits up against the head-board and grins at me the whole time while I eat my breakfast. I coerce him into letting me at least brush my teeth before we open presents, and he grudgingly agrees.

After I finishing freshening up, he pats the space in front of him, and while I can still see the excitement in those bright green eyes, I can also see . . . a little nervousness?

As soon as I sit down, Will produces a small box from behind his back, expertly wrapped—as if I would expect anything less from the man who makes me bouquets of flowers out of paper. His hand is shaking as he holds the box out, and I take it tentatively in both hands.

It's jewelry-light, and for about ten seconds, I panic that it could be an engagement ring—but no, he wouldn't do that this way, and I don't think either of us is ready. I look up at him, and he raises his chin to encourage me, his nervousness now written all over his face.

I rip the paper off quickly to reveal an off-white velvet box, and I take a deep breath, then open it. *Oh my!* It's a necklace! It's a red-purple gemstone carved in the shape of a heart, mounted and strung on a gold chain. *It's gorgeous!*

"The stone is alexandrite—my birthstone. I've given you my life, so I thought now it was time to give you my heart."

My breath catches, and I look up at him, tears already welling in my eyes. I can't believe that this man before me, who once didn't want me to know any more than his name, is giving himself to me so completely.

Suddenly, he lowers his eyes to watch his fingers play with the comforter. "That's cheesy, isn't it? I just thought—"

"No, it's not cheesy at all! It's the most romantic thing anyone has ever done for me. I love you, Will, and I want to have your heart and your soul and . . . anything else you're willing to give me! It's perfect."

He raises his eyes, and the smile he gives me is radiant and joyful. "Really?"

"Yes, really! Will you help me put it on?"

"Of course," he says, and I take it out of the box and hand it to him. He struggles a bit with the clasp, but he gets it open before I act on the urge to take it from him.

I turn around, and my heart nearly explodes from the look in his eyes. There's so much love there, I don't know what to do with it all.

"My heart looks good on you," he says playfully, and I laugh as I throw my arms around him.

"Everything of yours looks good on me," I answer, glancing down at his t-shirt that I wore to bed last night. "Thank you, Will, this is gorgeous. What an amazing gift!"

He beams at me. "That one I had help with, but this one I did all on my own," he says, turning slightly to retrieve a piece of Bristol board that was lying face down behind him.

I flip it over, and oh my God, it's a drawing of me! I've seen Will's drawings of me from his sketchbook, but this one isn't in charcoal; it's in color. The warm brown of my hair and eyes seems to jump off the page, and my lips and cheeks are a delicate shade of pink. He's captured me perfectly and in exquisite detail. *Wow, he thinks I'm this beautiful?*

"I couldn't really wrap it," he says, his fingers again busy.

"When did you—"

"When I was in the hospital. I asked Jason to bring me my Prismacolors so I could capture you better. I simply can't convey those brown eyes I get lost in in black and white."

I cover my mouth with my hand as my pulse starts to race. I can feel his love for me radiating off the page, and it's the most amazing feeling. Tears well in my eyes, and I struggle to hold them back. "Will, this is incredible! I can't— How do you *do* this? This is so perfect, I can't even—"

Abruptly, I give up trying, set the picture to the side, and climb into his lap, straddling him. I take his face in both my hands and kiss him for all I'm worth. Words can't express what I'm feeling, but maybe I can show him. My face feels wet, and I realize I'm crying, but I keep right on kissing him—using my body to say what's in my heart.

I sob against his lips, and Will grips my arms, pulling back quickly. "What is it? Are you all right?"

"Yeah. I'm just . . . happy," I say, sounding utterly pitiful, but I give him a watery smile.

"All right, then. Bring on the presents!" he exclaims, his smile spectacular. Damn, he's so adorable this morning, I can hardly stand it! I love seeing him like this, and it seems to be happening more and more the better he feels.

"Okay," I say, going to the closet and pulling out three wrapped boxes. I hand him the middle-sized one first, and he shakes it, but it makes no sound. He tears the paper off eagerly, then opens the box and rummages through the tissue paper. He chuckles as he holds up a t-shirt that says "I'm an artist. What is your superpower?"

"I saw it and couldn't resist. It reminded me so much of our discussions about comic book artists."

"Well, I guess if I had to name my superpower, it *would* be that I'm an artist," he admits, grinning. "I love it, Tori. Thank you."

I smile back at him, but my stomach is starting to knot with nerves. The remaining two, I'm not so sure of.

Next, I hand him an oblong box, and his brow furrows as he looks at it. It looks the right size for a wine or liquor bottle—is he wondering if there's alcohol in there? He knows I know better than that!

He shrugs and tears off the paper, and while I *have* put the item in a wine box, when he opens it, he pulls out a cylindrical object made of soft, light brown leather, held closed by a wraparound strap. He glances up at me, and I raise my chin this time, encouraging him to open it.

He flicks the clasp and unrolls it to reveal a selection of paintbrushes and tools, each inserted into its own slot.

"I thought it would be good for when you can paint outside again. Jason helped me with the supplies. He said you could use some new brushes since yours have sat unused for so long."

He stares at it, lost in another world, and after a few minutes, I start to get worried. Finally, he looks up at me, his gaze serious but peaceful. "Thank you, Tori. It's perfect." He still seems distant, as if I've stirred some deep emotion. I hope I didn't go too far somehow.

He glances at the final, large box, and now I'm *really* nervous. If that one got him upset, what will this one do? With slightly shaking hands, I hand it to him, and he tears the paper off slowly to reveal two blank canvases.

I take a deep breath, trying to steady myself before I begin. "I got you these because I know you're planning to start painting again now that you're home. When I thought about it, they kind of represent your life —you've been given a chance to start over, with a blank canvas in front of you to fill in however you wish. I knew you'd be starting smaller, so I thought these might be a good size. One is for you, to paint whatever you want on it as your first work in your new life. The other one is for me. I don't care what you paint on it, but I want to watch you work on that one because I love watching you create."

Again that deep emotion takes over his eyes, but he sets aside the canvases and leans in to hug me. He holds tight and buries his head in my shoulder, and he whispers "Thank you" against my collarbone. I rub his back gently and whisper back, "Merry Christmas, Will." He stays like that for a few moments, and when he sits back up, the sea of green is warm and tranquil.

"Do you have any idea what you might paint?"

Will looks down, a small smile on his face. "I have an idea for one of them."

CHAPTER 16

Day 76

I wake to soft kisses on my cheek, and I smile as I stretch innocently, tilting my head so my neck is more exposed. Warm lips slide over my jaw and tuck in under the bone, searching for that one certain spot—I cringe and stiffen as goosebumps shoot down my leg, and Will's deep chuckle reverberates underneath me.

"I love that." He purrs as I giggle and roll toward him, finally opening my eyes to be dazzled by my morning dose of brilliant green. Will's eyes sparkle with mischief as he watches me—playful and happy, and so much closer to whole.

Things have been going well since Christmas. Applesauce ended up being Will's turning point toward solid food again, and since then, he's been adding more and more items to his menu. There have been some incidents—eggs in particular didn't work out well—but he's now able to eat plain breads and pasta, and most fruits and vegetables. It'll still take a while before he can have dairy and fats, but the nausea is mostly gone, and he can eat more than a few bites at a time. As I watch him smiling at me this morning, I think the hollows in his cheeks look like they're filling in, but it's probably still too soon for that.

"What?"

"Nothing." I raise my finger and stroke the furrow in his brow until it disappears. "I was just thinking how much I like waking up this way with you."

He grins, and the twinkle in his eye and the sudden pink in his cheeks make my chest tighten and warm. "I like waking up with you too, but today, we actually have to get moving. You need to go to work this morning."

Oh, *shit*. That's right. I'm supposed to start going in at ten on days when Will doesn't have to go for a transfusion. I had been working only afternoons between Thanksgiving and Christmas, but now that he's so much better, we decided I should go back to at least a six-hour workday. I frown, but right away, there's a finger pulling at my lip until I can't help but smile.

"Hey, it's only six hours. And I have stuff to do today. I'm going to go into my studio this morning."

I raise my eyebrows at him, and he gives me his shy, little-boy smile. "That's a great idea, sweetheart! Do you think you'll try to paint today?"

"Yeah, I think I might, if I can get the space set up so I can use it. Since I can't stand for long periods, I'm hoping I can figure out a way to paint sitting down."

"That sounds like a good plan." *Oh my God, he's going to paint!* I whisper a silent prayer that this works for him; he could really use the boost after how sick he's been. And, oh, just the thought of watching him create! I adore watching him draw—he finally let me when he was in the hospital in December. As fantastic as that was, I know seeing him paint is going to be on a whole different level.

My thoughts are again interrupted by his lips—warm and soft as they press against mine. "Come on, let's get up. I'm hungry."

I shake my head and chuckle at him. Things are becoming so . . . normal. He still takes a lengthy afternoon nap, but he's steady on his feet, eating well, and he's not nearly as sore. He still has bad days, but he's had a few that were fantastic, and it's done so much to improve his outlook.

I roll out of bed but let him hobble into the bathroom first—he's still stiff first thing in the morning until his muscles and joints have a chance to loosen up. He can pretty much do for himself at this point, but he needs to take things slowly and rest often. I scurry off to use the hall bathroom so I can get a jump on his breakfast. It's not that often he tells me he's hungry.

We eat and shower, and I dawdle through getting ready for work because ten o'clock really isn't that early, and I don't want to leave him today after our lovely holiday together. He lies on the bed while I pick through the closet, and when I finally turn around with my selections, I nearly drop them as I take in the sight of him.

He's lying on our bed as he so often does, but today it's . . . different somehow. He's not lying there as if he's sick or sleeping but as though he's casually flopped himself down. He's wearing a short sleeve white t-shirt and jeans, and his arm rests casually over his now-flat belly. His other arm is cast to the side and bent at the elbow, resting against his forehead as he lies, head turned, watching me. The hair on his head is still short, but he's growing out the stubble on his chin, and his newly grown arm hair stands out dark against his t-shirt. He looks . . . hot— hot like I remember from those first days he smiled at me, and hot like I've imagined as I've waited for the pall of illness to let him go. His gaze is intense and heated, and my eyes widen as I freeze like a deer. *Oh, wow.*

Slowly, the hint of a smile warms the corners of his mouth, and I am *done for.* I drop the clothes I'm holding and crawl up from the bottom of the bed until I'm kneeling in the crook of his arm, and I take his face between both my hands and kiss him soundly. He grunts in surprise, but it quickly turns into a lusty moan as I thrust my tongue into his mouth, shivering with the need that blooms deep in my belly. I want him so badly—the stronger he gets and the more recovered he looks, it's easy to forget how fragile he still is, how defenseless to infection. But

I'm counting the days until Day 100. Twenty-four left to go, and if things keep going the way they are, he'll be cleared to touch me. And boy, do I plan on having him touch me—intimately and repeatedly.

We kiss until we're both panting for breath, and when he finally pulls back from me, his smile is spectacular. "Wow, what brought that on?"

"You," I answer, smirking at him. "Lying here all hot and come hither while I try to get ready for work."

"'Hot and come hither,' eh? That's a new one. When did I get that look?"

"About five minutes ago, as near as I can figure. And I'm thinking you should patent it—it may set records for how fast it can make me drop what I'm doing and jump you."

He laughs, sweet and deep, and my heart swells to near bursting.

"I'll take that under advisement. But as much as I'd like to explore what else my 'hot and come hither' look can do, right now I really should leave so you can get ready."

"You don't have to leave."

He cocks a sexy eyebrow at me. "Your clothes are on the floor, and you just tried to suck my tongue down your throat. I need to go."

"Okay, okay." I try to pout, but my lips betray me, and I grin anyway.

"Come kiss me before you leave," he tells me as he slides off the bed, grinning as if he's terribly pleased with himself.

When I finish getting ready, it doesn't take me long to find him, but I pause in the doorway of the studio to witness what's unfolding before me. Will is standing in front of one of his easels near the window, his back to me. He's lowered it so it's at a height where he can work sitting down, and he's pulled over his office chair from the corner and lined it with a few pillows from our bed. There's a canvas attached to the easel, but it's not one of the ones I got him. As I watch, he goes to the table next to the easel, and I spy the brush roll I got him for Christmas. He slowly unrolls it and begins examining the brushes one by one, holding them up to the light, then stroking a finger over the bristles to feel their texture. Watching him like this does strange things to my belly, little twists and flips of love and pride and heat. He's in his element at this moment, and it's something I've never seen. It's beautiful to behold.

He selects two brushes and lays them out, then steps to the side and stands, looking down at something. He caresses it with his fingers. I can't help but gasp when he picks up the palette that brought me to my knees all those months ago when I first truly glimpsed the depth of his creativity and talent, when I realized exactly what this world would be losing when he met his untimely death.

He startles and turns, his eyes widening as he takes me in, and he's across the room in an instant. "Are you all right? You look like you've seen a ghost!"

I chuckle-sob as a few tears escape. I have no intention of telling him how close to the truth he is.

"I'm fine," I say, swiping at my face hastily. "I'm just so happy you're able to be back in here, doing what you love."

"Well, that remains to be seen, but I'm going to give it my best shot."

I pull him into my arms and kiss him, thanking God again for the amazing gift I've been given in this sweet and wonderful man. But I need to go and let him do this for himself. "I should go. Good luck today. I hope you're able to work for a while and that it makes you happy."

"Oh, I'm already happy," he tells me, giving my waist a squeeze. "Have a good day, and come back to me as soon as you can. I'll miss you."

"I'll miss you too," I say, giving him one more kiss before I finally turn for the door.

The clock ticked in reverse today. I swear I saw it when I was with my two o'clock patient. I was listening, but I'm sure I saw that little hand move backward instead of forward. Maybe the fact that I spent the day thinking about Will painting had something to do with it. When four o'clock finally arrives, I hustle out of my office, anxious to find out how his day went. He was so excited and hopeful this morning—I hope he was able to do at least a little bit today.

I slip into the apartment quietly in case Will is sleeping, but the living room is empty. Putting down my bag and keys, I head down the hall and check our bedroom, but he's not there either. That only leaves one place, I realize, as my stomach does a nervous, excited flip.

I creep across the hallway, and as I approach, I can hear the soft strains of a violin floating from the room. Warmth and excitement pulse through me, and I close my eyes and draw in a deep breath, steadying myself for what I'm about to see. I've dreamed of seeing Will paint for months now, and I'm finally, *finally* going to get my wish.

It takes me a minute to get up the courage, then I slowly peek around the doorway. Will is standing in front of his easel, turned almost in profile toward me as he leans down, brush in one hand and palette in the other. He's changed since this morning—he's wearing an old pair of khakis with paint splotches on them and a sleeveless undershirt. My eyes follow a line from his hand, poised over the canvas, up his lean, smoothly muscled arm to the smattering of freckles on the top of his shoulder. He's absolutely stunning. I stare for a moment, watching the muscles ripple on his back as he moves the brush, until my eyes are drawn to his face. His concentration is absolute—his keen eyes focused on the gentle brushstrokes he's making, and I see his tongue poke out between his lips a little as he pauses.

I startle as he straightens up, but he's still completely absorbed in what he's doing and doesn't notice me as he sits down on the office chair and rolls it closer to his canvas. And finally, my eyes leave the masterpiece that is Will to take in what he's working on.

The entire canvas is already covered with paint, but it's indistinct and flowing. The top is shaded in blues, but it bleeds to mostly dark green in the middle and then a lighter, vibrant green at the bottom. Will is concentrating on the bottom right corner, and as I take a step closer, I see that he's painted a small area of water, and he's dotting rocks onto a riverbank. It's as if a camera lens has come into focus over that portion of the painting. I watch, mesmerized, as he finishes the rocks and picks up the smallest paintbrush I've ever seen. He dips it in green paint, and begins to painstakingly add individual blades of grass. It's like watching the hand of God as the picture comes to life before my very eyes—as *he* comes to life before my very eyes.

I drink him in as he creates, noting the curl of his thumb and index finger around the palette and the nimbleness of his long, thin fingers as they caress the brush and direct his featherlight, precision strokes. Emotion is building deep within me—powerful and intense—making my chest constrict and my stomach clench. He pauses, pulling the brush back and cocking his head to the side, and as he turns a little, I can see the tip of his tongue poised in concentration.

He begins again, and as his brush moves, I hear his warm, velvet voice humming along softly with the music, and my emotion reaches a crescendo along with the violin solo. I cover my mouth with my hand to keep from making any sound, but I'm overwhelmed by . . . love, pride, and such a vast and uncontainable joy that I can barely keep it in. This is Will—who he is, what he does—the person he is without cancer. The person he was always meant to be, and who he gets to *keep* being, now that he's healthy again, and I am desperately, hopelessly, and irrevocably in love with him.

I stand there forever, spellbound by his creative energy as he makes the meadow in his painting come alive with lupine and delicate purple blooms until suddenly, the spell is broken as he leans back against the chair, eyes closed. My sweet, breathtakingly amazing artist isn't fully recovered yet, and he's pushing himself too hard. I cross the room and put my arms around him from behind, startling him, but he recovers quickly and leans his cheek against my arm.

"Hello, sweetheart. You've been busy today."

"I have," Will says, grinning up at me. "It's been fantastic to get back in here and actually work on something."

"And what is it you're working on? This isn't one of the canvases I got you for Christmas."

"No, it's not." There's a mischievous smile on his face. "I have plans for those, but I wanted to start with something simpler and more relaxing for my maiden voyage back into painting."

I raise my eyebrows as I glance at what he's working on. "If this is simple and relaxing, I can't wait to see complicated and intense."

"You will," he says, grinning even wider. "But this . . . I want to take you here someday."

"Oh my God, it's an actual place?"

"Yes," he says, leaning against me again. "It's a few miles south of Cauterets, in the Pyrenees Mountains in the south of France. I'm sure I could find it again."

My chest expands with happiness as I realize he *can* take me there someday. By this time next year, he'll be well enough to travel, and we can go anywhere we want. He can show me all the amazing places he's been, and we can go to the cities he told me he wanted to paint. I lean down and kiss his cheek, smiling against the scruff I feel there. "That would be absolutely fantastic. I would love to go to Europe with you."

He smiles, but his eyes fall closed as he leans into me.

"Are you ready for a break? You've been at this for a while now."

He quirks an eyebrow. "You didn't just get home, did you?"

"No." My cheeks heat as I admit my transgression. "I've been watching you for a while."

"I get so absorbed in what I'm doing that I lose track of everything else. I had no idea you were back there."

"Well, I didn't want to disturb you, so I stayed as still and quiet as possible. But I've been here long enough to know you're getting tired."

He sighs heavily. "You're right. I am. I think I've reached my limit for today. I was in here this morning until Jason showed up, and then I rested after lunch and came back in about an hour ago."

"That's a long time for your first day."

"Yeah," he says, grinning sheepishly. "Like I said, I lose track of time."

My stomach does a giddy flip as I feel his smile against my cheek. Happiness is radiating off him even though he's tired. I reach down and take his palette from his hand, holding it reverently, and I can't help the crease that forms in my brow.

"What is it? You had that same look this morning when I was getting my things ready to paint."

"I came in here a few times when I was checking on your place while you were in the hospital. Seeing your work, this room, was hard when—"

"—when you thought I was going to die." He finishes for me, standing and squeezing my shoulder.

I nod and glance down at the object in my hand. "This, in particular, was hard to see because to me it embodied all your work—who you were."

He smiles as he takes it from me and walks over to his worktable, laying it on the edge and putting his brush down before returning to enfold me in his arms. "Well, it's still who I am, and I'm not going anywhere," he says, kissing me softly.

My lips move eagerly against his, and the memory of falling on my knees on this floor fades, crowded out by the feel and the taste of the man I love. We kiss for long moments until I pull away, and Will sways on his feet as he closes his eyes.

"Come on, let's get you settled in the recliner, and I'll make us some dinner. You've put in your day's work for today."

He just laughs and grins at me as he drapes an arm over my shoulder—for support or out of love, I can't tell, but I honestly don't care. As long as that smile stays on his face, he can do anything he wants.

The days go by in our new routine, and the change in Will is nothing short of miraculous. He's been pleased with our relationship since he told me he loved me, and his mood and attitude have been improving as he feels better, but it's as if painting again has added a whole new dimension to his personality. He's *happy*. And I don't mean a little bit. I mean singing and laughing and smiling like the world is his oyster. There's a light in his eyes that never graced the lonely man I met in the hospital; that flame was extinguished by his cancer. But it's been rekindled by his realization that he truly *has* been given a second chance. And he's determined not to waste a moment of it.

As the weeks of his confinement wane, Will is all about plans: where in Europe he wants to take me, cities he wants to paint, restaurants and places that are special to him that he wants me to see. His good mood is contagious, and I smile and sing and laugh right along with him, reveling in finally meeting the man I only saw glimpses of when he was in the hospital. And I fall a little deeper in love every day, if that's even possible.

One Saturday, about two weeks after he started painting again, I find myself drawn to his studio. It's eleven in the morning, and he's been in there for about an hour. I try to leave him alone so he can create without distraction, but I dearly love to watch him work! Although I often find him there when I get home from work, he usually closes up shop as soon as I get here, tired and wanting to spend time with me.

I approach the bedroom door slowly, creeping along and setting each foot down gently so as not to make a sound. Once I make it to the doorway, I stop, leaning against the frame as I stare dreamily at my very favorite sight.

Will is sitting before his easel, working on the painting he started two weeks ago of the meadow in France. He's a little frustrated by how slowly he's progressing with it, but after all, it's been months since he's painted, and he can only take an hour or two in here at a time before he tires. All in all, I think he's doing fantastic, and despite his grumbling, I suspect he agrees.

Today, he's working on the smoky white clouds in the center of the painting, and I realize with a start that he's almost finished. The detail of the painting is incredible—from the individual blades of grass in the meadow to every needle on the majestic evergreens to the craggy heights of the cobalt mountains in the background. I want to see this place so badly, but in all honesty, if I stare at the painting hard enough, I already feel like I'm there. Will has captured the essence of what he remembers so thoroughly that I can feel the crispness of the air and see the mist rising to cling to the branches of the fir trees.

"You can come in, you know," Will says with a smile in his voice, his hand not even pausing as he continues to paint wisps of cloud. I swear his eyes never left the canvas. How the hell does he *do* that?

"It looks amazing. Are you almost finished?"

"Actually, I think I am finished," he says, looking over his shoulder and grinning. "I think this one will fetch a pretty decent price. I'm glad you're here. I wanted to talk to you about something."

"A decent price?" I stammer, my eyes widening.

"Yes," he answers, drawing the word out. "That's how artists make their money—we paint things, and then we sell them."

"You *can't* sell this one. And if you insist, then I'm going to buy it."

"Tori—"

"Don't 'Tori' me," I say petulantly. "I am in love with this painting, and I won't let you sell it."

His smile is brilliant as he stands and put his arms around me. "You're in love with it, huh?"

"Yes. It's the first thing I ever saw you paint, you've been so happy working on it, and it's so beautiful and detailed that I already feel like I'm there even though you're planning to take me someday," I tell him, pulling out my best puppy dog eyes and my pouty lip for good measure.

He chuckles, then lowers his lips to mine—warm and sweet. When he pulls back, he grins at me affectionately. "Okay, we'll keep this one. But you do realize that eventually you're going to have to part with some of my work, right? I need to earn a living too, and there's only so much square footage of walls in this apartment."

"Then we'll get a bigger one," I say stubbornly, then dissolve into laughter as his eyes widen. "I know, I know! I'm just teasing you. I promise you can sell your work . . . but not this one."

"All right, fair enough."

I back him toward the chair until the back of his knees hit the pillows, and he gives me a knowing look but sits obediently. As he leans back to rest, I sit cross-legged on the floor in front of him. "You wanted to talk to me about something?"

"Oh, right," he says as his cheeks color.

I stare at him expectantly, and he takes a deep breath. "I was hoping to start working on one of the canvases you got me for Christmas now that I'm warmed up, but . . . I wanted to ask your permission to do something different than what you asked of me."

"How so?" I ask, intrigued.

His blush intensifies. "Well, you said the first one was for me to paint for myself, as my first work in my new life, but I painted the meadow first because I didn't feel ready to work on what you gave me yet. Now I am, and I'm planning to start on it, but . . . I'd like to have you watch me work on that one rather than the one I have in mind for you."

"Why?"

"Well, for my picture, I'd like to paint you, so I'd like you to pose for me, and I have . . . plans for yours that require me to keep it to myself. I promise it's going to be fantastic; I just can't let you see it until it's done."

What is he up to? But the smile on his face is so sweet and so hopeful—Mr. Romantic has got some plan up his sleeve, and I best let him do it his way. "Okay, sure. Wait, you want to paint . . . me?"

"Um, yes. I've drawn you so many times; I've been itching to capture you with my true talent."

My stomach flips, and it's hard to breathe as I think about Will painting me. Holy *shit*. "Of—of course, you can." I'm hardly able to get the words past the lump in my throat.

"And you'll sit for me?" His green eyes are alight with eagerness.

"Of course. When did you want to start?"

He ducks his head. "Um, today?"

I shake my head and chuckle at his eagerness. "Sure, but I'm hungry now, and I think you need to rest for a while. What about if we start after your nap this afternoon?"

Will sighs, but he knows the reality. "That's fine."

"Why don't you run through the shower, and I'll make us some lunch."

"Okay," he answers, grinning up at me as he takes my hand, and I pull him to his feet. He wobbles a little as he stands, and I slide a shoulder under his arm to steady him. "I'm all right; I'm just tired," he says as he

278

throws his arm over my shoulder and lets me lead him to the bathroom.

I head to the kitchen and make us both salads, but Will hasn't appeared yet even though it took me forever to get the vegetables cut. Wiping my hands on a towel, I go back to the bedroom, and I can't help but smile as I gaze down at him. He's obviously freshly showered, but somehow, he didn't make it past the bed, and he's sleeping peacefully, lying on top of the comforter and clutching his pillow. I fold the comforter over, covering him with what was on my side of the bed, and creep from the room. His salad will keep until he wakes up.

Three hours later, a very groggy Will joins me in the living room, and after eating his slightly wilted salad, he leads me back to his studio. He's completely awake now, and I can feel his excitement over painting me.

He lets go of my hand, and I stand and watch as he sets up a stool for me to sit on, affixes the canvas to his easel, then goes to his table to select brushes and paint. My stomach does little flips as I watch him choose colors and dot paint onto his palette, his eyes roving over me frequently as he determines what shades he'll need. *This is so exciting!*

Finally, he finishes and turns his attention to me. "I've thought about this, and with how slow I'm working at the moment, there's no way you're going to be able to sit for me the entire time while I paint your portrait. I'm too tired in the evenings, and if we do it only on the weekends, it's gonna take forever. So, I'm going to position you how I want you and take some pictures first, and then you can sit for me today and whenever else you want to when I'm working on it. Is that all right?"

"Sure," I tell him, all of a sudden a bit nervous and shy. I know it's only Will, but somehow, something changed as he spoke to me. *He* is the master here, and I'm just a girl who knows next to nothing about art but was lucky enough to have him fall for me. I've never really felt a balance of power between us, but whatever it was previously, it just shifted toward Will in a big way. He's in control here, and he knows what he's doing. And I smile, realizing this is truly the man he is without his cancer.

"What?" Will says, putting a hand on my waist.

"Nothing. I'm just enjoying watching you work."

His grin lights up the room. "And I'm enjoying working. It's beyond amazing to be back in here, doing what I love."

"And it's beyond amazing to be watching you because you're so much more than the man I fell in love with."

"Is that a good thing?" he asks, looking down.

"Of course it is!" I tell him, pulling him into my arms. "I loved you before when you weren't whole. The cancer had taken over half your life or more by the time I met you. But now, that part has been replaced by who you really are. You're whole again, and the flashes I saw of your true self aren't flashes anymore; they're you. And I love you more than ever."

His brow is furrowed in thought, but I kiss him before he can ponder it too deeply, telling him in no uncertain terms exactly what I think of who he is.

"I love you more than ever, too, Tori," he says, hugging me tightly. He holds me for a moment, and I feel like something more is going on, but as I'm about to ask, he releases me. "Let's get started, shall we?"

He seems fine now, so I allow him to lead me over to the stool and position me where he wants me. He has me sit at a precise angle to the window and asks me to look back over my shoulder as he rearranges strands of my hair, making it look exactly as he wants it. I can't help but blush as he fusses over me—the excitement of what we're doing and the raw sex appeal of watching Will in charge are conspiring to make me more than a little flustered.

Finally, he takes a few steps back and looks me over one more time. "Perfect," he says, picking up his camera. I smile at him, but he shakes he head. "No, not a smile. I want something . . . sexier. Think about eight days from now when I'm finally allowed to touch you."

As if I can think about anything else! But I do as he says and let my eyes rove over him, undressing him and reveling in what's underneath—the freckles smattered on his shoulders and chest, his flat stomach, his large and magnificent—

"Yes, that look right there!" Will exclaims and snaps a few rapid pictures before I reach a full, mortified blush. He doesn't notice, though; his eyes are on the view screen as he inspects the pictures he's taken. "These are perfect. Keep that look right there, and I'll start working."

I look down and grin, shaking my head as he gathers his palette and brushes. By the time he sits down, I'm reasonably composed, but that goes right out the window.

"So, what were you thinking about when I took the pictures?"

I swear I've raised the temperature in the room as my face bursts into flames, and Will's warm, sexy, and contagious laughter bounces around the space. "Oh God, Tori, that blush. Do you know what it makes me want to do to you?"

Impossibly, I blush even more, unable to contain my smile, and Will laughs again. "I was that good, was I?"

"You were fantastic," I say, pinning him with my stare. "I hope you can live up to it in real life because my fantasy Will is pretty amazing."

"That sounds like a challenge, Miss Somerset. I think I'm up to it, and I'll certainly have a lot of fun trying," Will declares with a grin and a wink.

Damn, he's really turning on the charm now, and I breathe deeply, trying to contain the urge to run over there and straddle him again.

Oblivious to my discomfort and slightly damp panties, Will begins to paint, and oh, sweet Jesus, it just got worse! I can see as he moves into that creative space in his mind, and he becomes serious—every fiber of his being focused on what he's doing. It's beyond erotic. His eyes caress me, warming and electrifying everywhere they touch, but he's unaware of the heat because he's focused on his work, and somehow, that makes it even more sexual and intense.

I squirm a little, rubbing my thighs together as I imagine what he's painting, what *he's* thinking as he works, and oh God, how am I going to sit here for a few hours when all I want to do is tackle him to the floor and— *Stop! You can do this! Yes, it makes you want to jump his bones, but it's also important to him. So set your mind on something else, and let the man work!* I scold myself, and somehow, I manage to cool the molten desire enough to remain seated so Will can paint.

An hour later, he leans back in his chair and smiles at me. "I think that's enough for today."

I launch from the stool, and before he knows what's happened, he's on the bed in our room, and I'm poised over him like a lioness over her prey. Will's really going to sleep well tonight.

CHAPTER 17

Day 100

"Lemme see! Lemme see!" I chant excitedly, nearly jumping up and down.

Will blushes, but he's grinning from ear to ear as he unbuttons his shirt and pulls it away. There's a bandage on his chest, covering the entry point where the central line was, but all the tubes and wires are gone. "We'll have to watch it closely and keep it sterile while it heals, but all that's left is a small incision wound," he says proudly.

I whoop and jump into his arms, being careful to snuggle against the opposite side of his chest. He winces, but he encircles me with his arms, and I can feel the strength there. "Is that everything?"

"Yes. I don't have to come back until next week."

I grin so broadly I think my face is going to split. He's come so far in such a relatively short time. I know that to him it seems like forever, but sometimes, I still can't believe that less than five months ago, I almost lost him, that he was literally on his deathbed, and he almost chose to let go.

I push the thoughts away as we head out to the car. We're both still beaming when we get in, so I decide it's time to unleash my surprise.

"We should celebrate tonight."

Will grins at me. "That sounds like an excellent idea. For the first time in a long while, I'm actually in the mood to celebrate."

"Good, because I have a plan," I tell him, my words tumbling out excitedly.

"I had a feeling," he says, smirking as I playfully swat his shoulder. "So what did you have in mind? Takeout and a movie?"

"Oh, I'm thinking bigger than that. We have reservations at Il Terrazzo Carmine at seven."

The smirk freezes on his face, and when I glance over, there's fear in his eyes. "Tori," he says uncertainly.

"Now wait just a minute; I'm not finished yet. When I called them yesterday, I booked the private alcove in the back so we won't be close to anyone, and it's Monday night, so they won't be that busy anyway. And I'll open the doors and handle the check and everything. I think as long as you don't touch anything more than you need to, everything will be fine."

He huffs out a breath, and forces his shoulders to relax. "You're right. I haven't been anywhere other than the apartment and the hospital in over six months—it's time for me to get out a little."

When we get to the apartment, I let him open the door, and he startles when he sees Jason and Jenny seated on the couch, grinning at him.

"Jason! Jenny! What are—Sebastian!" he exclaims, and a grey streak flies across the room and plants his forepaws on Will's jeans, stretching up Will's legs as far as possible and purring loudly. In that moment, I swear that cat is a dog, the way he reacts to Will. But Will's reaction isn't any less affectionate. He looks down and laughs a carefree, joyous laugh, his whole body softening. He starts to bend down, but freezes, turning questioning eyes to me.

"You can touch him; just don't touch your face. And you'll need to wash your hands afterward."

Will smiles even wider and plops down on the floor right where he is and begins scratching Sebastian behind the ears, making him purr even louder. "I've missed you, boy," he says, his tone warm and exuberant as Sebastian butts his head against Will's knee.

The cute is absolutely unbelievable, and I go to the couch and sit down next to Jenny so I can have a ringside seat for the reunion. Will focuses solely on Sebastian for a few moments as they reacquaint themselves with each other, and when he finally raises his eyes and sees the three of us staring at him, he blushes fiercely.

"Hi, Will, it's so nice to see you." Jason teases him, deepening Will's blush.

"It's nice to see you too, Jay, but I haven't seen Sebastian since July, so I'm a little more excited about him," Will answers, unashamedly stroking his cat.

"Well, it's obvious he's missed you, if this display is any indication."

"I guess so," Will says, chuckling. "How long can he stay?"

"He's home." Will's face lights up like a Christmas tree.

"Really? You're kidding! We really get to keep him now?"

"Yes, sweetheart, he can stay. His litter box has to go in the laundry room, and you're not allowed to touch it, but other than that, there are no restrictions. We are now a family of three."

Will's grin is spectacular, but he quickly turns it on Jason and Jenny. "Thank you so much for keeping him for so long; I'm sure it was a pain in the ass—"

"Nonsense!" Jason says, cutting him off. "As far as I'm concerned, Sebastian earned his keep when he kept you company through two rounds of chemo. He helped you through some pretty rough days, and I still consider myself in *his* debt."

Will chuckles and shakes his head, but he doesn't argue. We all know how true it is.

"How's Day 100 treating you?" Jenny asks.

"Well, I'm tube-free, I got my furry best friend back, and Tori's taking me out to dinner tonight. I'd say Day 100 gets a pretty high score."

"Good! You deserve it," Jenny answers. "Like I always said you did."

A look passes between them, and it's tender and sweet. They were so close when Will was in the hospital, and I know she cared for him in ways I don't even know about and never will. I hope their bond always remains strong.

Jenny and Jason stay and have lunch with us, and the conversation is light and easy. And every time Will gets up, Sebastian follows on his heels like a puppy. It's as if he's afraid Will is going to disappear if he lets him out of his sight, but I guess that's exactly what happened when Will got sick all those months ago.

Will excuses himself for his nap right after lunch; he's had a busy day already between the hours we spent at the hospital and Jenny and Jason's visit. After I see our guests out, I know I should take advantage of being off today and do some cleaning, but I just can't resist the thought of cuddling up with Will. We cuddle all the time, but this will be the first time with no tubes in his chest that I need to be careful of. We've both been waiting so long for this day—it seems unreal that it's finally here.

I round the corner into the bedroom and nearly laugh out loud at what I see. For the first time I've ever seen, Will is lying on his side. He's facing me, his legs curled up but not quite in the fetal position. And there, nestled in the hollow created by his body, is Sebastian. One of Will's hands is resting on his back as if he fell asleep while petting him, and as I step closer, I can hear Sebastian purring, even in sleep. They look so adorable—there's no way I can risk disturbing them. *But tonight, Sebastian, this man is all mine!*

We change and leave for the restaurant, and Will is . . . distracted. He's not upset exactly . . . just lost in his own thoughts. He smiles at me when I put a hand on his knee as I drive, so I let it go. If it's big enough, I'll hear about it eventually, and if it's not, then I don't need to know.

I smile at Will as we sit down at our table, but he's not looking at me. His eyes are darting everywhere—down to the table, meticulously set with dishes I didn't wash, across the room as a woman's laughter rings out, over to my other side as a glass clinks. His hands are in his lap below the table, but I know some part of him is in restless motion.

He jumps as I reach my hand toward him. "Sweetheart, are you nervous?"

The corner of his mouth turns up in a sheepish half-smile as his gaze finally falls on me. "Yeah . . . a little. I've been isolated for so long—this is going to take some getting used to."

It's been seven months since he's been out in public, and the restaurant is noisy and more crowded than I expected. Of course, he's a little overwhelmed—I would be, too, after that much time in quiet and solitude. "I'm sorry. I didn't think about how much this would be all at once. We can go home if you want to."

"No, I just need to settle down and get used to the sounds of life again," he says, threading his fingers into the short hair on the back of his head. "I want to do this with you. I'm ready."

"I think you're ready too," I tell him, smiling and squeezing his other hand. "Your cell counts are even higher than we expected at this point, and I know how much you want to start living your life again."

"Well, I kind of already am, with you," he replies, flashing a smile that melts my heart. "But it's time we start living our lives together, outside of the apartment."

I grin and nod, and Will's shoulders relax a bit. He starts looking around with interest instead of fear, and I feel my own tension begin to ebb. He can do this. We can do it together.

It takes a few minutes, but as he answers my questions about what he's been painting this week, he slowly begins to unwind. The noise and stimulation seem to bother him less and less, and by the time our meal arrives, it's as if the last seven months never happened. The only indication that it did is in what he's having for dinner. Although he can eat most things again, he couldn't order his favorite Rigatoni Bolognese—the acid and spices in the sauce would be too much for his still-healing stomach—so he's opted for a delicious-looking butternut squash risotto. But there's no difference at all in the sound he makes when he takes his first bite. As he groans in food-gasm ecstasy, I clench my thighs together and try not to whimper, my mind racing with thoughts of when I'll hear that sound again and what I might be doing to him when he makes it.

And so begins the fire in my belly. It starts as glowing embers—stolen glances at him as I eat my cannelloni, watching his strong, make-my-stomach-twinge-when-it-flexes jaw as he chews his food. *What would that stubble feel like against my inner thigh?* Argh, I need to stop *that* right now because that's the one thing we're still restricted from doing—the risk of infection from him putting his mouth on me is still too great. But that thought evaporates as Will offers me a bite of his risotto, his mischievous green eyes taking me back to that very first piece of popcorn. As I take his fork into my mouth, I slide my tongue under it the way I did his finger that day, imagining it's something else entirely, my tongue and lips caressing and gently sucking. Will swallows hard, shifting in his seat.

He pulls his fork back slowly, and I run my tongue over my lower lip, feeling the imprint of the tines and thinking about the smooth, velvety feel of the head of Will's cock.

"Jesus, Tori." He swears breathily, shifting again, and this time I'm pretty sure it's for friction. This is gonna get out of control quickly, and I don't even know if he wants this tonight, considering it's the very first day he's been cleared, and he had hardware removed from his chest this morning. I take a deep breath and try to tamp the fire down, but the smoldering ache in my belly stubbornly remains.

To Will, I offer a sweet smile, and his grin is . . . confused. But we still have half our meal to eat, so I return my attention to my food. Or, at least, I try to. I last a whole two minutes before my eyes are on him again, mesmerized by his casual grace and the delightful normalcy of having a meal out together. He pauses with his fork midway to his mouth and flashes me that panty-combusting grin he's recently developed. *Oh, my God, are we done with dinner yet?* I think for what feels like the hundredth time as my belly twinges and bursts into lustful, crackling flame.

"You know, technically, this is our first date." Will practically purrs as he slides closer to me, bringing my hand to his mouth and gently kissing a line from my knuckle to my wrist. "This is exactly how I wanted it to be. I'm sorry it's taken me so long."

He's being romantic again, but I can also hear the regret and wistfulness in his voice. And I don't want to hear that, now or ever.

"First dates are overrated. Both people are so nervous, and they usually don't know how they feel about each other—you don't really get to enjoy it. I like that we fell in love first," I tell him, rubbing my hand up and down his arm. Electricity zaps at my fingertips as I touch him, and I can feel my cheeks and ears getting warm as I lazily stroke.

He breathes out heavily and closes his eyes. When he opens them, the emerald green has darkened. "Do you know what I *do* like about this being our first date?"

I shake my head, lost in the intensity of his gaze.

He leans in close, taking my earlobe in his mouth and sucking seductively as I draw in a rapid breath. "Since I'm already in love with you, this can go much further than a first date with me usually would," he says huskily.

"Are . . . are you sure?"

"I've never been surer of anything in my life. I've waited so long to show you how much I love you. I can't wait anymore."

My eyes widen, and my heart threatens to jump out of my chest as he brushes his lips against mine. *Check, please.*

———————

I manage to settle the bill without jumping Will, but the minute we close the car doors, it feels as if the air is electrified around us. He's watching me. As I maneuver out of the parking garage, I can feel the heat of his gaze, and my hand has crept onto his thigh before I realize I gave it permission.

He puts his hand on top of mine, but I'm not interested in that kind of affection. I start to rub slow circles, and he sighs, but he draws in a sharp breath as I inch closer to my target with every languid stroke. He gasps when I finally make contact, exhaling with a delicious groan as I slide my hand firmly up and down his length. It's only three blocks to the apartment, but by the time I pull in, Will's a panting, writhing mess.

The minute I put the car in park, his hands are in my hair, pulling my lips to his and devouring me. My clit begins to pulse as he deepens the kiss, but before he thrusts his tongue into my mouth, he pulls back. "No, not in the car," he whispers, his eyes dark with desire.

"No," I agree, still breathless, and before I know it, he's opening the door and ushering me out. His hands are all over me as we walk—one buried at the nape of my neck and the other around my waist, his fingers rubbing gently, keeping the current flowing between us. I walk in front of him into the elevator, and as I turn around, he hits the button for the fourth floor without even looking, his gaze boring into me.

"Elevator's fine though." He almost growls, grabbing my face between his hands and pressing me against the back wall. He plunges his tongue into my mouth, greedily claiming me as my hands curl around his shoulders, pulling him closer. Will breaks away when the elevator stops, breathless but trying to appear casual as he grabs my hand and strolls down the hall, but as we approach our apartment, the heat begins to build between us again. He squeezes my hand before he lets go to unlock the door, and I rub my fingers together, the warmth and lingering charge like sparks to the still-glowing embers deep inside me.

The minute he shuts the door behind us, my desire comes roaring back, a blaze in the pit of my stomach. I want Will naked and moaning his pleasure, writhing and out of control . . . *now.*

I crash my lips to his, one hand wandering up the side of his neck and into his soft, new hair as the other presses his erection between us and slides down. Will gasps against my mouth and throws himself into the kiss, moaning deeply as I press and squeeze. But it's not enough, and I bring my other hand down, my lips never leaving his as I fumble blindly with the button and zipper. His cock springs free as I pull his pants and boxers down, and I fill my hands with smooth, velvet hardness.

"Ohhhh." He groans, and my belly twinges and flips, my kisses more insistent as I back him toward the couch. His calves hit the front, and I push him down gently, breaking our kiss but keeping my hands on him and landing on the floor between his knees. Before he realizes what's happened, I've taken him into my mouth, and he throws his head back against the cushion and cries out in pleasure.

"Fuck, Tori," he mumbles, his breath coming in pants as I lave my tongue around and over the soft head. He hisses as I take him all the way in, his hands gripping the cushion on either side of him, trying not to thrust into my mouth. The thought makes me smirk as I come back up, hollowing my cheeks with delicious suction that makes Will gasp and tense like a bowstring.

I start a slow rhythm, up and down, as the room fills with the sound of Will's pants and soft moans. He thrashes his head back and forth, unable to keep his hips still, and I'm all heat—in my chest from the satisfaction of giving him pleasure and in my center from what the sounds of his pleasure are doing to me.

"Ohhhh God," he whimpers, his leg muscles tensing, and I swear I almost come as his cock hardens even further in my mouth. "Stop."

The exhaled word is barely a whisper, but it brings me up short, and I release him from my mouth. "Did I hurt you?"

Will shakes his head, his eyes scrunched tightly closed, a grimace on his face, but it doesn't seem to be from pain.

I chuckle softly. "You're trying not to come, aren't you?"

He nods as he opens his eyes. "You're entirely too good at that."

"But I *want* you to come," I whine, puffing out my lower lip.

"I wanna come too, but not that way. Well . . . not tonight anyway," he says, his eyes dancing with mischief. "Tonight, I have other plans, but remind me I want to get back to that, repeatedly, and particularly when we're cleared to go all the way."

I snort and shake my head. "I seriously doubt I'll need to remind you. I have a feeling my performance made it into the 'memorable' category."

"And you'd be right," he says with a smirk, his breathing finally returning to normal. "But tonight, I want to worship you."

His words crawl down my spine with a delicious tingle, and I can't help the blush that colors my cheeks as he sits up and lets me pull him to his feet.

"Will you let me worship you, Tori?" His voice is deep and husky, dripping with eagerness and lust, and I melt. I nod numbly as he takes my hand, and I'm amazed my knees don't give out as he leads me to our bedroom.

He takes me to the foot of the bed, stepping back from me and raking his eyes from my chest down to my feet and back up again, my skin seeming to heat and tingle under the intensity of his gaze.

"So beautiful," he murmurs, his eyes finally locking with mine. "Have I told you that tonight, how beautiful you look?"

"No," I answer, cracking a smile as his brow furrows. "Sweetheart, you've told me at least a dozen times."

"Not nearly enough," he says, caressing my cheek with the backs of his fingers.

I lean into the touch, closing my eyes as heat flows from his fingertips to color my cheeks, creeping down onto my chest as I flush from the outside inward. Suddenly, he cups my face with both hands as he thrusts his tongue into my mouth, his excitement stirring my own and causing the flames to ignite again in my belly. My hands slide into his hair seemingly of their own accord, and he groans as I press against his scalp, pulling him closer.

His own hands have started to wander, sliding down to play idly over my collarbone as he continues to explore my mouth, his tongue twisting and tangling with mine. They journey down my sides, leaving a trail of goosebumps in their wake and landing at my waist, squeezing gently.

"I love this dress." His voice is a seductive purr as he fists the smooth fabric of my little black dress. "But right now I'd love to see it on the floor." He pulls and I barely have enough time to untangle my fingers from his hair and lift my arms before the fabric is passing in front of my eyes on the way to its new resting place—anywhere but here.

Will inhales sharply and lets out a low whistle as his gaze returns to me. But when he meets my eyes, and I see the lust burning there, I know the matching black lace panties and bra were totally worth it. I smirk as he tries to close the distance between us, but I stop him with a gentle hand on his chest.

"Oh, no. I want to feel you too. Please?" I ask, cocking my head to the side.

He huffs out a breath, but he allows me to slowly unbutton his shirt and push it off his shoulders. His chest is completely bare except for the bandage over his central line site, and I lean in and press a kiss over his heart, not wanting to disturb the other side. I think he gets the idea of where I wanted to put it, though. His smile is sweet and tender as he watches me, but it morphs into something else as I caress his abs, the muscles tightening under my fingers as I bring my hands to rest on the button of his dress pants.

His breathing is heavy as I unbutton them and they drop to the floor, but he stops my hand before I can soothe where he's aching for me. "Not yet," he whispers, and he steps close, trapping his erection between us and pressing his hard chest against mine. My nipples harden, and we both moan; we've never done this before. I've touched him a million times, but we've never held each other skin on skin like this. He was always so careful of his central line, and we both knew we couldn't go any further; we had a silent understanding to keep enough distance, and clothing, between us so that we could endure the wait. But now, oh now, nothing stands between us, and I press my cheek against him, feeling his heartbeat under my ear as I slide my arms around him, holding on tightly and reveling in the incredible closeness and intimacy of this moment.

"I love you," he murmurs, kissing the top of my head, but he doesn't stop there. He kisses a line down the side of my face, and my thighs clench as he reaches that spot right behind my ear. "Ohhhh," I groan as goosebumps shoot down my leg, and my head lolls to the side, offering my neck to him. He licks and sucks, his hands caressing my shoulders, and suddenly, I'm on my back on the bed and he's straddling me, kissing and licking every inch of skin and setting it on fire.

"Oh, Will . . ." I throw my head back and try to breathe, shivers rolling through me despite the searing heat of his lips. He reaches my shoulders and kisses a line beside the strap of my bra, and we both moan as he cups my other breast in his hand, tracing his finger over the black satin until my nipple peaks underneath.

"Please . . ." I arch my back as he slides his hand under me, releasing the clasp with a flick of his fingers. I cry out as he pulls my nipple into his mouth, rolling his tongue over the tip, then sucking just enough that—*oh,* fuck, *that feels good!* I writhe under him, arching even further and thrusting my nipple into his eager mouth. I roll my hips, and he groans deeply, his hot breath tightening my nipple even further as the sound makes my belly twinge hard in pleasure. *Yes.*

I roll against him again, but he slides down further, lapping and sucking his way down my stomach as his fingers continue their sweet torture of my nipples. *Oh, fuck, I'm gonna come before he even touches me down there.* I slide my thighs together, and I can feel the slickness as I move, trying to get some friction for my clit against something— anything! The heat and pressure are suddenly gone, and I gasp as I open my eyes to search for him. But Will hasn't left. He's on his knees beside me, sliding my panties down over my legs and staring at my sex as if he's about to devour me.

"No," I pant, and he stops and shakes his head, looking at me in bewilderment. "You can't. Not yet."

He growls in frustration, and even though I'm aching for him to taste me, I pull him back up to my lips, throwing everything I'm feeling into a searing kiss. Tongues tangle and teeth clash, but I break away in a gasp as his finger caresses my slit from back to front. He begins to rub in a gentle circle, and I arch against him, my breath coming in pants of sweet ecstasy as my walls tighten. "Oh God, more! Please, Will!" And he presses a little harder, circles a little faster, and I cry out again as he thrusts a finger deep inside.

My orgasm is beginning to build, my whole center tingling and tightening as Will's lips at my neck drive me wild, and I fly headlong toward my release.

"Come, Tori," he breathes against my neck, and I explode, pulsing against his fingers and rocking as wave after wave of pleasure overwhelms me.

"Whoa," Will says, his fingertips exploring my cheek. "That was—"

"Incredible." I finish for him, smiling and still panting.

"I've wanted to do that for so long." He's lying beside me, stretched out and glorious on his side, head resting on his arm as he watches me.

"And I've wanted you to." I trail my fingers down over his neck and collarbone, and he shivers and tenses as I brush them over his abs. "You really *are* beautiful, you know."

Will ducks his head and blushes, but he raises his eyes to mine almost immediately, brimming with intensity. "You've always made me feel that way. Do you know that? You made me feel whole even when I wasn't. It's as if you gave me a part of yourself to complete me when I no longer had enough pieces to complete myself. I needed you so much, and I still do. I always will."

My heart swells to bursting, and I gasp, unable to breathe, unable to do anything but marvel at the gentle perfection of the man I love as tears stream down my face. "I need you too, so much." I throw my arms around him and pull him close, reveling in the moment. Then his still-hard cock bumps my hip, and I remember why I was stroking my way down his body in the first place.

"I think you need me right now, actually," I say, grinning salaciously as I slide my hand over his erection and curl my fingers under his balls.

"Aunnngh." He groans, his eyes rolling back in his head, and even though I just had the orgasm of a lifetime, the sound rolls deliciously over all my girl parts and brings them to rapt attention.

He flexes his hips, jutting forward into my hand, and I'm rewarded with an erotic, guttural moan as I tighten my grip. But it's not enough—I want to *feel* him, so I lift his boxers down and away, and he arches off the bed so I can slide them down his legs. He rolls toward me, but my hand is on him again immediately, craving those fantastic sounds of pleasure he makes that set my world on fire.

I start a slow rhythm, my fingers curled in a tight circle, sliding up and down his length, turning and squeezing at the tip. He freezes and throws his head back, exposing his neck—his Adam's apple bobbing with a hard swallow and begging me to taste it.

"Oh God—" He pants between hard breaths as I lick and suck on his neck, my arousal mounting with every hum, whimper, and gasp. *His arousal is painted on my fingers, my speed increasing as we both become slick with the pre-cum dripping from his tip. I slide down one more time to massage his balls.

"Tori, stop! St—" He's completely out of breath, and for a moment, I worry we've gone too far somehow, but then his piercing green eyes meet mine, almost ferocious in their intensity. "I want to make love to you. Now. *Please.*"

I nod, my eyes not leaving his, caught like a mouse before a cobra, a sexy, beguiling, drop-dead gorgeous cobra who's about to redefine my existence. He rolls on his back toward the nightstand, pulling a condom out of the drawer and rolling it on himself. And then he kneels between my legs, arms braced on either side of me, hovering.

The world is reduced to his eyes as I stare so deeply into their green depths, and memories flood through me: the lazy, morphine-laden first smile he gave me that turned my world on end; our first gentle kiss, eyes closed and oh so tentative; his whispered "I love you," clinging to life because he wanted to be with me.

No words are spoken, but the wetness in the corners of his eyes matches my own as I reach down and gently guide him. He pushes halfway in and his eyes close, his face frozen in a soft gasp, then he pulls back and slowly slides all the way home, buried deep inside of me.

It's perfection.

Pure, unadulterated perfection.

We stare at each other for a moment, and I start to close my eyes to savor the moment. "No, Tori. Look right here." His whisper is deep and sexy, his eyes boring into me with so much love that I'm overwhelmed, and I forget to breathe. He pulls back slowly then pushes in again, groaning softly, and my breath escapes in a whoosh.

"Are you okay?"

"I'm . . . perfect," I stammer, still lost in the heat of his gaze.

"Me too." His smile is brilliant as he starts a slow rhythm, his eyes never leaving mine, and I swear I can hear his thoughts with every gentle thrust.

I love you.

I need you.

You're everything.

I'm home.

I'm whole.

Or maybe those are my thoughts, my words, because his smile grows ever wider as he loves me. The only sounds are our soft pants and the gentle creak of the bed as Will moves, the only light the reflected gleam of the lamp off the sheen of sweat on his skin. I wonder if we've stumbled into forever—because I surely wouldn't mind—until his eyes flutter closed, and he picks up his pace a bit.

"Ooohhh." He voices his pleasure, suddenly lost in his own world, and my clit begins to pulse as I watch him approach his orgasm. His breathing is rapid and uneven, his thrusts giving way to deep moans and whimpers, each caressing my sex and driving me toward my own climax.

"Tori," he pants, and the thought that he's close sends shivers down my spine and my fingers flying to my clit. I want to come with him. I press and rub as his thrusts become erratic, his soft cries urgent, and I spiral out of control ahead of him. He gasps as my walls tighten, thrusting twice more before he freezes, groaning each intense pulse of his release until he collapses against my chest. He winces as he makes contact, forgetting about the still-tender wound on his chest, and rolls us to our sides, still within me. And then he cuddles as close as he can, peppering my neck with kisses, although they're soft and languid.

"I love you so much," he murmurs against my neck, and I smile for what feels like the thousandth time today.

"I love you too. So much," I say, nuzzling my forehead against him, but I feel his nose wrinkle against me.

"Are you all right?"

"I'm perfect," he responds, echoing my own words and also taking me back to another day when he was cuddled on my shoulder, but this one is infinitely better.

"But?"

I feel his smile against my neck. "But my chest is sore, and I'm ... tired."

"I'm tired too," I tell him, and he smiles gratefully as I resist the urge to fuss over him. "Why don't you attend to matters while I grab you some pain meds, and we'll meet back here for a proper, no-tubes-involved cuddle?"

"That sounds fantastic," he says, kissing my nose as he slides out of bed and heads for the bathroom.

A short while later, we're snuggled up in the dark, him spooning behind me with his arm wrapped around me and our legs entangled.

"God, what a day," he mutters into my shoulder as he runs his lips over my bare skin.

"Was it a good one?"

"Best day I've ever had." A few seconds later, he sighs softly, and I know he's dropped off to sleep.

"Best day I've ever had too." I whisper to the darkness, burrowing deeper into the warmth of his embrace.

CHAPTER 18

Day 154

The rainy Seattle afternoon enfolds me, but instead of gloom, it brings comfort. It's warm today, the branches of the trees unable to hold back their buds in the face of such nurturing, and I'm on my way home early to do a little nurturing of my own. I smile as my thoughts stray to Will—home painting this afternoon, probably with the windows open to smell the rain and wearing those jeans that sit so gloriously low on his hips. *Well, I'm hoping I'm going to bring something up anyway. Is that close enough to nurturing?*

The last few weeks have been heaven after a trying February. Will's fledgling immune system had its first test about two weeks after Day 100 when he came down with a nasty cold. Naturally it scared the hell out of both of us, and we went straight to the ER, but Jill managed to calm us down. They took some blood and samples for culturing, but she said it was most likely a virus, so they loaded Will up with antiviral meds and sent us home to weather the storm.

He was miserably sick for more than two weeks, but Jenny came and checked on him every day before and after work, and we managed to keep him out of the hospital. His recovery was slow, and his cough still lingers even though it was almost a month ago, but his body was able to fight off the infection.

Since then, things have just been getting better and better. I'm working full days now, and Will is spending a good bit of his time painting. Jason still joins him for lunch, but it's more for companionship than help, and although Will still has to rest for a while in the afternoons, he's able to stay awake in the evenings with me.

And we've been going on dates! Will's not ready to brave the bars or a movie theater yet, but we've gone out to dinner several more times, including dates with Jenny and Jason, then come back to the apartment to watch a movie. It's not complete freedom, but he feels like a person with a life again.

He's also gotten quite a bit more . . . well, *adventurous*, shall we say? The first time we made love, it was sensual and sweet, but since then? I fan myself as I remember the sound of our skin slapping, warm and slick, as he bent me over the kitchen table a mere two nights ago. His favorite plan of attack is to corner me while I'm making dinner. He lets me start most nights because he wants to finish whatever he's working on, but the minute he reaches his stopping point, he's wrapped around me, his cock grinding against me and his warm breath in my ear.

But today, I'm going to beat him at his own game. My slow afternoon turned to fantasies of riding my lover like the prize stallion he is, so I left early, and I'm going to march right into his studio and not take no for an answer. I have a funny feeling I'll get no disagreement from him, and if I do, well then . . . I have my wicked ways.

I chuckle to myself as I turn the key in the lock, then drop my bag on the table. The living room is empty, as I expected, and I call out, "I'm home," to give him a moment's notice and so I don't scare the hell out of him. I learned my lesson once already about sneaking up on him when he has a brush in his hand. The painting ended up smudged, and I ended up with a blue nose.

"I'm in the studio," he calls back, and as I get to the doorway, I see he's working on the New York skyline painting for the first time since his last relapse. And it is, hands down, the hottest thing I've ever seen.

I fly across the room, sliding under his left arm as he steps backward, my fingernails scraping against his scalp as I assault his lips. He grunts, but his tongue is already seeking mine as I mold against his body, grinding my aching clit against the growing bulge in his jeans. He groans deeply, but it turns into almost a chuckle. I pull back, confused, to see his sparkling, boyish grin.

"Whoa, Tori! Did you miss me?" His words are innocent, but they stoke the blaze of my desire. My girl parts quiver and melt into a puddle of goo, drenched in my own juices and the low, husky rasp of Will's voice. I lean in to kiss him again, but he tilts his chin down and away, his sweet laugh sending my heart to join the other Tori goo on the floor.

"Hey, can I put down my palette and brush first? It's killing me not to be able to touch you when you're this . . . frisky."

I laugh, realizing that while I've been attacking him, he's been standing with his hands full. "Frisky? Is that what I am?"

"Well, personally, I think 'horny as hell' is a better description, but I was trying to be diplomatic about it."

"Put down that brush so I can show you exactly how 'horny as hell' I am." I challenge him, squeezing his bulge for the glorious moan it elicits as his eyes roll back in his head.

His fingers relax, and he nearly drops both palette and brush, but he catches them just in time. "Actually, I've got a better idea."

I raise my eyebrows, but now, he brings out the big guns, blushing a deep and delectable shade of red. His blushes turn me on almost as much as his moans do. I want to kiss every inch of tender, flushed skin, licking and sucking and—

"Tori!"

I've stepped forward again, and my lips are attached to his collarbone, laving at a spot that's now even redder from my ministrations. *Oops.*

"Jesus! You really *are* ready to go!"

I nod and blush my own shade of crimson, stepping back and allowing him to put his brush and palette on his art table. "What did you have in mind?" I ask, keeping my eyes on the floor because I know if I look at him, I'm going to jump him again.

"Well, I was wondering if I could . . . paint you."

I glance up, and his eyes are downcast now, but as he looks up at me through those glorious lashes, I know if he'd asked me if he could make love to me in a pile of wet leaves I'd have said yes. There's just one problem. "Will, you already *have* painted me."

"No, not like that," he says, coming to stand before me and taking my hand. "There's this project called Love and Paint that's run by a friend of Jason's." He kisses a line from my thumb down to my wrist. "The idea is that love is a form of art that can be captured on canvas . . . with paint."

I'm sure my eyebrows are so high, they're no longer attached to my forehead. "You mean we paint each other, and then we make love?"

"Uh huh. Or we paint each other while we make love. And when we're done, we have a piece of art to hang on the wall."

"Wow." A vision of Will naked and splattered with paint meanders sinfully through my head. *Oh my holy God.*

"It was just an idea," he says, letting my hand go.

"About the fucking hottest idea I've ever heard," I answer, picking up his hand again and trailing kisses from his palm to the scar on his wrist.

His eyes widen, and he draws in a rapid breath. "Really?"

Does he truly have no idea that the mere thought of him naked and painting is enough to make me jump him, or else need a shower really badly if I can't have him? *Really?* "*Hell*, yes! Is it safe? For you, I mean."

He huffs out a breath. There are still quite a few things we need to be careful about. "Yes, the paint is non-toxic, hypoallergenic, and they use a sterile process when they package it, considering the places it's likely to . . . end up." Now his blush is fierce, and I'm wondering if he's thinking about exactly where on me or in me he'd like that paint to end up.

"Yeah, I'd imagine their paint ends up in some interesting places."

"Oh, I can think of a few," he says, his eyes suddenly burning with lust.

"How long have you been planning this?" That look says there are some fully fleshed-out fantasies already in his mind, involving lots of flesh and not much else.

"Um . . . a while," he says, incinerating me with those searing green eyes. "I wanted to do this for Valentine's Day—"

"—but you were so sick."

"Yeah."

"Well, what's stopping you now?" I ask, smirking at him as I caress the front of his jeans.

He scrunches his eyes shut and hisses, but I know it has nothing to do with pain. "Ahnggh, nothing. Let me go get what we need," he answers, a little out of breath. I chuckle as he hurries from the room. *This is gonna be amazing.*

When he returns, he's all business for a few minutes, laying out a white sheet that looks like a drop cloth but thicker, and four medium-size cans of paint: blue, green, yellow, and red. Then he stands and goes to his art table, stroking his chin as he scrutinizes his paint can full of brushes. His gaze swings back, and his eyes rake over me, bright green laser beams of heat that slice through my blouse, hardening my nipples instantly. He smirks as he selects a few brushes, his long fingers hovering over the bristles as I imagine what it'll feel like when he's stroking them over my—his deep laugh rings out, and I realize I'm clenching my thighs. I need his clothes off. *Now.*

"Are you ready?" he asks, seductive and sweet and oh, so sexy.

I step forward and pull him to me so we're standing on the canvas, and the brushes fall from his hands as he grasps my cheeks, crushing his lips to mine, hot and wet and demanding entry. I open to him, tilting my head so I can reach deeper, swallowing his moan of pleasure as he grinds against my thigh.

My fingers slide beneath his t-shirt, his abs tensing as I tickle and tease. I continue upward, and he gasps as I circle his nipples with my index fingers, the little nubs hardening deliciously as his cock twitches against my leg. I want to suck on those nipples. *Now.*

I step back and tug on his shirt, and before he's managed to slip his arms out, I'm already pulling his nipple into my mouth, sucking hard as my hand slides down to cup and squeeze him.

"F-f-fuck-k-k." He's no longer touching me, and I press my advantage, undoing his jeans while I lap at his nipple. In seconds, my hands are filled with hard velvet heat, and he pants as I cup his balls and stroke up his length. But I want *more.* With practiced ease, I slide his jeans and boxers down, and while he's distracted by those, I hook an ankle behind his knee, then clasp his hands, lowering him to the floor.

He chuckles, but in an instant, I have his jeans and boxers off, and the sound turns to a deep, erotic groan as I go all the way down on him, pressing his tip to the back of my throat. "Gaa-ohhh." His head lolls to the side as I hollow my cheeks, sucking all the way to the tip before plunging down again.

"J-J-Jesus, Tori, you're going to have . . . me off . . . in two minutes . . . if you keep . . . that up." His breathing is ragged as his hands come to rest on my shoulders.

I love the feel of his cock on my tongue and how wild he can be while I'm pleasuring him, but he's right. We have new toys today, and we should play with them. When I reach his tip, I lave my tongue around it. I'm rewarded with a deep shiver and exhaled moan that set my clit to pulsing, but I release him, looking up to meet his blazing eyes.

"You're right, and I wouldn't want you coming before we play with our new toys." I crawl over his leg and sit beside him, and his look is such a combination of wonder and lust that it's almost comical.

Almost.

But he's lying naked beside me, his cock standing at attention and his smooth, soft skin calling to me, begging me to worship him. I pick up the nearest paintbrush and stroke my thumb over the soft bristles. "What kind of brush is this?"

"That's—" he swallows thickly, his eyes never leaving me, "—a mop brush."

"It looks kind of like a makeup brush. What do you use it for?"

"Well," he says, sitting up with a twinkle in his eye, "I use it to fill in large areas of color. It's very absorbent, and *very* soft." He takes the brush from me and holds it expertly, painting an imaginary stroke on my collarbone. I roll my head back, and Will's lips are on my neck, sending shivers down my spine and heating my chest and belly. "You're wearing too many clothes."

He unbuttons my blouse as he lays a line of hot, wet kisses from my jaw down to my breasts, and I can't help but moan.

I can feel his smile against my skin as he pulls my blouse off my shoulders and makes short work of my bra while he's back there. As I'm sliding my arms out of the straps, I gasp as Will trails the paintbrush between my breasts, heat and sensation erupting on my chest. I can't let him do this. Not yet. I'll lose my mind if I let him stroke that brush—*oh God*—over me just as he does with a canvas. I want it, but I want to try my hand at this first.

Grasping his hand that's holding the brush, I press it to his chest. "I want you to do that, *badly*, but I want to do it to you first. Please?"

A wicked, glorious grin spreads across his face, and he blushes deeply, causing my belly to twinge in anticipation.

"Okay, but whatever you're going to do, it has to be naked. You're still wearing too many clothes," he says, glaring at my khakis.

"Deal," I answer, standing and letting my pants and panties drop to the floor.

Will's eyes widen appreciatively, but I intercept his hand before he can turn the tables again. "Lie down on the canvas, please."

He smirks at me but complies, and I kneel beside him. I hold the brush poised over his belly and he tenses, his eyes boring into me and pulling me to look at him. "No, close your eyes."

The room has gone suddenly silent, and I can hear the unevenness of Will's breathing. The heat of his gaze melts me, but the part that really does me in is the trust I see there. He's trusted me with his secrets, his heart, his very life—he trusts me without thought or question. He closes his eyes, and my own breathing is uneven, and I choke back my emotion to focus on the task at hand—giving him as much pleasure as I can.

I move away from his abs, because he's expecting it, and stroke the brush lightly down his arm, from shoulder to wrist. He shivers, but he stays fairly still, so I decide to test his resolve. I bring the tip of the brush down on his peaked nipple and swirl gently. He gasps, convulsing inward, and his eyes fly open as he flops back on the canvas. "Now, Will, you have to stay *still*."

"While you're doing *that*?"

"Yes," I answer, eyeing the easel behind him. "And I think I know how to help you." I pick up a longer, slightly thinner brush with a pointed tip, and Will cocks his head at me curiously.

"Move back a bit." He does as I ask, but his brow is furrowed as I hand him the paintbrush. "Now, raise your arms over your head, slide the brush behind the leg of your easel, and grip the other end with your other hand."

He gasps, his mouth falling open in astonishment, but he moves quickly.

"Now, don't let go of the brush," I tell him, smirking. "It's not quite bondage, but it'll do in a pinch."

He blushes, the color soaring up his chest to kiss his cheeks. "Do you like that?"

"What?"

"Bondage."

"Well, I've never really done it before, but if you're asking if I want to tie you up and do dirty things to you, the answer is yes."

"Oh, fuck me," he mutters as he closes his eyes, and his cock gives a mighty twitch.

"We'll get to that," I answer, giggling, and I'm nearly knocked over backward as his lips crash into mine. I plunge my fingers into his hair, but I know this is going to get out of control, for both of us, if I don't stop it fast, so I push gently on his chest until he comes up for air. "Come on, sweetheart, let me make you feel good."

His grin is spectacular, his kisses chaste and sweet. "I *am* the luckiest man alive."

Warmth explodes in my chest, but now's not the time for being sentimental. I want to be *dirty*. "Not yet, but I'll *make* you the luckiest man alive if you'll just lie still!"

His chuckle is deep and sexy, and he lies back and grips the paintbrush the way I told him, his glorious body stretched out before me. "Close your eyes."

The lust in his gaze scorches me, but he complies, his muscles tensed in anticipation.

The room is silent—all I can hear is the harshness of Will's breath, waiting for me to pleasure him. A wave of euphoria crashes through me, and suddenly, all I want to do is mount him and ride until we're both screaming in ecstasy. But . . . now *I* have the chance to be in control, to do whatever I like and to squeeze every drop of pleasure out of this experience that I can, for both of us.

I poise the brush over his stomach, then trace a line up the center of his chest. He gasps, but he stays in place, so I begin to circle his nipple, stroking in wide arcs and slowly tightening them. Will's breath is coming in pants, and all the muscles on that side of his body are tense. I reach the center and he moans out a breath, making his cock twitch and my clit pulse at the same time. I want to hear that sound again, so I lift the brush and go straight for the kill on his other nipple, meanwhile leaning down to take the closer one into my mouth.

"Aahhh!" Will grunts as the paintbrush snaps against the leg of the easel, but he doesn't let go. I swirl my tongue around his nipple while painting the other with invisible strokes, and Will writhes underneath me, his breathing ragged. *Jesus Christ, what's he going to do when I do this to his cock?*

And suddenly, I really need to find out, so I begin moving downward, my lips and the brush painting lines down opposite sides of his chest as he whimpers above me, knowing exactly where I'm headed. My cheek bumps into his tip, already slick with anticipation as I begin to slide the bristles of my brush up his shaft. Will arcs up off the canvas with a deep groan, the sound of wood on wood ringing out again as the brush he's holding collides with the easel.

"Oh fuck! I can't . . . Doitagain."

I giggle, then slowly run the brush up the side of his cock, grinning as he squirms and undulates, his body angling toward the brush. I reach down and massage his balls as I do it again, and his guttural moan sends a shiver careening through me. I need to make him come. *Now.*

Continuing to fondle and squeeze him, I start running the brush up and down his length, from all angles, circling around and around as I watch his excitement build. He starts out slowly, rolling his hips and panting, but as I increase my pressure and speed, he begins to thrust upward to meet the downstroke of the brush. His pants turn to whimpers and moans, and I can hear the change in the sound as he bites down on his lip, pain to ground him and make the pleasure last a little longer.

So I watch as he gets closer and closer, his urgency making me clench and flex, my own heat building. But I think I can give him just a little more. I pull the brush away and push his hips back down to the floor, then flick the brush against that oh-so-sensitive spot right under the head of his cock, and he cries out in ecstasy. I use my other hand to stroke his length, and within seconds he's thrusting wildly.

"Tori . . . so good . . . I'm gonna come . . . I'm gonna come—" His words are cut short as he cries out sharply, and I hear another snap and a loud crunch. Will voices his pleasure with loud grunts as he explodes, painting his chest with streaks of pearl. He twitches with the aftershocks of his orgasm, trying to catch his breath as I smirk in triumph.

"Shit. I really liked that paintbrush," he says, bringing his hands down, half a brush in each one.

I bark out a laugh. "I'll buy you another one."

He chuckles as I wipe his chest and belly with a tissue, then he pulls me down to him, tucking me against his side. "Don't worry about it. Best use I've ever had for the thing! Goddamn, that was . . . Fuck, that was amazing! I'm still seeing stars!"

I giggle again and nuzzle against his still-heaving chest, feeling the warmth and life radiating from him. He's perfect and he's whole with only a little bit of healing left to do.

"I want to do that to you. So much. Just give me a minute." His eyes are closed, and there's a blissful smile on his face, and happiness surges through me like a tidal wave. This is what it's all about. These are the moments that make life worth living. I hope I have a million more, and Will shares in every single one.

We lie in contented silence until Will's breathing is slow and even, and I start to wonder if he's fallen asleep. Then his finger begins to make slow circles on my thigh. I shiver, but it feels so good that I can't pull away. "It's my turn now," he whispers into my ear, and goosebumps slide deliciously down my leg.

He rolls toward me and kisses me soundly, then sits up and gathers the brushes scattered around us. He shuffles through them, and an evil grin spreads across his face as he selects one.

"What's that one for?"

"This," he says, holding it aloft, "is a fan brush. It's used for blending and for fine details. Do you remember all those evergreens in the meadow painting?"

I nod.

He inclines his head. "This brush."

Swallowing thickly, I stare at it in wonder. How the hell does he create such beauty?

"But right now, I have a new use in mind for it," he says, winking at me. "Your turn to hold down the easel, Miss Somerset."

He hands me a brush similar to the one he broke, and I quickly lie back and get myself into position. I'm breathing faster, my heart thumping like a jackrabbit's as I watch him hover over me. He flashes that kid-on-Christmas grin of his and gets on his knees beside me. *Is he gonna make me—*

"Close your eyes, Tori. I'm going to make you feel so good."

Holy shit, I already feel good! My heart feels like it's going to jump right out of my chest, and every inch of my skin is sizzling with electricity just waiting for the spark of the brush to ignite the blaze.

His brilliant green eyes pierce me, seas of love and lust and teenage-boyish excitement. I giggle, then plunge myself into darkness, my other senses heightened by the loss. At first, all I can hear is the sound of my breathing, but once I steady myself, I can hear his too. It's soft and ragged and seems to be coming closer—I jump and snap the brush against the easel as Will's brush skims up the underside of my arm, ticklish at first but warm and tingly afterward.

He continues across my hands and down the other side, the bristles never leaving my skin, trailing fire in their wake. Now he slides onto my chest, and I shiver as he feathers across my collarbone, his strokes soft and reverent, as if I'm the canvas, and he's the master painter. *Holy fuck, he* is *the master painter,* I think as the brush swirls below the swell of my breast, and the image of his face as he paints, his complete and utter concentration, springs to mind. My belly twinges hard, and heat erupts deep inside me. *Oh God!* I'm *his work of art.*

I gasp as the brush teases my already peaked nipple, and his breath wafts over the skin below it. "Do you like that?"

"Yes. More." The brush glides over my skin, circling and teasing, hardening my nipples and stealing my breath as Will explores and re-creates me, his brush infusing crackling sensation into every millimeter of skin it touches. My breathing speeds up with the tempo of his strokes, and soon, I'm panting and aching for him, my thighs clenched as I writhe, my heaving, arousal-soaked body his masterpiece.

"Will. Please!" He chuckles—a deep, husky sound—but he's breathing hard too. I peek an eye open and inhale sharply at the beauty poised over me. He's rock hard again, his left hand driving me to ecstasy while his right teases his arousal with languid strokes. *Holy. Fucking. Shit.*

Searing heat erupts in my belly, and my only thought is to let go of the damn paintbrush and throw myself at him, but suddenly, I'm hanging on to it for dear life as soft bristles caress my slit from bottom to top. "Oh *God!*"

I squeeze the brush and feel it bow in my hands as he focuses in on my clit, but this brush is smaller, tighter. "Aannghh!" I don't care as long as he keeps flicking and circling and—oh, the tingling is building and—so tight— "Will—aaahh!" I shudder and shake as my orgasm rips through me, obliterating everything but the waves and waves of pleasure.

My head bounces gently off the floor as I come down, releasing one hand from the brush. I pant, too blissed out to open my eyes, but as I quiet, I hear Will's uneven breathing beside me. I open my eyes and midnight green is all I see—dark and smoky and burning with lust.

I'm on fire again, and I fill my hands with Will as I thrust my tongue into his mouth, nipping and sucking and squeezing and cupping, consumed by the need to pleasure and be pleasured. He grips my arms and his hands are . . . wet? My eyes fly open. His hands are covered with red and yellow, and he's spreading it over my arms and down onto my hips, and it's the most erotic thing I've ever felt. I plunge my hands into the blue and green, then into his hair, needing to claim him, to mark him as my own.

We touch and taste, and the paint spreads, covering us.

Red, my breasts that he squeezes and my ass that he grips as he plunders my mouth with scorching kisses.

Blue, his chest where my hands knead his pecs and circle his nipples, pulling moans from him as he grinds his arousal against me.

Yellow, my thighs, the muscles rippling as I hike my leg over his hip and he slides into me, pulling him home.

Green, his hips where I hold on so tightly as he plunges into me, thrusting hard.

Purple, where our chests meet as we writhe against each other, smooth and slick.

Brown, where our bodies join and slide together, the colors mixing so there's no end and no beginning.

My hand slides upward to grip his hair, and he rolls me onto my back, brilliant green eclipsing all the other colors as he devours me with his eyes. I'm lost there, both of us panting in time with the pleasure of each thrust, until the riot of color draws my eye.

His arms, blue and brown, the muscles flexing as he thrusts into me. His chest, glistening with sweat and purple and blue, heaving with passion and effort. His hips, slapping against mine, the colors merging and changing with each new stroke. *Holy fuck is this hot!* And suddenly, I can feel the heat building again deep in my belly, my breath coming fast and hard.

I reach up and bring his face down to mine, painting streaks of green and blue where my fingers stroke and slide. I thrust my tongue into his mouth, wanting to get closer, and he whimpers, his rhythm faltering.

Oh my God, I'm going to explode! is my only thought as I clench around him, and I can feel every delicious inch of him as he drives into me. He moans long and low at the change, making me clench even tighter, and he pulls away from my lips. Eyes closed, brow furrowed, his uneven pants turn to moans of pleasure, and I know he can't hold back much longer.

My finger finds my clit, and Will gasps as my walls clamp down on him. "Oh *Jesus!* Fuck. Fuck!" His words morph into an almighty groan, and he rolls his hips against me, giving me all he has as I shatter around him.

Eventually, the white noise in my ears gives way to the sound of Will's uneven breathing and the warm weight of him pressed against my belly and chest. I open my eyes to find sated, awestruck, adoring green eyes staring back at me.

"Wow."

He rolls us onto our sides, and I hike my thigh over his leg, pressing my foot to the back of his knee as my hands find purchase on his chest, and my lips tell him "wow" in return. The hand that's not trapped under me squeezes my ribs, pulling me tighter and closer as I give him everything

I have left, telling him with my kisses the things that words aren't enough to say.

His kisses become soft and sweet, and he pulls back slowly with a few pecks and rests his head on his arm, bent at the elbow, and stares at me thoughtfully.

I mirror his pose, and my face feels as if it's going to split from the smirk I can't contain. "Do you think we made a good painting?" I ask as I reach out and stroke his paint-covered cheek.

"Well, it certainly *felt* like a work of art," he answers, grinning.

We both chuckle, and we lie there for a while, touching and stroking, until I realize he's becoming aroused again.

I sit up slowly, then haul myself off the canvas, staring down at it as Will gets up and stands beside me. There's a riot of color before me, but I can make out our silhouette as he thrust into me on our sides and a bit of my red footprint from when I put my leg over his thigh. There are fragments of handprints where we both fisted the sheet, and a swath of reds and yellows where my hair fanned out as he drove into me, bringing us both to ecstasy.

"It's fantastic," he says, curling an arm around me. "I certainly know what I'm going to think of every time I look at it."

I giggle and blush to the roots of my hair, but I doubt he can tell for all the red paint that covers me. "Me too. But right now, I have another job to do," I tell him as I sheath his cock with my hand, the mix of blue and red on my fingers creating a deep purple as I stroke.

He inhales sharply and leans into me, his eyes closing and his head falling back to expose his delicious multi-colored neck. *Oh, yes, we're definitely ready for round two.*

"Now, I get to un-paint you."

CHAPTER 19

Day 169

I wake up to the feel of gentle fingers on my cheek, and I smile as I realize it's Saturday, and Will and I can spend the day doing whatever we want. *Now that it's April, it's getting warmer, and we really should*—and then it hits me—today is April sixth. The day my mother died. I haven't had a thought about it . . . in months. Not since Christmas. Not since the last time I felt a pang of guilt for not telling Will. Everything's been going so well for him, and we've been so focused on the future, I haven't thought about my own past in ages. But today, I will. I have no choice, really. But for the first time in four years, I'm not going to do it alone.

I know the smile has frozen on my face, but I pause and take a deep breath, knowing I won't be able to hide what's in my eyes. I open them slowly to find worried green staring back at me from under a deeply furrowed brow.

"Tori? What is it? You woke up and then . . . something changed."

Damn, he's good. We're so in tune now, our bodies and minds in balance and harmony with each other. I've disturbed the calm, and the little waves are rippling outward . . . but this isn't a breeze, it's a gale. "I . . . remembered what day it is," I say slowly, searching his eyes. *God, I hope he'll understand.*

He rolls on his side to face me and brings his hand back to my cheek. "It's Saturday."

"It's April sixth. I . . . need you to do something with me today. Say you will." My voice quavers with the urgency of my plea.

Now he sits up, and there's alarm in his eyes. "Of course I will. Tori, what's going on?"

I squeeze my eyes shut and will myself to come out with it already. It's long overdue, and I need his support. If he's angry, I'll just have to suck it up and deal because it's my own stupid fault. All of it's my fault. "I need . . . to go see . . . my mother."

His sharp intake of breath sounds like a cannon in my ears, and there's no noise after that, so I know he's frozen and staring at me. "Your mother," he whispers, shocked, shaken, but still I can't look at him. I can't bear to see pain or betrayal in his eyes on top of everything else I'm feeling right now; I'll shatter.

"Tori, where is your mother?"

"Calvary Cemetery."

This time he gasps, and my eyes fly open as he gathers me into his arms, but I bury my head in his chest. "Oh God, I thought—I mean, I just assumed . . . when?"

It takes me a minute to swallow past the lump in my throat. "Four years ago . . . today."

His arms tighten around me, but I have no tears to cry. I'm numb, and I don't want to be in this day. I hold this back always, *always*, and today is the only day I truly let myself feel it, but I don't want to feel it today. I don't want to burden him with it even if I should have done it long ago. He's had enough; he doesn't need any more.

"Will, I'm so sorry. I know this is a shock, but I don't let myself think about this. It's over and done with, and it only gets to me on this one day, and—"

"It's okay." His voice is soothing as he trails kisses along my jaw. "I know what it's like to not want to talk about things. I could teach a master class."

I snort and nuzzle under his neck, and he relaxes a little underneath me and rubs circles on my back.

"I'll go to the cemetery with you. And you don't need to tell me anything more—I know how hard it can be when you're in the moment. I'm here, whatever you need, okay?"

Finally, I muster the courage to look at him, and his gaze is warm and tender. If there was hurt there, he's managed to hide it, and for the first and probably only time in our relationship, I'm grateful for that. I feel like complete and total crap because there's so much I should tell him, but for now, I take the easy way out.

We get up and have our breakfast, and Will watches me thoughtfully. It's so rare for me to have anything on my mind that I don't just tell him. It feels . . . uncomfortable, as if I'm hurting him somehow even though he said it was okay. I push the thought away. This is all in the past; there's no point in reliving it. It's over. "Can we go right after breakfast? I want to do this and then . . ." I have no idea how to finish that sentence because I don't know what we'll do then. The last three years, I've spent this day wallowing in misery and drinking myself blind to dull the pain. Today will be quite different.

"Of course we can," Will says, covering my hand with his and looking deeply into my eyes. I can see the questions burning there, but he doesn't voice them, and it reminds me of myself not so many months ago. Touché, Mr. Everson. It appears we've come full circle.

We ride through downtown Seattle, and I stare out the window. I let Will drive this morning. He's thrilled to be behind the wheel again after so many months—one more step on his road to complete recovery and independence.

We drive past University of Washington Medical Center, and I don't think of the countless times I've brought Will here since November or all the days I've driven in to work—I think of the day I drove here blinded by tears to claim my mother's body, too late to say goodbye—too late to say anything that needed to be said. I hug my arms tighter around myself, and Will squeezes my knee, his warm green eyes seeking me out and holding nothing but comfort. I don't deserve his comfort today. I'm guilty. Guilty of doing to my own flesh and blood what I wouldn't let Will do to himself. What I can't stand to let anyone do, if I can help it.

As he turns into the cemetery, I direct him to make the first left and pull over to the side of the little road. I buried Mom here, in the section dedicated to Saint Raphael. He's the patron saint of people who need healing for their bodies, minds, or spirits and of the people who care for them—doctors, nurses, and counselors like me. I chose it because Mom fell into the former category, and I fell into the latter, but I realized later that because of her, I fall into both. I chose better than I could have ever imagined.

Will puts the car into park and glances over at me, but I'm frozen. I can see the gravestone from here, and I don't want to go any closer, but I have to. I have to give her today what I couldn't four years ago; I've promised myself that I will forevermore. I swallow thickly. "Sweetheart, can you please wait here? I . . . I need a few minutes."

His brow furrows slightly, and for a second, I wonder if it's hurt I see in his eyes, but it vanishes as he gives me a sympathetic smile. "Of course. I'll be right here."

I stare into the eyes of the man I love, and my heart clenches as I realize he's too good for me, too pure. He's come through hell and burned away all the demons from his past, yet I still carry mine and do their penance. He deserves better.

I shake my head and push my door open, forcing my legs to carry me from the car to the gravestone I chose. It's simple—rectangular with a small rise at the top, ivy etched into the sides. "Sharon Marie Hoffman, beloved Wife and Mother." I don't even know the man whose last name she took to the grave. They married and divorced during a period when I didn't see her, but she kept his name, so maybe she really did care about him—more than she did about me. At least, more than I believed she cared about me.

I must have fallen to my knees because suddenly, I'm enveloped in soft but strong arms, and my shins are cold against the frozen ground.

"Tori, are you all right?" Will asks, his warm breath washing over me, but it's not enough to calm me, not enough to help me contain the grief and the guilt and the *need* for him to understand.

I tuck my head against his chest, squeeze my eyes shut, and the words pour from my mouth like a monsoon, built up over so much time.

"She left when I was six, but that wasn't the end. She stayed away until I was twelve. Then one day, she turned up on the doorstep. She brought me presents and said she wanted me to live with her. I was thrilled, but after a few days, Dad sent her away. I didn't know why, and I was angry with him for months.

"She came back the following Christmas, but she was too happy, too excited. Dad told me she was high. I wanted so much just to have her in my life, but she and Dad argued, and she went away again. When I was fifteen, she came back clean, asked Dad to give her another chance, and she moved in with us for six months. On Christmas Eve, she came home high, and it started a cycle that ran for the next three years— she'd use until Dad caught her, then she'd run off for a few months, then she'd come back all clean with presents for me again, and the cycle would start over—until finally, on the last Christmas, she brought a man home with her, and Dad kicked her out.

"She made me so many promises during those years. So many times, she said she'd stay clean—that she loved me and Dad, that she'd always be there for me. But she wasn't. She ruined so many Christmases, she was too high to come to my high school graduation, and it went on and on and on. But I always gave her a chance. Again and again, through my early twenties, she came back, and I'd let her in, only to end up hurt and betrayed.

"And then I did my master's in psychology, and I started therapy for myself. I learned what I was enabling and how to stop it. I learned that after so many years, my only option was to save myself. And I did."

I pause, feeling myself beginning to shake, and Will holds on to me tighter. "F-f-five years ago, she came back again after being out of my life for three whole years. She was . . . calm. She said she was clean, and she wanted to start over with me, that things were different, and she'd seen the error of her ways. But I'd heard it all before. Things were never any different with her, and I always ended up hurt and betrayed. So, for the f-first time in my life, I t-told her no. I told her how much she h-hurt me, and that I never wanted to see her again. I told her I c-couldn't forgive her. She cried, but she s-said she understood, and she went away."

"Oh, Tori—"

I squeeze Will's arms, shaking like a leaf now, and I feel his warmth against me. And I cry. I cry so hard, but I force the words out over my tears. "That w-was the last t-time I saw her. She—she was dying. P-pancreatic cancer—she was clean, and she wanted to m-make peace with me, but she never told me she was sick. She wanted me to let her in, but not b-because she was dying. Because I loved her. And I didn't do it. She died alone, Will! She d-died in that hospital all alone because I was too stubborn and too stupid to see that she'd changed. She had n-no one because I turned my back on her. I made her die alone!"

I hear Will's gasp as I dissolve into a mass of keening misery, and he rocks me back and forth as he rubs my back, murmuring that it's going to be okay. I cry for ages, locked in my own hell, but the feel of Will's tears against my temple and the quaver in his voice as he comforts me bring me back to myself. He's crying for me. He's crying *with* me, and I just feel worse because I don't deserve this amazing gift I've been given.

Finally, my tears abate, and I pull Will as close to me as I can. I bury my nose in his newly regrown hair, and I thank God for him even if I don't deserve him. He senses the change in me, and he cocks his head down, trying to meet my eyes. I close them and bite my lip for a moment, but I know I have to let him ask me the things he needs to. Finally, I raise my eyes to his.

Now, there *is* hurt there, and although it twists my heart, I understand it.

"This is why you do what you do—befriend patients who are alone and dying. Tori, why? Why didn't you tell me?"

I sigh and smile at him through my tears. "You had enough to carry. I couldn't add to it—not when you were struggling and fighting so hard to save your own life."

Will drops his chin and sighs in exasperation. "Well, we're done with that. Now, I'll carry this with you—hell, I'll carry it *for* you. Oh God, what did I put you through? Pushing you away, almost making you watch me die alone—Jesus! I'm so fucking sorry!"

He rakes a hand through his hair, his expression distraught.

"No, Will," I say, reaching up and capturing his hand. "You were fighting your own battle, and I couldn't let what I've done affect that."

"What you've *done*? Don't tell me you actually believe you're guilty of something?"

I raise my eyes, and he flinches back as if I've slapped him. "Oh, Tori, no! Your mom spent a lifetime teaching you not to trust her! She gave you no reason to believe her when she came to you, and she didn't tell you she was sick. How could you have possibly known? She died alone because of the choices she made, not because of you."

"N-no. She tried to make it right, and I—"

"No, Tori. Just no," Will says angrily. "What happened to her was horrible, but it wasn't your fault. She knew she'd pushed you too far—that's why she didn't tell you she was sick. I bet she didn't feel she deserved to have you back in her life."

"But I had so much to tell her! I never thought that would be the end! The last thing I told her was that she didn't deserve my love. I was angry! I never thought that would be the last thing—" I dissolve into tears again, and Will holds me tight as I listen to his heart thrumming under my ear. The strong, steady beat calms me again, and I lie there, spent.

"You're doing penance, aren't you?" he whispers, laying a soft kiss on my forehead. "You befriend those who are dying alone to try to make up for what you didn't do for your mom."

I can't speak around the lump in my throat, so I nod against his chest.

"Tori, you saved me. If your mom hadn't died the way she did, you never would have come to me, and I would have died alone and terri- fied in the hospital. What happened with your mom was horrible, but it put you on the path to find me, to change both our lives and give us what we have now. Maybe . . . it was supposed to happen that way. Maybe she gave you . . . me."

I never thought about it that way. Will's right—if it weren't for what happened with my mom, I never would have gone to talk to him. All those others I befriended would have died alone, and Will would have died and not been cured. He would have suffered the same fate as my mother did. Of course, she couldn't have known, but could fate . . . Could this have all happened for a reason? To bring Will and me together?

"You can stop doing penance now. Not only did you keep me from dying alone, you helped me not to die at all. You've repaid the debt you think you owe—a life for a life. You lost your mom, but you saved me."

He lifts my chin, and my gaze locks with his, mesmerized. There's so much love and warmth and passion there—I can see the rest of my life in those brilliant green eyes, and it's happy and fulfilling. Maybe I *have* paid my debt, and I can stop now. Maybe I can stop trying to make up for what I lost and move forward with what's been given to me by the incredibly strong, amazing man in front of me. Maybe.

Will curls me tighter against him. "The ground is cold. Are you ready to go home?"

I rest my head against his chest and squeeze my eyes shut, trying to sort through pain and loss and love and redemption until my very soul seems to suddenly become quiet. I listen to the steady rhythm of Will's heart—the heart that would no longer be beating if it weren't for me—and I feel . . . peaceful. Maybe he's right. Maybe we saved each other.

"Let's go," I whisper, and he gathers me into his arms and makes to stand. "No—" I start to wriggle out of his grip, but he silences me with a stern look.

"Let me take care of you."

His gaze brooks no argument, but there's a softness to it too. He really wants to do this. I snuggle against him and hold on tight as he lifts me up and carries me to the car. He's a little out of breath when we get there, but no more so than I would expect any man to be, and it makes me smile. He really *is* whole and well again.

He gets me settled in my seat, and after he closes my door, I put my hand to the window, as if on top of the little gravestone I can still clearly see. "Thanks, Mom," I whisper as Will gets in, and we slowly drive away.

The ride home is quiet, and I can feel Will's eyes on me, but I'm not as upset anymore, I'm just . . . sad. No matter whose fault it is, and no matter how much of a fuckup she was, I still miss my mom, and I wish things could be different. But if she were here, then Will wouldn't be. I glance over at him, all wild bronze hair and fuzzy stubble and long artist's fingers curling around the steering wheel. I wish things could be different, but if I had to trade, I know I couldn't let go of Will. Not even for her.

Will keeps a protective arm around my waist all the way up to the apartment, and once we're inside, he pulls me back toward the bedroom.

"You look tired. Let's cuddle," he says, turning me around and coaxing me to sit, then kneeling down to take my shoes off. I run my fingers into his hair, and he sighs—it's still shorter than it was when I first met him but long enough that I can curl it around my fingers. He peers up at me from under his lashes, his gaze warm with concern. "Are you all right?"

"Yeah, I think I am. I'm just tired from crying so much." And I realize it really *is* true. This will always be a sad day, but now, I'll always wonder if Will was somehow my mother's gift to me—to take care of me and love me in the ways she couldn't.

Will circles around to his side of the bed, and I hear two muffled thumps and feel the bed dip beside me. Soft hands pull me backward, and he lays me on my stomach, then he curls up next to me and begins gently rubbing my back. I dream of fields of green, awash in sunlight and swaying in the breeze.

I wake up alone sometime later, and although I remember what day it is, all I can think about is the sweet man who held me through my tears, then carried me to the car. We're past the point where I worry that something bad has happened when I wake and Will isn't beside me, but I'm surprised he isn't still napping with me. Maybe he didn't sleep at all?

Rubbing a hand over my face, I yawn and head toward the sound of soft music coming from the living room. I freeze when I get to the end of the hallway, drinking in the glorious sight before me.

Will is in the kitchen, grooving to the beat of the music as he whirls around the small space, cooking. Once he recovered enough from his bout of graft-versus-host disease to be interested in food again, I assessed his skills in the kitchen and found them lacking. Well, nonexistent is more like it. So I slowly began teaching him the basics. He's surprised me by starting dinner a few times now, but whatever he's got going at the moment is way beyond that.

He dances back and forth, poking at this and stirring that, with Sebastian at his feet, weaving between his legs as he moves. I grin as I look at the pots to try to figure out what he's making, but my eyes are drawn to Will as he suddenly wiggles his ass in time to the music. It's ridiculously hot because his jeans are hugging him just right, but it's also so freaking cute—I don't know whether to jump him, hug him, or laugh my ass off.

Laughing my ass off wins because as he spins to open the fridge, I realize he's wearing my "Kiss the Cook" apron, big red lips and all. He stops mid-motion as I clap a hand over my mouth, his foot poised in mid-air with Sebastian underneath as they both stare at me, wide-eyed. The blush that floods Will's cheeks is furious, but when he drops his chin and gives me that shy smile, I fly across the room and into his arms.

I can feel the heat in his cheeks as he kisses me, and it makes me giggle, and he pulls his chin down and away, still blushing and grinning. As I look up into his laughing eyes, I can't help but run my hand up the back of his neck and pull him close again, kissing him for real this time as heat blooms in my belly. We both jump as the timer on the microwave beeps, and Will pulls back, glancing at the stove.

"*What* have you been doing? I thought we were taking a nap."

"Well, we were," Will says a little nervously. "But I woke up and I was hungry—we skipped lunch, you know—but you were still sleeping so peacefully that I didn't want to disturb you. I thought I would make us an early dinner."

My brow furrows, and he blushes again. "Well, not make exactly. I kind of thawed out some of your Bolognese sauce, so all I really needed to do was boil the pasta, but I *am* making my own garlic bread!" he says triumphantly, gesturing toward the counter where he was preparing to chop garlic.

I chuckle and shake my head, but I'm grinning from ear to ear. "Aw, sweetheart, you didn't have to do all this."

He steps close again and wraps his arms around my waist, gazing down into my eyes with love and adoration. "I just wanted to take care of you. You've spent so much time taking care of me. I wanted today to be my turn."

Warmth fills my chest as I gaze up at him, realizing for the first time he really *can* take care of me now. I can lean on him just as he's leaned on me; we can be there for each other. "Okay, sweetheart, you keep doing what you're doing, and I'll stay out of your way."

"I've got a better idea," Will says, turning to the cupboard and pulling out a wine glass.

I shake my head, but his pouty lip stills me.

"Come on, I know you like wine. And I don't mind. I don't miss it that much; I was only a social drinker anyway."

We always have wine around the apartment for when we have guests—which is fairly often because Will still isn't comfortable in crowded places—but I never have any because *he* can't. He pushes his lip out further, and I give in, smirking at him.

"That's my girl. And chianti goes well with red sauce."

I raise my eyebrows, and he narrows his eyes at me, but he can't hide his grin. "I know stuff. Red sauce, red wine—it's color-coded."

I laugh out loud, and he turns his back on me under the pretense of opening the wine, but I really think it's to hide the blush I can see on the back of his neck. I wonder if he knows he can't really hide it.

Wrapping my arms around him from behind, I stand on my tiptoes to kiss the heat above his shirt collar. "Of course you know stuff, particularly when it comes to color, but food and wine are *not* color-coded," I tell him, unable to keep the laughter out of my voice.

"Believe what you want," he says, glancing over his shoulder. "Chicken is white and you serve it with white wine. See? Color-coded."

I realize I'm not going to win this one, so I take the glass from him and set it down as he turns in my arms. "Okay, you win. It's color-coded just for you."

He sticks his tongue out at me, but I swallow it with my kiss, my arms curling around his shoulders as his fingers plunge into my hair. He moans against my lips, but the damn microwave beep stills him mid-grind.

"I don't want to burn the first dinner I've ever made for you, so why don't we continue this later?" he says, winking at me.

"All right, all right!" I know I'm whining, but I can't keep the smile off my face as I disentangle my fingers from his hair. "You owe me though."

"More than I can ever repay." I catch his soft whisper, but before I can pull him close, he turns toward the microwave. "Fine. I owe you," he says more loudly, and I know his first response wasn't intended for my ears. "Now take your wine and get out of my kitchen. Some of us are trying to chef here."

I chuckle, still standing there, but he raises his eyebrows at me and makes shooing motions until I scoop up my glass and retreat to the kitchen table.

Watching Will cook is hilarious, but it's so damn endearing that I can't laugh out loud at him, not wanting to hurt his feelings. But it's obvious that before today, he's never done most of what he's doing; his motions are awkward and stilted. He's learning, though, and watching him enjoy the simple things in life is just the balm I need to soothe my weary soul today.

My thoughts stray back to my mom for a moment, and for the first time, I don't feel the wave of crushing guilt that usually comes with any thought of her. The pain is still there, but it feels more like the ache of loss than the bitter stab of regret, and my subconscious helpfully supplies a vision of her sending Will to find me and take care of me. My eyes well up, but the thought of my mom as my guardian angel makes me smile through my tears. Maybe now, I can truly grieve for her instead of wrestling with her ghost.

I startle as Will sets a steaming pile of angel hair drowning in Bolognese sauce in front of me with a piece of garlic bread perched on the side of the plate. It smells *amazing*. Then I remember I made the sauce, so I already know how fantastic it's going to taste, but the apprehensive look on Will's face as he sits down across from me tells me he thinks this is all on him. Time to play with him a little bit.

Giving him a grateful smile as I pick up my fork, I twirl some pasta around it and pop it into my mouth. I make a show of swallowing, then quickly take a large gulp of my wine. Will's face falls, and by the time I set my glass down, he's staring forlornly at his own plate. Like a child playing hide and seek, I can't hold in my giggle, and his head snaps up, his eyes narrowing and his frown morphing into a murderous scowl.

"*You* are an evil, evil woman, Miss Somerset. Playing with a man's honor like that. It's just . . . Well, it's just downright *mean*."

I truly begin laughing then, and although Will's still trying to melt me with his death glare, his lips are turning up at the corners.

"Oh, sweetheart, of course it tastes wonderful! You're such an easy mark; sometimes I can't resist."

There goes that blush again as he glances down at his plate, trying to hide his smile. But he quickly looks back up at me. "It's good, really?"

"Yes, it's delicious. You cooked the pasta just the way I like it," I say, stroking his newborn culinary ego. Never mind the fact that all he did was boil water and heat up my sauce—this is important to him!

"Did you try the garlic bread?"

I try to hide my grin as I shift my eyes to my bread, but he sees right through me. "No fucking around this time. I mean it. My pride can only stand so much."

Covering his hand with mine, I take a bite of his homemade garlic bread and am pleasantly surprised by its tastiness—he had to have added something other than just garlic and butter to achieve this flavor.

Under his expectant and watchful gaze, I can't help but crack a smile. "Mmm, this is fantastic! What did you add to it other than garlic and butter?"

Will's smile could power a third world country. "I . . . am not telling," he answers, the smugness rolling off him in waves. "Maybe someday I'll tell you if you're very, very good."

I chuckle, but I'm not going to bite on that one. I'm actually hungry, and I want to finish this meal, not end up on the floor next to the kitchen table. "Well, I guess I'll have to be very good, then," I tell him, giving him a seductive smile as I pick up my fork.

He snorts and shakes his head, but he doesn't rise from his seat—he must be hungry too—and we may have made love in this very room not twenty-four hours ago. Now that Will's almost fully recovered, he's proving to have quite a bit of stamina and creativity in the love department. As I glance around the loft, I realize there are very few surfaces he hasn't had me on. I blush, and the heat seems to go down instead of up, so I steal a glance at Will, but he's busy eating his pasta. *Oh, right. Dinner.*

We eat in silence for a few moments, then Will seems to turn thoughtful, playing with his food more than eating it. "What is it?" I ask softly.

He glances up, and the words tumble out of his mouth. "Paul from Flatcolor called while you were sleeping."

Flatcolor is an art gallery a few blocks from here, but it happens to be one of the most sought-after exhibition galleries in Seattle. Will has been contacting galleries and sending out samples of his portfolio over the last few weeks, but he hasn't received any callbacks yet. I keep telling him they must be busy, but I can see his hope dwindling as the days go by. But right now, he's beaming and barely containing his excitement. "And?"

"And he wants me to bring my portfolio by next week."

I vault out of my chair and nearly knock him over sideways as I throw my arms around him. "Sweetheart, that's fantastic! I'm *so* excited for you! Oh my God, a gallery show! This is what you've been waiting for!"

"Well, I don't have a show *yet*, but Jason said they don't call you back unless they're really interested," Will says, but he's grinning as if he's won the Nobel Prize.

"Jason? Wait, am I the *last* person to know about this?" *How long was I asleep? Two hours, maybe?*

"Well . . . no," Will says sheepishly, ducking his chin and turning a delightful shade of red. "I mean, I didn't call my mom or anything. But I *had* to call Jay right away. You were asleep, and he's in the business with me . . ."

". . . and he's your best friend. I get it. I was just wondering what else went on during my two-hour nap," I say playfully.

I make to let him go, but Will rests his hands on my arms and scoots his chair out a bit. Then he grabs my leg behind my knee, and I straddle him, catching on quickly. The minute I'm settled on his lap, I take his face between my hands and kiss him thoroughly, my tongue plunging into his mouth and taking all he has to give, over and over. While I'm devouring him, I press my scorching hot center against his very prominent arousal.

Will tears his lips from mine, panting. "I missed you terribly; that's what went on."

"Mmm, yes . . . I can feel that you did," I say, rolling my hips against him until I'm rewarded with a moan so erotic my belly twinges almost painfully.

"I'm sorry I told Jay first. I was just so excited, and I knew you needed some downtime after the morning you had," Will says, nuzzling his nose under my chin so he can lay open-mouthed kisses on my neck.

"Ungh, I think I know how you can make it up to me." I lift my chin to give him better access, and the fire spreads from his lips to my every nerve ending.

We make love on the floor right beside the kitchen table, and it's sweet and playful. Will's excitement is contagious, and we laugh and tease until my orgasm demands our attention, and his follows soon afterward.

He's still trying to catch his breath as he lays his head on his arm beside me. "Well, that was a spot we hadn't christened before."

I raise my head and smirk at him. "Are you sure? I could have sworn—"

"Nope, I'm totally sure," he states, his green eyes twinkling at me. "We made love right there"—he points two feet to our right—"but definitely not right here."

"Please don't tell me you have a map of the floor somewhere, and this was merely another achievement in your little game."

"Of course not! But next time, I have to come over to your chair because —ow!" He jerks away, rubbing his chest where he just received a sound thwacking, but I grasp his chin and pull him back to me, kissing him soundly.

When he finally pulls away, he's flushed and winded again, but he's grinning from ear to ear. "Why don't we watch a movie? Let's just put away the leftovers and curl up on the couch. I'll do the dishes later."

I honestly can't think of a more perfect way to spend the rest of our evening, so I nod as he pulls me to my feet.

We put away the leftovers together, and Will smirks as he puts away the garlic bread. I shake my head and smile. A blowjob should be enough to weasel that particular secret out of him, but I'll let him think he has the upper hand for now.

I go into the living room to choose a movie, and Will doesn't follow, but I grin when I hear popping coming from the kitchen. Watching a movie without popcorn is sacrilege even if we recently finished dinner. But I remember the days when he'd eat three bites of something and tell me he couldn't manage any more. I light up every time I see him eating like a guy in his twenties should.

He rounds the corner humming to himself, bowl of popcorn in one hand and bag of Raisinets in the other, Sebastian following him like the second car in a parade. I can't help the laugh that bursts out of me— pure joy and giddiness over what I've been given—but Will doesn't miss a beat. He plops down on the couch before he realizes I'm laughing at him and raises his eyebrows. "What?"

"Nothing. This is turning out to be a better day than I thought it would be," I say as I sit down next to him and lay my head on his shoulder.

"Then everything's going according to plan," he whispers, kissing the top of my forehead as he presses play.

We snuggle and laugh, feeding each other Raisinets and popcorn until I think I'm going to burst, but Will keeps munching long after I've stopped. And for the rest of the evening, every time I get lost in my own thoughts, he's right there—acting silly and making me laugh, drawing me into some engaging conversation or kissing me until I forget I have any purpose on this planet other than to be molded to his lips.

Nothing we do is out of the ordinary, but he's somehow made it a perfect day spent together, a happy memory to lay against all the sad ones I have from growing up. And I know Will won't ever let this day pass without making it special for me and reminding me that if it weren't for Sharon, we both would have been lost.

When we finally climb into bed after another round of lovemaking on the couch, he maneuvers us until he's spooning behind me, his legs entwined in mine and his arm tucked around my waist. I relax back into his chest, and as his warm breath tickles my neck, all my worries, past and present, fall away. I'll never know for sure if my mom sent Will to me or if I would have somehow gotten here on my own, but one thing is certain: no matter how I got here, this is where I belong.

CHAPTER 20

Day 246

I awaken slowly—the glow behind the bedroom blinds letting me know I'm waking up later than usual. Opening my eyes, I get up immediately, eager to get the worst part of my day over with. I wince as the familiar soreness ripples through my muscles and joints. I usually wake before Tori since I still get more sleep than she does, and I get up, visit the bathroom, take my meds, and then crawl back in bed with her. And today will be no different, especially since it's Saturday.

Once I'm in the kitchen, I grab a granola bar since two of my morning meds cause nausea and wash it and the pills down with some orange juice. I shuffle slowly back down the hall and it sucks, but I know the pain meds will kick in in about twenty minutes. Morning used to be my favorite time of day because it was the only time I felt normal; now, it's the only time I *don't* feel normal. It's not as bad as it was a few months ago though. But I still look forward to the day when I wake up feeling like I'm thirty and not sixty.

Oh shit, I *am* thirty today. I honestly never thought I'd live to see this birthday. At this time last year, I was already sick with the infection that would land me in the hospital, but I had other plans for myself than how things ended up. At this time last year, I was devising a plan to keep everyone away so I could die alone, a bother to no one. I had given up on life, and I was convinced there was no hope for me, no way to beat the disease that was taking me apart piece by piece, and no one who wouldn't be better off without me. I've never been more wrong or happier to be so.

As I round the corner into the bedroom, I draw in a sharp breath as my eyes fall on absolute perfection. Waves of mahogany spill over the crisp white comforter and pool on the mattress beside her, baring the smooth, tender skin of her shoulder. My angel is sleeping on her stomach, arms tucked up under the pillow, her beautiful face turned away from me now but toward the place where she last knew I was.

I return to that place, lying down beside her as carefully as I can and trying not to grunt from the pain the movement causes me—I still have a good ten minutes left until I'll get my relief. But as soon as I'm settled, there's nothing in the world but her—dark, sculpted eyebrows arching over the delicate smudges of her eyelashes as they rest against her porcelain skin. I don't think I have a brush fine enough—or the skill—to paint such detail, such *beauty*. She's stunning, and that's with her eyes closed and some of her best features hidden from view. And her *very* best features are not even seen but felt—her amazingly giving heart, her stubborn courage, and her unbelievable kindness.

My chest tightens as I gaze down on her, the love I feel filling every millimeter of space so it's hard to breathe. She saved me. In every sense of the word—she took me from the brink of my own personal disaster and convinced me there were things worth living for, things worth *fighting* for, and she did all that just by being my friend. Just by standing by and being there when I needed her, even when I didn't know I did. She's the most amazing woman in the world, and I thank God every day that she came into my life. And today, even though it's *my* birthday, I'm going to show her just what she means to me.

I must have fallen back to sleep because the next thing I know, a soft hand is caressing my stubbly cheek. I plummet into a sea of deepest umber, and my smile is uncontainable, causing her to grin back.

"Good morning, birthday boy. How ya feelin'?"

"Fantastic." *Because even if I'm hurting, you're here with me.*

She smiles sweetly. "No pain today, then?"

"I've already been up." As I confess, her smile fades.

"Dammit, I'd hoped—"

"I'm fine," I tell her, and it's my turn to cup her cheek. "The codeine always does the trick." And it's the truth—I really *am* feeling better. *In fact, I'm feeling rather ready to go,* I think to myself as I shift my hips to give my rather prominent erection some more room and a little friction.

Tori glances downward, and a wicked grin dimples her cheeks. "Well, let me be the first to wish you a happy birthday, then." Her words are a sensual purr, wrapping around me just as her hand wraps around the back of my neck, and she crushes her lips to mine.

Heat floods my cheeks and groin as I thrust my tongue into her eager mouth, a moan escaping me as I pull her close and grind upward.

"Good morning to you, too," she murmurs against my lips as she slides a hand between us, stroking her fingers down either side of my length in the way she knows drives me wild.

I thrust against her—I honestly can't help it when she does that—and lose myself in the rhythm of our tangled tongues and rolling hips. My hand plunges under her tank top and squeezes the softest skin I've ever felt, and Tori moans deliciously against my mouth, her nipple hardening and causing a shiver to roll down my spine. My balls are already starting to tighten. *Jesus Christ, I'm going to come before we even get started.*

"Stop." I pant, pulling back a little although my body is screaming at me to go harder and faster.

She stops immediately, her brow furrowing in concern. "Are you all right?"

"Yeah, I—" I have to pant out a few breaths before I can continue, and I gasp a little at the end. "I didn't want to come like that."

She narrows her eyes, and an evil gleam appears there. "You're absolutely right. It's your birthday, and I know exactly how you should come."

And before I can even blink, she's ripped down the covers, rolled me onto my back, and is hovering over me. I throw my head back and close my eyes because just the thought of her warm lips around me makes my dick twitch. I want to make love to her, but I can wait a little longer, right? We're about to find out because while I've been contemplating my stamina, she's pulled down my sleep pants.

I gasp and arch my back as her scorching lips close over the head of my cock—*oh God, I can already feel my balls tightening again*, but I want to enjoy this. I want to come so badly, but I'm going to hold my orgasm back as long as I can.

Her lips slide downward, and I groan loudly, fisting the sheets to try to maintain some control, but it's so hard when she—"Aw, fuck! Do that again." She pulls back up to the tip, suctioning all the way, then she swirls her tongue around the head until I'm biting my lip to keep from crying out.

A soft chuckle sounds from between my legs. "I think you might be enjoying this."

I smile, but I'm immediately lost again as she repeats her patented "plunge and suck" maneuver, and I'm trying not to thrust into her mouth or grasp her cheeks to make her move faster. I clench my fists, and I know she's seen it because she increases her speed, plunging faster and sucking a little harder on each pass.

Waves of pleasure are rolling over my groin and into my stomach, the pressure slowly building as I pant and grunt every few breaths, riding the fine line between wanton pleasure and control. She suddenly takes me in as deep as she can, and I gasp as my tip hits the back of her throat. *Oh fuck, I'm gonna come.*

Tori molds her lips around me and deep-throats me again and again, and any thought of control is *gone*. All I can feel is the pressure building toward eruption in my groin; all I can hear are my urgent moans as I rocket toward ecstasy. "Tori, fuck, fu—" My words are overridden by a deep groan as my existence coalesces to a single point and explodes, pulses of pleasure almost too intense to bear as she swallows around me.

When I'm spent, I collapse against the mattress, all twitches and quivers as the adrenaline gives its last hurrah. "God, Tori. Happy birthday to *me*."

"That's right, sweetheart. All day long."

I open my eyes, and she's lying beside me, so I pull her close, my arm around her back and her head resting on my shoulder. "Well, we might as well just call it a day because I can't see how you're going to top that one."

Tori laughs and brings a hand to my cheek, and I press into it as I always do. "Oh, your special day has just begun, and I have *several* things to top that, or at least come pretty close."

"Can you tell me what we're doing yet?"

"No," she says, trying to play it cool, but I can feel the excitement radiating from her.

"But you want to."

"Yes, of course I want to! But I want it to be a surprise, and I've made it this long, so you're just going to have to wait."

I really hate surprises, but she's so excited, and she's never done anything for me that I haven't loved, so I just give her an indulgent smile.

"I love you," she says as she rests on her elbow and leans in to give me sweet, chaste kisses that turn long and hot and deep. We kiss until I feel myself hardening again, but I know we need to get up and get moving.

I'm pretty sure we're going somewhere or else someone is coming here, and there's . . . something I need to do first.

My stomach does an anxious flip. I've been planning this for weeks now. Everything is ready; *I'm* ready; I think *she's* ready, but I'm still a bundle of nerves when I think about it. I mean, after all we've been through together and all she's done for me, how could she possibly say no? Do all guys feel this way before they propose, no matter the situation? She's pledged her love to me so many times, but a ring somehow makes it official. She's *mine*, and she always will be. I want that so much, but damn, I hope I can get the words out. I hope I can manage to convey even a fraction of what she means to me.

"Hey," Tori says, stroking my cheek with the backs of her fingers. "Where'd you go? From the look on your face, it wasn't exactly a happy place."

Shit. I need to work on my poker face, seriously. I run a nervous hand through my hair. "I guess I just have a lot on my mind today. So much has changed since this time last year."

"For the better?" she asks, suddenly finding my right shoulder fascinating.

"Of course for the better! Last year, I was dying and trying to decide how best to end my life, and today, I'm spending my birthday with a beautiful woman and looking forward to a long future together. I was just thinking over everything I've been through—everything *we've* been through. It's been one hell of a year."

"It has," she says, her brown eyes now gazing into mine. "I'm so proud of you, Will. You've come so unbelievably far this year and accomplished so much. I can't even wrap my mind around the fact that you were dying at this time last year, that in a few short weeks, I'd be falling in love with you and trying to stop myself because I thought you wouldn't be here anymore."

"Really?"

"Well, I guess not *show* you I was in love with you would be more accurate. I think you had me from day one when you dazzled me with that morphine-laden smile and asked me to stay with you."

A blush heats my cheeks, and when she grins at me, I breathe in sharply, stunned by the force of her beauty and her love. *God, when she does that thing with her eyes . . .*

I glance down at the comforter but then force my eyes back up. "I really did think you were an angel that day. You were so fucking beautiful, and I was so lonely. I really thought God had sent you to comfort me."

Tears well in her eyes, but I don't think they're tears of sadness. "Maybe He did."

"He and your mom," I add softly, and her smile widens a bit. Even though I only found out about what happened with Tori's mom two months ago, I can see Tori's feelings have changed from that day to now. She felt so much guilt and anger when she finally told the story to me, but it's slowly been replaced by a gentle sadness and peace. She's even brought her mother up in conversation a few times and told me stories about her. I think she's finally grieving and scraping together in her mind what good times there were.

"Speaking of angels, I intend to be *your* angel all day today, so let's get moving. Will you take a shower with me?"

Her eyes turn smoky as she says this, and she slides her hand suggestively over my hip and side. I close my eyes, enjoying the tingling warmth on my skin, the feel of myself hardening for her. "Of course I will."

She grins and pulls me from the bed, and I come with her easily. Other than the tiredness, the only transplant-related symptom I still have is morning soreness, and once I get that under control, I'm pretty much good to go. It's so amazing to feel like a human being again, to know that I can do what I want when I want. And there's *so* much I want to do with Tori! But right now, all I want to do is rip off her tank top and those skimpy little sleep shorts and watch the water cascade over her glorious body.

As soon as my feet hit the tile floor, I slide my hands up her sides, pulling her tank top with me as I go. Tori glances over her shoulder demurely and winks at me, and I can't help but laugh. She can be so playful and so fucking sexy when she wants to be. And I just love it when she's in the mood to play.

She stops suddenly, and I groan as my erection slides against her ass, my hands drawn to her waist and then upward to the perfect breasts I've bared. *Oh, yes, we're definitely going to play.*

As I palm and knead the soft flesh in my hands, I ghost my lips along her shoulder and up the side of her neck, stopping just below her ear. "We're not going to get clean during this shower, are we?"

Her head falls back against me, and I take full advantage of the angle, covering every inch of pale skin with eager kisses.

"We are . . ." I arch an eyebrow at her. "Eventually," she finishes, stretching her arms upward so they're grasping the backs of mine.

I smile against her skin, continuing to lave my tongue over her collarbone and shifting from foot to foot so my dick will rub against her backside.

"But first I want to take care of you."

"Didn't you already do that this morning?" I ask, turning her in my arms so her fantastic breasts can be a feast for my eyes as well as my hands.

"Yes, I did, but I'm not done yet," she explains, laughing as she pulls my hands away from nipple nirvana and holds them together between us.

I can't help the growl that rumbles in my chest, and it turns feral as she sashays over to the shower stall, sliding her shorts down as she goes.

"Patience, sweetheart. I want to give you a massage first. Is that okay?"

Tori and I still shower together frequently, but if I take my medication as soon as I wake up, I'm usually pain-free by the time we get in, and I don't need a massage like I used to. And some days I have no pain at all, so massages are reserved for the really bad days. They don't happen too often anymore, but they haven't disappeared entirely. I *love* having her hands all over me, but she did it for so many months when I really needed it that I can't really bring myself to ask.

"That sounds fantastic," I tell her as I pull my t-shirt over my head.

Even though I'm expecting it, I still tense and hiss when her tongue swirls around my nipple while my arms are still tangled in my shirt. *Mmm . . . we need to do the paintbrush thing again, and soon.*

Her hands are at my waistband as I toss my shirt away, but they release me gently because she knows well enough that if she starts to stroke me now, I'm going to take her on the bathroom counter. I think we might be wearing a groove between the sinks.

She starts the water, and I remember so many days she did this for me while I sat on the toilet seat, trying to muster the energy to sit up long enough to let her take care of me. I'm so intensely glad those days are behind us, hopefully forever.

As soon as she turns, I lean down and suck a pert nipple into my mouth, and she arches her back and lets out a glorious moan. But her hands find their way to my shoulders and apply gentle pressure until I abandon my prize and raise my head to look at her.

"Mmm . . . not yet! It's *your* birthday, and I'm not done doing things for *you*, sweetheart!"

"But this *is* for me," I say, pointing out the obvious as I move my head down again, but her palm comes to rest on the bridge of my nose, stopping me in my tracks.

"Yes, and you can have it. *Later.* Right now I want to make *you* feel really good. Then you can give me my turn."

I smile and shake my head. When my girl makes up her mind about something, there's no stopping her. And a massage really would feel amazing right now.

We settle into a routine that we have memorized, and I sit on the shower bench while she massages from my fingers to my shoulders, slowly, gently, and with so much love, I can feel it radiating through her touch. I moan softly, lost in the feel of her hands, the depth of her love.

She moves to my feet, and while I'm still enjoying the hell out of it, I begin to harden again as she rubs up my body, her fingers roving ever closer to my dick. She stops midway up my thigh and moves to my other foot, but by now, I'm completely hard and thinking of ten different ways to make love to her and wondering which way she's going to let me.

The tension mounts as she moves up my leg, and I shift positions more than once to try to keep myself still and allow her to finish. But I can't keep my breathing steady, and I pant unevenly as she inches ever closer to where I now desperately need her.

My eyes are closed, but they snap open when I hear her chuckle. "You look like you're holding back Niagara Falls, sweetheart. Is it that hard to keep still?"

"Yes—when you've got me so horny I can barely stand not to touch myself!"

"Do it, then," she says, her eyes daring me as she continues to rub slow circles on my thigh.

My own eyes widen because she's never asked to watch me masturbate before, but fuck, just the thought of pleasuring myself with her watching . . . I melt into the wall as I grasp myself firmly at the base and pull upward, my own fingers finding the most sensitive spots and pulling moans and thrusts of my hips from me.

"Oh, *damn*, is that hot!" Tori exclaims, and I nearly jump from the bench as my balls tighten almost painfully, her talented fingers cupping and kneading them as I stroke.

We continue on like that until I'm moaning with each thrust, the tension built to where if we don't stop soon— "Fuck, I'm getting so close!" —and instantly her hand disappears from my sack as she straddles me. Both hands now plunge into my hair, her lips hot and demanding on mine.

I pull her as close to me as I can, her warm, wet pussy sliding over my shaft and doing nothing to slow things down. "Ohh . . . God," I moan, breaking the kiss to try to get a little control.

"That was . . . one of the hottest things . . . I've ever seen." Tori pants from above me, her eyes almost wild as her hands caress every bit of my skin they can reach. "I want you to fuck me, Will. *Right now.*"

My dick gives an almighty twitch as her words penetrate every fiber of my being and set me ablaze. I want to just lower her down on top of me, but I need to thrust so badly, there's no way I can handle her being in control. I stand up with her wrapped around me, and press her back against the opposite wall. Her legs are still gripping my waist, so it's easy to line myself up as she braces her arms on my shoulders.

I brush my tip against her clit, the tips of my fingers sliding between her folds, and she moans and throws her head back against the wall. Her neck is bared to me, her nipples taut and just begging for my lips, but more than anything, I need to be inside her right now. I need to feel the heat and delicious pressure as she takes in every inch of me. This woman drives me absolutely fucking crazy.

I inch forward, biting into my lip as her scorching heat surrounds me, molds to me, becomes part of me. My eyes want to close, but I keep them on her, watching as her brow furrows, her mouth falls open, and she arches upward, pressing into me even as I bury myself to the hilt.

"Oh, Will!" Her words are breathless—and God!—I hope she doesn't need me to wait because I just don't think I can.

"Tori, I need—"

"Fuck me. Will, please—"

With a deep groan, I pull out and push forward, faster this time, and she writhes above me, arching again, encouraging me. And I let loose, driving into her, grunting as the pressure builds each time I'm flush against her skin. The sound of the water is drowned out by harsh breaths and sounds of passion—deep, guttural moans and urgent pants, the sound of our skin as it slaps together. And all of it, *all of it* is driving me toward one hell of an orgasm.

My thrusts become erratic as my balls tighten, and I close my eyes, awash in pleasure and unable to focus on anything but my urgent need to explode. I roll my pelvis forward, trying to get even deeper, and I dimly register that Tori gasps, her fingernails suddenly digging into my back.

"Yes, right there!"

I nod, trying to hold on for just a few more thrusts, wanting her to come with me, around me. "Oh, Jesus—" Her walls clamp down on me and I moan in ecstasy. Just a few . . . more . . .

"Tori, I can't—" As I grind upward, she shatters, her thighs clamping tightly as she cries out. She pulses around me, and something deep inside lets go, my head snapping backward as my whole body seems to surge forward and out, each spurt a blinding wave of pleasure that ends in a moan I can't even begin to hold back.

When I'm finally spent, my knees feel weak and I'm dizzy, and the weight of Tori's thighs leaves my hips as her arms encircle me. I'm still trying to catch my breath as she nudges me until I sit, but I pull her down sideways onto my lap, laying my head against her heaving breasts.

Her chin comes to rest on the top of my head and we sit like that until the spots fade from behind my closed lids, and I can draw a full breath.

"That was fucking spectacular," I say into her chest, squeezing her tightly.

"You can say that again. I thought I killed you with shower sex."

"I thought you had too, for a moment there. That was the most intense orgasm I've had in a long time. Thanks for sitting us down before I dropped you."

Tori chuckles. "You would've dropped me?"

"Considering I couldn't really feel my legs, and I didn't know which way was up, I'd say it was pretty likely."

I feel her lips against my forehead as she ruffles my hair.

"Still having a good birthday?"

"The best."

"Did what just happened beat out this morning's blowjob?"

"Hands down."

"Are you ready to get clean before the hot water runs out?"

"Yeah, I guess we should," I reply, giving the nipple just below my chin a soft peck before I let her go. We wash each other, but our focus is now cleaning instead of playing, and taking my cue from Tori, I put on a pair of comfy cotton shorts and my "superpower" shirt that she got me for Christmas. She laughs when she sees me, but her kisses tell me she's happy I'm wearing it.

We have some breakfast and just hang out for a while, but Tori seems nervous. She keeps glancing back toward the hallway, and she's twisting her fingers in that way she does when she's anxious about something. I don't see it that often, but it's always a sure sign something's afoot, and even if it's only because she has some surprise for me, her nervousness is feeding *my* nervousness.

"Are you okay?" I ask after her fifteenth look down the hallway.

"What? Why?"

"Because I keep wondering when the zombies are going to come down that hallway to eat our brains. You're looking down there every two minutes."

She blushes and smiles at me shyly. "I'm sorry, I . . . Would you mind if I gave you your birthday presents now?"

"Of course not! But if there's someone hiding back there, I hope they're not my present."

Tori laughs, but it's a nervous sound as she goes not down the hallway but over to the table near the front door. She returns with an envelope in her hand, her eyes intent as she sits facing me on the couch.

"This should help cross a few things off our 'When the cancer's gone' list," she says as she hands me the envelope and rests her hand on my knee.

I grin at her and open it eagerly. Inside are two slips of paper, and I stare at them for a moment before I realize what they are. *Airline tickets to Paris?*

My eyes are wide as I raise them to her, my mind equal parts exhilaration and fear. I'm so excited to show her the places I've been and to paint new skylines in Europe, but I'm not ready. At least, not now.

"This is a promise. I know you're not ready yet, but I thought if we had the tickets, we could start planning, and you'd know how much I want to go with you. I didn't think we'd use them before next spring at the earliest—"

My heart melts in my chest. How does she always know just what I need, what will make me happy and inspire me to keep fighting to be well again, totally and completely. I've come a long way, but a trip to Europe would be the ultimate proof that I really *can* do anything.

"It's perfect! I want to take you to so many places I've been, and I *really* want to go to Rotterdam and paint the Erasmus Bridge at night, and—"

Her beautiful laughter drowns out the rest of my thought as she crawls onto my lap. "I'm so happy you're excited! You haven't talked much about going since February, and I was hoping you hadn't changed your mind."

February—when I got really sick, and it scared the shit out of me. I managed to stay out of the hospital, but I teetered on the edge of going to the ER for about five days when my fever just wouldn't break, and my cough sounded like it did when I had pneumonia. I was utterly miserable for weeks, and the whole affair put me off planning the future for a while—I was content just to be at home and try to keep myself healthy.

"No, I haven't changed my mind, but I got sidetracked for a while. I really want to plan this trip with you, and I'm excited to go when we can."

"Well, you just keep on getting stronger and healthier, and we'll be ready to go in no time," Tori says, molding her lips to mine. We kiss slowly and deeply, and I try to channel the love and gratitude I'm feeling into every stroke of my tongue, every caress of my fingers down her back. I think she feels it because she cuddles into my shoulder when we finally break apart.

"I have something else for you, too," she says softly. "I didn't plan it, I only meant to look, but . . . hopefully, when you see, you'll understand."

She stands up, uncertainty written all over her face, and turns toward the hallway. She stops at the laundry room and goes in, and I think I hear Sebastian meow, but—

I'm on my feet instantly as Tori reappears, cradling a kitten. It's half-white and half-calico—white on its paws, belly, chest, and around its nose and between its eyes, with a large black and tan calico patch on its back and masking its face. It's so tiny and feminine, somehow. A girl to balance out our little family.

My mouth falls open as the kitten flicks her ears toward me, meowing in greeting. I'm drawn to her just as I was to Sebastian, and I'm across the room and stroking gently under her chin before I even register that I've moved.

"Hey, girl." I coo at her, continuing to scratch as my smile threatens to split my face.

"This is Lily. I thought you and Sebastian might like a little more company during the day, so I went to the shelter just to see if they even had any kittens, and . . . she was there. They said the litter had been dumped in the street, and she was the last one left who wasn't adopted, and she was scheduled for euthanasia today if she didn't find a home –"

"She's absolutely gorgeous, and I'm so happy you didn't leave her there," I say, putting my arm around both of them.

"Really?" Those soulful eyes gaze up at me, and for a moment, I forget the kitten as Tori takes my breath away. She's just so beautiful and sweet, and God, when she looks at me that way . . .

Lily meows again, and I smile. "Yes, really. Can I—" I hold my hands out, and suddenly they're filled with cozy warm fluff. I immediately cradle her to my chest, laying her along my arm while I stroke over her ear with my other hand.

"Hello, Lily. What a beautiful girl you are, just like my Tori." And the universe consists of only Lily and me until Tori's soft laughter brings me back to the real world. I shake my head as I realize I'm sitting on the couch with Lily still cuddled into my chest, and Tori is sitting next to me with a peculiar look on her face.

"What?"

"I love watching you get caught up in things. The book you're reading, whatever you're painting or drawing, playtime with Sebastian—you have this singular focus that just amazes me."

I can feel my cheeks heat as I look down at Lily, but Tori grasps my chin so my gaze returns to hers. "It's a *good* thing. I think it's how you manage to do all the amazing things you do. It's incredible to watch."

"I can think of a few other things I do with singular focus," I say, waggling my eyebrows at her, and now it's her turn to blush as she squeezes my arm.

"Yes, you certainly do. You may even have as much skill in the bedroom as you do in the studio."

My eyebrows go up, and she laughs again. "Did I really say that? Let's quit before your ego explodes. So . . . can Lily stay?"

"Of course she can!" I exclaim, my fingers still running through her soft fur. "What a fantastic birthday present! Has she met Sebastian yet?"

"Yes, I had to steal her away from him to show her to you. They were sleeping together on Sebastian's bed in the laundry room."

"Always the ladies' man," I say, shaking my head. "Thank you, Tori. She's wonderful."

Tori smiles brilliantly and leans in, her kisses soft and sweet. "Happy birthday, Will."

The smile that spreads across my face is deep and genuine. It truly *is* a happy birthday.

Tori's nervousness evaporates once Lily is "out of the bag," but my own continues to grow as afternoon approaches. Tori orders in from Il Terrazzo Carmine, and I do my best to enjoy my Rigatoni Bolognese, but my stomach feels like it's in knots.

I'm so nervous about what I'm planning to do this afternoon that I realize I've fucked up my own birthday a bit. *First world problem, Will.*

You're not dying, and neither is anyone else. You're going to ask your girlfriend to marry you today? You poor thing. I chuckle and shake my head at my own ridiculousness. Unfortunately, that doesn't do anything to calm my nerves.

I'm quiet through lunch, and Tori watches me with a crease in her brow, but she doesn't say anything. She never pushes—she knows I'll tell her whatever it is when I can, and I'm so grateful for that, especially today.

She convinces me to lie down after lunch by telling me we're going out later, but as I lie there, my stomach churning and my pulse racing, I know there's not a chance in hell I'm going to be able to sleep.

I turn to face her, and I can tell she's been watching me.

"I know it's my birthday, but . . . I have something for you too."

Tori smiles, but that little crease forms between her eyebrows again. "You love giving me presents so much that you couldn't even have *one* day where you get them and I don't?"

I look at the floor as heat flairs on my cheeks. "Well . . . I'm kind of thinking of this birthday as a new leaf."

"I can tell," she says, stroking my cheek with her hand. "You've been doing entirely too much thinking today."

Oh, if you only knew. Well, you will *know in about five minutes if I can just get through this.* "Will you come back to the studio with me?"

She slips her hand into mine and squeezes. "Of course."

If she can feel the sweat on my palm, she doesn't say anything. The butterflies in my stomach threaten to make an escape, but I keep them down with a hard swallow. *Keep it together, Will!*

I lead her into the studio, where my two large easels stand covered with heavy cloths, just as I set them up while Tori was drying her hair this morning. Releasing her hand, I move to the side of the left one. "Today,

I want to show you what I did with the two canvases you gave me for Christmas."

The smile that lights up Tori's face is brilliant. "Oh! You've finished them both?"

Nodding, I pull the cloth off the easel deftly. "This is the painting I did for me."

I'm facing her and not the painting, so I get to see her eyes widen and her mouth fall open in a look of pure awe. She covers her mouth with her hand as tears well in her eyes. "It's . . . stunning. Oh my God, Will, it looks so real! I can't believe it's a painting and not a photograph. How on earth do you do that?"

I lower my eyes and shrug, but she's in my arms before I can find a focus point on the floor. "It's just what I do. Do you like it, really?"

"Sweetheart, it's positively breathtaking. There's no way I look that good."

I chuckle, and it helps to relieve some of my tension. "You're more beautiful than anything I could ever paint. I'm certain of that."

Her lips crash into mine, and I groan deeply, throwing myself into the kiss—another release for my nervous energy. I run my tongue along her lower lip, and she plunges hers into my mouth, her hands cupping my cheeks. As our tongues tangle and I press my throbbing erection against her, I forget everything—everything but the feel of her hands as they slide down my back, the taste of her lips as she devours me. I know I'm going to get lightheaded if I don't get some oxygen soon, so I pull back slightly then rest my cheek against her forehead.

"Will you let me display it at the gallery show?" Again, her eyes widen, but this time I think it's happiness and excitement.

"Of course! It's fantastic and I want everyone to see it. I want everyone to know how incredibly talented you are!"

Happiness and pride surge through me as yet again, warmth floods my chest and cheeks. Fuck, the way she makes me feel! No one has ever believed in me the way Tori does, and her enthusiasm is positively contagious.

"Thanks, Tori."

"So, do I get to see the other painting?"

I suck in a deep breath as my nerves flair. This is it; this is the moment. I swallow hard and slide my fingers over the outline of the ring in my front pocket. *Breathe. You've got this.*

"Yeah," I answer, taking her by the shoulders and positioning her in front of the easel. "Can you . . . close your eyes?"

She frowns at me; she suspects something is up, but she does as I ask anyway.

With a shaking hand, I lift the cloth, drop it to the side, then move to stand behind her. "Okay, you can look now."

I'm nearly hyperventilating as she stares at the picture. I hear her breath catch, but I have no idea what she's thinking because I can't see her face.

"Is this . . . for the gallery show?" she asks, her voice trembling a little.

"No, this is for you—for us. I hope it'll be our future." I look again at the canvas, but I've seen it so many times in my mind, I swear I could paint it again with my eyes closed. The scene is similar to the one in my sketchbook; Tori and I are standing close together, our eyes closed as our lips inch ever closer for an inevitable kiss. But this one is different —Tori's hair is pinned up into an intricate knot at the nape of her neck underneath a veil held by a pearl and silver comb, her shoulder covered in a fine white gown, and I'm wearing a tux with a white bow tie and a boutonniere.

She begins to turn, and as she does, I grasp her hands and slowly lower myself to one knee. She pulls in a gasping breath and holds it, and her eyes—God, her eyes! I fall headlong into an ocean of shock and love and joy and panic and amazement and—I look down and take a shaky breath, willing myself to go through with it, to say the words I've rehearsed so many times. *You survived high dose chemotherapy and beat cancer. You can tell the love of your life what she means to you.*

She squeezes my hands, and I choke out a strangled sob. I came so perilously close to dying so many times last year—and if I had, I would have missed out on . . . this. *But you didn't. You chose life, and you chose her.*

I raise my stinging eyes back to hers, blinking so the tears roll down my cheeks, and I can see again. "Tori." My voice breaks, but I keep going. She deserves for this to be perfect.

"Tori, from the first moment I saw you, you changed my life. I was broken and had given up, but you breathed life into me again and made me see I had so much to live for, so much to fight for. I can't even begin to explain how you changed my life, how you changed *me*. How you make me want to be the best person I can be, for me *and* for you.

"You saved me. You gave me everything you had, and now I want to give you everything I have in return. I've already given you my life and my heart—now I want to give you my soul and everything that I am. I want to bind myself to you in every way possible because you are my whole world.

"Tori Somerset, will you marry me?"

She takes a rapid breath and blinks, her own tears spilling down her cheeks, but I can't look anywhere but her eyes, waiting, hoping, praying. She falls to her knees, still gripping my hands, and she makes this laughing-sobbing sound as she bows her head. My breathing picks up, and I feel like I'm falling—she hasn't answered me yet. *What if*— And suddenly, her eyes pierce me, and her smile is the most beautiful thing I've ever seen.

"Yes! God, Will, yes! I'll marry you. I'll marry you!"

She flings herself into my arms, and I start to shake, unable to contain all the feelings inside me. It's like a tidal wave—incredible joy and sweet relief obliterating the uncertainty and doubt of the last few days, the fear and pain and sorrow of the whole last year. *This is my life now. She's mine forever, and all the heartache and suffering is over. I can really have this, with her. I am who and what she needs, just as she's always been for me.*

I realize we're both sobbing when she finds my cheek with her hand, pressing the wetness against my skin.

"Are you all right?"

Chuckling, I pull back and swipe a hand over each eye, watching as she does the same. "I'm . . . perfect. You just made me the happiest man alive. I love you so much, Tori."

"I love you so much too," she says as she leans forward, eyes on my lips.

I wipe my wet fingers on my jeans and feel something hard in my pocket. "Oh, jeez!" I exclaim, pulling out the ring. "I was so nervous I completely forgot this part."

"Will," she whispers as I slide it onto her finger, the diamonds glittering and sparkling in the sunlight. "It's gorgeous."

"The setting was actually my grandmother's—my dad's mom."

Tori raises her eyes from the ring, and they narrow a bit. "I've never told you about her . . . not *because* of her, but because I haven't wanted to think about my dad. She was a wonderful woman. She loved me very much, and she may have been the one person who knew or suspected what my dad was doing to me. She was always inviting me over to her house to spend weekends when I was in high school—she'd drive me wherever I needed to go to see my friends. She got sick when I was in Europe, and by the time I came back, she was close to death. When she said goodbye to me, she told me she'd taken care of me, and that she was sorry."

Tori puts her hand on my arm and squeezes, but I keep going, afraid I won't be able to start again if I stop.

"That didn't make any sense until a few months later when her will was read. She'd left me her ring, a few other family heirlooms, and a sizable trust fund. My dad was furious, but after he read the letter she left him, he was absolutely *livid*. He never got his hands on me after that, but I know he wanted to. There was nothing he could do about what she'd done, so the trust supported me when I was starting out in Seattle and when I had to stop working after I got sick. There won't be much of it left after we pay all my medical bills, but she certainly did take care of me. So I thought it seemed fitting I give this particular ring to you, the one person who's done even more than she did to take care of me."

Tori glances down at the ring again, but this time, her gaze is thoughtful. "Sweetheart, it's perfect. I'm honored to wear this, and I'm so happy she took care of you."

"I wish you could have known her. She was amazing."

"Me too," Tori says, turning her hand to admire the ring. She laughs, and for a second, I'm confused until I realize it's at nothing in particular —just the kind of sound you make when you're happy and can't contain it. I wrap an arm around her back and pull her close, my lips finding hers for the first time as her intended, and it feels more right than anything ever has.

We kiss hungrily, and she pulls me down so we're lying on the floor on our sides, stroking and fondling each other in just about the same place where we created our sensual masterpiece. *Damn, if we ever leave this apartment, we'll need to take this piece of floor with us—so much has happened here.*

Tori strokes the side of my face, both of us grinning like kids with a fabulous new toy. "I think I have some ideas for what we can do with those airline vouchers I got you."

After we got, um, finished on the floor, Tori pulled me into the bedroom and convinced me to lie down again to try to take a nap because we'd probably be out late. My curiosity about what she had planned was at an all-time high, but I was so relieved after I proposed and she accepted that I was able to sleep for a couple hours spooned around her.

When I awoke, she had shorts and a button-down shirt laid out for me, and she finally admitted we were going to Jenny's house. She wouldn't say why or what was happening after that, but at least now I knew *something*.

We got ready together, all smiles and stolen kisses, barely able to keep our hands off each other. And both our eyes kept straying to the ring on her finger, which would start the kissing all over again.

My eyes stray there now as Tori's hand grips the steering wheel, and I can see the diamond peeking over the top. I reach over and grasp her knee, and she giggles and puts her hand on top of mine. I've never seen her so happy.

"So, are we going to tell Jenny and Jason? Because I'm thinking we look a little 'happiness overkill' for just my birthday."

Tori chuckles. "I think you're right. Is it okay with you if we tell them?"

"I want the world to know how much I love you. Jenny and Jason are only the beginning."

"I think you're right about that," she says. *What does that mean?* Tori's smiling, so whatever it means, I'm probably going to like it.

I'm relieved we're only going to Jenny's house though. I was more than a little worried that Tori was planning something bigger, and I didn't know if I could handle it. Between being isolated for so long and the natural fear of getting sick that comes with willingly obliterating your own immune system, I've developed a bit of a fear of crowded places. I'm pretty good with restaurants, but we've only been out to one movie so far, and I was on edge the whole time. Just the thought of being at a bar or a concert is almost enough to give me a panic attack. We tried to meet my artist friends at a bar last month so I could introduce them all to Tori, but I got so worked up in the car on the way there that we ended up just going back home. Both Jenny and Jill have assured me this is not uncommon, given what I've been through. I need to try to overcome it though, and soon. I have a gallery show scheduled in just over a month, and there will be a room full of people I'll need to interact with. Just the thought of it makes my heart start to pound, but I swallow and take a few deep breaths. *I have time. It's not today.*

We park in front of Jenny's house, and I hold Tori's hand, my fingers brushing over her new accessory as we approach the door. Jason whips it open before we can even knock and pulls me into a one-armed hug.

"Happy birthday, Will!"

"Thanks, Jay!" I reply, gripping his shoulder tightly. Jason was the only person who saw me on my last birthday and only for a couple of hours. I was sick and didn't want to be bothered, but he insisted on coming over and cooking for me, then keeping me company for a while. I had intended for it to be the last time I ever saw him.

I squeeze my eyes shut tight as the painful memory lances through me, but that's not the way things ended. They didn't end at all, and we're both here to truly celebrate this year. He pulls back and looks at me carefully, but I've already tucked the past away. He grins and rubs my shoulder as Jenny pops up under my arm.

"Hello, birthday boy. I hope you're ready to party!" And she jumps up and plants a kiss on my cheek.

Tori chuckles as my cheeks burn, and I'm sure I'm six shades of red. Jenny's ability to make me blush is second only to Tori's.

They pull us into the house, and right away, Jason leads us through the living room and into the kitchen. "Before we go, I wanted to show you what Jenny had me plant for her."

As Jason opens the patio door, Tori grabs my hand, and hers is trembling. *What the hell is going—*

"Surprise! Happy birthday, Will!"

I startle badly and pull in a deep breath, my eyes widening as the panic takes rapid hold. I squeeze Tori's hand tighter, but she squeezes right back and reaches up to stroke my cheek as she whispers in my ear.

"Breathe, Will. You're okay. No one here is sick; everyone has washed their hands, and they know how hard this is for you. You'll need to do this with a room full of strangers next month, but these are your friends. Focus on their faces, Will. Focus and breathe, okay?"

I look around frantically, but I can't focus on anything. *There are so many people!* I take a ragged breath, already feeling light-headed. I'm trapped and I feel disjointed, numb.

Tori's touch on my cheek shocks me back to the present, but her voice is muffled and distant. "Come on, Will, you can do this! We're outside, and we can leave if you need to. Look for your mom, sweetheart."

Tori turns my head to the left, and my gaze settles on my mom, standing over by a big tree and holding a wine glass. She smiles brilliantly as I meet her eyes, and I take another breath. Tori strokes my cheek again, and I notice we're in Jenny's yard, and it's not fully enclosed. There's plenty of air and space out here, and I can escape if I need to.

I take another breath, and a bird chirps, shattering the unnatural silence I didn't even know I was cocooned in. I close my eyes and focus on breathing, letting the sounds of my friends and family wash over me. Jason is swearing behind us, and Kate is asking someone if I'm all right . . . and I realize I *am* all right. I'm standing here, and I'm breathing almost normally. Nothing bad has happened . . . and maybe nothing will.

Tori caresses my cheek again, and I open my eyes—still wide, but I'm breathing. "That's it. I knew you could do it!"

And suddenly, I can focus on what's around me again. We're in Jenny's back yard, and . . . *wow, look at all these people!* There's Kate and Julia, and Jill's here! No one seems to know how to react when I look at them, but Jeremy tips his beer bottle in my direction, and it catches my eye, and I can't help the smile that spreads across my face. I *can* do this! A laugh bubbles up from nowhere, and everyone claps as I smile and look around eagerly.

"Are you all right?" Tori asks. I rub my entwined fingers over hers and brush against the diamond I put on her finger this afternoon, and suddenly, all I'm feeling is warmth and love.

"Yes, I'm fine."

Jason drops his hand on my shoulder. "Thank God. You scared the hell out of me."

"You just brought yourself out of a panic attack. Good work, Will," Jill says as she walks up to us.

"Hi, Jill, thanks for coming!" I say, giving her a hug. "So . . . you knew they were going to do that to me?"

"Well, after I was invited to the party, I actually suggested they do that to you. Your claustrophobia and social anxiety are new and not ingrained in your psyche yet. New fears can often be overcome by exposure, and you needed to experience something like this before you walked into your gallery show next month to have an idea how you'd fare."

"And you were fantastic, sweetheart!" Tori says, grinning at me.

"You could've warned me," I complain, thinking that a little prep time might have done me some good.

"And what would you have done if I had? Say, on the car ride over here, for instance?"

"Well, I . . . I would have driven myself crazy over it and probably had a panic attack in the car," I admit, realizing how right she is. *Dammit.*

"Exactly. You think so much, and sometimes, you psyche yourself out. This way, you only had to deal with it for a moment, and you handled it beautifully."

I blush from Tori's compliment and the fact that my psychological problems are the topic of party conversation, and the women around me chuckle.

"I'm thrilled to see you so happy and healthy though, Will," Jill tells me.

Tori and I chat our way around the yard, and we finally make it over to where all my closer Seattle friends are congregated. The minute I turn to the group, Jeremy gives me a tight bro hug. "It's nice to see you up close and personal this time. I don't even feel like throwing peanuts."

"Ha, ha, ha, fucker." I taunt him, hugging him back and smirking. "Just be glad you don't have to spend your time in a cage."

"Yeah, but would I get to spend it with her?" he asks, and I pull back and put my arm around Tori.

"Nope, she's all mine. Jeremy, this is my Tori."

Jeremy raises an eyebrow and gives Tori his best "smolder" as he lifts her hand to kiss the back and freezes when he comes nose to nose with the glittering diamond on Tori's finger. Kate gasps, but Tori just giggles at the sudden attention surrounding us.

Here we go . . .

"Jason!" Jeremy bellows, still holding Tori's hand, and Jason makes his way through the crowd to us.

"What's up?" he asks, but his own eyes widen as Jeremy raises Tori's hand toward him.

"Did you know about this?"

"Umm . . . I do now." Jason is dumbfounded, his eyes shifting rapidly from Tori to me, both of us grinning like idiots now.

"Ohmygod, ohmygod, ohmygod!" Jenny exclaims as she skitters to a halt beside Jason.

"When did this happen?" Jason asks.

"Earlier today," Tori replies, nearly bouncing.

"Woohoo!" Jeremy lets out a whoop, then he raises his voice. "Hey, everyone, this isn't just a birthday party; it's an engagement party! Will proposed to Tori today!"

The cheers and applause are loud and enthusiastic, and as Tori takes my hand again, I realize there are some things I need to say.

"Jeremy, would you?" I don't even have to finish my sentence—Jeremy knows he's the mouth of the group.

"Hey now, Will has something he wants to say! Pipe down!"

The group laughs, and Jeremy bows deeply, yielding the floor to me.

"Um, well, thank you all for coming to celebrate with me today," I say, stumbling over my words a bit. But Tori squeezes my hand, and as I look into her eyes, I find the strength to continue.

"This is a very special birthday for me. I'm turning thirty, and that's a big thing, but the bigger thing is, I never expected to see this birthday. At this time last year, I'd given up on life. My lymphoma had come back for the third time. I was sick and getting sicker, and I was only looking for the fastest way to end things for myself.

"But then I met this woman." The guys start ribbing each other, and a few of them whistle, but Jeremy shushes them with an exaggerated scowl. I smile at him, but my eyes go right back to Tori, and I keep going, letting the story pour out of me.

"She was beautiful and kind. She came to me like an angel, and just by being there when I needed her, she slowly convinced me to talk to her. She taught me that death isn't about sparing your friends and family at your own expense; it's about coming to terms with your past, righting wrongs, and mending relationships, but most of all, it's about taking what *you* need and allowing others to give it to you."

Tori's eyes shine bright, and as she blinks, a tear rolls down each cheek, and I have to swallow past the lump in my throat.

"But then she taught me something else. She taught me that some things are worth fighting for, worth *dying* for. That sometimes it's worth trying as hard as you can because even if you don't succeed, the fact that you tried makes a difference. I chose to fight my cancer because I fell in love with this amazing woman, and I wanted to spend the rest of my days—a lifetime of days—with her.

"Tori, I love you . . . more than I ever thought it was possible to love another person. You're my first thought in the morning, my last whisper before sleep, and then you wander through my dreams—you're all I see and all I'll ever need. I'm here because you walked into my hospital room and changed me forever, because you believed in me even when I didn't and when I couldn't. You saved me, and now, I'm going to spend the rest of my life doing everything in my power to give you even a fraction of the happiness and joy you bring to me. Thank you for doing me the tremendous honor of becoming my wife."

She stares at me for a moment, her eyes alight with so much love, I swear I can feel the force of it. Then the dam breaks, and she throws her arms around me, sobbing into my shoulder and squeezing me as hard as she can. When she lifts her head, her lips find mine, and everything falls away.

And in my mind, all I see is her, telling me stories of her childhood as she sits beside me; holding my hand, her eyes a reflection of the terror I'm feeling as I gasp for breath; watching me slyly while we're supposed to be watching a movie, sitting side by side on my hospital bed; kissing me as my heart threatens to explode in my chest; comforting me as I cry, lost in despair; telling me she loves me through a haze of fever; holding my very soul together as I beg her to let me die. I see her under my shoulder, supporting me as I take painful steps; urging me to eat just a little more; sitting for me, a sparkle in her eyes as I paint her; writhing under me, a fire in her eyes as our love paints her; smiling that absolutely perfect smile as I slip a ring on her finger.

When we finally pull back amid the applause, neither of us has dry eyes. *Holy shit, when did I get so emotional?* I know it's because I've gone through more trauma in a year than most people go through in a lifetime, but I've also been luckier than few ever hope to be. And as I look around at the smiling faces of my family and friends, I realize I'm happy—happier than I ever believed I could be.

What's happening today, and as I get better, isn't a happy ending though. It's a happy beginning.

I was meant to be with Tori. And I hope fate will give us all the tomorrows we deserve.

ACKNOWLEDGMENTS

Mom and Dad, you're right at the top, of course. Your encouragement and pride has brought me to this moment and helped me to achieve what was once only a little girl's fantasy. I can't ever thank you enough for that!

Jared, you've stood by my side and supported me every step of the way on this perilous path to publishing. I know it hasn't been easy—it's added stress to our lives and jobs to your list—and sometimes the most important one has been holding me together. All that you do means more to me than I can say, and it always will.

Noah and Tori, thank you for your pats on the head, your hugs (especially your wiggle hugs), and your understanding of how important this is to me. I love you both so much!

Sue, you have quickly become my mainstay in this adventure. I come to you first with the good and the bad, and you're always there with a cheer or a consoling hug. Oh yeah, and you're also my editor. The success of this belongs to both of us—I hope you know that.

Jada, thank you for this glorious cover! It truly *is* a work of art. Thank you for letting me play with it until we had more versions than we could keep track of. The final product is just perfect.

Belynda, Beth, Jennifer, Jennifer, and Sally—ladies, you're my team. I come to each of you for different things, but the one you share in common is that you're always there, whatever I need. Your friendship and support mean more than I can say.

Thank you to everyone who read, reviewed, and discussed this story in its first incarnation, both in my group and elsewhere on the web. And to those who shared their own stories with me along the way—I hold your loved ones in my heart. I wish more than anything that I could give them a happily ever after.

Dear Readers, thank you for making it to this page with me. I hope the Embrace Tomorrow Duet was a journey you'll never forget. I also hope to see you again for our next adventure.

ABOUT THE AUTHOR

Amy Argent is the author of the *Embrace Tomorrow* Duet: *Come Back Tomorrow* and its sequel, *Whatever Tomorrow Brings*. Amy can honestly say she writes day and night—clinical trial documents as a medical writer by day and contemporary romance as a novelist by night . . . and possibly into the wee hours of the morning. She has a PhD in Genetics that she agonized entirely too much over, but it did result in a fascinating day job—the details of which tend to creep into her fiction.

Amy can be found in Raleigh, North Carolina, with her husband, two teenagers, and two hedgehogs, where she's most likely planning her next departure from reality—destination: Dragon Con, the closest Renaissance Faire, or the nearest book.

Made in the USA
Monee, IL
09 October 2021